D0913938

THE CLAY SANSKRIT LIBRARY

FOUNDED BY JOHN & JENNIFER CLAY

GENERAL EDITOR

Sheldon Pollock

EDITED BY

Isabelle Onians

www.claysanskritlibrary.com

www.nyupress.org

Artwork by Robert Beer.
Typeset in Adobe Garamond Pro at 10.25 : 12.3+pt.
XML-development by Stuart Brown.
Editorial input from Dániel Balogh,
Csaba Dezső, Ridi Faruque, Chris Gibbons,
Tomoyuki Kono, Guy Leavitt & Eszter Somogyi.
Printed and bound in Great Britain by
T.J. International, Cornwall, on acid-free paper.

PRINCESS KĀDAMBARĪ

VOLUME ONE

by BĀṆA

EDITED AND TRANSLATED BY

David Smith

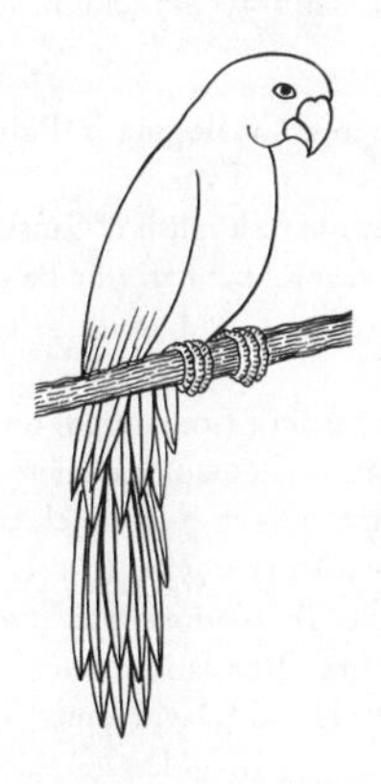

NEW YORK UNIVERSITY PRESS

JJC FOUNDATION

2009

First Edition 2009

The Clay Sanskrit Library is co-published by
New York University Press
and the JJC Foundation.

Further information about this volume
and the rest of the Clay Sanskrit Library
is available at the end of this book
and on the following websites:
www.claysanskritlibrary.com
www.nyupress.org

ISBN-13: 978-0-8147-9558-3 (cloth : alk. paper)
ISBN-10: 0-8147-9558-7 (cloth : alk. paper)

Library of Congress Cataloging-in-Publication Data
Bāṇa.
[Kādambarī. English & Sanskrit]
Princess Kadámbari / by Bana ;
translated by David Smith. -- 1st ed.
p. cm.
In English and Sanskrit (romanized) on facing pages.
Includes bibliographical references.
ISBN-13: 978-0-8147-9558-3 (cl : alk. paper)
ISBN-10: 0-8147-9558-7 (cl : alk. paper)
1. Bana--Translations into English.
2. Aryasura--Translations into English.
I. Smith, David (David James), 1944-
II. Title.
PK3791.B188K33 2009
891.2'3--dc22
2009019754

CONTENTS

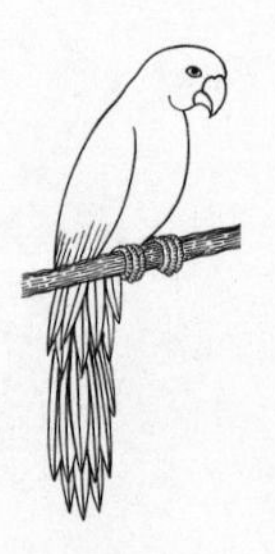

CSL CONVENTIONS

Sanskrit Alphabetical Order

Vowels:	*a ā i ī u ū ṛ ṝ ḷ ḹ e ai o au ṃ ḥ*
Gutturals:	*k kh g gh ṅ*
Palatals:	*c ch j jh ñ*
Retroflex:	*ṭ ṭh ḍ ḍh ṇ*
Dentals:	*t th d dh n*
Labials:	*p ph b bh m*
Semivowels:	*y r l v*
Spirants:	*ś ṣ s h*

Guide to Sanskrit Pronunciation

a	b*u*t
ā, â	f*a*ther
i	s*i*t
ī, î	f*ee*
u	p*u*t
ū, û	b*oo*
ṛ	vocalic *r*, American p*ur*dy or English p*re*tty
ṝ	lengthened *ṛ*
ḷ	vocalic *l*, ab*le*
e, ê, ē	m*a*de, esp. in Welsh pronunciation
ai	b*i*te
o, ô, ō	r*o*pe, esp. Welsh pronunciation; Italian s*o*lo
au	s*ou*nd
ṃ	*anusvāra* nasalizes the preceding vowel
ḥ	*visarga*, a voiceless aspiration (resembling the English *h*), or like Scottish lo*ch*, or an aspiration with a faint echoing of the last element of the preceding vowel so that *taiḥ* is pronounced $taih^{i}$
k	lu*ck*
kh	blo*ckh*ead
g	*g*o
gh	bi*gh*ead
ṅ	a*n*ger
c	*ch*ill
ch	mat*chh*ead
j	*j*og
jh	aspirated *j*, he*dgeh*og
ñ	ca*ny*on
ṭ	retroflex *t*, *t*ry (with the tip of tongue turned up to touch the hard palate)
ṭh	same as the preceding but aspirated
ḍ	retroflex *d* (with the tip

	of tongue turned up to touch the hard palate)
ḍh	same as the preceding but aspirated
ṇ	retroflex *n* (with the tip of tongue turned up to touch the hard palate)
t	French *t*out
th	ten*t h*ook
d	*d*inner
dh	guil*dh*all
n	*n*ow
p	*p*ill
ph	u*ph*eaval
b	*b*efore
bh	a*bh*orrent
m	*m*ind
y	*y*es
r	trilled, resembling the Italian pronunciation of *r*
l	*l*inger
v	*w*ord
ś	*sh*ore
ṣ	retroflex *sh* (with the tip of the tongue turned up to touch the hard palate)
s	hi*ss*
h	*h*ood

CSL Punctuation of English

The acute accent on Sanskrit words when they occur outside of the Sanskrit text itself, marks stress, e.g., Ramáyana. It is not part of traditional Sanskrit orthography, transliteration, or transcription, but we supply it here to guide readers in the pronunciation of these unfamiliar words. Since no Sanskrit word is accented on the last syllable it is not necessary to accent disyllables, e.g., Rama.

The second CSL innovation designed to assist the reader in the pronunciation of lengthy unfamiliar words is to insert an unobtrusive middle dot between semantic word breaks in compound names (provided the word break does not fall on a vowel resulting from the fusion of two vowels), e.g., Maha·bhárata, but Ramáyana (not Rama·áyana). Our dot echoes the punctuating middle dot (·) found in the oldest surviving samples of written Indic, the Ashokan inscriptions of the third century BCE.

The deep layering of Sanskrit narrative has also dictated that we use quotation marks only to announce the beginning and end of every direct speech, and not at the beginning of every paragraph.

CSL Punctuation of Sanskrit

The Sanskrit text is also punctuated, in accordance with the punctuation of the English translation. In mid-verse, the punctuation will not alter the sandhi or the scansion. Proper names are capitalized. Most Sanskrit meters have four "feet" (*pāda*); where possible we print the common *śloka* meter on two lines. In the Sanskrit text, we use French *Guillemets* (e.g., *«kva saṃcicīrṣuḥ?»*) instead of English quotation marks (e.g., "Where are you off to?") to avoid confusion with the apostrophes used for vowel elision in sandhi.

SANDHI

Sanskrit presents the learner with a challenge: *sandhi* (euphonic combination). Sandhi means that when two words are joined in connected speech or writing (which in Sanskrit reflects speech), the last letter (or even letters) of the first word often changes; compare the way we pronounce "the" in "the beginning" and "the end."

In Sanskrit the first letter of the second word may also change; and if both the last letter of the first word and the first letter of the second are vowels, they may fuse. This has a parallel in English: a nasal consonant is inserted between two vowels that would otherwise coalesce: "a pear" and "an apple." Sanskrit vowel fusion may produce ambiguity.

The charts on the following pages give the full sandhi system.

Fortunately it is not necessary to know these changes in order to start reading Sanskrit. All that is important to know is the form of the second word without sandhi (pre-sandhi), so that it can be recognized or looked up in a dictionary. Therefore we are printing Sanskrit with a system of punctuation that will indicate, unambiguously, the original form of the second word, i.e., the form without sandhi. Such sandhi mostly concerns the fusion of two vowels.

In Sanskrit, vowels may be short or long and are written differently accordingly. We follow the general convention that a vowel with no mark above it is short. Other books mark a long vowel either with a bar called a macron (*ā*) or with a circumflex (*â*). Our system uses the

VOWEL SANDHI

Final vowels: a	ā	i	ī	u	ū	ṛ	e	ai	o	au	Initial vowels:
' â	" â	y a	y a	v a	v a	r a	e '	ā a	o '	āv a	a
' ā	" ā	y ā	y ā	v ā	v ā	r ā	a ā	ā ā	a ā	āv ā	ā
' ê	" ê	' î	" î	v i	v i	r i	a i	ā i	a i	āv i	i
' ē	" ē	' ī	" ī	v ī	v ī	r ī	a ī	ā ī	a ī	āv ī	ī
' ô	" ô	y u	y u	' û	" û	r u	a u	ā u	a u	āv u	u
' ō	" ō	y ū	y ū	' ū	" ū	r ū	a ū	ā ū	a ū	āv ū	ū
a' r	a" r	y ṛ	y ṛ	v ṛ	v ṛ	' ṝ	a ṛ	ā ṛ	a ṛ	āv ṛ	ṛ
' âi	" âi	y e	y e	v e	v e	r e	a e	ā e	a e	āv e	e
' āi	" āi	y ai	y ai	v ai	v ai	r ai	a ai	ā ai	a ai	āv ai	ai
' âu	" âu	y o	y o	v o	v o	r o	a o	ā o	a o	āv o	o
' āu	" āu	y au	y au	v au	v au	r au	a au	ā au	a au	āv au	au

CONSONANT SANDHI

Permitted finals: k	ṭ	t	p	ṅ	n	m	(Except āḥ/aḥ) ḥ/r	āḥ	aḥ	Initial letters:
k	ṭ	t	p	ṅ	n	ṃ	ḥ	āḥ	aḥ	k/kh
g	ḍ	d	b	ṅ	n	ṃ	r	ā	o	g/gh
k	ṭ	c	p	ṅ	ṃś	ṃ	ś	āś	aś	c/ch
g	ḍ	j	b	ṅ	ñ	ṃ	r	ā	o	j/jh
k	ṭ	ṭ	p	ṅ	ṃṣ	ṃ	ṣ	āṣ	aṣ	ṭ/ṭh
g	ḍ	ḍ	b	ṅ	ṇ	ṃ	r	ā	o	ḍ/ḍh
k	ṭ	t	p	ṅ	ṃs	ṃ	s	ās	as	t/th
g	ḍ	d	b	ṅ	n	ṃ	r	ā	o	d/dh
k	ṭ	t	p	ṅ	n	ṃ	ḥ	āḥ	aḥ	p/ph
g	ḍ	d	b	ṅ	n	ṃ	r	ā	o	b/bh
ṅ	ṇ	n	m	ṅ	n	ṃ	r	ā	o	*nasals* (n/m)
g	ḍ	d	b	ṅ	n	ṃ	r	ā	o	y/v
g	ḍ	d	b	ṅ	n	ṃ	*zero*[1]	ā	o	r
g	ḍ	l	b	ṅ	l̃[2]	ṃ	r	ā	o	l
k	ṭ	c ch	p	ṅ	ñ ś/ch	ṃ	ḥ	āḥ	aḥ	ś
k	ṭ	t	p	ṅ	n	ṃ	ḥ	āḥ	aḥ	ṣ/s
gg h	ḍḍ h	dd h	bb h	ṅ	n	ṃ	r	ā	o	h
g	ḍ	d	b	ṅ/ṅṅ[3]	n/nn[3]	m	r	ā	a[4]	*vowels*
k	ṭ	t	p	ṅ	n	m	ḥ	āḥ	aḥ	*zero*

[1]ḥ or r disappears, and if a/i/u precedes, this lengthens to ā/ī/ū. [2]e.g. tān+lokān=tāl̃ lokān.
[3]The doubling occurs if the preceding vowel is short. [4]Except: aḥ+a=o '.

macron, except that for initial vowels in sandhi we use a circumflex to indicate that originally the vowel was short, or the shorter of two possibilities (*e* rather than *ai*, *o* rather than *au*).

When we print initial *â*, before sandhi that vowel was *a*

î or *ê*,	*i*
û or *ô*,	*u*
âi,	*e*
âu,	*o*
ā,	*ā*
ī,	*ī*
ū,	*ū*
ē,	*ī*
ō,	*ū*
ai,	*ai*
āu,	*au*
', before sandhi there was a vowel *a*	

When a final short vowel (*a*, *i*, or *u*) has merged into a following vowel, we print ' at the end of the word, and when a final long vowel (*ā*, *ī*, or *ū*) has merged into a following vowel we print " at the end of the word. The vast majority of these cases will concern a final *a* or *ā*. See, for instance, the following examples:

What before sandhi was *atra asti* is represented as *atr' âsti*

atra āste	*atr' āste*
kanyā asti	*kany" âsti*
kanyā āste	*kany" āste*
atra iti	*atr' êti*
kanyā iti	*kany" êti*
kanyā īpsitā	*kany" ēpsitā*

Finally, three other points concerning the initial letter of the second word:

(1) A word that before sandhi begins with *ṛ* (vowel), after sandhi begins with *r* followed by a consonant: *yatha" rtu* represents pre-sandhi *yathā ṛtu*.

(2) When before sandhi the previous word ends in *t* and the following word begins with *ś*, after sandhi the last letter of the previous word is *c*

and the following word begins with *ch*: *syāc chāstravit* represents pre-sandhi *syāt śāstravit*.

(3) Where a word begins with *h* and the previous word ends with a double consonant, this is our simplified spelling to show the pre-sandhi form: *tad hasati* is commonly written as *tad dhasati*, but we write *tadd hasati* so that the original initial letter is obvious.

COMPOUNDS

We also punctuate the division of compounds (*samāsa*), simply by inserting a thin vertical line between words. There are words where the decision whether to regard them as compounds is arbitrary. Our principle has been to try to guide readers to the correct dictionary entries.

Exemplar of CSL Style

Where the Devanagari script reads:

कुम्भस्थली रक्षतु वो विकीर्णसिन्धूररेणुर्द्विरदाननस्य ।
प्रशान्तये विघ्नतमश्छटानां निष्ठ्यूतबालातपपल्लवेव ॥

Others would print:

kumbhasthalī rakṣatu vo vikīrṇasindūrareṇur dviradānanasya /
praśāntaye vighnatamaśchaṭānāṃ niṣṭhyūtabālātapapallaveva //

We print:

kumbha|sthalī rakṣatu vo vikīrṇa|sindūra|reṇur dvirad'|ānanasya
praśāntaye vighna|tamaś|chaṭānāṃ niṣṭhyūta|bāl'|ātapa|pallav" êva.

And in English:

May Ganésha's domed forehead protect you! Streaked with vermilion dust, it seems to be emitting the spreading rays of the rising sun to pacify the teeming darkness of obstructions.

("Nava·sáhasanka and the Serpent Princess" I.3)

Wordplay

Classical Sanskrit literature can abound in puns (*śleṣa*). Such paronomasia, or wordplay, is raised to a high art; rarely is it a *cliché*. Multiple meanings merge (*śliṣyanti*) into a single word or phrase. Most common are pairs of meanings, but as many as ten separate meanings are attested. To mark the parallel senses in the English, as well as the punning original in the Sanskrit, we use a *slanted* font (different from *italic*) and a triple colon (⁝) to separate the alternatives. E.g.

yuktaṃ Kādambarīṃ śrutvā kavayo maunam āśritāḥ
Bāṇa|dhvanāv an|adhyāyo bhavat' îti smṛtir yataḥ.

It is right that poets should fall silent upon hearing the Kadámbari, for the sacred law rules that recitation must be suspended when *the sound of an arrow ⁝ the poetry of Bana* is heard.

(Soméshvara·deva's "Moonlight of Glory" 1.15)

INTRODUCTION

There is no Sanskrit poet more interesting than Bana, none more original, none greater; and his prose poem "Princess Kadámbari" is his supreme achievement. Always held in India to be the best prose poem, Bana's *Kādambarī*, which was concluded by his son Bhúshana after his death, is a masterpiece of classical Sanskrit literature, unrivaled in richness and depth. It has everything. It is a love story doubled and redoubled in rebirth, a romance so influential that its title became the word for "a novel" in some modern Indian languages. It is at the same time a poem in free form verse, an experimental poem of enormous originality and prodigious vigor, with sympathetic and sharp-sighted observation of real life intermingled with judicious helpings of the high flown superworld of ornate Sanskrit metrical poetry, where flowers and mythology reign supreme. All is integrated into a single aesthetic unit, achieved in a complex but perfectly coherent structure with a breathtaking conclusion. The passion of young lovers is set in the context of a highly detailed portrayal of royal courts; nor is the animal kingdom neglected, the reader being treated to intimate presentations of parrot, horse, and elephant. The action proceeds over several lives, in a series of tales boxed one within the other, with tight cohesion and truly luminous artistic control on the part of both Bana and his son Bhúshana. The reader is given perhaps the fullest presentation of classical India available in a single work.

Albrecht Weber noted in 1853 that "Princess Kadámbari" is "a rather extensive work, about three times as long as" Dandin's "What Ten Young Men Did" (*Daśakumāra-carita*).[1] And "Princess Kadámbari" is again almost triple the size of Bana's other prose poem, "The Deeds of Harsha" (*Harṣacarita*), its closest rival in terms of quality. "Princess Kadámbari" is not only long, it is difficult. In 1984 LIENHARD declared, "Bāṇa is undoubtedly one of the most difficult poets in Sanskrit, and even a well-educated Indian will find his two novels hard to read" (1981: 256). Bana's long sentences, enormous range of reference, and use of puns (*śleṣa*) are the principal components of the difficulty he presents.[2] However, this Clay Sanskrit Library translation and edition sets out to show that the difficulty of Bana's poetry has been overstated; and once Bana's genius is appreciated, the only regret will be that his "Princess Kadámbari" is not longer.

Bana was a contemporary of the king Harsha·várdhana, who reigned between 606 and 647. In his "Deeds of Harsha," he describes his meeting with the king. The Chinese Buddhist pilgrim Hsuan Tsang, who visited India between 630 and 647, gives a detailed eyewitness account of Harsha's kingdom. As a result, we are exceptionally well informed about the life and times of Bana. Although "Princess Kadámbari" is a story prose poem (*kathā*) rather than a factual narrative prose poem (*ākhyāyikā*) like "The Deeds of Harsha," clearly the royal courts described in the former bear some relation to the court of Harsha.

The first point to be made about Bana's style of writing is that it has strong affinities with the style of royal proclamations, as SHELDON POLLOCK has noted. The main source of Indian history is the large number of inscriptions preserved on stone and metal. POLLOCK's recent study, "The Language of the Gods in the World of Men," is an attempt to make sense of this "inscriptional discourse," which "was the way power spoke at every royal court for a millennium or more all across the Sanskrit cosmopolis, and it spoke this way not because other discursive options, like the factual-referential or the vernacular, were unavailable but because they were thought to be unsuitable in many contexts. ...its preeminent goal was to make the real superreal, so to speak, by coding reality in the apparent impossibilities of poetic figuration" (2006: 146). Bana's use of punning was indeed significant, POLLOCK claims:

> Sustained use of bitextual poetry does not predate the Gupta period, when the Sanskrit cosmopolitan style crystallized; it was perfected by the poet Bāṇa at the end of the midseventh-century court of Harṣavardhana of Kānyakubja, and from there—no doubt through the circulation of Bāṇa's *Harṣacarita* itself—was transmitted across the cosmopolitan space, profoundly influencing the way power enunciated itself in public. (2006: 139)

But "Princess Kadámbari" seems always to have been the more popular of Bana's two works, and no doubt the specific reference of "The Deeds of Harsha" limited its appeal. And it is in "Princess Kadámbari" that we get a fascinating mention of the royal clerkdom at work:

> Thousands of edicts were being written down
> by the court clerks, who knew the name of every village
> and city, and who were as familiar with the whole world
> as if it were a single dwelling;

in as much as they were writing down all the world's
transactions, they seemed to be demonstrating
what goes on in the city of Death, the King of Justice.
(p. 401)

The reader new to Bana will certainly be helped by a fuller understanding of Bana's bitextuality, his punning (*śleṣa*). While some poems were resolutely bitextual throughout, in an extreme case retelling both the "Ramáyana" and the "Maha·bhárata," each verse referring punningly to both texts, and Bana's predecessor Subándhu used punning continuously through his prose poem, Bana is in fact quite sparing in his use of it. He employs it towards the end of his long descriptions, following on from detailed realistic description and after an array of comparisons and metaphors. There is a kind of surreal wildness in the random items that similarity of sounds pulls together in the latter stages of his long descriptions. The *śleṣa* affirms an underlying unity at the heart of things, however disparate those things may seem to be. Often punning references are to the epics, so that Bana's poem enjoys an underlying consistency with the grandest statements of Sanskrit epic poetry. Thus in describing the silk-cotton tree where the parrot lives Bana mentions that birds are found on it, and punningly refers to Shákuni, a character in the "Maha·bhárata" whose name is a common word for "bird:"

Like Duryódhana who showed *partisanship*
for Shákuni, it *has birds*
which can be seen flapping their wings. (p. 107)

Shákuni was brother-in-law of the blind king Dhrita·rashtra, and maternal uncle of the arch-villain Duryódhana, a skillful gambler who cheated Yudhi·shthira in the game of dice that is the armature of the "Maha·bhárata." This punning reference in "Princess Kadámbari" places the silk-cotton tree in the context of the epic, and hints at the tree's significance in the structure of the plot, and above all at the disastrous turn of events that will befall the parrots living in the tree. A similar pun is used in a quite opposite sense a little later, when the parrot who survives the catastrophe that strikes the tree is lucky enough to be brought to a peaceful hermitage:

> *The only killing of birds* in that place
> was *the killing of Shákuni*
> that occurs in the "Maha·bhárata." (p. 187)

There is nothing difficult about this pun. What the reader must learn to do is to be sensitive to the richness of Bana's intention.

Another problem the modern reader faces in reading Bana is the idiosyncratic botany and zoology of Sanskrit poetry's superreal reality, not so much what POLLOCK calls "apparent impossibilities of poetic figuration," but actual impossibilities. Bana not only gives extensively realistic descriptions, but also luxuriates in extensive reference to lotuses, bees, and all the unreal paraphernalia of classical Sanskrit poetry (*kāvya*). H.H. WILSON long ago remarked, "incidental reference to a deity by one of his many titles, and fanciful allusions to a flower or plant, constitute half, or more than half, of the poetry of the Hindus. Their mythology is the main structure, their botany the chief decoration, of their poetical compositions."[3] This early modern characterization of Sanskrit poetry needs considerable amplification before the special attractions of this poetry can be properly appreciated.

Perhaps the most prominent seemingly extraneous factor in Sanskrit poetry, Bana's included, is the lotus, in its many botanical forms. The reader should understand that the lotus here is a support, a provider of coherence, moving through poems with a binding and strengthening force. "Through its pervasive invasion of the subject matter of *kāvya*, it creates a poetic universe that obeys its own laws—or should we speak rather of a universe that simply succumbs to the dominance of the lotus and does not question its obtrusive presence."[4] Its delicate purity, symbol of the divine world and at the same time of femininity, arises from the mud beneath the surface of the water. The lotus is a highly charged symbolic force, and to understand the poetry the reader must be sensitized to the modulations of the lotus.

Bana's treatment of another favorite of *kāvya*, the elephant, is particularly varied. The frontal lobes of elephants are seen by Sanskrit poets to resemble the breasts of women, and their way of walking resembles women's. Other characteristics commonly referred to are distinctively male: the pearls said to be contained within those lobes are surely emblematic of male semen, and the rut or must that oozes from those lobes is another form of semen. Elephants in the real world were the foundation of royal power, its most graphic expression. The emperor Harsha was said to have 60,000 elephants at his disposal. In cosmological terms, the world is supported by the elephants standing at the cardinal points, who have themselves nothing to stand on—or, as Bana puts it, are "carried" by each cardinal point (p. 393). A good instance of the interplay between graphic description of the world of story and the superior universe of ornate poetry is Bana's account of the female doorkeeper who is about to usher in an outcaste young woman, whom we later discover to be an incarnation of the Goddess Shri:

> She was lovely in form but formidable.
> With her breasts whitened
> with a thick coating of sandal paste,
> she was like the heavenly Ganga
> with the two frontal lobes of Indra's elephant,
> Airávata, rising up from her waters. (p. 29)

Here we see Bana's precise visual eye and his strong sense of color values combining with the hyperreal world of the heavenly and mythological, and also *kāvya*'s special understanding of elephant physiology which stresses the lobes on elephants' heads. And this potent figure of the female doorkeeper is about to announce the arrival of the Goddess Shri in the form of a *mātaṅga* female, *mātaṅga* here a particular outcaste tribe, but also meaning "elephant."

> Like a forest lotus pool *which is destroyed*
> *by a herd of elephants,*
> she *was contaminated by her matánga family,* (p. 45)

is how the visitor who is about to be introduced to the king's court is subsequently described. We have been led back to punning. In contrast to these examples of the superreal is Shuka·nasa's entirely natural and well-observed comment that kings treat givers of good advice with disdain, closing their eyes to them like an elephant who is switching off from human antics:

> And when they do listen to elders
> who are giving them good advice,
> they show their contempt by closing their eyes
> in the way an elephant does. (p. 479)

Beyond the problem of punning and the superreal forms of nature, perhaps the most difficult thing with "Princess Kadámbari" is the length of Bana's sentences. WEBER's complaint on this score and his comparison of "Princess Kadámbari" to an Indian forest has ever since been referred to whenever Bana is presented:

> a mannerism, already apparent in the *Daśakumâracharitra*, is here carried to excess: the verb is kept back to the second, third, fourth, nay, once to the sixth page, and all the interval is filled with epithets and epithets to these epithets: moreover these epithets frequently consist of compounds extending over more than one line: in short, Bâna's prose is an Indian wood, where all progress is rendered impossible by the undergrowth until the traveler cuts out a path for himself, and where, even then, he has to reckon with malicious wild beasts in the shape of unknown words that affright him. (WEBER, loc. cit., translated by P. PETERSON 1899–1900: 37)

Not just the verb, but more significantly the subject, is kept till the end of Bana's long sentences. Those of Bana's sentences that are long have a clear purpose. The subject is held back till the end, and the effect is to bring multiplicity into unity, a unity that is not manifested until the end of the sentence is reached. Metrical poetry is forced to work at the level of the single verse, though groups of verses may be strung together, and meter forces exact measurement of length, while the prose poet is entirely freed from external restraint, a freedom in which Bana exults. But though Bana's prose lacks external constraint, it has its own rhythms and structure. And the repetition of similar case endings provides frequent rhyming that assists understanding. Printed versions of the text have hitherto presented solid blocks of text, following the practice of manuscripts.[5] But such presentation in continuous unbroken lines is not used in the case of metrical poets, though their manuscripts too do not break up the lines. This edition and translation aims to allow Bana to speak in English as I believe he would have wished had he, master of the novel of rebirths, been reborn today. Bana's difficulty largely evaporates once he is set out in line lengths that mirror the rhythms and rhymes of his prose, which in fact is free form verse.

Nor is WEBER's analogy of a jungle totally unhelpful. It reminds us that there is a great deal about getting lost in Bana's story (*kathā*). "Princess Kadámbari" is a jungle in that it is hard to know where the narrative is going, and one is surprised and overwhelmed by the variety of impressions that are forced on one. Like a jungle, the text has a seamless unity: there are no divisions, no chapters or sections formally marked out. The only division, between the part written by the father and the part written by the son, is brought about by the author's death, but even here the unity of the text as a whole is maintained by the fact that it is the author's chosen son who completes it[6] and all the puzzles of the preceding part are solved and explained. The text lacks formal divisions because of the overriding concern to make the richly diverse text a single unit; and at the level of the sentence the same concern can be found. At the level of the whole poem, the diverse characters and narratives are finally explained in the dénouement where all complications are explained. At the level of the sentence, multiple and contesting parts only make full sense when the noun is reached at the very end. The reader is, as it were, in front of a giant IMAX cinema screen, where so much is going on at once that it takes a while before one can get one's bearings.

In WEBER's graphic phrase, the reader of "Princess Kadámbari" is lost in a kind of jungle, but that this is so is Bana's deliberate intention. Although the wild *śabara* hunters who so frighten the young parrot have no trouble following the trails of various wild beasts, Bana provides very little to help the reader find their way. The work as a whole and its individual sentences pull as many disparate lives, reincarnations, and things as possible into a unity made out of baffling complexity.

When the minister Shuka·nasa lectures Prince Chandrapída on the dangers of being young, he tells him:

> And like disorientation *sending one on the wrong road,*
> excessive attachment to sense objects destroys a man,
> *sending him morally astray.* (p. 475)

This disorientation (*diṅ/moha*) is what Bana deliberately brings about in the reader of "Princess Kadámbari," and disorientation is experienced by his own characters, when the parrot escapes from the clutches of the *śabara* hunter, when Chandrapída out hunting gets separated from his parasol bearer, when Chandrapída again gets lost hunting the *kiṃnara* couple. Likewise, there is a problem of mapping when Chandrapída returns to the royal palace after his ten year stint in college, and has to be directed through his father's palace, and that of the minister Shuka·nasa, the palaces evidently seeming almost as new to him as Harsha's to Bana himself when he was summoned to the Emperor's presence, as detailed in "The Deeds of Harsha."

The problem of finding one's way spatially echoes the temporal problem of who was who in the last birth and in the next; and is further compounded by transpositions of things from one element to another in *kāvya*'s similes and metaphors. Bana's world moves effortlessly from painterly descriptions of visual reality to literary confections of extravagant tropes and punning literary reference, to the epics, *purāṇa*s, and the story literature which is the milieu of the plot of "Princess Kadámbari."

The traditional saying that the whole world is the leavings (*ucchiṣṭam*) of the "Maha·bhárata" has also been applied to Bana. KUNHAN RAJA in the introduction to his abbreviated version of "Kadámbari" expresses it in this way: "There is nothing in the world which Bana has not munched, ... everything in the world is what he had munched and thrown out later" (KUNHAN RAJA 1963: 7). Bana himself in the autobiographical beginning of his "Deeds of Harsha" has a friend refer to the account of Harsha that Bana is about to recite as a second "Maha·bhárata;"

and there is some humor in Bana's choice of name for the parrot who retails the second phase of "Princess Kadámbari," that is to say the name of the person who is reincarnated in the parrot—Vaishampáyana, the narrator of the "Maha·bhárata." Like many other poets, Bana frequently refers to the "Maha·bhárata," and the "Ramáyana," mainly in the form of puns so that details of the epic narratives occasionally irradiate his story. In Bana's case the weight and dignity of his own artistic endeavor are not unbalanced by these references, but carry them in their stride. Bana also makes passing reference to the "Long Story" (*Bṛhatkathā*), a cycle of stories that may have been the source of the plot of "Princess Kadámbari."

Bana wrote several works. The natural assumption is that "Princess Kadámbari" is his last work, but it remains to be proven on internal grounds that it is later than "The Deeds of Harsha." Bana also wrote a series of verses in praise of the Goddess Durga, the *Caṇḍīśataka*. Some sixty other verses are credited to him in anthologies. He may have written a play on the marriage of Shiva and Párvati, the *Pārvatīpariṇaya*, closely based on Kali·dasa's "Birth of Kumára" (*Kumārasaṃbhava*),[7] and a very early work if his. Something of Bana's liveliness is suggested in this play by Shiva's suggestion, entirely absent from the play's inspiration and model, that rather than waiting for a regular wedding, he and Párvati should make love at once, performing what was known as a fairy wedding (*gandharva/vivāha*). Párvati's female companion tells him that he must wait for a regular ceremony at Párvati's father's house.

It is not impossible that Bana was the author of the three plays generally supposed to be have been written by Harsha, the king he served. The poetician Mámmata referred to the fact that Bana earned lots of money from Harsha, and the commentator Uddyóta·kara offered the explanation that Bana was the real author of Harsha's "Lady of the Jewel Necklace" (*Ratnāvalī*).[8] It has not, I believe, previously been noticed that the episode of a monkey escaping from the horse stable in Tarapída's palace is very like the parallel event in "The Lady of the Jewel Necklace;" and in both cases this commotion is followed by a reference to talking birds revealing embarrassing secrets. Since this is part of the plot of "The Lady of the Jewel Necklace" it is more likely that this work is the source of the similar passage in "Princess Kadámbari." G.C. JHALA noticed in 1967 that the women in Tarapída's harem imitating the actions of the king is "exactly illustrated" by the play within the play in the third act of "The Lady of the Jewel Necklace." Both in itself and in relation to other works, the literary study of "Princess Kadámbari" has a long way to go. Excellent beginnings were made by GWEN LAYNE and ROBERT HUECKSTEDT more than twenty years ago, both of them clearly inspired by Bana's original genius.

This book is dedicated to past and future editors and translators of Bana's *Kādambarī*.

Notes

1 "*ein ziemlich umfangreiches Werk, etwa dreimal so stark als der Daçakumàra*," (WEBER 1853: 582).

2 In tribute to the rich complexity of his two great prose poems Bana is often called "Bana the Master," *Bāṇa/bhaṭṭa* or *bhaṭṭa/Bāṇa*.

3 *A Dictionary, Samscrit and English,* Calcutta, 1819, p. xlvi.

4 See SMITH (2000: 211).

5 The printed editions are, it is true, paragraphed in varying ways by different editors, but the overall effect is of solid text—PETERSON, for instance has 352 paragraphs for 369 pages of text.

6 On Bana's choice of the son who was to complete "Princess Kadámbari" see introduction to vol. 3.

7 Translated by DAVID SMITH, Clay Sanskrit Library, 2005.

8 Translated by WENDY DONIGER, Clay Sanskrit Library, 2007.

Bibliography

The Sanskrit text of this edition is based on PETER PETERSON's edition of *Kādambarī*, 1899–1900.

CONCORDANCE OF PAGE NUMBERS WITH PAGE NUMBERS OF PETERSON'S EDITION

CSL	PETERSON	CSL	PETERSON
2	4	260	55
20	6	280	59
40	10	300	64
60	14	320	69
80	19	340	74
100	22	360	79
120	26	380	83
140	31	400	87
160	36	420	91
180	40	440	95
200	43	460	99
220	48	480	104
240	52	500	108

Peterson page numbers are additionally given in the margin to the present edition, every five Peterson pages.

I have also consulted one manuscript on difficult passages: India Office Sanskrit 3300 (IOSan3300). Devanagari. "Old writing (17th century?) from Western India."

For a detailed bibliography of editions and translations of *Kādambarī* up to 1936 see Scharpé (1937).

EDITIONS

Kādambarī. (ed.) Madanamohana Tarkālaṃkāra. Calcutta, (*saṃvat* 1906) 1849.

Kādambarī. (ed.) T. Tarkavācaspati Bhaṭṭācārya. Calcutta, (*śaka* 1793) 1871.

Kādambarī. (ed.) Peter Peterson (Bombay Sanskrit Series, 24), Third Edition, Part i, text, 1900. Part ii, Introduction and notes. 1899. Bombay: Government Central Book Depôt. This edition is based on two manuscripts collated with the two Calcutta editions and four other manuscripts. As this edition is exceedingly rare, I quote Peterson's introduction from his second edition, Bombay, 1889.

Kādambarī Pūrvabhāga. (ed.) M.R. Kale. with the *Bālābodhinū* Sanskrit commentary by the editor. Delhi: Motilal Banarsidass, 1968. (Includes English translation of the *Pūrvabhāga*.)

Kādambarī (*Pūrvabhāga* pp. 1–124 of Peterson's edition). Edited with introduction, notes and appendices by P.V. Kane. First edition. Published by the author. Bombay, 1920.

Kādambarī (*Pūrvabhāga*, pp. 124–237 of Peterson's edition). Edited with introduction, notes and appendices by P.V. Kane. Third edition. Published by the author. Bombay, 1921.

Kādambarī (*Uttarabhāga*). Edited with introduction, notes and appendices by P.V. Kane. First edition. Published by the author. Bombay, 1913.

Kādambarī. (ed.) Kāśīnāth Pāṇḍurang Parab, with the commentaries of Bhānuchandra and his disciple Siddhachandra. Ninth edition revised with his own commentary named Chaṣaka by Mathuranāth Śāstrī, Bombay: Nirṇaya Sāgar Press, 1948.

Kādambarī. (ed.) P.L. VAIDYA Critical text as per PETERSON's edition with an introduction in Sanskrit. 2nd edition. Poona: Oriental Book Agency, 1951.

Kādambarī of Bāṇabhaṭṭa. Edited with the *Candrakalā* Sanskrit commentary and a Hindi translation by KRISHNAMOHANA ŚĀSTRĪ. Kashi Sanskrit Series 151, 7th edition. Varanasi: Chaukhambha Sanskrit Sansthan: 2000.

Kādambarī (*Uttarārdha*) of Son of Bāṇabhaṭṭa. Edited with the *Candrakalā* Sanskrit commentary and a Hindi translation by RĀM CHANDRA MIŚRA. Kashi Sanskrit Series 151 (Part II), 4th edition. Varanasi: Chaukhambha Sanskrit Sansthan: 2000.

SRIVASTAVA, UMA. *An edition of Arjuna-Paṇḍita's commentary on the Kādambarī (Uttarabhāga) (with an introduction and notes in English)*. PhD thesis, University of Toronto, 1979.

TRANSLATIONS

GRINTSER, P.A. (trans.) 1995. *Kadambari*. Moskva: Ladomir, Nauka. (A complete translation of the *Pūrvabhāga* into Russian, with a summary of the *Uttarabhāga*.)

KALE, M.R. (ed.) 1968. *Kādambarī Pūrvabhāga* with the *Bālābodhinū* Sanskrit commentary by the editor. Delhi: Motilal Banarsidass. (Includes English translation of the *Pūrvabhāga*.)

KUNHAN RAJA, C. (trans.) 1963. *Kadambari*. Bombay: Bharatiya Vidya Bhavan. (An abridged and simplified translation.)

LAYNE, GWENDOLYN. (trans.) 1991. *Kadambari: a classic Sanskrit story of magical transformations*, with illustrations by VIRGIL BURNETT. New York, London : Garland.

RIDDING, C.M. (trans.) 1896. *The Kādambarī of Bāṇa*. London: Royal Asiatic Society.

SCHARPÉ, ADRIAAN ALBERICK MARIA. 1937. *Bāṇa's Kādambarī*. Dissertation, Utrecht. Leuven: N. v. de Vlaamsche Drukkerij, 1937. (Translation into Flemish of those parts of *Kādambarī* untranslated or abbreviated by RIDDING.)

OTHER WORKS

AGRAWĀLA, VĀSUDEVAŚARAṆA. 1970. *Kādambarī: ek sāṃskṛtik adhyayan.* Vidyabhawan Rashtrabhasha Granthamala 14. Second edition. Varanasi: Chowkhamba Vidyabhavan.

BIARDEAU, M. AND M.-C. PORCHER (trans.) 1999. *Le Rāmāyaṇa de Vālmīki.* Paris: Gallimard.

COWELL, E.B. and F.W. THOMAS (trans.) 1897. *The Harsacarita of Bāna.* London: Royal Asiatic Society; rpt. Delhi: Motilal Banarsidass, 1961.

DIXIT, S.V. 1963. *Bāṇabhaṭṭa: His Life and Literature.* Belgaum: A.S. Dixit.

GEROW, EDWIN. 1971. *A Glossary of Indian Figures of Speech.* The Hague: Mouton.

HALL, FITZEDWARD. (ed.) 1859. *The Vásavadattá: a romance by Subandhu, accompanied by Śivaráma Tripáthin's perpetual gloss, entitled Darpaṇa.* Bibliotheca Indica no. 30, Calcutta: Asiatic Society of Bengal.

HUECKSTEDT, ROBERT A. 1985. *The Style of Bāṇa: An Introduction to Sanskrit Prose Poetry.* Lanham, New York, London: University Press of America.

JHALA, C.C. 1967. "A note on Bāṇa's *Kādambarī* and Harṣa's *Priyadarśikā.*" *Indian Antiquary* 2(1): 40–41.

KARMAKAR, R.D. 1964. *Bāṇa.* Dharwar: Karnatak University.

KRISHNAMOORTHY, K. 1976. *Bāṇabhaṭṭa.* New Delhi: Sahitya Akademi.

LAYNE, GWENDOLYN LOUISE. 1979. *Kādambarī: a Critical Inquiry into a Seventh Century Sanskrit Narrative.* PhD Dissertation, University of Chicago.

———. 1980–81. "*Kādambarī* and the Art of Framing Lies: a Study in Storytelling." *Jadavpur Journal of Comparative Literature* 18/19: 98–118.

———. 1982. "Orientalists and literary critics: East is East, West is West, and it is in the professional interest of some to keep it that way." *The Western Humanities Review,* xxxvi/2: 165–75.

LIENHARD, SIEGFRIED. 1984. *A History of Classical Poetry: Sanskrit—Pali—Prakrit.* Wiesbaden: Otto Harrassowitz.

Patil, Sharad. 1974. "Earth Mother." *Social Scientist* 2(21): 31–58.

Pollock, Sheldon. 2006. *The Language of the Gods in the World of Men*. Berkeley: University of California Press.

Sharma, Neeta. 1968. *Bāṇabhaṭṭa: a Literary Study*. Delhi: Munshiram Manoharlal.

Smith, David. 2000. "An alternative poetics of the lotus." In Jaroslav Vacek (ed.) *Pandanus: Natural Symbolism in Indian Literatures*. Prague: Signeta, pp. 211–29.

Tieken, H. Forthcoming. "Bāṇa's Death in the Kādambarī."

Trikha, Raj Kumari. 1982. *Alaṃkāras in the Works of Bāṇabhaṭṭa*. Delhi: Parimal Publications.

van Buitenen, J.A.B. (trans.) 1981. *The Mahābhārata, Volume 2, Book 2: The Book of Assembly; Book 3: The Book of the Forest*. Chicago: University of Chicago Press.

Weber, A. 1853. "Analyse der *Kādambarī*." *Zeitschrift der Deutschen Morgenländischen Gesellschaft* 7: 582–89.

PRINCESS KADÁMBARI
VOLUME I

RAJO|JUṢE JANMANI, sattva|vṛttaye,

sthitau prajānāṃ, pralaye tamaḥ|spṛśe,

Ajāya sarga|sthiti|nāśa|hetave

trayīmayāya tri|guṇ'|âtmane namaḥ!

jayanti Bāṇ'|âsura|mauli|lālitā

Daśāsya|cūḍā|maṇi|cakra|cumbinaḥ

sur'|âsur'|âdhīśa|śikh'|ânta|śāyino

bhava|cchidas Tryambaka|pāda|pāṃsavaḥ.

jayaty Upendraḥ sa cakāra dūrato

bibhitsayā yaḥ kṣaṇa|labdha|lakṣayā

dṛś" âiva kop'|âruṇayā ripor uraḥ

svayaṃ bhayād bhinnam iv' âsra|pāṭalam.

Combining with the quality of activity
in giving birth to living beings,
acting with the quality of goodness
in maintaining their existence,
coming into contact with the quality
of darkness in their dissolution,
to the unborn one,
cause of creation, maintenance, destruction,
consisting of the triple Vedas,
composed of the three qualities,
to that Brahman,
glory!
The dust of Tryámbaka Shiva's feet triumphs,
caressed by the demon Bana's[1] crown,
kissing the circle of ten-headed Rávana's crest jewels,
resting on the crests of the lords of gods and demons,
cutting through becoming.
Vishnu as the Man-lion triumphs,
with just his eye, red with anger,
focussed for a moment
on the chest of his foe
in a desire to split it open,
from a distance making
the chest blood red,
as if it had split open
of its own accord,
through fear.

namāmi Bharvoś caraṇ'|âmbuja|dvayaṃ

sa|śekharair Maukharibhiḥ kṛt'|ârcanam

samasta|sāmanta[2]|kirīṭa|vedikā|

viṭaṅka|pīṭh'|ôlluṭhit'|āruṇ'|āṅguli.

a|kāraṇ'|āviṣkṛta|vaira|dāruṇād

a|saj|janāt kasya bhayaṃ na jāyate,

viṣaṃ mah"|âher iva yasya durvacaḥ

su|duḥsahaṃ saṃnihitaṃ sadā mukhe?

kaṭu kvaṇanto mala/dāyakāḥ khalās

tudanty alaṃ bandhana|śṛṅkhalā iva

manas tu *sādhu/dhvanibhiḥ pade pade*

haranti santo maṇi|nūpurā iva.

subhāṣitaṃ hāri viśaty adho galān

na durjanasy' Ârkaripor iv' âmṛtam.

tad eva dhatte hṛdayena saj|jano

Harir mahā|ratnam iv' âtinirmalam.

I bow down to the lotus feet of Bharvu,[3]
which are honored by the crowned Máukharis,
his toes red from rubbing on
what serves as a lofty stool:
the platform of the crowns
of the assembled tributary kings.
Who does not fear the wicked critic
fierce in the enmity he displays
without cause,
with abuse always ready in his mouth
like a great snake,
very difficult to withstand?
Rogues *given to harsh criticism spreading calumny*
like fetters of iron
harshly clanking at every step,
staining with rust,
bruise,
while the good *with their applause at every word*
like jeweled anklets,
sounding just right at every step
delight the mind.
Charming, well chosen words of poetry
penetrate an evil person
no further than his throat,
like nectar the throat of Rahu[4], enemy of the sun.
The good person bears them in his heart
as Vishnu bears the entirely spotless gem,
the great Káustubha,[5]
on his chest.

sphurat|kal'|ālāpa|vilāsa|komalā

karoti rāgaṃ hṛdi kautuk'|âdhikam

rasena śayyāṃ[6] *svayam abhyupāgatā*

kathā janasy' *âbhinavā* vadhūr iva

haranti kaṃ n' *ôjjvala|dīpak"|ôpamair*

navaiḥ pad'|ârthair upapāditāḥ kathā

nir|antara|śleṣa|ghanāḥ su|jātayo

mahā|srajaś campaka|kuḍmalair iva.

babhūva Vātsyāyana|vaṃśa|saṃbhavo

dvijo jagad|gīta|guṇo 'graṇīḥ satām,

aneka|Gupt'|ârcita|pāda|paṅkajaḥ

Kubera|nām' âṃśa iva Svayaṃbhuvaḥ.

Tenderly manifesting erotic grace
in melodious conversation,
an *innovatory katha* story,
such as is the work which follows,
stringing words fluently together
in harmonious combination
with aesthetic emotions—
just like a *new* bride *coming lovingly*
of her own accord to her husband's bed—
arouses passion in the heart of its audience,
heightened by curiosity.
Whom do *katha* stories not captivate,
made up out of *new* things
in which zeugmas and similes shine forth clearly
dense with unabated punning,
splendid with realistic description
like large garlands of *jasmine flowers*
tightly knotted,
made up with *fresh chámpaka* buds
resembling brilliant lamps?
There was a brahmin
belonging to Vatsyáyana's lineage,
his virtues sung throughout the world,
leader of the good,
his lotus feet worshipped by several Gupta princes;[7]
Kubéra by name, he seemed a portion
of Self-born Brahma.

uvāsa yasya śruti|śānta|kalmaṣe
sadā puroḍāśa|pavitrit'|âdhare
Sarasvatī soma|kaṣāyit'|ôdare
samasta|śāstra|smṛti|bandhure mukhe

jagur[8] gṛhe 'bhyasta|samasta|vāṅmayaiḥ
sa|sārikaiḥ pañjara|vartibhiḥ śukaiḥ
nigṛhyamāṇā baṭavaḥ pade pade
yajūṃṣi sāmāni ca yasya śaṅkitāḥ

Hiraṇyagarbho bhuvan'|âṇḍakād iva,
kṣapā|karaḥ kṣīra|mah"|ârṇavād iva,
abhūt Suparṇo Vinat'|ôdarād iva,
dvijanmanām Arthapatiḥ patis tataḥ.

vivṛṇvato yasya visāri vāṅ|mayaṃ
dine dine śiṣya|gaṇā *navā navāḥ*
uṣaḥsu *lagnāḥ śravaṇe* 'dhikāṃ śriyaṃ
pracakriye candana|pallavā iva.

vidhāna/saṃpādita/dāna/śobhitaiḥ
sphuran/mahā/vīra/sanātha/mūrtibhiḥ
makhair a|saṃkhyair ajayat sur'|ālayaṃ
sukhena yo *yūpa/karair* gajair iva.

Sarásvati, Goddess of Speech,
ever dwelled in his mouth,
which was purified of sin by the Vedas,
his lips sanctified by sacrificial cake,
his palate reddened by the *soma* drink,
his mouth adorned with all sciences
and codified knowledge.
In his house the boys recited the hymns
of the "Yajur Veda" and the "Sama Veda."
Checked on every word[9]
by caged parrots and mynah birds
who'd mastered all forms of literature,[10]
they were anxious boys.[11]
Like Hiránya·garbha from the world egg,
like the moon from the milk ocean,
like beautiful-winged Gáruda from Vínata's womb,
Artha·pati,[12] chief of the twice-born,
was born from him.[13]
Daily at dawn as he expounded
the broad range of verbal knowledge
ever new throngs of pupils
added to his glory,
intent on hearing him,
like *really fresh* sandal shoots *on his ear.*
He easily conquered heaven
with innumerable sacrifices
adorned with gifts properly bestowed,
blazing spectacularly with Great Hero[14] *fires,*
where *sacrificial posts were hands to achieve the goal,*
as if with innumerable elephants

sa Citrabhānuṃ tanayaṃ mah"|ātmanāṃ

sut'|ôttamānāṃ śruti|śāstra[15]|śālinām

avāpa madhye *sphaṭik'|ôpal'|âmalaṃ*[16]

krameṇa Kailāsam iva *kṣamā|bhṛtām.*

mah"|ātmano yasya *su|dūra|nirgatāḥ*

kalaṅka|mukt'|êndu|kal"|âmala|tviṣaḥ

dviṣan|manaḥ prāviviśuḥ kṛt'|ântarā

guṇā nṛ|siṃhasya nakh'|âṅkurā iva.

diśām alīk'|âlaka|bhaṅgatāṃ gatas

trayī|vadhū|karṇa|tamāla|pallavaḥ

cakāra yasy' âdhvara|dhūma|saṃcayo

malīmasaḥ śuklataraṃ nijaṃ yaśaḥ.

Sarasvatī|pāṇi|saroja|saṃpuṭa|

pramṛṣṭa|homa|śrama|śīkar'|âmbhasaḥ

yaśo|'ṃśu|śuklī|kṛta|sapta|viṣṭapāt

tataḥ suto Bāṇa iti vyajāyata.

adorned with the rut produced by proper fodder,
their tremendous bodies carrying mighty warriors,
their trunks like sacrificial posts.
In due course, he obtained a son,
Chitra·bhanu, "Bright Light,"
as pure as a piece of crystal,
appearing amid his other noble and most excellent
sons[17] *who where patient by nature,*
like Kailása *as bright as a piece of crystal*
amid the other mountains.
That noble one's merits
spreading far and wide
entered his enemies' hearts,
like Man-lion Vishnu's curved claws,
shining as brightly as the digit of a moon
that has no stain,
penetrating most deeply
into the heart of his enemy,
Hiránya·káshipu.
The dark mass of smoke from his sacrifices
curling like locks of hair on the quarters' brows,
tamála shoots for the ear
of the threefold Veda as bride,
made his fame the brighter.
When Sarásvati with her folded lotus hands
had wiped away the drops of sweat he'd shed
from the effort of the *soma* sacrifice,
and he'd whitened the seven worlds[18]
with the rays of his glory,
to him was born a son, Bana by name.

P5 dvijena ten' â|kṣata|kaṇṭha|kauṇṭhyayā

mahā|mano|moha|malīmas'|ândhayā

a|labdha|vaidagdhya|vilāsa|mugdhayā

dhiyā nibaddh' êyam atidvayī kathā.

āsīd a|śeṣa|nara|pati|śiraḥ|samabhyarcita|śāsanaḥ

Pāka|śāsana iv' âparaś,

catur|udadhi|mālā|mekhalāyā bhuvo bhartā,

pratāp'|ânurāg'|âvanata|samasta|sāmanta|cakraś,

cakra|varti|lakṣaṇ'|ôpetaś,

cakra|dhara iva

kara|kamal'|ôpalakṣyamāṇa|śaṅkha|cakra|lāñchano,

Hara iva *jita/Manmatho,*

Guha iv' *â/pratihata/śaktiḥ,*

kamala|yonir iva *vimānī/kṛta/rāja/haṃsa/maṇḍalo,*

jaladhir iva *Lakṣmī/prasūtir,*

That brahmin, albeit with his mind undiminished in dullness of expression, blind in the great darkness of his mental delusion, naïve, never having attained the charm of wit, composed this story that has no parallel.[19] P5

There was a king whose commands
were honored by the bowed heads of all kings,
as if he were another Indra, punisher of Paka.
He was the lord of the earth whose girdle
is the four oceans.
The whole circle of neighboring princes
bowed down in loving submission to his valor,
and he was endowed with the marks
that showed him born to be universal emperor:
like Vishnu who holds the discus,
the marks of conch and lotus were discernible
on his lotus-like hands.
Like Shiva the destroyer *who overcame Kama,*
god of love, he'd *conquered passion within himself.*
Like Guha, the Secret One, Shiva's son,
whose *spear is irresistible,*
his *power met with no opposition.*
Like lotus-born Brahma,
who *took his mount from the circle of royal geese,*
he *humbled the circle of excellent kings.*
Just as the ocean was *the source of the Goddess Lakshmi,*
he was *the source of wealth.*

Gaṅgā|pravāha iva Bhagīratha|patha|pravṛtto,

ravir iva pratidivas'|ôpajāyamān'|ôdayo,

Merur iva

sakala|bhuvan'|ôpajīvyamāna|pāda|cchāyo,

dig|gaja iv'

ân|avarata|pravṛtta|dān'|ārdrī|kṛta|karaḥ,

kartā mah"|āścaryāṇām,

āhartā kratūnām,

ādarśaḥ sarva|śāstrāṇām,

utpattiḥ kalānāṃ,

kula|bhuvanaṃ guṇānāṃ,

āgamaḥ kāvy'|âmṛta|rasānām,

udaya|śailo mitra|maṇḍalasy',

ôtpāta|ketur ahita|janasya,

pravartayitā goṣṭhī|bandhānām,

āśrayo rasikānāṃ,

pratyādeśo dhanuṣmatāṃ,

dhaureyaḥ sāhasikānām,

agraṇīr vidagdhānāṃ,

Vainateya iva

Vinat"|ānanda|janano,

Like Ganga's stream,
he followed in Bhagi·ratha's[20] path.
Just as the sun rises every day,
day by day his prosperity increased.
As with Meru, all the world lived submissively
in the shadow of his feet.
Like one of the eight elephants at the cardinal points,
who support the world,
its trunk wet with the ichor it unceasingly emitted,
his hand was wet with the gifts[21] *he unceasingly gave out.*
He was the performer of great and wonderful deeds.
The offerer of sacrifices,
mirror of all the sciences,
origin of the arts,
the ancestral home of good qualities,
the source of poetry's nectareous aesthetic emotions.
To the circle of his friends he brought rock-solid success,
like the mountain of sunrise
to the disc of the sun, mankind's friend.
To his foes, he was a comet of calamity.
He was the organizer of literary societies,
the patron of men of taste,
he threw archers into the background,
he was the foremost of the bold,
the leader of intellectuals,[22]
Like Gáruda, Vínata's son,
who gave joy to his mother Vínata,
he *gave joy to those to who bowed down to him.*

Vainya iva
cāpa|koṭi|samutsārita|sakal'|ârāti|kul'|âcalo
rājā Śūdrako nāma.
nāmn" âiva yo nirbhinn'|ârāti|hṛdayo
viracita|Nārasiṃha|rūp'|āḍambaram
eka|vikram'|ākrānta|sakala|bhuvana|talo
vikrama|tray'|āyāsitaṃ ca jahās' êva Vāsudevam.
aticira|kāla|lagnam atikrānta|ku|nṛpati|sahasra|saṃparka|
kalaṅkam iva kṣālayantī
yasya vimale kṛpāṇa|*dhārā*|jale
ciram uvāsa rāja|lakṣmīḥ.
yaś ca manasi Dharmeṇa,
kope Yamena,
prasāde Dhanadena,
pratāpe Vahninā,
bhuje Bhuvā,
dṛśi Śriyā,
vāci Sarasvatyā,
mukhe śaśinā,
bale marutā,
prajñāyāṃ sura|guruṇā,
rūpe Manasijena,
tejasi Savitrā vasatā,
sarva|devamayasya prakaṭita|viśva|rūp'|ākṛter[25]
anukaroti bhagavato Nārāyaṇasya.

Like Prithu[23], son of Vena, with the points of his bow
he rooted up all the mountain chains that were his foes.
Súdraka[24] was the name of the king.
He seemed to laugh at Krishna, Vasu·deva's son,
in that he broke his foes' hearts by his name alone
while Krishna had to put on the show
of assuming the form of the Man-lion,
and he overran the whole surface of the world
in a single heroic campaign
while Krishna in his dwarf incarnation
had to tire himself with his three giant steps.
As if washing away the stain—clinging to her all too long—
from excessive contact with thousands of bad kings,
the goddess of royal glory long dwelled
in the water *of the stream* that was his sword *blade.*
Moreover, since Dharma dwelled in his mind,
Yama, god of death, in his anger,
Kubéra, god of wealth, in his kindness,
Agni, god of fire, in his splendor,
the goddess Earth on his arm,
the goddess of Beauty in his glance,
Sarásvati in his speech,
the moon in his face,
the wind in his strength,
Brihas·pati, guru of the gods, in his wisdom,
the god of Love in his handsome body,
the vivifying sun in his glory,
he, composed of all the gods,[26]
resembled the blessed lord Naráyana
who manifests his form in the shape of the universe.

yasya ca mada|kala|kari|kumbha|pīṭha|pāṭanam ācarato

lagna|sthūla|muktā|phalena dṛḍha|muṣṭi|nipīḍanān

niṣṭhyūta|*dhārā*|jala|bindu|dantureṇ' êva kṛpāṇen'

ākṛṣyamāṇā

subhaṭ'|ôraḥ|kapāṭa|vighaṭita|kavaca|sahasr'|

ândhakāra|madhya|vartinī kari|karaṭa|taṭa|galita|

mada|jal'|āsāra|durdināsv abhisārik" êva samara|niśāsu

samīpam a|sakṛd ājagāma rāja|Lakṣmīḥ.

yasya ca hṛdaya|sthitān api patīn didhakṣur iva

pratāp'|ânalo viyoginīnām api ripu|sundarīṇām

antar|janita|dāho divā|niśaṃ jajvāla.

yasmiṃś ca rājani jita|jagati paripālayati mahīṃ

citra|karmasu *varṇa|saṃkarā,*

rateṣu keśa|grahāḥ,

kāvyeṣu *dṛḍha|bandhāḥ,*

śāstreṣu *cintā,*

svapneṣu vipralambhāś,

And as he performed the splitting
of the temple lobes of rutting elephants,
royal Glory was drawn to him by his sword
which seemed inlaid with drops of water
squeezed out from the *river* of its *blade*
because his fist held it so tightly,
when in reality big pearls were clinging to it.
She, living amid the darkness of thousands of breastplates
torn from the broad chests of great warriors
in the nights of battle, stormy with the showers of rut
flowing from the broad temples of elephants,
like a woman who goes in the night to her lover,
came to him.
And as if it wished to burn up
the memory of their husbands
that the lovely women of the foe
alone though they were,
had left in their hearts,
the fire of his valor blazed night and day,
making them suffer.
And while that king who'd conquered the universe
was protecting the earth,
for his subjects *mixtures of caste* occurred
only in paintings *as mixing of colors;*
pulling hair only in love-making;
rigorous imprisonment only in poetry
as rigid rules of composition;
worry only in respect of *deliberation*
about the forms of secular knowledge;
separations only in dreams;

chattreṣu *kanaka/daṇḍā,*

dhvajeṣu prakampā,

gīteṣu *rāga/vilasitāni,*

kariṣu *mada/vikārāś,*

cāpeṣu *guṇa/cchedā,*

gavākṣeṣu *jāla/mārgāḥ,*

śaśi|kṛpāṇa|kavaceṣu kalaṅkā,

rati|kalaheṣu dūta|saṃpreṣaṇāni,

śāry|akṣeṣu *śūnya/gṛhāḥ* prajānām āsan.

yasya ca para|lokād bhayam,

antaḥ|purik"|âlakeṣu *bhaṅgo,*

nūpureṣu *mukharatā,*

vivāheṣu *kara/grahaṇam,*

an|avarata|makh'|âgni|dhūmen' âśru|pātas,

turaṃgeṣu kaś"|âbhighāto,

Makaradhvaje cāpa|dhvanir abhūt.

tasya ca rājñaḥ

Kali|kāla|bhaya|puñjī|bhūta|Kṛta|yug'|ânukāriṇī

tri|bhuvana|prasava|bhūmir iva vistīrṇā,

fines in gold only *as golden poles in parasols;*
trembling only in flags;
manifestations of passionate emotion only in songs
as performances of musical ragas;
deterioration of behavior through intoxication
only in the case of *the perturbation of* elephants *in rut;*
absence of merits only in bows *when their strings snapped;*
deceitful practices only *as latticework* in windows;
stains were found only on armor, swords, and the moon;
messengers were sent only in the case of love quarrels,
not to declare war;
the only *deserted houses* were *empty squares*
on the boards of chess and dice games.
And for him there was fear only of the next world,
frustration only *as the curve*
in the curls of the women of his harem,
garrulity only *as the noisiness* of anklets,
imposing taxes only *as taking the hand in marriages,*
shedding tears only from the smoke
from the fires of ceaseless sacrifices,
the lash of the whip only on horses,
the twang of the bow only on the part
of *mákara*-bannered Kama.
Resembling the Golden Age huddled up
through fear of the time of the demon Kali, the fourth age,
extensive, as if it had been the place of origin
of the three worlds,

majjan|Mālava|vilāsinī|kuca|taṭ'|āsphālana|jarjarit'|

ōrmi|mālayā jal'|âvagāhan'|āyāta|jaya|kuñjara|kumbha|

sindūra|saṃdhyāyamāna|salilay" ônmada|kalahaṃsa|kula|

kolāhala|mukharita|kūlayā Vetravatyā saritā parigatā

Vidiś"|âbhidhānā nagarī rāja|dhāny āsīt.

sa tasyām avajit'|âśeṣa|bhuvana|maṇḍalatayā

vigata|rājya|cintā|bhāra|nirvṛto

dvīp'|ântar'|āgat'|âneka|bhūmi|pāla|

mauli|mālā|lālita|caraṇa|yugalo

valayam iva līlayā bhujena

bhuvana|bhāram udvahan,

amara|gurum api prajñay" ôpahasadbhir

aneka|kula|kram'|āgatair

a|sakṛd|ālocita|nīti|śāstra|nirmala|manobhir a|lubdhaiḥ

snigdhaiḥ prabuddhaiś c' āmātyaiḥ parivṛtaḥ,

samāna|vayo|vidy"|âlaṃkārair,

aneka|mūrdh'|âbhiṣikta|pārthiva|kul'|ôdgatair,

akhila|kalā|kalāp'|ālocana|kaṭhora|matibhir,

encircled by the Vétravati river
whose garlands of waves broke up in collision with
the lovely Málava women's breasts as they bathed,
and whose waters took on the glow of evening
thanks to vermilion from the temples
of the victorious war elephants
come to dip themselves in its waters,
its banks resounding with the cackle of flocks
of impassioned *kala·hansa* geese—
such was his capital city. Vídisa[27] was its name.
In that city he was at ease,
freed from the burden of worry about his kingdom
because he'd conquered the whole circle of the world.
His feet were cherished with the garland of the crowns
of many kings who'd come from other continents,
and he was carrying the burden of the world on his arm
with graceful ease, as if it were a bangle.
Putting to shame by their wisdom
even Brihas·pati, adviser to the gods,
the hereditary ministers from several families
who surrounded him, their minds refined
by frequent reflection on the science of politics,
were free from greed, loyal, and enlightened.
His equals in age, learning, and adornment;
sprung from the families of many anointed kings;
their intellects rigorous from study
of the whole assemblage of the arts;

atipragalbhaiḥ,

kāla|vidbhiḥ,

prabhāv'|ânurakta|hṛdayair,

a|grāmya|parihāsa|kuśalair,

iṅgit'|ākāra|vedibhiḥ,

kāvya|nāṭak'|ākhyānak'|ākhyāyik"|ālekhya|vyākhyān'|ādi|

kriyā|nipuṇair,

atikaṭhina|pīvara|skandh'|ōru|bāhubhir

a|sakṛd|avadalita|samada|ripu|gaja|ghaṭā|pīṭha|bandhaiḥ

kesari|kiśorakair iva,

vikram'|âika|rasair api vinaya|vyavahāribhir

ātmanaḥ pratibimbair iva,

rāja|putraiḥ saha ramamāṇaḥ prathame vayasi

sukham aticiram uvāsa.

tasya c' âtivijigīṣutayā mahā|sattvatayā ca

tṛṇam iva laghu|vṛtti straiṇam ākalayataḥ

prathame vayasi varta|mānasy' âpi rūpavato 'pi

saṃtān'|ârthibhir amātyair apekṣitasy' âpi

surata|sukhasy' ôpari dveṣa iv' āsīt.

saty api rūpa|vilās'|ôpahāsita|Rati|vibhrame

lāvaṇyavati vinayavaty anvayavati

hṛdaya|hāriṇi c' âvarodha|jane

utterly self-confident;
knowing the proper time for things;
their hearts in love with valor;
skilled in joking without being vulgar;
understanding gestures and expressions;
expert in poetry, drama, tales, romances,
sketches, essays, and other such works;
their shoulders, arms and thighs very hard and muscular,
like young lions they'd often smashed open
the temple lobes of herds of their enemies' rutting elephants;
though deeds of valor were their sole delight,
their conduct was modest
—like mirrors of himself, such were the princes
with whom he sported and with whom he lived happily
in the flush of youth for a remarkably long time.
And because he had an extreme desire for conquest
and great strength of character
he counted womankind
as something trivial, like mere grass.
Although he was in the flush of youth,
although he was handsome, he seemed to have
a hatred for the pleasures of love-making,
notwithstanding the expectations of his ministers
who were concerned about the continuation of his lineage.
Even though he did have a harem of women
who put to shame Rati's charms
with the grace of their beauty,
being deliciously good-looking, modest in behavior,
of good lineage, and altogether captivating—

sa kadā cid an|avarata|dolāyamāna|ratna|valayo
ghargharik"|āsphālana|prakampa|jhaṇajhaṇāyamāna|
maṇi|karṇa|pūraḥ svayam ārabdha|mṛdaṅga|vādyaḥ
saṃgītaka|prasaṅgena,
kadā cid a|virala|vimukta|śar'|āsāra|śūnyī|kṛta|kānano
mṛgayā|vyāpāreṇa,
kadā cid ābaddha|vidagdha|maṇḍalaḥ
kāvya|prabandha|racanena,
kadā cic chāstr'|ālāpena,
kadā cid ākhyānak'|ākhyānik"|êtihāsa|
purāṇa'|ākarṇanena,
kadā cid ālekhya|vinodena,
kadā cid vīṇayā,
kadā cid darśan'|āgata|muni|jana|caraṇa|śuśrūṣayā,
kadā cid akṣara|cyutaka|mātrā|cyutaka|bindumatī|
gūḍha|caturtha|pāda|prahelikā|pradān'|ādibhir
vanitā|saṃbhoga|sukha|parāṅ|mukhaḥ
suhṛta|parivṛto divasam anayat.
yath" âiva ca divasam evam ārabdha|vividha|krīḍā|
parihāsa|caturaiḥ suhṛdbhir upeto
niśām anaiṣīt.

sometimes, his jeweled bracelets swinging[28] incessantly,
his jeweled earrings jingling
with the shaking of their little bells each time he struck,
he himself played the *mridánga* drum,
in his fondness for concerts;
sometimes, hunting was his occupation,
and he emptied the forests with showers of arrows
released in continuous succession;
sometimes, it was composition of works of poetry,
and he called together a circle of critics;
sometimes, it was discussion of the *shastra*s;
sometimes, it was listening to tales, romances,
epics or the *purána*s;[29]
sometimes, it was the amusement of painting;
sometimes, it was the *vina;*
sometimes, it was revering the feet
of sages who had come to see him;[30]
sometimes, it was in setting literary puzzles
such as finding the missing syllable,[31]
finding the missing character,[32]
supplying missing consonants,[33]
uncovering the last quarter of a verse and so on—[34]
thus it was, averse to the pleasures
of the enjoyment of women,
surrounded by his male friends,
he spent the day.
And as he spent the day so the night,
with his friends skilled in undertaking
all sorts of games and jokes.

ekadā tu n' âtidūr'|ôdite

nava|nalina|dala|saṃpuṭa|bhidi

kiṃcid|unmukta|pāṭalimni

bhagavati sahasra|marīci|mālini

rājānam āsthāna|maṇḍapa|gatam

aṅganā|jana|viruddhena vāma|pārśv'|âvalambinā

kaukṣeyakeṇa saṃnihita|viṣa|dhar" êva

candana|latā bhīṣaṇa|ramaṇīy'|ākṛtir,

a|virala|candan'|ânulepana|dhavalita|stana|taṭ" ônmajjad|

Airāvata|kumbha|maṇḍal" êva Mandākinī,

cūḍā|maṇi|pratibimba|cchalena rāj'|ājñ" êva mūrtimatī

rājabhiḥ śirobhir uhyamānā,

śarad iva *kalahaṃsa|dhaval'|âmbarā*,

Jāmadagnya|paraśu|dhār" êva

vaśī|kṛta|sakala|rāja|maṇḍalā,

Vindhya|vana|bhūmir iva vetra|latāvatī,

rājy'|âdhidevat" êva vigrahiṇī pratīhārī samupasṛtya

kṣiti|tala|nihita|jānu|kara|kamalā

sa|vinayam abravīt.

One day, when the blessed sun garlanded
with its thousand rays was not very far risen,
splitting open the petal cups of the young lotuses,
its rosiness only partially cast off,
and he was in his audience hall, there came up to him
a woman with what was forbidden to women,
a sword hanging from her left side,
like a sandal creeper with a poisonous snake beside it.
She was lovely in form but formidable.
With her breasts whitened
with a thick coating of sandal paste,
she was like the heavenly Ganga
with the two frontal lobes of Indra's elephant,
Airávata, rising up from her waters.
In the guise of her reflection in their crest-jewels,
she was like the embodiment of the king's command
being carried by the kings' heads.[35]
Like *a fall sky white with kala·hansa geese,*
she *wore a goose-white garment.*
Just as the axe blade of Jamad·agni's son, Párashu·rama,[36]
subdued the circle of kings, so too did she.
Like the Vindhya forest which has bamboo canes,
so too did she have a bamboo cane.
She was a female doorkeeper who was like
the presiding goddess of the kingdom in human form.
Kneeling and touching the ground with her lotus hands,
she respectfully addressed the king.

«deva, dvāra|sthitā

sura|lokam ārohatas Triśaṅkor iva

kupita|Śatamakha|huṃkāra|nipātitā

rāja|lakṣmīr dakṣiṇā|pathād āgatā

cāṇḍāla|kanyakā pañjara|sthaṃ śukam ādāya

devaṃ vijñāpayati.

‹sakala|bhuvana|tala|sarva|ratnānām

udadhir iv' âika|bhājanaṃ devo

vihaṃgamaś c' âyam āścarya|bhūto

nikhila|bhuvana|tala|ratnam iti kṛtvā

deva|pāda|mūlam ādāy' āgat" âham icchāmi

deva|darśana|sukham anubhavitum› iti.

etad ākarṇya devaḥ pramāṇam»

ity uktvā virarāma.

upajāta|kutūhalas tu rājā

samīpa|vartināṃ rājñām ālokya mukhāni

«ko doṣaḥ, praveśyatām» ity ādideśa.

atha pratihārī nara|pati|vacan'|ânantaram utthāya

tāṃ mātaṅga|kumārīṃ prāveśayat.

praviśya ca sā nara|pati|sahasra|madhya|vartinam

aśani|bhaya|puñjita|kula|śaila|madhya|gatam iva

kanaka|śikhariṇam,

"Your Majesty, there stands at the doorway,
like Tri·shanku's[37] royal glory brought down to earth
by wrathful Indra's roaring
when he was rising up to the world of the gods,
an outcaste maiden who's come from the south.
She brings a parrot in a cage
and respectfully informs Your Majesty,
'As the ocean is the unique receptacle of all the jewels
on the whole surface of the world, so too is Your Majesty,
and realizing that this is a marvelous bird,
a jewel equal to any from the whole surface of the world,
I have come to lay it at Your Majesty's feet.
I wish to enjoy the happiness
of an audience with Your Majesty.'
Your Majesty has heard. Let Your Majesty decide."
So saying, she fell silent.
The king, for his part, his curiosity aroused,
looked at the faces of the nearby kings, and declared,
"There's no harm in letting her in. Bring her in."
Then the female doorkeeper rose
as soon as the king spoke
and ushered in the *matánga* maiden.
And on entering she beheld him.
Amid the thousand kings he was like Meru,
the golden mountain,
amid the mountain chains
in fear of Indra's thunderbolt[38]
crowded together around him for protection.

aneka|ratn'|ābharaṇa|kiraṇa|jālak'|ântarit'|âvayavam
Indr'|āyudha|sahasra|saṃchādit'|âṣṭa|dig|bhāgam iva
jala|dhara|samaya|divasam
avalambita|sthūla|muktā|kalāpasya
kanaka|śṛṅkhalā|niyamita|maṇi|daṇḍikā|catuṣṭayasya
gagana|sindhu|phena|paṭala|pāṇḍurasya
n' âtimahato dukūla|vitānasy' âdhastād
indu|kānta|maṇi|paryaṅkikā|niṣaṇṇam
uddhūyamāna|kanaka|daṇḍa|cāmara|kalāpam,
unmayūkha|mukha|kānti|vijaya|parābhava|praṇate
śaśin' îva sphaṭika|pāda|pīṭhe vinyasta|vāma|pādam,
indra|nīla|maṇi|kuṭṭima|prabhā|
saṃparka|śyāmāyamānaiḥ
praṇata|ripu|niḥśvāsa|malinī|kṛtair iva
caraṇa|nakha|mayūkha|jālair upaśobhamānam,
āsan'|ôllasita|padma|rāga|kiraṇa|pāṭalī|kṛten'
â|cira|mṛdita|Madhu|Kaiṭabha|rudhir'|âruṇena
Harim iv' ōru|yugalena virājamānam,
amṛta|phena|dhavale
go|rocanā|likhita|haṃsa|mithuna|sanātha|paryante
cāru|cāmara|pavana|pranartita|daśe dukūle vasānam,

With his limbs hidden in a thicket of rays
emitted from his many jewel ornaments,
he was like a day in the rainy season
when all eight quarters of the horizon
are swathed in thousands of rainbows.
Beneath a canopy of silk festooned with big pearls,
held up by four jeweled posts joined by golden chains,
as white as a mass of foam of the heavenly Ganga
but not very large,
he was seated on a couch of moonstones.
Several gold-handled chowries
were being waved over him.
His left foot was placed on a crystal footstool
that seemed like the moon bowed down in submission
to the triumphant beauty of his beaming face.
He was resplendent with the networks of rays
from his toes; these rays, darkened in hue from contact
with the luster of the sapphire pavement
seeming as if they were clouded over by the sighs
of the foes who bowed down before him.
His thighs reddened by the rays from the rubies
gleaming on his throne,
he shone forth like Hari with his thighs red
with the blood of Madhu and Káitabha[39]
when he'd just crushed them.
He was wearing a pair of silken garments
white as nectar's foam,
bordered with pairs of geese painted in cow-yellow,[40]
their ends fluttering in the wind of the lovely chowries.

atisurabhi|candan'|ânulepana|dhavalit'|ôraḥ|sthalam
upari|vinyasta|kuṅkuma|sthāsakam
antar"|ântarā|nipatita|bāl'|ātapa|cchedam iva
Kailāsa|śikhariṇam
apara|śaśi|śaṅkayā nakṣatra|mālay" êva
hāra|latayā kṛta|mukha|pariveṣam,
aticapala|rāja|Lakṣmī|bandha|nigaḍa|kaṭaka|śaṅkām
upajanayat" êndra|nīla|keyūra|yugalena
malayaja|rasa|gandha|lubdhena bhujaṃga|dvayen' êva
veṣṭita|bāhu|śikharam,
īṣad|ālambi|karṇ'|ôtapalam,
unnata|ghoṇam,
utphulla|puṇḍarīka|locanam,
amala|kala|dhauta|paṭṭ'|āyatam
aṣṭamī|candra|śakal'|ākāram
aśeṣa|bhuvana|rājy'|âbhiṣeka|salila|pūtam
ūrṇā|sanāthaṃ lalāṭa|deśam udvahantam,
āmodita|mālatī|kusuma|śekharam uṣasi
śikhara|paryasta|tārakā|puñjam iva paścim'|âcalam,
ābharaṇa|prabhā|piśaṅgit'|âṅgatayā
lagna|Hara|hut'|āśam iva
Makara|dhvajam;

The expanse of his chest, whitened
with a smearing of very fragrant sandal paste
and with an application of saffron on top of that,
was like Mount Kailása with patches
of early morning sunlight on it here and there.
His face was encircled by a pearl necklace
as if by the zodiac of stars
under the impression that it was another moon.
Two sapphire armlets were wrapped around his biceps,
like two snakes greedy for the smell of sandal paste,
giving the impression they were the links of a chain
to bind royal Fortune who is all too fickle.
A lotus drooped down a little over one ear.
His nose was nobly prominent.
His eyes were *pundaríka* lotuses in bloom.
His broad forehead was a shining expanse of gold,
shaped like the eighth day moon,
hallowed by the water that inaugurated
his rule of the entire world;
and between the eyebrows was a circle of hair,
mark of a world-ruler.
He wore a chaplet of sweet-smelling jasmine flowers,
as if he were the western mountain at dawn
with a cluster of stars ranged around its peak.
Because his body was rendered tawny
by the luster of his ornaments
he was like *mákara*-bannered Love
with the fire of Shiva[41] the destroyer clinging to him.

āsanna|vartinībhiḥ sarvataḥ sev"|ârtham āgatābhir iva

dig|vadhūbhir vāra|vilāsinībhiḥ parivṛtam,

amala|maṇi|kuṭṭima|saṃkrānta|sakala|deha|pratibimbatayā

pati|premṇā vasuṃdharayā hṛdayen' êv' ôhyamānam,

a|śeṣa|jana|bhogyatām upanītay" âpy

a|sādhāraṇayā

rāja|Lakṣmyā samāliṅgita|deham,

a|parimita|parivāra|janam apy a|dvitīyam,

ananta|gaja|turaga|sādhanam api khaḍga|mātra|sahāyam,

P10 eka|deśa|sthitam api vyāpta|bhuvana|maṇḍalam,

āsana|gatam api dhanuṣi niṣaṇṇam,

utsādit'|â|śeṣa|dviṣad|indhanam api jvalat|pratāp'|ânalam,

āyata|locanam api sūkṣma|darśanaṃ,

mahā|doṣam api

sakala|guṇ'|âdhiṣṭhānaṃ,

ku|patim api

kalatra|vallabham,

Dancing girls surrounded him on all sides,
waiting at hand,
as if they were the horizon-women
come to worship him.
Because his whole body had been transferred
as reflection to the shining jeweled pavement,
he seemed to be carried in her heart
by the earth out of love for her lord.
Although he'd made *her give herself to all men*
and made *all his subjects enjoy prosperity,*
once royal Fortune embraced his body
she remained exclusive to him.
Though his retinue was innumerable,
he was without a second.
Though he had countless elephants
and horses at his disposal,
he trusted only to his own sword.
Though he stood in one place,
he pervaded the whole earth. PIO
Though seated on the throne, he rested on his bow.
Though all the fuel that was his enemies was destroyed,
the fire of his valor still blazed.
Though his eyes were long,
he saw the subtlest things.
There was no question of him having *great faults*—
he was home of all virtues, *his arms were long.*
There was no question of him being *a bad husband*—
he was the darling of his wives, *the husband of the earth.*

a|virata|pravṛtta|*dānam* apy

a/madam,

atiśuddha|svabhāvam api

Kṛṣṇa/caritam,

a/karam api hasta|sthita|sakala|bhuvana|talaṃ,

rājānam adrākṣīt.

ālokya ca sā dūra|sthit" âiva pracalita|ratna|valayena

rakta|kuvalaya|dala|komalena pāṇinā

jarjarita|mukha|bhāgāṃ veṇu|latām ādāya

nara|pati|prabodhan'|ârtham

a|sakṛt sabhā|kuṭṭimam ājaghāna.

yena sakalam eva tad|rājakam eka|pade

vana|kari|yūtham iva tāla|śabdena

tena veṇu|latā|dhvaninā

yuga|pad|āvalita|vadanam avani|pāla|mukhād ākṛṣya

cakṣus tad|abhimukham āsīt.

«avani|patis tu dūrād ālokay'» êti abhidhāya

pratīhāryā nirdiśyamānāṃ tāṃ

vayaḥ|pariṇāma|pāṇḍura|śirasā rakta|rāj" îv'

ēkṣaṇ'|âpāṅgen' ân|avarata|kṛta|vyāyāmatayā

Though his *rut* flowed unceasingly,
he was *free from rut*—
that is to say, his *generosity* flowed unceasingly
and he was *free from arrogance.*
Though his nature was very bright,
it appeared contradictory that *his deeds were black,*
but in fact they were *parallel to those of Krishna.*
It wasn't true that *he had no hands*—
the fact of the matter was that even though
he held the whole world in the palm of his hand,
he didn't levy taxes.
Such was the king she beheld.
And on beholding him, while still standing at a distance,
she took in her hand, soft as a red lotus petal,
a bamboo cane, the end of which was worn
and, her jeweled bracelets shaking,
she struck the pavement of the assembly hall with it
more than once to gain the king's attention.
At the sound of her bamboo cane,
the whole assemblage of kings,
like a herd of wild elephants
at the sound of a falling coconut,[42]
at one and the same moment simultaneously
turned their faces and withdrew their gaze
from the king's face to her direction.
The female doorkeeper directed her
to look at him from afar.
Before her went a male attendant, white-haired with age,
the corners of his eyes red as red lotuses.
From constant exercise, though no longer young,

yauvan'|âpagame 'py a|śithila|śarīra|saṃdhinā saty api
mātaṅgatve n' âtinṛśaṃs'|ākṛtin" ânugṛhīt'|ārya|veṣeṇa
dhavala|vāsasā puruṣeṇ' âdhiṣṭhita|puro|bhāgām
ākul'|ākula|kāka|pakṣa|dhāriṇā
kanaka|śalākā|nirmitam apy antar|gata|śuka|prabhā|
śyāmāyamānaṃ marakata|mayam iva pañjaram udvahatā
cāṇḍāla|dārakeṇ' ânugamyamānām,
asura|gṛhīt'|âmṛt'|âpaharaṇa|
kṛta|kapaṭa|paṭu|vilāsinī|veṣasya śyāmatayā
bhagavato Harer iv' ânukurvatīṃ
saṃcāriṇīm iv' êndra|nīla|maṇi|putrikām,
āgulph'|âvalambinā nīla|kañcuken' âvacchanna|śarīrām
upari rakt'|âṃśuka|racit'|âvaguṇṭhanāṃ
nīl'|ôtpala|sthalīm iva nipatita|saṃdhy"|ātapām,
eka|karṇ'|âvasakta|danta|pattra|prabhā|
dhavalita|kapola|maṇḍalām
udyad|indu|kiraṇa|cchurita|mukhīm iva vibhāvarīm,
ākapila|gorocanā|racita|tilaka|tṛtīya|locanām
Īśāna|racit'|ânuracita|kirāta|veṣām iva Bhavānīm,

his joints were supple.
Though a *matánga* outcaste,
his aspect wasn't terribly ferocious.
He had dressed himself respectably,
wearing white garments.
Behind her came a *chandála* outcaste boy
with tousled hair falling to his shoulders.
He was carrying a cage
which though constructed with golden rods
seemed made of emerald since it was turned dark green
by the luster of the parrot contained within it.
By her darkness she seemed to be imitating divine Hari
when he adopted the disguise of a seductive woman
to take back the nectar the demons had seized.
She looked like a figurine made of sapphire
moving about.
Her body covered with a blue dress
which reached her ankles, and wearing red silk as a shawl,
she looked like a bed of blue water-lilies
on which evening sunlight was falling.
The circle of her cheek whitened
by the luster of the ivory leaf hanging from one ear,
she was like the night with its face
strewn with the rays of the rising moon.
She had a third eye in the form of a forehead mark
made with brownish cow-yellow,
as if she were Bhaváni, Shiva's spouse,
adopting the wild mountaineer dress of Shiva the lord.

uraḥ|sthala|nivāsa|saṃkrānta|Nārāyaṇa|deha|prabhā|

śyāmalitām iva Śriyaṃ,

kupita|Hara|hut'|āśana|dahyamāna|

Madana|dhūma|malinī|kṛtām iva Ratim,

unmada|Hali|hal'|âpakarṣaṇa|bhaya|

prapalāyitām iva Yamunām,

atibahala|piṇḍ'|ālaktaka|rasa|rāga|

pallavita|pāda|paṅkajām

a|cira|mṛdita|Mahiṣ'|âsura|rudhira|

rakta|caraṇām iva Kātyāyanīm,

ālohit'|âṅguli|prabhā|pāṭalita|nakha|mayūkhām

atikaṭhina|maṇi|kuṭṭima|sparśam a|sahamānāṃ

kṣiti|tale pallava|bhaṅgān iva nidhāya saṃcarantīm,

āpiñjareṇ' ôtsarpiṇā nūpura|maṇīnāṃ prabhā|jālena

rañjita|śarīratayā Pāvaken' êva bhagavatā rūpa eva

pakṣa|pātinā Prajāpatim a|pramāṇī|kurvatā

jāti|saṃśodhan'|ârtham āliṅgita|dehām,

She was like Shri, goddess of beauty, darkened
by the luster of Naráyana's body
reflected on her as she sits on his chest.
She was like Rati, obscured by the smoke
from her husband Love being burned up
by the fire of Shiva the destroyer
when he'd angered him.
She was like the river Yámuna when the river fled
in fear of being dragged into a new course
by the plow of drunken Bala·rama, the plow-bearer.
Her lotus feet turned into blossom
by the red dye of very thick lumps of lac,
she was like Katyáyani with her feet reddened
by the blood of the Mahisha, the buffalo demon,
just after she'd trampled him to death.
The rays of light from her toe-nails made pink
by the luster from her reddish toes,
she seemed to be scattering pieces of petals
on the surface of the ground as she walked,
being unable to bear the touch
of the very hard jeweled paving.
Because her body was reddened by the network of rays
from her anklet jewels, reddish and rising upwards,
it seemed as if the blessed god of fire
took the side of beauty in its own right,
and paying no attention
to the standards set by the Creator
was embracing her body in order to purify her caste.

Anaṅga|vāraṇa|śiro|nakṣatra|mālāyamānena

roma|rāji|lat"|ālavālakena mekhalā|dāmnā

parigata|jaghana|sthalām,

atisthūla|muktā|phala|ghaṭitena

śucinā hāreṇa Gaṅgā|srotas" êva Kālindī|śaṅkayā

kṛta|kaṇṭha|grahām,

śaradam iva vikasita|puṇḍarīka|locanām,

prāvṛṣam iva *ghana/keśa/jālām*,

Malaya|mekhalām iva candana|pallav'|âvataṃsām,

nakṣatra|mālām iva *citra/śravaṇ'/ābharaṇa/bhūṣitām*,

Śriyam iva hasta|sthita|kamala|śobhām,

mūrchām iva *mano/hāriṇīm*,

araṇya|bhūmim iv' *âkṣata/rūpa/sampannām*,

divya|yoṣitam iv' *ā/ku/līnām*,

nidrām iva locana|grāhiṇīm,

araṇya|kamalinīm iva *mātaṅga/kula/dūṣitām*,

Her hips were spanned by the cord of her girdle —
a zodiac-necklace ornament
for the head of Love's elephant,
a watering basin for the creeper
that was the line of hair on her stomach.
Her neck was encircled by a bright necklace
made with very big pearls, as if Ganga's flowing waters
had mistaken it for Yámuna, Kalínda's daughter.
Like the fall, her eyes were lotuses in bloom.
Like the rainy season *with its coiffured hair of clouds,*
she *had a thick mass of hair.*
Like the slopes of the Málaya mountain,
she had a garland of sandal blossom.
Like the zodiac adorned with the lunar asterisms
Chitra, Shrávana, and Ábharana,
she was *adorned with wonderful ear ornaments.*
Like the goddess Shri she had the beautiful characteristic
of holding a lotus in her hand.
Like a swoon which *removes consciousness,*
she was *ravishing.*
Like a forest *endowed with dice trees,*
she *had perfect beauty.*
Like an heavenly nymph, an *ápsaras,*
who is not attached to the earth,
she *was not of good family.*
Like sleep, she seized the eyes.
Like a forest lotus pool *which is destroyed*
by a herd of elephants,
she *was contaminated by her matánga family.*

a|mūrtām iva sparśa|varjitām,

ālekhya|gatām iva darśana|mātra|phalāṃ,

madhu|māsa|kusuma|samṛddhim iva *vijātim,*

Anaṅga|kusuma|cāpa|lekhām iva muṣṭi|grāhya|madhyāṃ,

yakṣ'|âdhipa|lakṣmīm iv' *Âlak'|ôdbhāsinīm,*

acir'|ôparūḍha|yauvanām,

atiśaya|rūp'|ākṛtim

a|nimeṣa|locano dadarśa.

samupajāta|vismayasya c' ābhūn manasi mahī|pateḥ.

«aho Vidhātur a|sthāne rūpa|niṣpādana|prayatnaḥ!

tathā hi. yadi nām' êyam

ātma|rūp'|ôpahasit'|â|śeṣa|rūpa|saṃpad utpāditā,

kim artham apagata|sparśa|saṃbhoga|sukhe

kṛtaṃ kule janma?

manye ca Mātaṅga|jāti|sparśa|doṣa|bhayād

a|spṛśat" êyam utpāditā Prajāpatinā.

anyathā katham iyam a|kliṣṭatā lāvaṇyasya?

na hi kara|tala|sparśa|kleśitānām avayavānām

īdṛśī bhavati kāntiḥ.

Like a thing without form she couldn't be touched.
Like a figure in a painting,
her only purpose was to be looked upon.
Like the rich abundance of flowers in the month of spring,
when the jasmine flower doesn't appear,
she *was of no caste.*
Like bodiless Love's flower bowstock,
her waist could be grasped by the fist.
Like the *Yaksha* Lord's royal fortune
resplendent in Álaka, his capital,
she was *resplendent with her curls.*
She was but newly a woman.
She was excessively beautiful in form.
The king gazed at her with unblinking eyes.
And the king was astonished.
He turned the matter over in his mind.
"Alas the Creator has exerted himself
only to produce beauty in the wrong place.
The thing is this. If indeed this woman has been created
such that her loveliness puts to shame
the excellence of all loveliness,
why did she have to be born in a family
that can never enjoy the happiness of being touched?
And I think Praja·pati the Creator produced her
without touching, fearing the sin of touching
one of the *matánga* caste.
Otherwise how came about
this absence of defect in her loveliness?
For such beauty as this doesn't come about
for limbs spoiled by the touch of hands.

sarvathā dhig Vidhātāram a|sadṛśa|saṃyoga|kāriṇam.
atimanohar'|ākṛtir api
krūra|jātitay" êyam
asura|śrīr iva
satata|nindita|suratā
ramaṇīy" âpy
udvejayati!»
ity evam|ādi cintayantam eva rājānam
īṣad|avagalita|karṇa|pallav'|âvataṃsā
pragalbha|vanit" êva kanyakā praṇāma.
kṛta|praṇāmāyāṃ ca tasyāṃ
maṇi|kuṭṭim'||ôpaviṣṭāyāṃ
sa puruṣas taṃ vihaṃgam ādāya pañjara|gatam eva
kiṃ cid upasṛtya rājñe nyavedayad abravīc ca.
«deva, vidita|sakala|śāstr'|ârtho,
rāja|nīti|prayoga|kuśalaḥ,
purāṇ'|êtihāsa|kath"|ālāpa|nipuṇo,
veditā gīta|śrutīnāṃ,
kāvya|nāṭak'|ākhyāyik|ākhyānaka|prabhṛtīnām
a|parimitānāṃ subhāṣitānām adhyetā svayaṃ ca kartā,
parihās'|ālāpa|peśalo,
vīṇā|veṇu|muraja|prabhṛtīnāṃ
vādya|viśeṣāṇām a|samaḥ śrotā,

Fie in every way upon the Creator
who brings about such an improper combination.
Even though her form is exceedingly lovely,
the fact that she belongs to a savage tribe
makes her disgusting, however beautiful she may be.
She's like the royal fortune of the demons
who is always casting aspersions on the gods—
making love to her will always be reprehensible."
While the king was thinking along these lines,
the girl bowed to the king like a mature woman,
the sprout that formed her ear ornament
slipping slightly out of place as she did so.
And after she'd made her bow
and sat down on the jeweled paving,
her male attendant took the bird,
still confined within the cage,
approached the king and showed it to him, saying,
"Your Majesty, he knows the purport of all *shastra*s.
He is expert in the application
of the rules of statesmanship.
He is skilled in telling stories from the *purána*s and epics.
He has mastered the twenty-two *shruti*s of singing.
He recites and has himself composed
literary works beyond number,
poems, plays, romances, tales, and the like.
He has the knack of telling jokes.
He is a peerless connoisseur
of all sorts of musical instruments,
such as the *vina*, the flute and the drum.

nṛtta|prayoga|darśana|nipuṇaś,

citra|karmaṇi pravīṇo, dyūta|vyāpāre pragalbhaḥ,

praṇaya|kalaha|kupita|kāminī|prasādan'|ôpāya|caturo,

gaja|turaga|puruṣa|strī|lakṣaṇ'|âbhijñaḥ,

sakala|bhū|tala|ratna|bhūto

'yaṃ Vaiśampāyano nāma śukaḥ,

sarva|ratnānāṃ c' ôdadhir iva devo bhājanam iti

kṛtv" âinam ādāy' âsmat|svāmi|duhitā

deva|pāda|mūlam āyātā.

tad ayam ātmīyaḥ kriyatām.»

ity uktvā nara|pateḥ puro nidhāya pañjaram

asāv apasasāra.

apasṛte ca tasmin sa vihaṃga|rājo

rāj'|âbhimukho bhūtvā

samunnamayya dakṣiṇaṃ caraṇam

atispaṣṭa|varṇa|svara|saṃskārayā girā

kṛta|jaya|śabdo rājānam uddiśy'

āryām imāṃ papāṭha.

«stana|yugam aśru|snātaṃ

samīpatara|varti hṛdaya|śok'|âgneḥ

carati *vimukt'|āhāraṃ*

vratam iva bhavato ripu|strīṇāṃ.»

He is proficient in performing and appreciating dance,
a master painter, and a bold gambler.
He is ready in resources to win over
women angered in love quarrels.
He is familiar with the characteristics
of elephants, horses, men, and women.
This parrot is called Vaishampáyana.
He is the gem of the whole earth.
And in the thought that you, like the ocean,
are proper receptacle of all jewels,
our chief's daughter has brought him to set at your feet.
So, please accept him as your own."
With these words he placed the cage before the king
and withdrew.
And when he was gone,
the king of birds turned to face the king
and lifting up his right foot cried,
"Victory to the king,"
and recited this *arya* verse in a voice in which syllable,
accent, and grammatical purity were extremely clear:
"The breasts of your enemies' women,
bathed in tears,
situated all too near the fire
that's the grief of their hearts,
necklaces abandoned,
seem to have *given up food,*
in performance of a vow."

rājā tu tāṃ śrutvā saṃjāta|vismayaḥ sa|harṣam
āsanna|vartinam
atimah"|ârtha|hem"|āsan'|ôpaviṣṭam,
amara|gurum iv' âśeṣa|nīti|śāstra|pāra|gam,
ativayasam agra|janmānam,
akhila|mantri|maṇḍale pradhānam amātyaṃ
Kumārapālita|nāmānam abravīt.
«śrutā bhavadbhir asya vihaṃgamasya spaṣṭatā
varṇ'|ôccāraṇe svare ca madhuratā.
prathamaṃ tāvad idam eva mahad āścaryam
a|saṃkīrṇa|varṇa|pravibhāgām
abhivyakta|mātr'|ânusvāra|saṃskāra|yogāṃ
viśeṣa|saṃyuktāṃ yad ayam
atiparisphuṭ'|âkṣarāṃ giram udīrayati.
tatra punar aparam abhimata|viṣaye tiraśco 'pi
manujasy' êva saṃskāravato buddhi|pūrvā pravṛttiḥ.
tathā hi. anena samutkṣipta|dakṣiṇa|caraṇen'
ôccārya jaya|śabdam
iyam āryā mām uddiśy' âtisphuṭ'|âkṣaraṃ gītā.
prāyeṇa hi pakṣiṇaḥ paśavaś ca
bhay'|āhāra|maithuna|nidrā|saṃjñā|mātra|vedino bhavanti.
idaṃ tu mahac citram.»

The king, for his part, when he'd heard this
was astonished and delighted,
and to the man who sat beside him,
seated on a gold throne
of the greatest value like the guru of the gods,
who'd mastered the further reaches of politics,
aged brahmin,
foremost in the whole circle of counselors,
his minister Kumára·pálita,
to him he said,
"You've heard this bird's clearness in enunciating syllables
and the sweetness in his tone.
The first thing to be said is that it is indeed a great marvel
that this bird gives forth a voice
in which the division of letters is not muddled up,
and syllable lengths, nasals, and grammatical purity
are clearly differentiated,
a voice in which every syllable is perfectly clear,
a voice of distinction.
Moreover, in his case, there is something more.
Though he's an animal, his behavior is intelligent,
like that of a man of refinement,
in respect of a matter of interest to him.
What I mean is that he lifted up his right leg
and hailed me as triumphant king
before singing this *arya* verse with perfectly clear syllables,
a verse which had specific refcrence to me.
It's generally the case that birds, and animals in general,
have their knowledge limited to fear, food,
copulation, sleep and wakefulness.

ity uktavati bhū|bhuji, Kumārapālitaḥ
kiṃ cit smita|vadano nṛpam avādīt:
«deva, kim atra citram?
ete hi śuka|sārikā|prabhṛtayo vihaṃgama|viśeṣā
yathā|śrutāṃ vācam uccārayant" îty
adhigatam eva devena.
tatr' âpy ‹anya|janm'|ôpātta|saṃskār'|ânubandhena vā
puruṣa|prayatnena vā saṃskār'|âtiśaya upajāyata› iti
n' âticitram.
anyad eteṣām api purā puruṣāṇām iv'
âtiparisphuṭ'|âbhidhānā vāg āsīt.
Agni|śāpāt tv a|parisphuṭ'|ālāpatā śukānām
upajātā kariṇāṃ ca jihvā|parivṛttiḥ.»
ity evam uccārayaty eva tasminn a|śiśira|kiraṇam
ambara|talasya madhyam'|ārūḍham āvedayan
nāḍikā|ccheda|prahata|paṭu|paṭaha|nād'|ânusārī
madhy'|âhna|śaṅkha|dhvanir udatiṣṭhat.
tam ākarṇya ca samāsanna|snāna|samayo
visarjita|rāja|lokaḥ
kṣiti|patir āsthāna|maṇḍapād uttasthau.
atha calati mahī|patāv anyonyam atirabhasa|saṃcalana|
cālit'|âṅgada|pattra|bhaṅga|makara|koṭi|pāṭit'|âṃśuka|
paṭānām ākṣepa|dolāyamāna|kaṇṭha|dāmnām

This, then, is a great wonder."
When the king said this, Kumára·pálita
gave a slight smile and said,
"Your Majesty, what is surprising in this?
For certain kinds of birds—parrots, mynahs and others—
as Your Majesty well knows, can repeat
what they've heard spoken.
In that respect it's hardly very remarkable if
either in consequence of training
received in a previous birth
or by the efforts of some man
a special refinement is produced.
Another thing is that formerly these birds
used to have voices
which enunciated perfectly clearly, just like men's.
But through Agni's curse,
parrots' talking became indistinct,
and elephants' tongues were turned back to front."[43]
Even as he thus pronounced,
the shrill beat of the kettle drum marking the half hour[44]
was followed by the blare of the midday conch
announcing the sun had reached the zenith.
And hearing this, the king dismissed all the kings
from the assembly hall and rose up,
for it was time for him to bathe.
Then as the king moved
they in their sudden corresponding movement
knocked their armlets against each other,
and ripped their silken robes on the sharp points
of the *mákara*s on each other's armlets' leaf-work,

aṃsa|sthal'|ôllasita|kuṅkuma|paṭa|vāsa|dhūli|

piñjarita|diśām

ālola|mālatī|kusuma|śekhar'|ôtpatad|ali|kadambakānām

ardh'|āvalambibhiḥ karṇ'|ôtpalaiś

cumbyamāna|gaṇḍa|sthalānāṃ

gamana|praṇāma|lālasānām ahamahamikayā

vakṣaḥ|sthala|preṅkholita|hāra|latānām uttiṣṭhatām

āsīd atimahān saṃbhramo mahī|patīnām.

itaś c' êtaś ca niṣpatantīnāṃ

skandha|deś'|âvasakta|cāmarāṇāṃ cāmara|grāhiṇīnāṃ

kamala|madhu|pāna|matta|jarat|kalahaṃsa|

nāda|jarjareṇa pade pade

raṇita|maṇīnāṃ maṇi|nūpurāṇāṃ ninādena,

vāra|vilāsinī|janasya saṃcarato

jaghana|sthal'|āsphālana|rasita|ratna|mālikānāṃ

mekhalānāṃ manohāriṇā jhaṃkāreṇa,

nūpura|rav'|ākṛṣṭānāṃ ca

dhavalit'|āsthāna|maṇḍapa|sopāna|phalakānāṃ

bhavana|dīrghikā|kalahaṃsakānāṃ kolāhalena,

their garlands round their necks
swinging to and fro from the collision.
They reddened the quarters
with the perfumed saffron powder
thrown up from their shoulders.
As their garlands of jasmine flowers shook,
swarms of bees flew up from them.
The lilies on their ears half slipped off,
and kissed their cheeks.
Each thought only of himself
in his eagerness to bow down
at the king's going.
As the kings jumped up,
bouncing the pearl necklaces on their chests,
great was their confusion.
And as the chowrie bearers,
resting their chowries on their shoulders,
were pouring out on this side and that side,
there was the jangling sound of their jeweled anklets
tinkling at every step, a sound distorted
by the sound of the old *kala·hansa* geese
intoxicated from drinking lotus wine.
As the dancing girls went by, lovely was the tinkling
of their girdles as the strings of gems on them
sounded out on striking against their buttocks.
And there was cackling from the palace ponds'
kala·hánsaka geese whitening the slabs
of the steps that led to the assembly hall,
attracted by the noise of the anklets.

rasanā|rasit'|ôtsukitānāṃ ca tāratara|virāviṇām
ullikhyamāna|kāṃsya|kreṃkāra|dīrgheṇa
gṛha|sārasānāṃ kūjitena,
sarabhasa|pracalita|sāmanta|śata|caraṇa|tal'|âbhitasya c'
āsthāna|maṇḍapasya
nirghāta|nirghoṣa|gambhīreṇa
kampapyat" êva vasumatīṃ dhvaninā,
pratīhāriṇāṃ ca puraḥ sa|saṃbhramaṃ
samutsārita|janānāṃ daṇḍināṃ samārabdha|helam
uccair uccārayatām
«ālokayat' ālokayat'» êti tāratara|dīrgheṇa
bhavana|prāsāda|kuñjeṣ' ûccarita|pratiśabdatayā
dīrghataratām upagaten' āloka|śabdena,
rājñāṃ ca sa|saṃbhram'|āvarjita|mauli|lola|cūḍā|maṇīnāṃ
praṇamatām amala|maṇi|śalākā|danturābhiḥ
kirīṭa|koṭibhir
ullikhyamānasya maṇi|kuṭṭimasya svanena,
praṇāma|paryastānām atikaṭhina|maṇi|kuṭṭima|
nipatita|raṇaraṇāyitānāṃ ca maṇi|karṇa|pūrāṇāṃ
ninādena,
maṅgala|pāṭhakānāṃ ca puro|yāyināṃ
«jaya jīv'» êti madhura|vacan'|ânuyātena
paṭhatāṃ dig|anta|vyāpinā kalakalena,

There was the cry of the house cranes excited
by the tinkling of girdles
and calling out all the more loudly
with their sustained sound of bell-metal being scratched.
Deep as the rumbling of an thunderstorm,
there was the sound, seeming to make the earth tremble,
of the assembly hall being struck
by the soles of the feet of hundreds of feudatories
hurriedly on the move.
And there was the warning cry of the gatekeepers
with their staffs, pushing the people pell-mell before them,
contemptuously shouting out loud and long,
"Look out, look out!"
a warning the longer because its echo
resounded all the way
to the arbors on the roof terraces of the palace.
And as the kings bowed down, their crest jewels
wobbling as they hastily inclined their heads,
there was the sound of the jeweled paving
scraped by the sharp points of their crowns,
jagged with shining slivers of jewels.
And there was the tinkling
of their jeweled ear ornaments,
tossed about as they made their obeisance,
and jangling as they fell
on to the very hard jeweled pavement.
And as the bards went in front,
the hubbub of their recitation, reaching the horizon,
was punctuated by the agreeable cry of
"Victory, long live the King!"

pracalita|jana|caraṇa|śata|saṃkṣobha|bhayād
apahāya kusuma|prakaram utpatatāṃ ca madhulihāṃ
huṃkṛtena,
saṃkṣobhād atitvarita|pada|pravṛttair avani|patibhiḥ
keyūra|koṭi|tāḍitānāṃ
kvaṇita|mukhara|ratna|dāmnāṃ ca
maṇi|stambhānāṃ raṇitena
sarvataḥ kṣubhitam iva tad āsthāna|bhavanam abhavat.
atha visarjita|rāja|loko «viśramyatām» iti
P1 5 svayam ev' âbhidhāya tāṃ cāṇḍāla|kanyakāṃ
«Vaiśampāyanaḥ praveśyatām abhyantaram» iti
tāmbūla|karaṅka|vāhinīm ādiśya
katipay'|āpta|rāja|putra|parivṛto
nara|patir abhyantaraṃ prāviśat.
apanīt'|âśeṣa|bhūṣaṇaś ca
divasa|kara iva vigalita|kiraṇa|jālaś
candra|tārakā|samūha|śūnya iva gagan'|ābhogaḥ
samupāhṛta|samucita|vyāyām'|ôpakaraṇāṃ
vyāyāma|bhūmim ayāsīt.
sa tasyāṃ ca samāna|vayobhiḥ saha rāja|putraiḥ
kṛta|madhura|vyāyāmaḥ
śrama|vaśād unmiṣantībhiḥ kapolayor
īṣad|avadalita|sinduvāra|kusuma|mañjarī|vibhramābhir,

And the bees hummed as they left the mass of flowers
and flew up in the air through fear of the turmoil
of hundreds of feet of people on the move.
There was the ringing sound of the jeweled pillars,
their festoons of jewels jangling loudly
when struck by the sharp points of the armlets
of the kings pushing past with hasty step.
With these sounds the assembly hall
seemed shaken in every direction.
Then, the assembly of kings dismissed, the king himself
told the *chandála* girl to rest herself, P15
and ordered the maid who carried his betel box
to bring Vaishampáyana into the inner apartments.
Accompanied by a few favorite princes
the king entered into the inner apartments.
And taking off all his ornaments,
looking like the sun divested of all his rays,
or the expanse of the sky bereft
of the moon and the clusters of stars,
he went to the exercise hall which was equipped
with all the necessary apparatus for physical exercise.
There he undertook pleasant exercise
with princes of his own age.
As a result of his exertion, his body was ornamented
with lines of drops of sweat, breaking out
on his cheeks as the semblance of clusters
of slightly opened *sinduvára* flowers;

urasi nirdaya|śrama|cchinna|hāra|vigalita|
muktā|phala|prakar'|ânukāriṇībhir,
lalāṭa|paṭṭake 'ṣṭamī|candra|śakala|tal'|ôllasad|
amṛta|bindu|viḍambinībhiḥ
sveda|jala|kaṇikā|saṃtatibhir alaṃkriyamāṇa|mūrtir,
itas tataḥ snān'|ôpakaraṇa|saṃpādana|sa|tvareṇa
puraḥ pradhāvatā parijanena tat|kālaṃ
virala|jane 'pi rāja|kule samutsāraṇ'|âdhikāram ucitam
ācaradbhir daṇḍibhir upadiśyamāna|mārgo,
vitata|sita|vitānām
aneka|cāraṇa|gaṇ'|âvabadhyamāna|maṇḍalāṃ
gandh'|ôdaka|pūrṇa|
kanaka|maya|jala|droṇī|sanātha|madhyām
upasthāpita|sphāṭika|snāna|pīṭhām
ekānta|nihitair atisurabhi|gandha|salila|pūrṇaiḥ
parimal'|âvakṛṣṭa|madhu|kara|kul'|ândhakārita|mukhair
ātapa|bhayān nīla|karpaṭ'|âvaguṇṭhita|mukhair iva
snāna|kalaśair upaśobhitāṃ
snāna|bhūmim agacchat.
avatīrṇasya jala|droṇīṃ
vāra|vilāsinī|kara|mṛdita|sugandh'|âmalak'|ôpalipta|śiraso

on his chest imitating a profusion of pearls
scattered from a necklace
broken by his strenuous exercise;
on the expanse of his forehead
looking very much like drops of nectar
shining forth from the surface of the half moon
of the first half of the lunar fortnight.
Then from there he went to the bathing place,
way being made for him
by his attendants running on ahead,
expeditious in preparing materials for his bath,
and by his staff-bearers performing their customary duty
of pushing people aside, though at that time
the royal palace had few people in it.
A white canopy was stretched over the bathing place.
Many bands of bards formed a circle around it.
In the middle of it was set a golden tub
filled with scented water.
A crystal bath seat was in position.
And it was adorned with golden water-vessels
set in one corner
full of very fragrant scented water
with their openings darkened
by swarms of bees the perfume attracted,
so that they seemed to have their openings covered
with dark blue cloths from fear of the heat.
When the king had got into the tub,
the dancing girls crushed fragrant *ámalaka* fruit
and smeared his head with them.

rājñaḥ samantāt samupatasthur

aṃśuka|nibiḍa|nibaddha|stana|parikarā

dūra|samutsārita|valaya|bāhu|latāḥ

samutkṣipta|karṇ'|ābharaṇāḥ

karṇ'|ôtsārit'|âlakā gṛhīta|jala|kalaśāḥ

snān'|ârtham abhiṣeka|devatā iva vāra|yoṣitaḥ.

tābhiś ca *samunnata/kuca/kumbha/maṇḍalābhir*

vāri|madhya|praviṣṭaḥ

kariṇībhir iva vana|karī parivṛtas

tat|kṣaṇaṃ rājā rarāja.

jala|droṇī|salilād utthāya ca snāna|pīṭham

amala|sphaṭika|dhavalaṃ

Varuṇa iva rāja|haṃsam āruroha.

tatas tāḥ kāś cin marakata|kalaśa|prabhā|śyāmāyamānā

nalinya iva mūrti|matyaḥ pattra|puṭaiḥ,

kāś cid rajata|kalaśa|hastā rajanya iva

pūrṇa|candra|maṇḍala|vinirgatena jyotsnā|pravāheṇa,

kāś cit kalaś'|ôtkṣepa|śrama|sved'|ārdra|śarīrā

jala|devatā iva

sphāṭikaiḥ kalaśais tīrtha|jalena,

They surrounded him, ready to bathe him,
holding pitchers of water,
their silken garments pulled tight
against their ample breasts,
their armlets pushed high up their creeper-like arms,
ear-ornaments thrown back,
hair pulled back behind their ears,
looking like goddesses come to consecrate him.
Immersed in the water up to his waist,
with them surrounding him, *the round pots*
of their breasts uplifted—
at that moment the king splendidly resembled
a wild elephant surrounded by female elephants,
the breast-like round protrusions
on their foreheads raised high.
And rising from the water in the tub,
he mounted the white bath slab of shining crystal
as Váruna, god of the oceans, mounts his royal goose.
Then one after another the dancing girls
poured water on the king.
Some, darkened by the luster of their emerald pots
looked like lotus plants in bodily form, with petal-cups.
Some, with silver pots in their hands,
were each like the night with a flood of moonlight
issuing from the disk of the full moon.
Some with crystal pots with holy water
from pilgrimage sites,
their bodies wet with sweat
from the exertion of pouring the pots,
were like mermaids.

kāś cin malaya|sarita iva
candana|rasa|miśreṇa salilena,
kāś cid utkṣipta|kalaśa|pārśva|vinyasta|hasta|pallavāḥ
prakīryamāṇa|nakha|mayūkha|jālakāḥ
pratyaṅguli|vivara|vinirgata|jala|dhārāḥ
salila|yantra|devatā iva,
kāś cij jāḍyam apanetum
ākṣipta|bāl'|ātapen' êva
divasa|śriya iva kanaka|kalaśa|hastāḥ
kuṅkuma|jalena
vār'|âṅganāḥ krameṇa rājānam abhiṣiṣicuḥ.
anantaram udapādi ca sphoṭayann iva śruti|patham
aneka|prahata|paṭu|paṭaha|jhallarī|mṛdaṅga|
veṇu|vīṇā|gīta|ninād'|ânugamyamāno
bandi|vṛnda|kolāhal'|ākulo
bhuvana|vivara|vyāpī
snāna|śaṅkhānām āpūryamāṇānām
atimukharo dhvaniḥ.
evaṃ ca krameṇa nirvartit'|âbhiṣeko
viṣa|dhara|nirmoka|parilaghunī dhavale paridhāya
dhauta|vāsasī śarad|ambar'|âika|deśa iva
jala|kṣālana|vimala|tanur
atidhavala|jala|dhara|ccheda|śucinā
dukūla|paṭa|pallavena
tuhina|girir iva gagana|sarit|srotasā kṛta|śiro|veṣṭanaḥ

Some with water mixed with liquid sandal paste,
were like the rivers on the Málaya mountain.
Some, with their leaf-tender hands
holding the sides of the pots they'd lifted up,
and scattering networks of rays from their nails,
were like fountain statues of deities
with water streaming down
from gaps between their fingers.
Some holding golden pots sprinkled
the king with saffron water,
each like day's triumphant beauty
pouring out morning sunshine
to dispel the king's coldness.
And thereupon there arose the very loud noise
of the bath-time conches being blown,
almost shattering people's eardrums,
filling the hollows of the universe,
added to by the hubbub of the throng of bards,
and accompanied by the multiple sounds
of loudly beaten kettledrums, cymbals,
mridánga drums, flutes, *vinas*, and singing.
And thus his bathing completed in due order,
he put on two white garments, freshly washed,
as light as shed snakeskin,
his body spotless from his water cleansing
likc a portion of the sky in fall,
he wrapped his head in a turban of silken cloth,
blossom fine, as pure as a wisp of very white cloud,
and looked like Himálaya, the snow mountain,
with the heavenly Ganga wrapped round its peak.

saṃpādita|pitṛ|jala|kriyo mantra|pūtena toy'|âñjalinā
divasa|karam abhipraṇamya deva|gṛham agamat.
uparacita|Paśupati|pūjanaś ca
niṣkramya deva|gṛhān
nirvartit'|âgni|kāryo,
vilepana|bhūmau jhaṃkāribhir ali|kadambakair
anubadhyamāna|parimalena
mṛga|mada|karpūra|kuṅkuma|vāsa|surabhiṇā
candanen'|ânulipta|sarv'|âṅgo,
viracit'|āmodi|mālatī|kusuma|śekharaḥ,
kṛt'|âmbara|parivarto ratna|karṇa|pūra|mātr'|ābharaṇaḥ
samucita|bhojanaiḥ saha bhū|patibhir āhāram
abhimata|ras'|āsvāda|jāta|prītir avani|po nirvartayām āsa.
paripīta|dhūpa|dhūma|vartir upaspṛśya ca gṛhīta|tāmbūlas
tasmāt pramṛṣṭa|maṇi|kuṭṭimāt praveśād utthāya
n' âtidūra|vartinyā sa|saṃbhrama|pradhāvitayā
pratīhāryā prasāritam avalamby'
ân|avarata|vetra|latā|grahaṇa|prasaṅgād
atijaraṭha|kisalay'|ânukāri kara|talaṃ kareṇ'[45]
âbhyantara|saṃcāra|samucitena parijanen'
ânugamyamāno

With a handful of water purified by mantras
he performed the water offering to his ancestors,
bowed to the sun, and made his way to the temple.
When he'd worshipped Shiva, lord of animals,
he left the temple
and made the customary offering to Agni, god of fire.
In the perfuming room his whole body
was smeared with sandal paste sweetened
with the fragrance of musk,
camphor and saffron,
swarms of humming bees following its scent.
He put on a chaplet made of fragrant jasmine flowers,
changed his clothes;
and, a pair of jeweled ear-rings his only ornaments,
the king took his meal with the kings
who were his usual dining companions,
delighting in tasting his favorite flavors.
He smoked a fragrant cigar,[46]
rinsed his mouth and took his betel.
When the jeweled floor had been cleaned,
as he rose from his place
a nearby female door-keeper hastily ran up to him
and put out her arm and he leaned on it.
Followed by the attendants
privileged to pass into the inner apartments,
the palms of their hands resembling toughened shoots
from having to constantly grasp their cane staffs,
he made his way to the assembly hall.

dhaval'|âṃśuka|javanikā|parigata|paryantatayā
sphaṭika|maṇi|maya|bhitti|baddham iv' ôpalakṣyamāṇam,
atisurabhiṇā mṛga|nābhi|parigaten' āmodinā candana|vāriṇā
sikta|śiśira|maṇi|bhūmim, avirala|viprakīrṇena
vimala|maṇi|kuṭṭima|gagana|tala|tārā|gaṇen' êva
kusum'|ôpahārena nirantara|nicitam,
utkīrṇa|śāla|bhañjikā|nivahena
saṃnihita|gṛha|devaten' êva
gandha|salila|kṣālitena kala|dhauta|mayena
stambha|saṃcayena virājamānam,
atibahal'|âguru|dhūpa|parimalam,
akhila|vigalita|jala|nivaha|dhavala|jala|dhara|śakal'|
ânukāriṇā kusum'|āmoda|vāsita|pracchada|paṭena
paṭṭ'|ôpadhān'|âdhyāsita|śiro|dhāmnā
maṇi|maya|pratipādukā|pratiṣṭhita|pādena
pārśva|stha|ratna|pāda|pīṭhena
tuhina|giri|śilā|tala|sadṛśa|śayanena
sanāthī|kṛta|vedikaṃ,
bhuktv" āsthāna|maṇḍapam ayāsīt.
tatra ca śayana|tala|niṣaṇṇaḥ kṣiti|tal'|ôpaviṣṭayā
śanaiḥ śanair utsaṅga|nihit'|âsi|latayā khaḍga|vāhinyā
nava|nalina|dala|komalena kara|saṃpuṭena
saṃvāhyamāna|caraṇas tat|kāl'|ôcita|darśanair
avani|patibhir amātyair mitraiś ca saha
tās tāḥ kathāḥ kurvan muhūrtam iv' āsāṃ cakre.

Because its sides were draped in white silk
it looked as if enclosed with walls of precious crystal.
Its jeweled floor was cool, being sprinkled
with fragrant sandal water
heavy scented, being infused with musk,
and covered over with thickly scattered flower offerings,
as if they were the hosts of stars in the sky
that was the bright pavement of precious stones.
It was resplendent with numerous pillars made of gold
and washed down with scented water,
with countless images sculpted on them,
so that it seemed that the household deities
were assembled.
It was fragrant with very dense aloe incense.
There was a platform provided with a couch
like a slab of stone from the snow mountain,
like a fragment of white cloud
which has shed all its water;
its covering, flower scented cloth,
a pillow of fine linen at the head.
The couch stood on jeweled pedestals;
beside it was a jeweled footstool.
Such was the assembly hall he went to after he'd eaten.
And there as he reclined on the couch,
the maid who carried his sword,
seated on the ground with the sword in her lap,
very slowly massaged his feet
with her joined hands as soft as fresh lotus petals.
He spent about an hour
chatting about various things with his friends,

tato n' âtidūra|vartinīm
«antaḥ|purād Vaiśampāyanam ādāya āgacch'» êti
samupajāta|tad|vṛttānta|praśna|kutūhalo
rājā pratīhārīm ādideśa.
sā kṣiti|tala|nihita|jānu|kara|talā
«yath" ājñāpayati deva» iti
śirasi kṛtv" ājñāṃ yath"|ādiṣṭam akarot.
atha muhūrtād iva Vaiśampāyanaḥ
pratīhāryā gṛhīta|pañjaraḥ
kanaka|vetra|lat"|âvalambinā kiṃ cid
avanata|pūrva|kāyena
sita|kañcuk'|âvacchanna|vapuṣā
jarā|dhavalita|maulinā gadgada|svareṇa
manda|manda|saṃcāriṇā
vihaṃga|jāti|prītyā jarat|kalahaṃsen' êva kañcukin"
ânugamyamāno rāj"|ântikam ājagāma.
kṣiti|tala|nihita|kara|talas tu kañcukī rājānaṃ vyajñāpayat.
«deva, devyo vijñāpayanti:
‹dev'|ādeśād eṣa Vaiśampāyanaḥ snātaḥ kṛt'|āhāraś ca
deva|pāda|mūlaṃ pratīhāry" ānītaḥ.› »
ity abhidhāya gate ca tasmin rājā
Vaiśampāyanam apṛcchat:

counselors and such kings as were usually
granted audience with him at that time.
Then the king ordered the nearby female doorkeeper
to bring Vaishampáyana from the inner apartments,
for his curiosity was aroused and
he wanted to question the parrot about his history.
She knelt, put her palms to the ground,
and bowed her head to his command.
Saying, "As Your Majesty commands,"
she did as she was bade.
Then in a short while Vaishampáyana
came into the king's presence.
His cage was carried by the female doorkeeper,
and he was escorted by a chamberlain
who looked like an aged *kala·hansa* goose
following him because of fellow feeling
for a member of the bird species,
his upper body slightly stooping,
leaning on his golden cane-staff,
his body clothed in a white coat,
his head white with age,
his voice faltering, walking very slowly.
Placing the palms of his hands on the ground
the chamberlain informed the king,
"Your Majesty, their majesties the queens
inform Your Majesty
that by Your Majesty's command
this Vaishampáyana has been bathed and fed,
and is now brought to Your Majesty's feet
by the doorkeeper."

«kaccid abhimatam āsvāditam abhyantare bhavatā
kiṃ cid aśana|jātam?» iti.
sa pratyuvāca. «deva! kiṃ vā n' āsvāditam?
āmatta|kokila|locana|cchavir nīla|pāṭalaḥ kaṣāya|madhuraḥ
prakāmam āpīto jambū|phala|rasaḥ.
hari|nakhara|bhinna|matta|mātaṅga|kumbha|mukta|
rakt'|ārdra|muktā|phala|tviṣi khaṇḍitāni dāḍima|bījāni.
nalinī|dala|harinti drākṣā|phala|svādūni ca dalitāni
sv'|êcchayā prācīn'|āmalakī|phalāni.
kiṃ vā pralapitena bahunā? sarvam eva devībhiḥ
svayaṃ kara|tal'|ôpanīyamānam amṛtāyate.»
ity evaṃ|vādino vacanam ākṣipya nara|patir abravīt.
«āstāṃ tāvat sarvam ev' êdam. apanayatu naḥ kutūhalam.
āvedayatu bhavān āditaḥ prabhṛti kārtsnyen' ātmano janma
kasmin deśe bhavān kathaṃ jātaḥ?
kena vā nāma kṛtam?
kā mātā? kas te pitā?
kathaṃ vedānām āgamaḥ?
kathaṃ śāstrāṇāṃ paricayaḥ?
kutaḥ kalāḥ samāsāditāḥ?
kiṃ janm'|ântar'|ânusmaraṇam uta vara|pradānam?
athavā vihaṃga|veṣa|dhārī
kaś cic channaṃ nivasasi?

When he'd said this and gone,
the king asked Vaishampáyana,
"I hope you've eaten food sufficient and to your taste
in the inner apartments?"
He replied, "Your Majesty, what have I not tasted?
I've drunk my fill of the juice of *jambu* fruit,
the color of a drunken *kókila*'s eye,
bluish red, bitter-sweet.
I've cracked pomegranate seeds
the color of pearls wet with blood
released from the temples of rutting elephants
split open by lions' claws.
I've crushed ripe myrobalan fruit to my heart's content,
as green as lotus leaves and sweet as grapes.
But what more can I say?
Everything the queens brought with their own hands
tasted of nectar."
Thus did he speak, but the king cut him short, saying,
"Never mind all this. You must satisfy our curiosity.
Please tell us from the beginning in full detail,
how and where were you born?
Who gave you your name? Who was your mother,
who was your father?
How came about your attainment of the Vedas?
Your knowledge of the *shastras*?
How did you master the fine arts?
Was it remembering former lives,
or the granting of some boon?
Or are you someone living in disguise,
having taken on the garb of a bird?

kva vā pūrvam uṣitam? kiyad vā vayaḥ?

kathaṃ pañjara|bandhaḥ?

kathaṃ cāṇḍāla|hasta|gamanam?

iha vā katham āgamanam?» iti.

Vaiśampāyanas tu svayam upajāta|kutūhalena

sa|bahu|mānam avani|patinā pṛṣṭo

muhūrtam iva dhyātvā s'|ādaram abravīt.

«deva, mahat" îyaṃ kathā.

yadi kautukam ākarṇyatām:

asti pūrv'|âpara|jala|nidhi|velā|vana|lagnā,

madhya|deś'|âlaṃkāra|bhūtā mekhal" êva bhuvo,

vana|kari|kula|mada|jala|seka|saṃvardhitair

ativikaca|dhavala|kusuma|nikaram

atyuccatayā tārā|gaṇam iva śikhara|deśa|lagnam

udvahadbhiḥ pādapair upaśobhitā,

mada|kala|kurara|kula|daśyamāna|marica|pallavā,

kari|kalabha|kara|mṛdita|tamāla|kisalay'|āmodinī,

madhu|mad'|ôparakta|Keralī|kapola|komala|cchavinā

saṃcarad|vana|devatā|caraṇ'|ālaktaka|rasa|rañjiten' êva

pallava|pracayena saṃcchāditā,

And where did you live? And how old are you?
How did you come to be shut in a cage?
How did you fall into the hands of *chandála* outcastes?
And how came you to be here?"
Vaishampáyana, for his part,
questioned so respectfully by the king himself,
whose curiosity he'd aroused,
pondered for a while and then respectfully said,
"Your Majesty, the tale is long. If you are curious,
let it be heard!
There is a forest that extends as far as the trees
on the shores of both the eastern and the western oceans.
It is the adornment of the Middle Region,
the very girdle of the earth.
It is resplendent with its trees grown high,
watered with the rut of wild elephants,
trees so lofty that the mass
of white flowers in full bloom they carry
seems to be the throng of stars clinging to their tops.
Ospreys whistle in delight
as they nibble the fronds of its pepper plants.
It is fragrant with *tamála* branches
crushed by the trunks of young elephants.
Foliage, the delicate color
of Kerala women's wine-flushed cheeks,
seemingly reddened by the lac melting
from the feet of roaming woodland deities,
envelopes it.

śuka|kula|dalita|dāḍimī|phala|drav'|ārdrī|kṛta|talair,

aticapala|kapi|kampita|kakkola|cyuta|

pallava|phala|śabalair,

an|avarata|nipatita|kusuma|reṇu|pāṃsulaiḥ,

pathika|jana|racita|lavaṅga|pallava|srastarair,

atikaṭhora|nālikera|ketakī|karīra|kesara|parigata|prāntais,

tāmbūlī|lat"|âvanaddha|pūga|khaṇḍa|maṇḍitair,

vana|lakṣmī|vāsa|bhavanair iva virājitā latā|maṇḍapair,

unmada|mātaṅga|kapola|sthala|galita|mada|salila|sikten' êva

nirantaram elā|latā|vanena mada|gandhin" ândhakāritā,

nakha|mukha|lagn'|êbha|kumbha|muktā|phala|lubdhaiḥ

śabara|senā|patibhir abhihanyamāna|kesari|śatā

pret'|âdhipa|nagar" îva

sadā|saṃnihita|mṛtyu|bhīṣaṇā

mahiṣ'|âdhiṣṭhitā ca,

samar'|ôdyata|patākin" îva

bāṇ'|āsan'|āropita|śilīmukhā

vimukta|siṃha|nādā ca,

Their floors wet with juice from pomegranates
bitten into by flocks of parrots;
dappled with fruit and leaves
fallen from *kakkóla* trees
shaken by frenetic monkeys;
dusty with the pollen falling unceasingly;
where travelers make themselves beds of clove leaves;
bordered by full grown *nalikéra,*
kétaki, *karíra*, and *késara* trees,
adorned with clumps of areca trees
encircled by *tambúli* creepers—
such are the creeper bowers which adorn the forest,
looking like residences for the woodland Lakshmi.
The forest is darkened with cardamom creepers
that smell like rut,
as if sprinkled everywhere with liquid rut flowing
from the surfaces of the cheeks of rutting elephants;
tribal war lords are killing hundreds of its lions,
greedy for the pearls from elephants' temples
clinging to the tips of their claws.
Like the city of Yama, lord of the dead,
ever-present death makes the forest frightening,
and *just as he has his buffalo to ride on*
the forest *is frequented by buffalo.*
Like an army ready for battle,
arrows fitted to bows, and voicing battle cries,
it *has bees placed on its bana* and *ásana trees,*
and lions' roars are emitted.

Kātyāyan" îva

pracalita|khaḍga|bhīṣaṇā,

rakta|candan'|âlaṃkṛtā ca,

Karṇīsuta|kath" êva

saṃnihita|Vipul'|Âcalā

śaś'|ôpagatā ca,

kalp'|ânta|pradoṣa|saṃdhy" êva

pranṛtta|nīla|kaṇṭhā pallav'|âruṇā c',

âmṛta|mathana|vel" êva

Śrī|drum'|ôpaśobhitā

Vāruṇī|parigatā ca,

prāvṛḍ iva *ghana|śyāmal"|*

âneka|śata|hrad'|âlaṃkṛtā ca,

candra|mūrtir iva

satatam ṛkṣa|sārth'|ânugatā

hariṇ'|âdhyāsitā ca,

Like the goddess Katyáyani *who is frightening*
and waves a sword,
and who is smeared with red sandal paste,
the forest *is frightening with rhinoceroses wandering about,*
and adorned with red sandal trees.
Like the story of the famous thief Karni·suta
and his companions Vípula and Áchala,
along with his guru Shasha,
the forest *is flanked by extensive mountains*
and populated with hares.
Like the evening twilight of the end of the world age
red as blossom, when blue-necked Shiva has begun to dance,
the forest *has peacocks dancing in it*
and is red with blossom.
Like the time of the churning of nectar,
adorned with the goddess Shri
and the wish-granting tree, and *accompanied*
by Váruna's wife, goddess of spirituous liquor,
the forest *was adorned with bilvas, Shri's trees,*
and accompanied by durva grass.
Like the rainy season, *which is dark with clouds*
and ornamented with much lightning,
the forest *has thick growths of shyámala* vines *and*
is ornamented with many hundred ponds.
Like the orb of the moon,
which is everywhere accompanied by the hosts of stars
and is inhabited by the deer,
the forest *throughout is thronged with hordes of bears*
and is inhabited by deer.

rājya|sthitir iva camara|mṛga|bāla|vyajan'|ôpaśobhitā

sa|mada|gaja|ghaṭā|paripālitā ca,

giri|tanay" êva

Sthāṇu/saṃgatā mṛga/pati/sevitā ca,

Jānak" îva

prasūta/Kuśa/Lavā

niśā/cara/parigṛhītā ca,

kāmin" îva

candana/mṛga/mada/parimala/vāhinī

P20 *rucir'/âguru/tilaka/bhūṣitā* ca,

s'|ôtkaṇṭh" êva

vividha/pallav'/ânila/vījitā

sa/madanā ca,

bāla|grīv" êva

vyāghra/nakha/paṅkti/maṇḍitā

gaṇḍak'/ābharaṇā ca,

pāna|bhūmir iva

prakaṭita/madhu/kośaka/śatā

prakīrṇa|vividha|kusumā ca

Like kingship, the forest is beautified by yaktail fans
and protected by herds of rutting elephants.
Like Párvati, daughter of the mountain,
who is accompanied by Shiva the rigid ascetic,
and served by the lord of beasts, her lion,
the forest is *full of tree trunks and frequented by lions.*
Like Sita, Jánaka's daughter,
who gave birth to Kusha and Lava,
and who was earlier seized
by the night-roaming demon, Rávana,
the forest *produces clumps of* ***kusha*** *grass*
and is the haunt of nocturnal creatures.
Like a woman in love,
who wears the scent of sandal and musk,
and *is adorned with a forehead mark of bright aloe paste,*[47]
the forest is *fragrant with sandal and musk,*
and is *adorned with vivid aloe and tílaka* trees. P20
Like a woman longing for her lover,
fanned by the wind of various leaves
and *full of passion,*
the forest, *likewise fanned by the wind of various leaves,*
is also *full of hallucinatory thorn apple trees.*
Like a child's neck, *adorned with a row of tiger claws*
and *having a rhinoceros horn as ornament,*
the forest has *the tracks of tigers' claws*
and *is ornamented with rhinoceroses.*
Like a drinking hall, *which has hundreds*
of wine goblets on display,
the forest has *hundreds of honey combs in evidence*
and both drinking hall and forest

kvacit pralaya|vel" êva

mahā|varāha|damṣṭrā|samutkhāta|

dharaṇi|maṇḍalā,

kva cid Daśamukha|nagar" îva

caṭula|vānara|vṛnda|bhajyamāna|

tuṅga|śāl'|ākulā,

kva cid acira|nirvṛtta|vivāha|bhūmir iva

harita|kuśa|samit|kusuma|śamī|palāśa|śobhitā,

kva cid udvṛtta|mṛga|pati|nāda|bhīt" êva

kaṇṭakitā,

kva cin matt" êva

kokila|kula|pralāpinī,

kva cid unmatt" êva

vāyu|vega|kṛta|tāla|śabdā,

kva cid vidhav" êv'

ônmukta|tālapattrā,

are strewn with all sorts of flowers.
In some places, like the time of doomsday,
when the great boar form of Vishnu
lifts up on its snout
the circle of the earth,
the forest *has circles of earth dug up*
by the snouts of great boar.
In some places, like the city of ten-headed Rávana,
which was full of *lofty halls* being broken up
by the troops of restless monkeys,
so too is the forest with its *lofty shala trees.*
In some places, like the scene of a recent wedding,
the forest is adorned with green *kusha* grass,
firewood, flowers, and *shami* leaves.
In some places, the forest *is prickly with thorns*
as if, terrified of the roaring of proud lions,
its hair stood on end.
In some places, *when it gave voice*
through the flocks of kókila birds,
it seems like a drunken woman
speaking incoherently to the flocks of kókila birds.
In some places, like a madwoman
clapping her hands in her delirium,
the forest *is made to rustle its palm leaves*
by the force of the wind.
In some places, like a widow *shedding*
her tala·pattra ornaments,
the forest *sheds its palm leaves.*

kva cit samara|bhūmir iva

śara/śata/nicitā,

kva cid amara|pati|tanur iva

netra/sahasra/saṃkulā,

kva cin Nārāyaṇa|mūrtir iva

tamāla/nīlā,

kva cit Pārtha|ratha|patāk" êva

vānar'/ākrāntā,

kva cid avani|pati|dvāra|bhūmir iva

vetra/latā/śata/duṣpraveśā,

kva cid Virāṭa|nagar" îva

Kīcaka/śat'/āvṛtā,

kva cid ambara|śrīr iva

vyādh'/ânugamyamāna/

tarala/tāraka/mṛgā,

kva cid gṛhīta|vrat" êva

darbha/cīra/jaṭā/valkala/dhāriṇy,

In some places like battlefield *filled*
with hundreds of arrows,
it *is overgrown with reed-beds.*
In some places like the body of Indra, lord of the gods,
which is covered with a thousand eyes,
the forest is filled with thousands of netra trees.
In some places like the form of Naráyana
which is as dark as a tamála tree
the forest *is dark with tamála trees.*
In some places like the chariot banner of Árjuna,
descendant of Pritha, *blazoned with a monkey,*
the forest *is overrun with monkeys.*
In some places like a king's gatehouse
which is hard to pass through on account
of *the hundreds of officials holding cane staffs,*[48]
the forest is *difficult of access* because of
the large amount of reeds and creepers.
In some places like Viráta's city
which is thronged with Kíchaka people,
the forest is *full of hollow bamboos.*
In some places like the glorious beauty of the sky
where the constellation of Capricorn
with its twinkling stars is followed by Orion the hunter,
the forest has *tremulous-eyed deer pursued by hunters.*
In some place like a woman who has undertaken a vow,
and wears bark, and has matted locks
and garments of darbha grass,
the forest *produces strips of kusha* grass,
fibrous roots, and bark.

aparimita|bahula|pattra|saṃcay" âpi

sapta/parṇa/bhūṣitā,

krūra/sattv" âpi

muni|jana|sevitā,

puṣpavaty api

pavitrā,

Vindhy'|āṭavī nāma.

tasyāṃ ca Daṇḍak'|āraṇy'|ântaḥ|pāti

sakala|bhuvana|tala|khyātam

utpatti|kṣetram iva bhagavato Dharmasya,

sura|pati|prārthan"|āpīta|sakala|sāgara|salilasya,

Meru|matsarād gagana|tala|prasārita|vikaṭa|śiraḥ|sahasreṇa

divasa|kara|ratha|gamana|patham apanetum abhyudyaten'

âvagaṇita|sakala|sura|samūha|vacasā Vindhya|giriṇ" âpy

an|ullaṅghit'|ājñasya,

jaṭhar'|ânala|jīrṇa|Vātāpi|dānavasya,

sur'|âsura|mukuṭa|makara|pattra|koṭī|cumbita|

caraṇa|rajaso,

dakṣiṇ'|āśā|mukha|viśeṣakasya,

Though it has a vast quantity of leaves of different sorts,
only seven leaves adorn it,
that is to say, *it is adorned with, among others,*
sapta·parna trees, the seven-leafed tree.
Though *of a cruel disposition* it is honored by ascetics,
that is to say, *having wild animals and so being remote,*
it is resorted to by ascetics.
Although *a menstruating woman* it is pure,
that is to say, *it is full of flowers* and is pure.
The name of it is the Vindhya forest.
And in that forest,
there was, within the confines of Dándaka's wood,
a place famous throughout the world,
as if it were the birthplace of Dharma itself,
and it belonged to the person who
at the request of the lord of the gods
drank up all the water in the ocean.
When in rivalry with Meru
the Vindhya had its thousand mighty heads
stretching across the surface of the sky,
straining to interrupt the course of the sun's chariot,
scorning the voice of the whole assembly of gods,
even that mountain chain
did not contravene his command.
The fire in his belly digested the demon Vatápi.[49]
The dust of his feet was kissed
by the protrusions of the *mákara* leaf-work
on the crowns of the gods and the demons.
He was the forehead mark of the face
of the woman who is the southern quarter.

sura|lokād
eka|huṃkāra|nipātita|Nahuṣa|prakaṭa|prabhāvasya,
bhagavato mahā|muner Agastyasya
bhāryayā Lopāmudrayā
svayam uparacit'|ālavālakaiḥ
kara|puṭa|salila|seka|saṃvardhitaiḥ
suta|nirviśeṣair upaśobhitaṃ pādapais,
tat|putreṇa ca gṛhīta|vraten' āṣāḍhinā
pavitra|bhasma|viracita|tri|puṇḍrak'|ābharaṇena
kuśa|cīvara|vāsasā
muñja|mekhalā|kalita|madhyena
gṛhīta|harita|parṇa|puṭena
pratyuṭajam aṭatā bhikṣāṃ
Dṛḍhadasyu|nāmnā pavitrī|kṛtam
atiprabhūt'|êdhm'|āharaṇāc ca
yasy' Êdhmavāha iti pitā dvitīyaṃ nāma cakāra.
diśi diśi śuka|haritaiś ca kadalī|vanaiḥ
śyāmalī|kṛta|parisaraṃ
saritā ca kalaśa|yoni|paripīta|sāgara|mārg'|ânugatay" êva
baddha|veṇikayā Godāvaryā parigatam
āśrama|padam āsīt.

His might was manifest when he made
Náhusha[50] tumble down from heaven
by making a single roar of concentrated power.
Such is the great and blessed sage Agástya;
and his wife Lopa·mudra it was who herself
made the watering basins and reared
by pouring water from her own cupped hands
the trees that adorned the hermitage,
treating them no differently from her sons.
It was hallowed also by his son,
who'd taken the vow
and carried the *palásha* staff,
drawing on his forehead with purifying ash
the insignia of the three horizontal lines,
wearing a garment woven from *kusha* grass,
fastened round his waist a belt of *munja* grass,
holding a green leaf cup as he went round
begging alms from every hut.
Dridha·dasyu was his name, 'Demon-restrainer,'
but because he collected so much firewood,
his father gave him a second name:
Idhma·vaha, 'Firewood-carrier.'
In every direction plantain trees as green as parrots
make the environs of the place dark green.
And, circling round it,
the river Godávari's *stream was uninterrupted,*
as if, *with her hair in a widow's single braid*
she were following the path of her husband the ocean
who was drunk up by Agástya, the pot-born.[51]
Such was the hermitage.

yatra ca Daśaratha|vacanam anupālayann utsṛṣṭa|rājyo Daśa|vadana|lakṣmī|vibhrama|virāmo Rāmo mahā|munim Agastyam anucaran saha Sītayā Lakṣmaṇ'|ôparacita|rucira|parṇa|śālo Pañcavaṭyāṃ kaṃ cit kālaṃ sukham uvāsa.

cira|śūnye 'dy' âpi yatra śākhā|nilīna|nibhṛta|pāṇḍu|kapota|paṅktayo lagna|tāpas'|âgnihotra|dhūma|rājaya iva lakṣyante taravaḥ.

bali|karma|kusumāny uddharantyāḥ Sītāyāḥ kara|talād iva saṃkrānto yatra rāgaḥ sphurati latā|kisalayeṣu.

yatra ca pīt'|ôdgīrṇaṃ jala|nidhi|jalam iva muninā nikhilam āśram'|ôpānta|vartiṣu vibhaktaṃ mahā|hradeṣu.

yatra Daśaratha|suta|niśita|śara|nikara|nipāta|nihata|rajani|cara|bala|bahula|rudhira|sikta|mūlam ady' âpi tad|rāg'|āviddha|nirgata|palāśam iv' ābhāti nava|kisalayam araṇyam.

There too, in what is the Pancha·vati region,
giving up his kingdom and keeping his father's promise,
Rama, who was to be the end of the lascivious behavior
of ten-faced Rávana's royal fortune,
dwelled happily for some time with Sita,
attending on the great sage Agástya,
and living in a charming leaf-hut Lákshmana had made.
There, even today,
though the hermitage has long been empty,
its trees, with rows of white pigeons softly nestling
in their boughs, seem to have clinging to them
columns of smoke from ascetics' fire sacrifices.
There redness bursts out in creepers' leaves
as if transferred from Sita's palms
when she picked flowers for offerings.
And there all the water of the ocean—
which having drunk
the ascetic must have had to dispel—
seems to have been shared out among all the large pools
in the vicinity of the hermitage.
There Dasha·ratha's son
slew hosts of night-roaming demons,
raining down on them his sharp arrows,
and watering the roots of the forest
with their copious blood,
so that even today
when the forest shines with fresh shoots
it seems as though its foliage
were saturated with that crimson.

adhun" âpi yatra jala|dhara|samaye gambhīram
abhinava|jala|dhara|nivaha|ninādam ākarṇya
bhagavato Rāmasya tri|bhuvana|vivara|vyāpinaś
cāpa|ghoṣasya smaranto na gṛhṇanti śaṣpa|kavalam,
ajasram aśru|jala|lulita|dīna|dṛṣṭayo
vīkṣya śūnyā daśa diśo
jarā|jarjarita|viṣāṇa|koṭayo
Jānakī|saṃvardhitā jīrṇa|mṛgāḥ.
yasminn an|avarata|mṛgayā|nihata|śeṣa|vana|hariṇa|
protsāhita iva kṛta|Sītā|vipralambhaḥ
kanaka|mṛgo Rāghavam atidūraṃ jahāra.
yatra ca Maithilī|viyoga|duḥkha|duḥkhitau
Daśa|vadana|vināśa|piśunau
candra|sūryāv iva *Kabandha|grastau*
samaṃ Rāma|Lakṣmaṇau
tri|bhuvana|bhayaṃ mahac cakratuḥ.
atyāyataś ca yasmin Daśaratha|suta|śara|nipātito
Yojanabāhor bāhur Agastya|prasādan'|
āgata|Nahuṣ'|âjagara|kāya|śaṅkām akarod ṛṣi|janasya.

Even now, when it's the rainy season,
and they hear the deep rumble
of banks of gathering rain clouds
they remember the twang of divine Rama's bow
resounding through the three worlds
and they won't nibble the grass;
sad eyes dimmed with tears
they keep looking in the ten directions
and find them empty,
those old deer, horn tips crumbling with age,
whom Sita, Jánaka's daughter, reared.
There it was the golden deer,
as if incited by such wild deer
as had survived Rama's incessant hunting,
brought about Rama's separation from Sita,
and led him, Raghu's descendant,
far far away.
And there, portending the destruction
of ten-faced Rávana,
as if they were the sun and moon
swallowed by Rahu in a dual eclipse,
Rama and Lákshmana, grieving for the bitter loss of Sita,
were both seized *by the demon Kabándha, 'Just-a-trunk,'*
and caused great fear in the three worlds.
And there the very long arm
of the demon known as Yójana·bahu,
'Three-leagued Arm,'
sliced off by the arrow of Rama
made the sages suppose
it was Náhusha's boa constrictor body[52]

Janaka|tanayā ca bhartrā

viraha|vinodan'|ârtham

uṭaj'|âbhyantara|likhitā yatra

Rāma|nivāsa|darśan'|ôtsukā

punar iva dharaṇi|talād ullasantī

vana|carair ady' âpy ālokyate.

tasya c' âivaṃvidhasya saṃpraty api

prakaṭ'|ôpalakṣyamāṇa|pūrva|vṛttāntasy' Âgasty'|āśramsya

n' âtidūre jala|nidhi|pāna|prakupita|Varuṇ'|ôtsāhiten'

Âgastya|matsarāt tad|āśrama|samīpa|varty

apara iva Vedhasā mahā|jala|nidhir utpāditaḥ,

pralaya|kāla|vighaṭit'|âṣṭa|dig|bhāga|saṃdhi|bandhaṃ

gagana|talam iva bhuvi nipatitam,

Ādi|varāha|samuddhṛta|dharā|maṇḍala|sthānam iva

salila|pūritam,

an|avarata|majjad|unmada|śabara|kāminī|

kuca|kalaśa|lulita|jalam,

come back to propitiate Agástya.
And there even today Jánaka's daughter,
her portrait painted inside the leaf hut
by her husband as solace for separation from her
is looked at by the people who live in the forest—
she seems to be rising up out of the ground again,
longing to see Rama's dwelling.
Such is Agástya's hermitage even now,
its past history clearly to be seen.
Not very far from it,
like another great ocean,
deliberately brought into being
right beside his hermitage,
by Brahma the creator—
urged on by Váruna, God of the waters,
out of malice towards Agástya,
angered by his drinking up the oceans—
there was a lake of red lotuses.
It was like the sky fallen to the earth,
connections to the eight points of the compass
shattered at the time of universal dissolution.
It seemed like the place on the circle of the earth,[53]
now filled up with water,
where Vishnu as the primal boar
lifted up the world on his snout.
Its waters are constantly agitated by the pot-like breasts
of the *shábara*-tribal mistresses as they bathe,
lovely women, intoxicated.

utphulla|kumuda|kuvalaya|kahlāram,

unnidr"|âravinda|

madhu|bindu|nisyanda|baddha|candrakam,

ali|kula|paṭal'|ândhakārita|saugandhikam,

ārasita|sa|mada|sārasam,

amburuha|madhu|pāna|

matta|kalahaṃsa|kāminī|kṛta|kolāhalam,

aneka|jala|cara|pataṃga|śata|saṃcalana|cañcalita|

vācāla|vīci|mālam,

anil'|ôllāsita|kallola|śikhara|śīkar'|

ārabdha|durdinam,

a|śaṅkit'|âvatīrṇābhir ambhaḥ|krīḍā|rāgiṇībhiḥ

snāna|samaye

vana|devatābhiḥ keśa|pāśa|kusumaiḥ surabhī|kṛtam,

eka|deś'|âvatīrṇa|muni|jan'|āpūryamāṇa|

kamaṇḍalu|kala|jala|dhvani|manoharam,

unmiṣad|utpala|vana|madhya|cāribhiḥ

sa|varṇatayā rasit'|ânumeyaiḥ

kādamba|kadambakair āsevitam,

abhiṣek'|âvatīrṇa|pulinda|rāja|sundarī|

kuca|candana|dhūli|dhavalita|taraṃgam,

Kúmuda, *kúvalaya*, and *kahlára* lotuses bloom in it.
The moonlike whorls on peacocks' tail feathers
are formed in it by the drops of honey
trickling from the full-blown *aravínda* lotuses.
Swarms of bees darken its *saugándhika* lotuses.
Impassioned *sárasa* birds screech.
Drunk from drinking lotus wine,
female *kala·hansa* birds
make a tremendous noise.
Garlanded in noisy waves
the movements of many hundred
aquatic birds set in motion,
it turns into a rainy day with the spray
from the peaks of its waves
whipped up by the wind.
The woodland goddesses make it fragrant
with the flowers on their hair-knots,
boldly plunging in when it's time to bathe,
delighting in water sports.
Charming it is with the pleasing sound of water splashing
into the pots the ascetics are filling at one place
where they've got down to the river.
It's the resort of flocks of *kadámba* birds
moving amid its blooming blue-water-lily beds
and because they're the same color
they're distinguishable only by their cries.
Its waves are whitened by sandalwood powder
from the breasts of the beautiful women
of the *pulínda* tribal kings gone down to bathe.

upānta|jāta|ketakī|rajaḥ|paṭala|
baddha|kūla|pulinam,
āsann'|āśram'|āgata|tāpasa|kṣālit'|
ārdra|valkala|kaṣāya|pāṭala|taṭa|jalam,
upataṭa|viṭapi|pallav'|ânila|vījitam,
avirala|tamāla|vīthik"|ândhakāritābhir,
Vāli|nirvāsitena saṃcaratā pratidinam
Ṛṣyamūka|vāsinā Sugrīveṇ'
âvalupta|phala|parilaghu|latābhir,
uda|vāsi|tāpasānāṃ
devat"|ârcan'|ôpayukta|kusumābhir,
utpataj|jala|cara|pataṃga|pakṣa|
puṭa|vigalita|jala|bindu|
seka|sukumāra|kisalayābhir,
latā|maṇḍapa|tala|sthita|
śikhaṇḍi|maṇḍal'|ārabdha|tāṇḍavābhir,
aneka|kusuma|parimala|vāhinībhir
vana|devatābhiḥ śvāsa|vāsitābhir iva
vana|rājibhir uparuddha|tīram,
apara|sāgar'|āśaṅkibhiḥ salilam ādātum
avatīrṇair jaladharair iva
bahala|paṅka|malinair vana|karibhir
an|avaratam āpīyamāna|salilam,

Masses of pollen from the *kétaki* trees native to the vicinity
have formed sand banks along its shore.
Its shore waters are reddened by the stain
of the wet bark garments washed by the ascetics
come from the nearby hermitages.
It's fanned by breezes
from the foliage of the trees on its banks.
Dense groves of *tamálas* darken them;
when Sugríva, banished by Valin,
was dwelling in Rishya·muka,
he wandered there everyday
and lightened their branches by plucking their fruit;
the ascetics living near the water use their flowers
for worshipping the gods;
their sprouts when tender are sprinkled
with spray shaken from the outspread wings
of the aquatic birds as they take off from the water;
circles of peacocks commence their wild *tándava* dancing
on the ground within the dance pavilions
formed by their creepers;
carrying the fragrances of their many flowers,
as if perfumed by the breath of the woodland deities—
such are the groves which cover the shores of the lake.
As if they were clouds come down to take its water,
supposing it to be another ocean,
wild elephants dirty with thick mud
incessantly drink its waters.

a|gādham an|antam a|pratimam
apāṃ nidhānaṃ
Pamp'|âbhidhānaṃ padma|saraḥ.
yatra ca vikaca|kuvalaya|prabhā|śyāmāyamāna|
pakṣa|puṭāny ady' âpi
mūrtimad|Rāma|śāpa|grastān' îva
madhya|cāriṇām[54]
ālokyante cakra|nāmnāṃ mithunāni.
tasy' âivaṃvidhasya padma|sarasaḥ paścime tīre
Rāghava|śara|prahāra|jarjarita|
jīrṇa|tāla|taru|khaṇḍasya ca samīpe
dig|gaja|kara|daṇḍ'|ânukāriṇā jarad|ajagareṇa
satatam āveṣṭita|mūlatayā baddha|mah"|ālavāla iva,
tuṅga|skandh'|âvalambibhir
anila|vellitair ahi|nirmokair
dhṛt'|ôttarīya iva,
dik|cakravāla|parimāṇam iva
gṛhṇatā bhuvan'|ântarāla|viprakīrṇena
śākhā|saṃcayena
pralaya|kāla|tāṇḍava|prasārita|bhuja|sahasram
uḍu|pati|śakala|śekharam iva
viḍambayitum udyataḥ,

Such is the lake of lotuses, bottomless,
endless, incomparable reservoir of water;
and Pampa is its name.
And there, even today, the pairs of *chakra·vaka* ducks
moving in the middle of the lake,
their wings darkened by the luster
of the fully open blue water-lilies,
seem swallowed up
by Rama's curse[55] in physical form.
Such is the lotus lake, and on its western shore,
near the group of tala trees, now grown old,
which the arrow of Rama, Raghu's descendant,
ripped through, there's an aged python
that resembles a world-supporting elephant's
outstretched trunk.
Because it's always wrapped round the root of a tree,
it seems to form a great irrigation basin for the tree.
Snakes' sloughs, trembling in the wind,
hang from the tree's massive branches,
so that it seems to be wearing an upper garment.
With its mass of branches stretched out
to the edges of the world,
as if taking the measurement of the horizon,
the tree seems striving to imitate
the one who has the crescent of the lord of the stars,
the moon, as his crest,
when his thousand arms are outstretched
in his wild *tándava* dance
at the time of universal dissolution.

purāṇatayā patana|bhayād iva
gagana|skandha|lagno,
nikhila|śarīra|vyāpinībhir atidūr'|ônnatābhir
jīrṇatayā śirābhir iva parigato vratatibhir,
jarā|tilaka|bindubhir iva kaṇṭakair ācita|tanur,
itas tataḥ paripīta|sāgara|salilair gagan'|āgataiḥ
pattra|rathair iva śākh"|ântareṣu nilīyamānaiḥ kṣaṇam
ambu|bhār'|âlasair ārdrī|kṛta|pallavair
jala|dhara|paṭalair apy
a|dṛṣṭa|śikhara|deśas,
tuṅgatayā Nandana|vana|śriyam iv'
âvalokayitum abhyudyataḥ,
samīpa|vartinām upari saṃcaratāṃ
gagana|tala|gamana|khed'|āyāsitānāṃ
ravi|ratha|turaṅgamāṇāṃ sṛkka|parisrutaiḥ phena|paṭalaiḥ
saṃdehita|tūla|rāśibhir dhavalī|kṛta|śikhara|śākho,
vana|gaja|kapola|kaṇḍūyana|lagna|mada|nilīna|
matta|madhukara|mālena
loha|śṛṅkhalā|bandha|niścalen' êva
kalpa|sthāyinā mūlena samupetaḥ,

Because of its great age, it seems to rest
on the shoulders of the sky, in fear of falling down.
With the creepers that pervade its whole body,
it seems traversed with veins far protruding
through old age.
Nodules have gathered on its surface, like old age's moles.
Coming through the sky from here and there
when they've drunk the ocean's waters
and nestling for a moment
like birds between its branches,
weary with their burden of water,
dampening the foliage,
even the banks of clouds don't see
the region of the tree's summit.
Its great height makes it seem on tiptoe
to gaze at the glory
of Indra's Nándana grove in heaven.
Passing nearby as they go overhead
for they're weary from the effort
of crossing the sky's expanse,
from the corners of their mouths
the sun's chariot horses drop gobbets of foam
which look like balls of cotton
and whiten the branches on the tree's summit.
Garlanded with drunken bees
clinging to the wild elephants' rut
which sticks to it
after they scratch their cheeks against it,
and consequently looking immovable
because seemingly held down by chains of iron,

koṭar'|âbhyantara|niviṣṭaiḥ sphuradbhiḥ

sajīva iva madhukara|paṭalair,

Duryodhana iv'

ôpalakṣita|*Śakuni/pakṣa/pāto,*

Nalinanābha iva

vana/māl'/ôpagūḍho,

nava|jala|dhara|vyūha iva

nabhasi darśit'/ônnatir,

akhila|bhuvana|tal'|âvalokana|prāsāda iva

vana|devatānām,

adhipatir iva Daṇḍak'|âraṇyasya,

nāyaka iva sarva|vanaspatīnāṃ,

sakh" êva Vindhyasya,

śākhā|bāhubhir upagūhy' êva Vindhy'|âṭavīm,

avasthito mahāñ jīrṇaḥ śālmalī|vṛkṣaḥ.

tatra ca śākh"|âgreṣu koṭar'|ôdareṣu pallav'|ântareṣu

skandha|saṃdhiṣu jīrṇa|valkala|vivareṣu

mah"|âvakāśatayā viśrabdha|viracita|kulāya|sahasrāṇi

the root the tree is endowed with
will last an eon.
It seems alive with the hosts of bees
who've gone into its hollows
and are swarming out.
Like Duryódhana who showed *partisanship*
for Shákuni, it *has birds*
which can be seen flapping their wings.
Like lotus-naveled Vishnu *who has*
his garland of wild flowers,
it is surrounded by woodland.
Like an army of fresh rain-clouds
which *shows its ascendancy in Nabhas,*
the month of rains,
it *manifests its elevation in the sky.*
Like the woodland deities' watch-tower for surveying
the whole surface of the earth;
like the monarch of the Dándaka forest;
like the commander of all trees,
lords of the forest that they are;
like the bosom friend of the Vindhya mountain;
seeming to embrace the lady who is the Vindhya forest
with the arms of its branches,
it stands firm,
a great and aged silk-cotton tree.
And in it, at the tips of its branches,
in the cavities of its hollows,
in the depths of its foliage,
in the crotches of its trunk,
in holes in its aged bark,

dur|ārohatayā vigalita|vināśa|bhayāni
nānā|deśa|samāgatāni śuka|śakuni|kulāni
prativasanti sma.
yaiḥ pariṇāma|virala|dala|saṃhatir api
sa vanaspatir a|virala|dala|nicaya|śyāmala iv'
ôpalakṣyate divā|niśaṃ nilīnaiḥ.
te ca tasmin vanaspatāv
ativāhy' âtivāhya rajanīm ātma|nīḍeṣu,
pratidinam utthāy' ôtthāy' āhār'|ânveṣaṇāya
nabhasi viracita|paṅktayo,
mada|kala|Haladhara|hala|mukh'|ôtkṣepa|
vikīrṇa|bahu|srotasam ambara|tale
Kalinda|kanyām iva darśayantaḥ,
sura|gaj'|ônmūlita|vigalad|ākāśa|Gaṅgā|
kamalinī|śaṅkām upajanayanto,
divasa|kara|ratha|turaga|prabh"|ânuliptam iva
gagana|talam upapādayantaḥ,
saṃcāriṇīm iva marakata|sthalīṃ viḍambayantaḥ,
śaivala|pallav'|āvalim iv' âmbara|sarasi prasārayanto,
gagana|vitataiḥ pakṣa|puṭaiḥ kadalī|dalair iva
dina|kara|khara|kara|nikara|

families of parrots
came from various parts of the country
and dwelled there because there was so much space,
confidently making nests by the thousand,
losing all sense of danger
because it was so difficult to climb up.
That tree, though on account of its age
its foliage is sparse,
with the parrots perching on it night and day
looked green with dense leaves.
And they invariably spent the night
in their own nests on that tree,
and everyday invariably flew out to look for food,
forming lines in the sky.
Seeming to represent in the sky Yámuna,
Kalínda's daughter,
scattered into many streams when drawn
by the end of the plow of Bala·rama,
the Plowbearer, as he drunkenly went his way;
giving the impression of being a *kámala* lotus bed
of the heavenly Ganga uprooted
by the elephant of the gods
and flying through the air;
making the surface of the sky seem smeared
with the green luster of the sun's chariot horses;
seeming to imitate an emerald floor on the move;
seeming to spread a layer of duckweed
over the lake of the sky;
seeming, with their wings spread out in the heavens
like plantain leaves, to fan the faces of the quarters

parikhedit'|āśā|mukhāni vījayanto,
viyati visāriṇīṃ śaṣpa|vīthīm iv' āracayantaḥ,
s'|Êndr'|āyudham iv' ântarikṣam ādadhānā
vicaranti sma śuka|śakunayaḥ.
kṛt'|āhārāś ca punaḥ pratinivṛty'
ātma|kulāy'|âvasthitebhyaḥ śāvakebhyo
vividhān phala|rasān kalama|mañjarī|vikārāṃś ca
prahata|hariṇa|rudhir'|ânurakta|
P25 śārdūla|nakha|koṭi|pāṭalena cañcu|puṭena
dattvā dattv" âdharī|kṛta|sarva|snehen' â|sādhāraṇena
guruṇ" âpatya|premṇā tasminn eva
kroḍ'|ântar|nihita|tanayāḥ kṣapāḥ kṣapayanti sma.
ekasmiṃś ca jīrṇa|koṭare
jāyayā saha nivasataḥ paścime vayasi vartamānasya
katham api pitur aham ev' âiko vidhi|vaśāt sūnur abhavam.
atiprabalayā c' âbhibhūtā
mam' âiva jāyamānasya prasava|vedanayā
jananī me lok'|ântaram agamat.
abhimata|jāyā|vināśa|śoka|duḥkhito 'pi khalu
tātaḥ suta|snehād antar nigṛhya
paṭu|prasaram api śokam
ekākī mat|saṃvardhana|para ev' âbhavat.

who're pained by the mass of the sun's keen rays;
seeming to construct a grassy path
stretching across the sky;
seeming to give the sky a rainbow
as they roamed about—
such were these parrot birds.
And when they'd eaten, returning again
they invariably gave to their young ones
who'd remained in their nests
various juicy fruits and portions of the ears of *kálama* rice
from their beaks red as the points of tigers' claws P25
red with blood of the deer they've slain,
with their great and unparalleled love for their offspring
subordinating all other affection;
and in this very tree they spent their nights,
their offspring tucked under their wings.
And in an old hollow of that tree,
where my father lived in his old age with his wife,
somehow, as fate would have it, I was born,
his only son. Even as I was being born,
overcome by the very severe pain of giving birth,
my mother passed on to the next world.
Though assuredly overwhelmed with grief
at the death of his beloved wife, my father,
out of love for his son, repressed his grief,
deep and severe though it was,
and devoted himself to bringing me up on his own.

atipariṇata|vayāś ca kuśa|cīr'|ânukāriṇīm
alp'|âvaśiṣṭa|jīrṇa|piccha|jāla|jarjarām
avasrast'|âṃsa|deśa|śithilām
apagat'|ôtpatana|saṃskārāṃ
pakṣa|saṃtatim udvahann,
upārūḍha|kampatayā ca saṃtāpa|kāriṇīm
aṅga|lagnāṃ jarām iva vidhunvann,
a|kaṭhora|śephālikā|kusuma|nāla|piñjareṇa
kalama|mañjarī|dalana|masṛṇita|kṣīṇ'|âpānta|lekhena
sphuṭit'|âgra|koṭinā cañcu|puṭena
para|nīḍa|nipatitābhyaḥ śāli|vallarībhyas
taṇḍula|kaṇān ādāy' ādāya
taru|mūla|nipatitāni śuka|kul'|âvadalitāni
phala|śakalāni samāhṛtya
paribhramitum aśakto
mahyam adāt.
pratidivasam ātmanā ca mad|upabhukta|śeṣam
akarod aśanam.
ekadā tu prabhāta|saṃdhyā|rāga|lohite
gagana|tala|kamalinī|madhu|rakta|pakṣa|saṃpuṭe
vṛddha|haṃsa iva Mandākinī|pulinād
apara|jala|nidhi|taṭam avatarati candramasi,
pariṇata|raṅku|roma|pāṇḍuni vrajati viśālatām āśā|cakravāle,

He was very advanced in age,
and his wings resembled a garment made of *kusha* grass;
decrepit, the few remaining feathers of his plumage
worn out,
they hung limply from his drooping shoulders,
and had lost the power of flight.
And as he was always trembling all over
he seemed to be trying to shake off
the old age that gripped his body and caused him pain.
His beak had its edges blunted and worn away
by breaking open ears of *kálama* rice;
its pointed tip was broken off.
It was reddish like the stalk of a *shephálika* flower
not yet hardened; and with it,
not able to roam about,
unfailingly he collected grains of rice
from ears of *shali* rice stalks
that had fallen from the nests of others
and collected the bits of fruit
that had fallen to the root of the tree
while being nibbled by flocks of parrots
and gave them to me.
And every day he made his meal on what was left
after I'd eaten my fill.
One day, blushing with first light of dawn,
like an old goose with its wings reddened
by the honey from the lotus pool of the sky,
the moon was descending
to the shore of the western ocean
from the sandbank of the celestial Ganga;

gaja|rudhira|rakta|hari|saṭā|loma|lohinībhir
ātapta|lākṣika|tantu|pāṭalābhhir āyāminībhir
aśiśira|kiraṇa|dīdhitibhiḥ
padma|rāga|ratna|śalākā|saṃmārjanībhir iva
samutsāryamāṇe gagana|kuṭṭima|kusuma|prakare
tārā|gaṇe,
Saṃdhyām upāsitum uttar'|āś"|âvalambini
Mānasa|saras|tīram iv' âvatarati sapta|ṛṣi|maṇḍale,
taṭa|gata|vighaṭita|śukti|saṃpuṭa|viprakīrṇam
aruṇa|kara|preraṇ'|âdho|galitam
uḍu|gaṇam iva muktā|phala|nikaram udvahati
dhavalita|pulina|taṭam udanvati pūrv'|êtare,
tuṣāra|bindu|varṣiṇi
vibuddha|śikhi|kule
vijṛmbhamāṇa|kesariṇi
kariṇī|kadambaka|prabodhyamāna|sa|mada|kariṇi
kṣapā|jala|jaḍa|kesaraṃ kusuma|nikaram
Udayagiri|śikhara|sthitaṃ savitāram iv' ôddiśya
pallav'|âñjalibhiḥ samutsṛjati kānane,

when the horizon,
pale white like the hair of a full grown antelope,
was widening out;
when the host of stars—
a heap of flowers on the paved floor of heaven—
was being swept away,
as if with brooms of slivers of ruby
by the rays of the sun,
red as threads of heated lac,
red as the hairs on the mane of a lion
reddened with elephants' blood;
when the circle of the Seven Sages
hanging over the northern horizon
seemed to be descending to the shore of the Mánasa lake
to offer worship to Sandhya, the twilight;
when the western ocean was holding out a mass of pearls
which, whitening its beaches, lay scattered
in the hollows of open shells on its shore,
as if it were the host of stars dropped down
impelled by the red-rayed sun;
when, dripping dew, peacocks awake, lions yawning,
rut elephants roused from slumber
by their harems of female elephants,
the forest with its leaves as cupped hands
seemed to be offering up a mass of flowers,
filaments torpid with night dew,
in the direction of the sun
on the peak of the Rising Mountain, Údaya·giri;

rāsabha|roma|dhūsarāsu

vana|devatā|prāsādānāṃ tarūṇāṃ

śikhareṣu pārāvata|mālāyamānāsu

dharma|patākāsv iva samunmiṣantīṣu

tapo|van'|âgnihotra|dhūma|lekhāsv,

avaśyāya|śīkariṇi lulita|kamala|vane

rati|khinna|śabara|sīmantinī|sveda|jala|kaṇik'|âpahāriṇi,

vana|mahiṣa|romantha|phena|bindu|vāhini,

calita|pallava|latā|lāsy'|ôpadeśa|vyasanini,

vighaṭamāna|kamala|khaṇḍa|madhu|śīkar'|āsāra|varṣiṇi

kusum'|āmoda|tarpit'|âli|jāle,

niś"|âvasāna|jāta|jaḍimni

manda|manda|saṃcāriṇi

pravāti prābhātike mātariśvani,

kamala|vana|prabodha|maṅgala|pāṭhakānām

ibha|gaṇḍa|ḍiṇḍimānāṃ madhu|lihāṃ

kumud'|ôdareṣu ghana|ghaṭamāna|dala|puṭa|

nibaddha|pakṣa|saṃhatīnām

uccaratsu huṃkāreṣu,

when there appeared, gray as an ass's hair,
stretching out like rows of doves, on the tops of trees—
tops of the palaces of the woodland deities—
lines of smoke,
like the banners of righteousness,
from the sacrificial fires in the penance groves;
charged with drops of dew,
ruffling the lotus beds,
stealing away the drops of sweat
from the *shábara* tribal women
worn out with sexual pleasure,
scooping up drops of foam
from the rumination of the wild buffalo;
giving itself up to teaching the *lasya* dance
to the creepers waving their leaves,
scattering a thick honey mist
from the beds of *kámala* lotuses as they opened up,
gratifying the networks of bees with the scent of flowers,
turning cold at the end of the night,
moving very very slowly—
the morning wind was blowing.
There were cries of rage issuing
from the bees in the wombs of *kúmuda* lotuses,
their wings beating against the petal cups
now firmly closing upon them,
bees who were wont to be reciters of auspicious hymns
to awaken the day lotus-beds,
and whose other regular role
was drumming on elephants' temples.

prabhāta|śiśira|mārut'|āhatam
uttapta|jatu|ras'|āśliṣṭa|pakṣma|mālam iva
sa|śeṣa|nidrā|jihma|tāraṃ cakṣur unmīlayatsu śanaiḥ śanair
ūṣara|śayyā|dhūsara|kroḍa|roma|rājiṣu vana|mṛgeṣv,
itas tataḥ saṃcaratsu vana|careṣu,
vijṛmbhamāṇe śrotra|hāriṇi
Pampā|saraḥ|kalahaṃsa|kolāhale,
samullasati nartita|śikhaṇḍi|maṇḍale
manohare vana|gaja|karṇa|tāla|śabde,
krameṇa ca gagana|tala|mārgam avatarato
divasa|kara|vāraṇasy'
âvacūla|cāmara|kalāpa iv' ôpalakṣyamāṇe
mañjiṣṭhā|rāga|lohite kiraṇa|jāle śanaiḥ śanair udite
bhagavati savitari.
Pampā|saraḥ|paryanta|taru|śikhara|saṃcāriṇy
adhyāsita/giri/śikhare
divasa/kara/janmani hṛta/tāre
punar iva kap'|īśvare
vanam abhipatati bāl'|ātape,

Struck by the cold wind of morning,
their eyelashes seeming glued together with molten lac,
their pupils sideways, astray,
abstracted with sleep still left in them,
only very slowly did the wild deer open their eyes,
the lines of hair on their bellies
gray from their beds of saline soil.
The creatures of the wood started to move here and there.
On the Pampa lake, commotion of the *kala·hansa* geese
broke out and pleased the ear.
The charming sound of wild elephants
flapping their ears arose
and made the circles of peacocks dance;
and the divine sun was very slowly rising,
its network of rays the red of madder,
beginning to look like the arrangement of fly-whisks
forming the forehead ornament
of the elephant that was the sun
ambling down his route across the sky.
When the early sunshine, *born of the sun,*
moving across the tops of the trees round Lake Pampa
and *taking up residence on the mountain top,*
vanquishing the stars
was finally falling on the woods,
just like Sugríva, the monkey king
son of Surya, the sun god,
his wife Tara stolen from him,
exiled to the mountain top,
again taking to the woods;

spaṣṭe jāte pratyūṣasi

na|cirād iva divas'|âṣṭa|bhāga|bhāji

spaṣṭa|bhāsi bhāsvati bhūte,

prayāteṣu yath"|âbhhimatāni dig|antarāṇi śuka|kuleṣu

kulāya|nilīna|nibhṛta|śāvaka|sanāthe 'pi

niḥśabdatayā śūnya iva

tasmin vanaspatau,

sva|nīḍ'|âvasthita eva tāte mayi ca

śaiśavād a|saṃjāta|bala|samudbhidyamāna|pakṣa|puṭe

tātasya samīpa|vartini koṭara|gate,

sahas" âiva tasmin mahā|vane

saṃtrāsita|sakala|vana|caraḥ,

sarabhasam utpatat|patatri|pakṣa|puṭa|śabda|saṃtato,

bhīta|kari|pota|cīt|kāra|pīvaraḥ,

pracalita|lat"|ākulita|matt'|âli|kula|kvaṇita|māṃsalaḥ,

paribhramad|udghoṇa|vana|varāha|rava|ghargharo,

giri|guhā|supta|prabuddha|siṃha|nād'|ôpabṛṃhitaḥ,

kampayann iva tarūn,

Bhagīrath'|âvatāryamāṇa|Gaṅgā|pravāha|kala|kala|bahalo,

bhīta|vana|devat"|ākarṇito

mṛgayā|kolāhala|dhvanir udacarat.

the early dawn became clearer,
quickly passing through the eighth part of the day,
and the sun shone brightly and clearly.
When the flocks of parrots had set off
in every direction for their favorite places,
though the young birds were resting quietly in their nests,
because of the silence
that tree seemed empty.
While my father was still in his nest
and I was beside him in the hollow,
for being young my strength had not developed,
and my wings were still breaking forth,
all of a sudden in that great wood
terrifying every forest creature,
prolonged by the noise of the wings
of birds flying up in panic;
amplified by the screams of frightened young elephants;
magnified by the humming of swarms of drunken bees
disturbed on the creepers that were shaken;
rumbling with the snorting of wild boar
roaming around with raised snouts;
reechoing with the roars of lions awoken
from sleep in their mountain caves;
seeming to shake the trees;
as deep as the surging roar of Ganga's flood
when she was brought down to the earth by Bhagi·ratha;
terrifying the woodland deities as they listened to it—
the tumultuous commotion of hunting rose up.

ākarṇya ca tam aham a|śruta|pūrvam
upajāta|vepathur arbhakatayā
jarjarita|karṇa|vivaro bhaya|vihvalaḥ
samīpa|vartinaḥ pituḥ pratīkāra|buddhyā
jarā|śithila|pakṣa|puṭ'|ântaram aviśam.
anantaraṃ ca sarabhasam
‹ito gaja|yūtha|pati|lulita|kamalinī|parimala.›
‹itaḥ kroḍa|kula|daśyamāna|bhadramustā|ras'|āmoda.›
‹itaḥ kari|kalabha|bhajyamāna|sallakī|kaṣāya|gandha.›
‹ito nipatita|śuṣka|pattra|marmara|dhvanir.›
‹ito vana|mahiṣa|viṣāṇa|koṭi|kuliśa|
bhidyamāna|valmīka|dhūlir.›
‹ito mṛga|kadambakam.›
‹ito vana|gaja|kulam.›
‹ito vana|varāha|yūtham.›
‹ito vana|mahiṣa|vṛndam.›
‹itaḥ śikhaṇḍi|maṇḍala|virutam.›
‹itaḥ kapiñjala|kula|kala|kūjitam.›
‹itaḥ kurara|kula|kvaṇitam.›
‹ito mṛga|pati|nakha|bhidyamāna|kumbha|
kuñjara|rasitam.›
‹iyam ārdra|paṅka|malinā varāha|paddhatir.›

And hearing this sound, such as I'd never heard before,
I began to tremble and my ears were deafened,
for I was very young.
Overcome with fear, and thinking father,
there beside me, could help me,
I crept under his wing,
slack as it was from old age.
And immediately after, vehemently,
'Here's the scent of a lotus pool
trampled by the bull elephant and his herd.'
'This way's the juicy aroma of *bhadra·musta* grass
being chewed by a group of hogs.'
'This way's the sharp smell of *sállaki* trees
broken by young elephants.'
'This way's the rustling sound
among fallen dry leaves.'
'This way's the dust from anthills being broken up
by the diamond-hard points of wild buffalo horns.'
'This way there's a herd of deer.'
'This way there's a troop of wild elephants.'
'This way's a band of wild boar.'
'This way a throng of wild buffaloes.'
'This way's the shriek of a pride of peacocks.'
'This way there's the murmur of a covey of partridges.'
'This way there's the whistling of a flight of ospreys.'
'This way's the trumpeting of a bull elephant
as a lion's claws split open his temple.'
'This way's a boar track dirty with fresh mud.'

‹iyam abhinava|śaṣpa|kavala|rasa|śyāmalā
hariṇa|romantha|phena|saṃhatir.›
‹iyam unmada|gandha|gaja|gaṇḍa|kaṇḍūyana|parimal'|
ālīna|mukhara|madhukara|virutir.›
‹eṣā nipatita|rudhira|bindu|sikta|
śuṣka|pattra|pāṭalā ruru|padavy.›
‹etad dvirada|caraṇa|mṛdita|viṭapa|pallava|paṭalam.›
‹etat khaḍgi|kula|krīḍitam.›
‹eṣa nakha|koṭi|vilikhita|vikaṭa|pattra|lekho
rudhira|pāṭalaḥ kari|mauktika|dala|danturo
mṛga|pati|mārga.›
‹eṣā pratyagra|prasūta|vana|mṛgī|garbha|
rudhira|lohinī bhūmir.›
‹iyam aṭavī|veṇik"|ânukāriṇī
pakṣa|carasya yūtha|pater
mada|jala|malinā saṃcāra|vīthī.›
‹camarī|paṅktir iyam anugamyatām.›
‹ucchuṣka|mṛga|karīṣa|pāṃsulā
tvaritataram adhyāsyatām iyaṃ vana|sthalī.›
‹taru|śikharam āruhyatām.›
‹ālokyatāṃ dig iyam.›
‹ākarṇyatām ayaṃ śabdo.›
‹gṛhyatāṃ dhanur.›
‹avahitaiḥ sthīyatāṃ.›
‹vimucyantāṃ śvāna.›

'This is a mass of foam from ruminating deer,
dark green from the juice of mouthfuls of fresh grass.'
'This is the humming of bees
noisy because they're sticking
to the scent of elephants in rut scratching their cheeks.'
'That is the track of an antelope, red
with dry leaves sprinkled with drops of its blood.'
'That mass of branches and shoots
has been crushed by elephants' feet.'
'That is where rhinoceroses have been playing.'
'This is a lion's track,
studded with pieces of elephants' pearls,
red with blood, with huge leaflike patterns
drawn by the points of its claws.'
'That is ground reddened with blood from the womb
of a wild deer that's recently given birth.'
'This is the stampede route—
like the braid of hair of the woman who is the forest—
dirty with the liquid of his rut,
taken by the leader of a herd, who's gone off on his own.'
'We must follow this string of yaks.'
'We should occupy this glade as quickly as possible,
it's dusty with deers' dried up droppings.'
'Climb to the top of this tree, survey this region.'
'Listen to this noise.'
'Take up your bows.'
'Stand at the ready.'
'Loose the hounds.'

ity anyonyam abhivadato mṛgay"|āsaktasya
mahato jana|samūhasya taru|gahan'|ântarita|vigrahasya
kṣobhita|kānanaṃ kolāhalam aśṛṇavam.

atha n' âticirād iv' ânulepan'|ārdra|mṛdaṅga|dhvani|dhīreṇa
giri|vivara|vijṛmbhita|pratināda|gambhīreṇa
śabara|śara|tāḍitānāṃ kesariṇāṃ ninādena,
saṃtrasta|yūtha|muktānām ekākināṃ ca saṃcaratām
an|avarata|kar'|āsphoṭa|miśreṇa
jala|dhara|rasit'|ânukāriṇā
gaja|yūtha|patīnāṃ kaṇṭha|garjitena,
sarabhasa|sārameya|vilupyamān'|âvayavānām
ālola|kātara|tarala|tārakāṇām eṇakānāṃ ca
karuṇa|kūjitena,
nihata|yūtha|patīnāṃ viyoginīnām
anugata|kalabhānāṃ ca sthitvā sthitvā
samākarṇya kalakalam utkarṇa|pallavānām
itas tataḥ paribhramantīnāṃ
pratyagra|pati|vināśa|śoka|dīrgheṇa kariṇīnāṃ cīt|kṛtena,
katipaya|divasa|prasūtānāṃ ca khaḍgi|dhenukānāṃ
trāsa|paribhraṣṭa|pot'|ânveṣiṇīnām
unmukta|kaṇṭham atikaruṇam
ārasantīnām ākranditena,

Thus was the pandemonium I heard, shaking the forest,
of a great crowd of men, their bodies
hidden in the thick of the trees,
as they called to each other,
totally absorbed in their hunting.
Then it wasn't very long before there was,
deep as the boom of a freshly moistened *mridánga* drum,
the roar of lions struck by the *shábara* tribesmen's arrows,
all the deeper with its echo
swelling in the mountain's caves;
the trumpeting of elephant herd leaders
resembling thunder
mixed with the continuous lashing about of their trunks
as they wandered about alone,
deserted by their terrified herds;
the piteous cry of the deer, their shy and restless eyes
rolling wildly as their limbs
are torn off by excited hounds.
Their herd leaders killed, separated from one another,
wandering about here and there
followed by their young ones,
the cow elephants kept stopping
and lifting their ears to listen to the din,
and their high-pitched trumpeting
was long drawn out in their grief
for the recent death of their lords.
There was the lamentation of the rhinoceroses in milk,
who'd given birth only a few days previously,
their necks outstretched as they sought their offspring
lost in the panic, bellowing most piteously.

taru|śikhara|samutpatitānām ākul'|ākula|cāriṇāṃ ca
pattra|rathānāṃ kolāhalena,
rūp'|ânusāra|pradhāvitānāṃ ca mṛgayūnāṃ yugapad
atirabhasa|pāda|pāt'|âbhihatāyā
bhuvaḥ kampam iva janayatā caraṇa|śabdena,
karṇ'|ânt'|ākṛṣṭa|jyānāṃ ca
mada|kala|kurara|kāminī|kaṇṭha|kūjita|kalena
śara|nikara|varṣiṇāṃ dhanuṣāṃ ninādena,
pavan'|āhati|kvaṇita|dhārāṇāṃ asīnāṃ ca
kaṭhina|mahiṣa|skandha|pīṭha|pātināṃ raṇitena,
śunāṃ ca sarabhasa|vimukta|ghargharā|dhvanīnāṃ
van'|ântara|vyāpinā dhvānena sarvataḥ pracalitam iva
tad araṇyam abhavat.
acirāc ca praśānte tasmin mṛgayā|kalakale
nirvṛṣṭa|mūka|jala|dhara|vṛnd'|ânukāriṇi
mathan'|âvasān'|ôpaśānta|vāriṇi sāgara iva
stimitatām upāgate kānane
mandī|bhūta|bhayo 'ham upajāta|kutūhalaḥ
pitur saṅgād īṣad iva niṣkramya koṭara|stha eva
śiro|dharāṃ prasārya
saṃtrāsa|tarala|tārakaḥ śaiśavāt kim idam iti
samupajāta|didṛkṣas tām eva diśaṃ
cakṣuḥ prāhiṇavam.

There was the hullabaloo of birds flying up
from the tops of trees and wheeling about in confusion.
There was the sound of the hunters' feet
which seemed to make the earth quake
with the violent pounding of their steps
as they ran after the wild beasts.
There was the twang of bows drawn back to the ear tip
and showering masses of arrows,
as melodious as the whistling
from the throats of impassioned female ospreys.
There was the sound of swords,
blades whizzing through the air and slicing
into the muscular shoulders of buffaloes.
And there was the noise penetrating all the recesses
of the forest of dogs barking viciously.
By these noises that forest seemed shaken in every direction.
And when, not long after,
the din of the hunt had died away,
and the forest had become motionless,
resembling a bank of clouds
silent after raining down its water,
like the ocean when its waters became still
at the conclusion of the churning, my fear diminished,
and I became curious.
I moved out a little from my father's embrace,
and while remaining in the hollow, stuck out my neck,
my eyes darting here and therc in fear.
Because of my youth, I wondered what was happening,
and keen to see for myself, I cast my eyes
in that direction whence the noise had gone.

abhimukham āpatac ca tasmād van'|ântarād
Arjuna|bhuja|daṇḍa|sahasra|viprakīrṇam iva
Narmadā|pravāham,
anila|vaśāc calitam iva tamāla|kānanam,
ekī|bhūtam iva kāla|rātrīṇāṃ yāma|saṃghātam,
añjana|śilā|stambha|saṃbhāram iva
kṣiti|kampa|vighūrṇitam,
andhakāra|puñjam iva ravi|kiraṇ'|ākulitam,
Antaka|parivāram iva paribhramantam,
avadārita|rasā|tal'|ôdbhūtam iva dānava|lokam,
aśubha|karma|samūham iv' âikatra samāgatam,
aśeṣa|Daṇḍak'|āraṇya|vāsi|muni|jana|
śāpa|sārtham iva saṃcarantam,
an|avarata|śara|nikara|varṣi|Rāma|nihata|Khara|Dūṣaṇa|
bala|nivaham iva tad|apadhyānāt piśācatām upagataṃ,
Kali|kāla|bandhu|vargam iv' âikatra saṃgatam,
avagāha|prasthitam iva vana|mahiṣa|yūtham,
acala|śikhara|sthita|kesari|kar'|ākṛṣṭi|patana|viśīrṇam iva
kāla|megha|paṭalam,
akhila|rūpa|vināśāya dhūma|ketu|jālam iva samudgatam,

And coming towards me out from the wood,
like the stream of the Nármada broken up
by Árjuna's thousand arms,
Árjuna the son of Krita·virya;[56]
like a grove of *tamála* trees set in motion by the wind,
like all the nights of the dark fortnight
compressed into one,
like a colonnade of pillars of solid collyrium
hurled about in an earthquake,
like a heap of darkness bothered by the sun's rays,
like Death's entourage on the march,
like demons bursting through their netherworld
and rising up,
like collected impure deeds assembled in one place,
like a moving caravan formed from all the curses
uttered by the sages dwelling in the Dándaka wood,[57]
like all the troops of Khara[58] and Dúshana[59]
who'd been slain
by Rama ceaselessly showering his mass of arrows,
and had now become flesh-eating goblins
out of hatred for him,
like all the friends of the Kali age
gathered together in one place,
like a band of wild buffaloes about to take their bath,
like massed black storm clouds riven by the swipes
of a lion's paw as he stands up on a mountain peak,
like a network of smoke-bannered meteors risen up
to signal the destruction of all wild beasts,

andhakārita|kānanam aneka|sahasra|saṃkhyam
atibhaya|jananam utpāta|vetāla|vrātam iva
śabara|sainyam adrākṣam.
madhye ca tasy' âtimahataḥ śabara|sainyasya
prathame vayasi vartamānam,
atikarkaśatvād āyasam iva nirmitam,
Ekalavyam iva janm'|ântar'|āgatam
udbhidyamāna|śmaśru|rājitayā
prathama|mada|lekhā|maṇḍyamāna|gaṇḍa|bhittim iva
gaja|yūtha|pati|kumārakam,
asita|kuvalaya|śyāmena deha|prabhā|pravāheṇa
P30 Kālindī|jalen' êva pūrit'|āraṇyam,
ākuṭil'|âgreṇa skandh'|âvalambinā kuntala|bhāreṇa
kesariṇam iva gaja|mada|malinī|kṛtena
kesara|kalāpen' ôpetam,
āyata|lalāṭam atituṅga|ghora|ghoṇam,
eka|karṇ'|ābharaṇatām upanītasya bhujaṃga|phaṇa|maṇer
āpāṭalair aṃśubhir ālohitī|kṛtena parṇa|śayan'|âbhyāsāl
lagna|pallava|rāgeṇ' êva vāma|pārśvena virājamānam,
acira|prahata|gaja|kapola|gṛhītena
saptacchada|parimala|vāhinā kṛṣṇ'|âguru|paṅkeṇ' êva
surabhiṇā madena kṛt'|âṅga|rāgam,
upari tat|parimal'|ândhena bhramatā
māyūr'|ātapatr'|ânukāriṇā madhu|kara|kulena

turning the wood into darkness,
many thousand in number, inspiring great dread
like an army of ghouls portending disasters,
was the army of *shábaras* I beheld.
And in the midst of it was a man in the prime of youth,
from his excessive hardness seeming made of iron,
like Eka·lavya[60] reborn.
From the line of his beard breaking forth
he seemed like a young elephant
already leader of the herd,
with the surface of his cheeks adorned
with his first line of rut, filling the forest
with the flowing current of the luster of his body
dark as a blue lotus,
as if with the waters of Yámuna, Kalínda's daughter. P30
With his head of hair curling at the ends
and hanging down to his shoulders,
he resembled a lion with its mane
soiled in elephant rut.
His forehead broad,
his nose jutting out and fierce,
shining on the left-hand side
for it was reddened by the reddish rays
from the snake-hood gem
he wore as ornament in one ear,
as if the color of leaves clung to him
from him frequently making his bed on leaves.
He'd colored his body with fragrant elephant rut
taken from the cheeks of elephants he'd recently slain,
bearing the fragrance of the *sapta·cchada* plant,

tamāla|pallaven' êva nivārit'|ātapam,

ālola|karṇa|pallava|vyājena

bhuja|bala|nirjitayā bhaya|prayukta|sevayā

Vindhy'|âṭavy" êva kara|talen'

âpamṛjyamāna|gaṇḍa|sthala|sveda|lekham,

āpāṭalayā hariṇa|kula|kṣaya|rātri|saṃdhyāyamānayā

śoṇit'|ārdray" êva dṛṣṭyā rañjayantam āśā|vibhāgān,

ā|jānu|lambena kuñjara|kara|pramāṇam iva gṛhītvā

nirmitena Caṇḍikā|rudhira|bali|pradān'|ârtham

asakṛn niśita|śastr'|ôllekha|viṣamita|śikhareṇa

bhuja|yugalen' ôpaśobhitam,

antar"|ântarā|lagn'|āśyāna|hariṇa|rudhira|bindunā

sveda|jala|kaṇikā|citena guñjā|phala|vimiśraiḥ

kari|kumbha|muktā|phalair iva racit'|ābharaṇena

Vindhya|śilā|tala|viśālena

vakṣaḥ|sthalen' ôdbhāsamānam,

avirata|śram'|âbhyāsād ullikhit'|ôdaram,

ibha|mada|malinam ālāna|stambha|yugalam

upahasantam iv' ōru|daṇḍa|dvayena,

lākṣā|lohita|kauśeya|paridhānam,

as if it were sweet-smelling black aloe paste.
The heat was kept off him by a swarm of bees
hovering blindly around that scent of his,
resembling a parasol of peacock feathers,
or like *tamála* leaves.
Under the guise of a leaf
bobbing up and down on his ear,
it seemed the Vindhya forest herself
with her own hand was wiping away
the lines of sweat on his cheeks,
serving him out of fear.
With his red eyes seeming wet with blood,
the twilight of the night of doom for herds of deer,
he was reddening the horizon all around.
He was splendid with his two long arms
hanging down to his knees,
as if a mature elephant's trunk
had been the measure
for making them, and his upper arms
were roughened with scars from sharp swords when
he'd made frequent offerings of his blood to Chándika.
Shining with the expanse of his chest
broad as a slab of rock of the Vindhya mountain
ornamented as if with pearls from elephants' temples
intermixed with *gunja* fruit,
dried drops of deer's blood sticking here and there
and covered with drops of sweat,
his abdomen rippled with muscles from unceasing exercise,
with his two long thighs he seemed to be putting to shame
a pair of tying posts dirty with elephants' rut.

a|kāraṇe 'pi krūratayā
baddha|tri|patāk'|ôgra|bhru|kuṭi|karāle
lalāṭa|phalake
prabala|bhakty|ārādhitayā mat|parigraho 'yam iti
Kātyāyanyā triśūlen' êv' âṅkitam,
upajāta|paricayair anugacchadbhiḥ
śrama|vaśād dūra|vinirgatābhiḥ sva|bhāva|pāṭalatayā
śuṣkābhir api hariṇa|śoṇitam iva kṣarantībhir jihvābhir,
āvedyamāna|khedair vivṛta|mukhatayā
spaṣṭa|dṛṣṭa|dant'|âṃśūn
daṃṣṭr'|ântarāla|lagna|kesari|saṭān iva
sṛkka|bhāgān udvahadbhiḥ,
sthūla|varāṭaka|mālikā|parigata|kaṇṭhair
mahā|varāha|daṃṣṭrā|prahāra|jarjarair,
alpa|kāyair api mahā|śaktitvād
an|upajāta|kesarair iva kesari|kiśorakair
mṛga|vadhū|vaidhavya|dīkṣā|dāna|dakṣair aneka|varṇaiḥ
śvabhir atipramāṇābhiś ca
kesariṇām a|bhaya|pradāna|yācan'|ârtham āgatābhiḥ
siṃhībhir iva
kauleyaka|kuṭumbinībhir anugamyamānam,
kaiś cid gṛhīta|camara|bāla|gaja|danta|bhāraiḥ,
kaiś cid a|cchidra|parṇa|baddha|madhu|puṭaiḥ,
kaiś cin mṛga|patibhir iva
gaja|kumbha|muktā|phala|nikara|sanātha|pāṇibhiḥ,

His silk garment was reddened with lac.
On the surface of his forehead corrugated
in a fierce three-pointed frown due to his cruel nature
even though there was no occasion for it,
he seemed to be marked by Katyáyani with her trident
to show that this man belonged to her,
because he'd propitiated her with deep devotion.
Following close on his heels, his familiar friends,
from weariness tongues far extended,
and such was their natural redness, though dry
seeming to drip deers' blood;
their exhaustion shown by mouths wide open;
the corners of their mouths with the rays
from their teeth clearly visible on them,
as if the hair from lions' manes
was stuck between their fangs,
necklaces of big cowries round their necks;
scarred by wounds from the tusks of great boars;
though their bodies were small, from their great energy
like young lions before their manes appear;
adept in imposing the initiation of widowhood
upon the wives of deer;
of many colors—
Such were the dogs who followed him; and with them
their bitches, immense, looking like lionesses
coming to beg an amnesty for the lions.
Some carried bundles of yaks tails and elephant tusks,
some carried honey combs closely wrapped in leaves,
some like lions had their hands full
of masses of pearls from elephants' temples,

kaiś cid yātudhānair iva gṛhīta|piśita|bhāraiḥ,

kaiś cit pramathair iva kesari|kṛtti|dhāribhiḥ,

kaiś cit kṣapaṇakair iva mayūra|piccha|vāhibhiḥ,

kaiś cic chiśubhir iva kāka|pakṣa|dharaiḥ,

kaiś cit kṛṣṇa|caritam iva darśayadbhiḥ

samutkhāta|vidhṛta|gaja|dantaiḥ,

kaiś cij jalad'|āgama|divasair iva

jala|dhara|cchāyā|malin'|âmbarair,

aneka|vṛttāntaiḥ śabara|vṛndaiḥ parivṛtam,

araṇyam iva *sa/khaḍga/dhenukam,*

abhinava|jaladharam iva

mayūra/piccha/citra/cāpa/dhāriṇaṃ,

Baka|rākṣasam iva

gṛhīt'/Âikacakram,

Aruṇ'|ânujam iv'

ôddhṛt'/âneka/mahā/nāga/daśanaṃ,

Bhīṣmam iva *Śikhaṇḍi/śatruṃ,*

nidāgha|divasam iva

satat'/āvirbhūta/mṛga/tṛṣṇaṃ,

vidyā|dharam iva *Mānasavegaṃ,*

Parāśaram iva

Yojanagandh'/ânusāriṇaṃ,

some like ghouls carried loads of flesh,
some like the tormentors, Shiva's attendants,
wore lion-skins,
some like Jain fasting monks carried peacock feathers,
some like boys wore their hair to their shoulders
in the crows wing style,
some, as if they were representing the life of Krishna,
carried elephant tusks they'd ripped out,
some, like days when clouds come and all the sky is dark,
had dirty garments the color of rain clouds—
such were the multifarious bands of *shábara*s
who surrounded him.
As a forest *has its female rhinoceroses*, he *had a dagger*,
like a fresh rain cloud *with its rainbow*
as bright as a peacock's feather
he *carried a bow ornamented with peacock feathers.*
Like Baka the demon *who'd taken Eka·chakra's city,*
he'd *taken a single discus.*
Like Áruna's younger brother, Gáruda,
who'd drawn out many serpents' fangs,
he'd *extracted tusks from many elephants.*
Like Bhishma who was *Shikhándin's foe,*
he *was the enemy of peacocks.*
Like a summer's day *when mirages are always appearing,*
he *was always showing his thirst for deer.*
Like the *vidya·dhara* Mánasa·vega,[61]
he *was as fast as thought.*
Like Paráshara *following his wife Yójana·gandha,*
he *could follow a scent from a mile away.*

Ghaṭotkacam iva

Bhīma/rūpa/dhāriṇam,

acala|rāja|kanyakā|keśa|pāśam iva

Nīlakaṇṭha/candrak'/ābharaṇaṃ,

Hiraṇyākṣa|dānavam iva

mahā/varāha/daṃṣṭrā/vibhinna/vakṣaḥ/sthalam,

atirāgiṇam iva

kṛta/bahu/bandī/parigrahaṃ,

piśit'|āśanam iva

rakta/lubdhakaṃ,

gīta|kalā|vinyāsam iva

niṣād'/ânugatam,

Ambikā|triśūlam iva

mahiṣa/rudhir'/ārdra/kāyam,

abhinava|yauvanam api

kṣapita/bahu/vayasaṃ,

kṛta/sāra/meya/saṃgraham api

phala|mūl'|āśanaṃ,

Kṛṣṇam apy *a/Sudarśanaṃ,*

Like Ghatótkacha, *who resembled his father Bhima,*
he was *dreadful in form.*
Like the long hair tied in a knot
of the daughter of the king of mountains
which is adorned by blue-necked Shiva's
moon crescent ornament,
he *was adorned by the bright circles on his peacock feathers.*
Like the *dánava* demon Hiránya·aksha, *whose chest*
has been split open by the tusk of Vishnu as the great boar,
his chest *was scarred by the tusks of great boars.*
Like a very musical man who surrounds himself
with many singing bards,
he *had many captured women in his harem.*
like a flesh-eating demon *greedy for blood,*
he *delighted in hunting.*
Like the arrangement of notes in the art of music,
where the nish/ *nishāda* notes follow,*
he *was followed by Nishāda tribesmen.*
Like the goddess Ámbika's trident
wet with the blood
of the buffalo demon,
his *body was wet with buffaloes' blood.*
Though he was in fresh youth,
it might seem *he'd gone through a long span of life,*
but in fact *he'd killed many birds.*
Though *it might seem he had great wealth,*
and yet dined on fruits and roots,
it was a pack of dogs that he possessed.
Though it might seemed strange that he was *Krishna*
and yet had no Sudárshana discus,

svacchanda|pracāram api
durg'|âika|śaraṇaṃ,
kṣiti|bhṛt|pād'|ânuvartinam api
rāja|sev"|ânabhijñam,
apatyam iva Vindhyasy',
âṃś'|âvatāram iva kṛt'|ântasya,
sah'|ôdaram iva pāpasya, sāram iva Kali|kālasya,
bhīṣaṇam api
mahāsattvatayā gambhīram iv' ôpalakṣyamāṇam,
an|abhibhavanīy'|ākṛtiṃ,
Mātaṅgaka|nāmānaṃ śabara|senā|patim apaśyam.
abhidhānaṃ tu paścāt tasy' âham aśrauṣam.
āsīc ca me manasi:
‹aho moha|prāyam eteṣāṃ jīvitaṃ
sādhu|jana|vigarhitaṃ ca caritam.
tathā hi, puruṣa|piśit'|ôpahāre dharma|buddhiḥ.
āhāraḥ sādhu|jana|nindito
madhu|māṃs'|ādiḥ.
śramo mṛgayā. śāstraṃ śivā|rutam.
samupadeṣṭāraḥ sad|asatāṃ kauśikāḥ.
prajñā śakuni|jñānam. paricitāḥ śvānaḥ.
rājyaṃ śūnyāsv aṭavīṣu.

in fact *he was black in color* and *ugly to look at.*
Though he roamed at will,
he *shut himself up in a fortress,*
but really *it was Durga who was his only refuge.*
Though he *followed the feet of a king,*
yet he had no experience in service of a king,
for in reality he *sojourned in the foothills of mountains.*
He was like the offspring of the Vindhya mountain,
the partial avatar of Death, the born brother of sin,
the essence of the Kali age.
Though he was frightening to behold,
his strength of character seemed profound,
his physical form unsurpassable.
Such was the leader of the *shábara* outcaste army.
Matángaka was his name, but his name I heard only later.
And what I thought was,
'Alas, full of folly are these peoples' lives,
and good people censure their behavior.
For look at what they do: their conception of religion
is to make offerings of human flesh.
Their sustenance good people despise:
it's wine, meat and suchlike.
Hunting is their occupation.
The howling of jackals is their scripture.
Owls are their advisers on what is good and what is bad.
Wisdom for them is knowing about birds.
Dogs are their bosom companions.
Their kingdom lies in empty forests.

āpānakam utsavaḥ.
mitrāṇi krūra|karma|sādhanāni dhanūṃṣi.
sahāyā viṣa|digdha|mukhā bhujaṃgā iva sāyakāḥ.
gītam utsāda|kāri mugdha|mṛgāṇām.
kalatrāṇi bandī|gṛhītāḥ para|yoṣitaḥ.
krūr'|ātmabhiḥ śārdūlaiḥ saha saṃvāsaḥ.
paśu|rudhireṇa devat"|ârcanam.
māṃsena bali|karma. cauryeṇa jīvanam. bhūṣaṇāni bhujaṃga|maṇayaḥ. vana|gaja|madair aṅga|rāgaḥ.
yasminn eva kānane nivasanti
tad ev' ôtkhāta|mūlam aśeṣataḥ kurvate.›
iti cintayaty eva mayi sa śabara|senā|patir aṭavī|bhramaṇa|samudbhavaṃ śramam apaninīṣur āgatya tasy' âiva śālmalī|taror adhaś chāyām avatārita|kodaṇḍas tvarita|parijan'|ôpanīta|pallav'|āsane samupāviśat.
anyatamas tu śabara|yuvā sa|saṃbhramam avatīrya tasmāt kara|yugala|parikṣobhit'|âmbhasaḥ saraso vaidūrya|drav'|ânukāri
pralaya|divasa|kara|kiraṇ'|ôpatāpād
ambar'|âika|deśam iva vilīnam,
indu|maṇḍalād iva prasyanditaṃ,
drutam iva muktā|phala|nikaram
atyacchatayā sparś'|ânumeyaṃ hima|jaḍam,
aravinda|kośa|rajaḥ|kaṣāyam ambhaḥ
kamalinī|pattra|puṭena

Their idea of a festival is a drinking bout.
Their friends are their means to cruel deeds: their bows.
Their helpers, like snakes, faces smeared with poison,
are their arrows.
When they sing, it is to entrap the silly deer.
Their wives are other men's women they've taken captive.
Tigers, cruel by nature, are their companions.
Their worship of the gods is with the blood of beasts.
Their offerings are flesh. They make their living by theft.
Their ornaments are jewels from the hoods of snakes.
They use rut of wild elephants as their cosmetic.
Whichever forest they inhabit they completely uproot.'
While I was thinking along these lines,
that *shábara* general, wishing to dispel the fatigue
of roaming through the forest,
coming to the shade beneath that very silk-cotton tree,
put down his bow and seated himself on a seat of leaves
hurriedly gathered by his attendants.
A certain *shábara* youth from among them
dashed down to the lake,
agitated its waters with his hands
and from it brought water resembling liquid lapis lazuli,
like a piece of the sky liquefied
by the heat of the rays of the sun of universal dissolution,
seeming to have oozed from the disc of the moon,
like a lump of melted pearls, so clear,
only touch showed it was there, as cold as ice,
fragrant with the pollen of lotus buds,
in a cup of *kámalini* lotus leaves;
and freshly pulled lotus shoots

pratyagr'|ôddhṛtāś ca dhauta|paṅka|nirmala|mṛṇālikāḥ
samupāharat.
āpīta|salilaś ca senā|patis tā mṛṇālikāḥ
śaśi|kalā iva Saiṃhikeyaḥ krameṇ' âdaśat.
apagata|śramaś c' ôtthāya paripīt'|âmbhasā
sakalena tena śabara|sainyen' ânugamyamānaḥ
śanaiḥ śanair abhimataṃ dig|antaram ayāsīt.
ekatamas tu jarac|chabaras tasmāt pulinda|vṛndād
an|āsādita|hariṇa|piśitaḥ piśit'|âśana iv' âtivikṛta|darśanaḥ
piśit'|'ârthī tasminn eva taru|tale
muhūrtam iva vyalambata.
antarite ca śabara|senā|patau
sa jīrṇa|śabaraḥ pibann iv' âsmākam āyūṃṣi
rudhira|bindu|pāṭalayā
kapila|bhrū|latā|pariveṣa|bhīṣaṇayā dṛṣṭyā,
gaṇayann iva śuka|kula|kulāya|sthānāni,
śyena iva vihag'|āmiṣ'|āsvāda|lālasaḥ,
suciram āruruksus taṃ vanaspatim ā mūlād apaśyat.
utkrāntam iva tasmin kṣaṇe
tad|ālokana|bhītānāṃ śuka|kulānām asubhiḥ.

with the mud washed off and shining.
And when he'd drunk the water
the commander ate those lotus shoots one by one,
as Rahu, son of Sínhika swallows the digits of the moon.
And, fatigue abated, he rose,
and followed by all his *shábara* army,
which had also been drinking water, very slowly
went off in the next direction that took his fancy.
But one old *shábara* there was
from that crowd of *pulínda* tribals,
who hadn't got hold of any venison
though he looked horrid enough
to be a flesh-eating demon,
and seeking meat for himself
delayed for a while
at the foot of that very tree.
And when the *shábara* commander was out of sight
that old *shábara,* seeming to drink in our lives
through his blood red eyes
terrible beneath overhanging tawny brows,
seeming to count up the places
where the families of parrots had built their nests,
eager as a hawk to taste the flesh of birds,
desiring to climb the tree,
long examined it from its root up,
that tree where at that very moment
so terrified were the parrot families
by him simply looking at them
their lives seemed to have left them at that very moment.

kim iva hi duṣkaram a|karuṇānām,
yataḥ sa tam aneka|tāla|tuṅgam
abhraṃkaṣa|śākhā|śikharam api sopānair iv'
â|yatnen' âiva pādapam āruhya
tān an|upajāt'|ôtpatana|śaktīn
kāṃś cid alpa|divasa|jātān garbha|vipāṭalāñ
chālmakī|kusuma|śaṅkām upajanayataḥ,
kāṃś cid udbhidyamāna|pakṣatayā
nalina|saṃvartik"|ânukāriṇaḥ
kāṃś cid arka|phala|sadṛśān,
kāṃś cid lohitāyamāna|cañcu|koṭīn
īṣad|vighaṭita|dala|puṭa|pāṭala|mukhānāṃ
kamala|mukulānāṃ śriyam udvahataḥ,
kāṃś cid an|avarata|śiraḥ|kampa|vyājena
nivārayata iva pratīkār'|â|samarthān
ek'|âikatayā phalān' îva tasya vanaspateḥ
śākh"|ântarebhyaḥ koṭarebhyaś ca śuka|śāvakān agrahīt.
apagat'|āsūṃś ca kṛtvā kṣitāv apātayat.
tātas tu taṃ mahāntam akāṇḍa eva prāṇa|haram
a|pratīkāram upaplavam upanatam ālokya
dvi|guṇa|tar'|ôpajāta|vepathur maraṇa|bhayād
udbhrānta|tarala|tārakāṃ viṣāda|śūnyām
aśru|jala|plutāṃ dṛśam itas tato dikṣu vikṣipann
ucchuṣka|tālur ātma|pratīkār'|â|kṣamas

Indeed what's hard for the hard-hearted, since that tree
was as tall as many palm trees one on top of another,
its topmost branches scraped the clouds,
and yet he climbed it with ease,
as if he were using a ladder.
Those who were not yet able to fly,
some of them just a few days old,
pink from the womb, making you think
they were silk-cotton flowers,
some with their wings beginning to sprout
looked like young lotus leaves still curled up,
some resembled *arka* fruits,
some with the tips of their beaks beginning to redden
had the beauty of lotus buds when their red tops
push just a little through their leaf cups,
some under the guise of non-stop nodding of their heads
seemed to be forbidding him,
unable to resist though they were—
one by one, as if they were fruit,
he took those baby parrots
from among the branches
of that tree, and from its hollows,
and killing them, threw them to the ground.
My father, for his part, when he saw this great disaster
come upon us, totally unexpected, fatal, unavoidable,
more than redoubled his usual trembling.
In his fear of death, he cast his gaze from here to there,
in all directions, eyes twitching and rolling,
unfocussed in panic, bathed in tears, his palate dried up,
unable to do anything to protect himself.

trāsa|srasta|saṃdhi|śithilena pakṣa|saṃpuṭen'
ācchādya māṃ
tat|kāl'|ôcita|pratīkāraṃ manyamānaḥ
sneha|para|vaśo mad|rakṣaṇ'|ākulaḥ
kiṃ|kartavyatā|vimūḍhaḥ
kroḍa|vibhāgena mām avaṣṭabhya tasthau.
asāv api pāpaḥ krameṇa śākh"|ântaraiḥ saṃcaramāṇaḥ
koṭara|dvāram āgatya
jīrṇ"|âsita|bhujaṃga|bhoga|bhīṣaṇaṃ prasārya
vividha|vana|varāha|vasā|visra|gandhi kara|talaṃ
kodaṇḍa|guṇ'|ākarṣaṇa|vraṇ'|âṅkita|prakoṣṭham
antaka|daṇḍ'|ânukāriṇaṃ
vāma|bāhum atinṛśaṃso
muhur muhur datta|cañcu|prahāram
utkūjantam ākṛṣya tātam
apagat'|āsum akarot.
māṃ tu sv|alpatvād bhaya|saṃpiṇḍit'|âṅgatvāt
s'|âvaśeṣatvād āyuṣaḥ katham api
pakṣa|saṃpuṭ'|ântara|gataṃ n' âlakṣayat.
uparataṃ ca tam avani|tale śithila|śiro|dharam
adho|mukham amuñcat.
aham api tac|caraṇ'|ântarāle praveśita|śiro|dharo
nibhṛtam aṅka|nilīnas ten' âiva sah' âpatam.

With the fold of his wing, loose as it was,
with his muscles even weaker through fear,
he covered me up, thinking that
the most fitting remedy for the occasion.
Swayed wholly by love, intent on protecting me,
not knowing what to do, he stood,
clutching me to his chest.
That wicked one, moving systematically
from branch to branch,
came to the entrance of our hollow.
Reaching in with his left arm
as frightening as the coil of an old black snake,
resembling Death's staff—
his palm reeking
from the flesh and marrow of many a wild boar,
his forearm scarred from drawing the bowstring—
the brute pulled out my father
who was repeatedly striking him
with his beak and crying out,
and squeezed the life out of him.
But me, wrapped in the folds of my father's wing,
because I was very small,
and had shrunk my body in terror,
and because I had the rest of my life to live,
somehow he did not notice.
And he dropped him, headfirst,
broken-necked, dead,
to the ground.
As for me, my neck wedged between his feet,
hidden in his lap,

avaśiṣṭa|puṇyatayā tu pavana|vaśa|sampuñjitasya

mahataḥ śuṣka|pattra|rāśer upari

patitam ātmānam apaśyam.

aṅgāni yena me n' âśīryanta.

yāvac c' âsau tasmāt taru|śikharān n' âvatarati

tāvad aham avaśīrṇa|parṇa|savarṇatvād

a|sphuṭ'|ôpalakṣyamāṇa|mūrtiḥ

pitaram uparatam utsṛjya nṛśaṃsa iva

prāṇa|parityāga|yogye 'pi kāle bālatayā

kāl'|ântara|bhuvaḥ sneha|rasasy' ân|abhijño

janma|saha|bhuvā bhayen' âiva kevalam abhibhūyamānaḥ

kiṃ cid upajātābhyāṃ pakṣābhyām īṣat|kṛt'|âvaṣṭambho

luṭhann itas tataḥ kṛt'|ânta|mukha|kuharād iva

vinirgatam ātmānaṃ manyamāno

n' âtidūra|vartinaḥ

śabara|sundarī|karṇa|pūra|racan'|ôpayukta|pallavasya

Saṃkarṣaṇa|paṭa|nīla|cchāyay" ôpahasata iva

Gadādhara|deha|cchavim,

acchaiḥ Kālindī|jala|cchedair iva viracita|cchadasya,

vana|kari|mada|salilair iv' ôpasikta|kisalayasya,

Vindhy'|âṭavī|keśa|pāśa|śriyam udvahato,

I fell down with him, without a sound.
Thanks to my merit earned in former lives
not being entirely used up,
I found that I'd fallen on top of a big pile of dry leaves
heaped up by the wind, so my limbs weren't broken.
And before he got down from the top of that tree,
I, not clearly visible since I was the same color
as the withered leaves,
like a brute abandoned my dead father—
though the right thing to have done at the time
was to die myself—
since I was a child
and didn't know the emotion of loving affection
that comes with the passing of time,
being overcome solely by natural inborn terror.
Supporting myself a little on my undeveloped wings,
lurching from side to side, I realized I had escaped
from the yawning jaws of Death.
Not very far away was a *tamála* tree, its leaves
used to make ear ornaments for *shábara* beauties,
with its dark shadow as dark a blue
as Bala·rama the plowman's garment,
seeming to scorn the color
of the body of Vishnu the club-bearer,
seeming to have clad itself in gleaming portions
of the waters of Kalínda's daughter, the Yámuna.
With its sprouts it seemed sprinkled
with the liquid rut of wild elephants.
It had the beauty of the hair knot
of the woman who is the Vindhya forest.

div" âpy andhakārita|śākh"|ântarasy'
â|praviṣṭa|sūrya|kiraṇam atigahanam
aparasy' êva pitur utsaṅgam
atimahatas tamāla|viṭapino
mūla|deśam aviśam.
avatīrya sa tena samayena
kṣiti|tala|viprakīrṇān saṃhṛtya tāñ chuka|śiśūn
eka|latā|pāśa|saṃyatān ābadhya parṇa|puṭe
'titvarita|gamanaḥ senā|pati|gaten' âiva
vartmanā tām eva diśam agacchat.
māṃ tu labdha|jīvit'|āśaṃ
pratyagra|pitṛ|maraṇa|śoka|śuṣka|hṛdayam
atidūra|pātād āyāsita|śarīraṃ saṃtrāsa|jātā
P35 sarv'|âṅg'|ôpatāpinī balavatī pipāsā para|vaśam akarot.
anayā ca kāla|kalayā sudūram atikrāntaḥ sa pāpa|kṛd
iti parikalayya kiṃ cid unnamita|kaṃdharo
bhaya|cakitayā dṛśā diśo 'valokya
tṛṇe 'pi calati punaḥ pratinivṛtta iti
tam eva pade pade pāpa|kāriṇam utprekṣamāṇo
niṣkramya tasmāt tamāla|taru|mūlāt
salila|samīpam upasartuṃ prayatnam akaravam.
ajāta|pakṣatayā ca n' âtisthira|caraṇa|saṃcārasya
muhur muhur mukhena patato muhus tiryaṅ|nipatantam
ātmānam ekayā pakṣa|pālyā saṃdhārayataḥ

And even by day, the space between its branches
was in darkness.
Into the very deep root region of this very great tree,
where the rays of the sun never entered,
I entered, as if into the lap of another father.
By now he'd got down
and collected all those young parrots
scattered on the ground,
tied them together with a creeper-rope,
and wrapped them up in a basket of leaves;
and with hasty steps
along the path taken by his commander
he went off in the same direction.
But as for me, who'd begun to hope I would live,
my heart was dried up in grief at my father's recent death,
my body was in pain from my long long fall,
and, torturing all my limbs, a powerful thirst, P35
brought on by fright, overcame me.
And calculating that enough time had gone by
for the evil-doer to have gone far away,
I lifted up my head a little,
and looked all around,
my eyes still unsteady from fear,
and when a blade of grass trembled
I thought he'd come back again.
Imagining I saw the evil-doer at every step,
I came out of that *tamála* tree root
and made a determined effort to reach water.
Since my wings were not fully grown,
I was unsteady on my feet,

kṣiti|tala|saṃsarpaṇa|bhram'|āturasy' ân|abhyāsa|vaśād

ekam api dattvā padam an|avaratam

unmukhasya sthūla|sthūlaṃ śvasato dhūli|dhūsarasya

saṃsarpato mama samabhūn manasi.

‹atikaṣṭāsv apy avasthāsu jīvita|nirapekṣā

na bhavanti khalu jagati sarva|prāṇināṃ pravṛttayaḥ.

n' âsti jīvitād anyad abhimatataram iha jagati

sarva|jantūnām. evam uparate 'pi sugṛhīta|nāmni tāte

yad aham avikal'|êndriyaḥ punar eva prāṇimi.

dhiṅ mām a|karuṇam atiniṣṭhuram akṛta|jñam.

aho soḍha|pitṛ|maraṇa|śoka|dāruṇaṃ yena mayā jīvyate.

upakṛtam api n' âpekṣyate.

khalaṃ hi khalu me hṛdayam.

mayā hi lok'|ântara|gatāyām ambāyāṃ niyamya

śoka|vegam ā prasava|divasāt pariṇata|vayas" âpi satā

tais tair upāyair mat|saṃvardhana|kleśam

atimahāntam api sneha|vaśād a|gaṇayatā

yat tātena paripālitas tat sarvam eka|pade vismṛtam.

and kept falling on my face.
But gradually, when I lurched to one side,
I managed to support myself on one wing.
Not used to exercise, I was giddy
from moving along the surface of the ground.
Just making one step I was gasping,
my face constantly lifted up for air.
Gray with dust, as I moved along,
these were the thoughts that crossed my mind.
'Even in the worst of times, no creature in this world,
for sure, acts in a way that disregards its own safety.
Nothing here in this world
is dearer to all creatures than life.
Thus even though my father,
blessed be his name, is dead,
it's the case that I'm still living,
my senses unimpaired.
Shame on me for being so pitiless, cruel and ungrateful.
It's shameful that I can put up with the grief
of my father's death
and heartlessly remain alive.
What he did for me, I'm ignoring.
Hard and callous is my heart, that's for sure.
For I've forgotten how
when my mother had gone to the next world,
he restrained his bitter grief,
and from the day of my birth,
despite being really old, did everything for me.
In his love for me he reckoned lightly
the very great trouble of rearing me.

atikṛpaṇāḥ khalv amī prāṇāḥ, yad upakāriṇam api tātam

ady' âpi kv' âpi gacchantaṃ n' ânugacchanti.

sarvathā na kaṃ cin na khalī|karoti jīvita|tṛṣṇā,

yad īdṛg|avastham api mām ayam āyāsayati jal'|âbhilāṣaḥ.

manye c' â|gaṇita|pitṛ|maraṇa|śokasya nirghṛṇat" âiva

kevalam iyaṃ mama salila|pāna|buddhiḥ.

ady' âpi dūra eva saras|tīram.

tathā hi, jala|devatā|nūpura'|ânukāri dūre

'dy' âpi kalahaṃsa|virutam etat.

a|sphuṭāni śrūyante sārasa|rasitāni.

ayaṃ ca viprakarṣād āśā|mukha|visarpaṇa|viralaḥ

saṃcarati nalinī|khaṇḍa|parimalaḥ.

divasasya c' êyam atikaṣṭā daśā vartate.

tathā hi, ravir ambara|tala|madhya|vartī

sphurantam ātapam an|avaratam anala|dhūli|nikaram iva

vikirati karaiḥ.

adhikām upajanayati tṛṣām

ātapa|sparśa|saṃtapta|pāṃsu|paṭala|durgamā bhūmiḥ.

atiprabala|pipās"|âvasannāni

It was he who protected me.
All that I forgot in one moment.
Truly my life's worthless
since it doesn't follow my father,
my benefactor, wherever he goes.
It's absolutely true there's no one
thirst for life doesn't turn into a villain,
since this longing for water
overwhelms me even in such a condition as I am in.
And I think this obsession
with drinking water on my part,
when I'm paying no attention
to the grief I ought to feel at the death of my father
is sheer heartlessness.
Even now, the lake shore is far off.
Thus it is that the cries of the *kala·hansa* geese,
resembling the sound of water fairies' anklets,
are still far off even now.
The cries of the water birds I hear are indistinct.
And this scent of masses of *nálini* lotuses
is from so far away that it has grown very faint
as it reaches as far as the faces of the quarters.
And this is the worst time of day. What I mean is this:
the sun, right in the middle of the sky,
scatters with its rays throbbing, unabating heat
that's like a mass of burning charcoal.
Ever increasing thirst is produced by the earth,
difficult to traverse, its spreading dust
heated by the touch of the sunlight.
My little limbs are overpowered by overwhelming thirst

gantum alpam api me n' âlam aṅgakāni.
a|prabhur asmy ātmanaḥ. sīdati me hṛdayam.
andhakāratām upayāti cakṣuḥ.
api nāma khalo vidhir
an|icchato 'pi me maraṇam ady' ôpapādayet.›
ity evaṃ cintayaty eva mayi tasmāt saraso
n' âtidūra|vartini tapo|vane Jābālir nāma
mahā|tapā muniḥ prativasati sma.
tat|tanayaś ca Hārīta|nāmā tāpasa|kumārakaḥ
Sanatkumāra iva sarva|vidy"|âvadāta|cetāḥ
sa|vayobhir aparais tapo|dhana|kumārakair
anugamyamānas ten' âiva pathā
dvitīya iva bhagavān Vibhāvasur
atitejasvitayā dur|nirīkṣya|mūrtir,
udyato divasa|kara|maṇḍalād iv' ôtkīrṇas,
taḍidbhir iva racit'|âvayavas, tapta|kanaka|draveṇ' êva
bahir upalipta|mūrtir āpiśaṅg'|âvadātatayā
deha|prabhayā sphurantyā sa|bāl'|ātapam iva
divasaṃ sa|dāv'|ânalam iva vanam upadarśayann
uttapta|loha|lohinīnām aneka|tīrth'|âbhiṣeka|pūtānām
aṃsa|sthal'|âvalambinīnāṃ jaṭānāṃ nikareṇ' ôpetaḥ,
stambhita/śikhā/kalāpaḥ
Khāṇḍava|vana|didhakṣayā
kṛta|kapaṭa|baṭu|veṣa iva bhagavān Pāvakas,

and cannot go even a little way.
I've no control over myself.
My heart sinks. My eyes dim.
Surely wicked fate
is going to bring about my death today, willy-nilly.'
While I was thinking thus,
the fact was that in a penance grove
not very far from that lake
was living a sage of great ascetic power,
Jabáli by name.
And his son—Haríta was his name—a young ascetic,
like Sanat·kumára, the shining youth,[62]
his mind refined by all sciences,
with other ascetics of his own age following him,
came along by the very path I was on,
his form hard to look upon
such was its radiance, like a second blessed sun,
seeming carved from the rising disc of the sun,
maker of the day,
his limbs seeming fashioned from lightning flashes,
the surface of his body smeared with molten gold.
With the yellowish-whitish luster of his body gleaming,
he made the day seem to have the light of early morning,
the forest to be on fire.
Glowing like heated iron,
hallowed by bathing in many sacred places
were the matted locks
that hung down to his shoulders
in a mass.
His topknot was tied up

tapo|vana|devatā|nūpur'|ânukāriṇā
dharma|śāsana|kaṭaken' êva
sphāṭiken' âkṣa|valayena
dakṣiṇa|śravaṇ'|âvalambinā virājamānaḥ,
sakala|viṣay' ôpabhoga|nivṛtty|artham upapāditena
lalāṭa|paṭṭake tri|satyen' êva
bhasma|tri|puṇḍrakeṇ' âlaṃkṛto,
gagana|gaman'|ônmukha|balāk'|ânukāriṇā
svarga|mārgam iva darśayatā
satatam udgrīveṇa sphaṭika|maṇi|kamaṇḍalun"
âdhyāsita|vāma|kara|talaḥ,
skandha|deś'|âvalambinā kṛṣṇ'|âjinena nīla|
pāṇḍu|bhāsā tapas|tṛṣṇā|nipīten' ântar|niṣpatatā
dhūma|paṭalen' êva parīta|mūrtir,
abhinava|bisa|sūtra|nirmiten' êva
parilaghutayā pavana|lolena
nirmāṃsa|virala|pārśvaka|pañjaram iva gaṇayatā
vām'|âṃs'|âvalambinā yajñ'|ôpavīten' ôdbhāsamāno,
devat"|ârcan'|ârtham āgṛhīta|vana|latā|kusuma|
paripūrṇa|parṇa|puṭa|sanātha|śikhareṇ' āṣāḍha|daṇḍena
vyāpṛta|savy'|êtara|pāṇir,
viṣāṇa|śikhar'|ôtkhātām udvahatā
snāna|mṛdam upajāta|paricayena

as if he were the divine purifier, Agni, god of fire,
the mass of flames from his head held back,
disguised in the dress of a young brahmin
in his desire to burn down the Khándava forest.
He was shining with a crystal rosary
hanging over his right ear,
resembling the anklet of the goddess of the ascetics' grove,
like a compilation of the teachings of *dharma.*
On his broad forehead he was adorned
with the three-lined mark in white ash
like the triple vow of word, thought, and deed
made to abstain from all sensory enjoyment.
His left hand carried a jeweled crystal pot
that with its neck always upward
seemed to be showing the path to heaven,
resembling a crane looking up, about to fly into the sky.
Hanging down from his shoulders, a black antelope skin
pale blue in color, like a mass of smoke he'd drunk in
through his thirst for ascetic power,
encircled his body.
Seemingly made of young lotus fibers,
in its lightness trembling in the wind,
as if counting the ribs of his fleshless ribcage,
hanging from his left shoulder
his sacred thread shone out.
In his right hand, he carried a staff of *ashádha* wood
with a basket of leaves at the top filled with flowers
from wild creepers for worshipping the gods.
Carrying clay that would be used for his bath
on the tips of its horns,

nīvāra|muṣṭi|saṃvardhitena

kuśa|kusuma|lat"|āyāsyamāna|lola|dṛṣṭinā

tapo|vana|mṛgeṇ' ânuyāto,

viṭapa iva komala|valkal'|āvṛta|śarīro,

girir iva *sa/mekhalo,*

Rāhur iv'

â/sakṛd/āsvādita/somaḥ,

padma|nikara iva

divasa|kara|marīci|po,

nadī|taṭa|tarur iva

satata/jala/kṣālana/vimala/jaṭaḥ,

kari|kalabha iva

vikaca/kumuda/dala/śakala/sita/daśano,

Drauṇir iva

Kṛp'/ânugato,

nakṣatra|rāśir iva

Citra/Mṛga/Kṛttik"/Āśleṣ'/ôpaśobhito,

gharma|kāla|divasa iva

kṣapita/bahu/doṣo,

those tips which had dug up the clay,
reared by himself on handfuls of wild rice,
its restless eyes flitting
from *kusha* grass to flowers to creepers,
a tame deer from the penance grove followed after him.
Like a tree, his body was covered by soft bark.
Like a mountain *with its sloping sides, he had his girdle.*
Like Rahu *who repeatedly swallows the moon,*
he *had often tasted soma juice.*
Like a bed of the red *padma* lotuses
which bloom in the day,
he when fasting drank the rays of the sun.
Like a tree on a river bank
with its roots exposed by constant washing by the water,
his matted locks were shining
from their constant washing in water.
Like a young elephant
with its tusks white with gleaming shreds of lotus shoots,
his teeth were as white as gleaming shreds of lotus shoots.
Like Drona's son, Ashva·tthaman,
followed by the warrior Kripa,[63]
compassion was second nature to him.
Like the zodiac *which is adorned*
with the Chitra, Mriga, and Ashlésha constellations,
he *was adorned by the loose fitting hide of a dappled deer.*
Like a day in the hot season
when the length of night is greatly curtailed,
he'd eradicated most of his faults.

jala|dhara|samaya iva
praśamita/rajaḥ/prasaro,
Varuṇa iva
kṛt'/ôda/vāso,
Harir iv'
âpanīta/Naraka/bhayaḥ
pradoṣ'|ārambha iva
saṃdhyā/piṅgala/tārakaḥ,
prabhāta|kāla iva
bāl'/ātapa/kapilo,
ravi|ratha iva
dṛḍha/niyamit'/âkṣa/cakraḥ,
su|rāj" êva
nigūḍha/mantra/sādhana/kṣapita/vigraho,
jala|nidhir iva
karāla/śaṅkha/maṇḍal'/āvarta/garto,
Bhagīratha iv'
âsakṛd/dṛṣṭa/Gaṅg"/âvatāro,
madhu|kara iv'
âsakṛd/anubhūta/puṣkara/vana/vāso,
vana|caro 'pi
kṛta/mah"/ālaya/praveśo,

Like the rainy season *which allays the flying dust,*
he'd *limited the extent of his passion.*
Like Váruna *who lives in the waters,* he'd
practiced the austerity of standing a long time in water.
Like Hari *who'd removed the fear*
the demon Náraka[64] *inspired,*
he *dispelled the fear of hell.*
Like the beginning of dawn, *when the stars are tawny*
with the twilight, his eyes were tawny like twilight.
Like dawn, *tawny red with early morning sunshine,*
he *was tawny red like early morning sunshine.*
Like the sun's chariot
with its axles and wheels well set in place,
he *firmly restrained the circle of his sense apertures.*
Like a good king *who puts an end to the possibility*
of conflict with secret plans and a strong army,
he *kept his body lean by the use of secret mantras*
for getting superhuman powers.
Like the ocean *with its masses of gaping conches*
and cavernous whirlpools
he *had deep round indentations in his bony temples.*
Like Bhagi·ratha,
who'd *seen Ganga's original descent from the heavens,*
he'd *often seen the descent of Ganga from the Himálaya.*
Like a bee *often visiting beds of blue lotuses,*
he *often stayed in the wood beside the Púshkara lake.*
Though living in the woods,
he might have been said
to live in a great house,
but in fact *he was absorbed in the supreme soul.*

'|saṃyato 'pi

mokṣ'/ârthī,

sāma/prayoga/paro' pi

satat'/âvalambita/daṇḍaḥ,

supto 'pi

prabuddhaḥ,

saṃnihita|netra|dvayo 'pi

parityakta/vāma/locanas,

tad eva kamala|saraḥ sisnāsur upāgamat.

prāyeṇ' â|kāraṇa|mitrāṇy atikaruṇ'|ārdrāṇi ca

sadā khalu bhavanti satāṃ cetāṃsi.

yataḥ sa māṃ tad|avastham ālokya samupajāta|dayaḥ

samīpa|vartinam ṛṣi|kumārakam anyatamam abravīt.

‹ayaṃ katham api śuka|śiśur a|saṃjāta|pakṣa|puṭa eva

taru|śikharād asmāt paricyutaḥ.

śyena|mukha|paribhraṣṭena v" ânena bhavitavyam.

tathā hi. atidavīyastayā prapātasy' âlpa|śeṣa|jīvito 'yam

āmīlita|locano muhur muhur mukhena patati

muhur muhur atyulbaṇaṃ śvasiti

muhur muhuś cañcu|puṭaṃ vivṛṇoti.

na śaknoti śiro|dharāṃ dhārayitum.

tad ehi yāvad ev' âyam asubhir na viyujyate

Though unrestrained, *he desired to be set free;*
but in fact *he desired release from rebirth.*
Though *intent on the practice of peace,*
he *continually relied on violence,*
but in fact *he was intent on the ritual of the "Sama Veda,"*
and *always had his staff for support.*
Though he slept at night, he *was awake;*
that is to say, he was *enlightened.*
Though he had two eyes in place,
he'd abandoned his left eye;
that is to say,
he'd *renounced women with their lovely eyes.*
Intending to bathe in that very same lotus lake,
he came along.
It's generally the case, surely, that the hearts of the good
are friendly without ulterior motive
and tender with lots of compassion.
For, seeing me in that condition,
his compassion was aroused
and he said to one of the young ascetics who were nearby,
'Somehow or other this infant parrot whose wings
are not yet grown has fallen from the top of this tree.
Or he might have dropped from the mouth of a hawk.
Just see, from the very great length of his fall,
he's little life left, his eyes are closed.
He keeps falling on his face,
frantically trying to breathe
he opens his beak again and again.
He can't hold his neck up.
Come then, before life leaves him,

tāvad eva gṛhāṇ' êmam avatāraya salila|samīpam.›

ity abhidhāya tena māṃ saras|tīram anāyayat.

upasṛtya ca jala|samīpam eka|deśa|nihita|daṇḍa|kamaṇḍalur

ādāya svayaṃ māṃ mukta|prayatnam

uttānita|mukham aṅgulyā kati cit salila|bindūn apāyayat.

ambhaḥ|kṣoda|kṛta|sekaṃ ca samupajāta|navīna|prāṇam

upataṭa|prarūḍhasya nalinī|palāśasya

jala|śiśirāyāṃ chāyāyāṃ nidhāya

samucitam akarot snāna|vidhim.

abhiṣek'|âvasāne c' âneka|prāṇāyāma|pūto

japan pavitrāṇy agha|marṣaṇāni

pratyagra|bhagnair unmukho rakt'|âravindair

nalinī|patra|puṭena bhagavate savitre dattv"

ârgham udatiṣṭhat.

āgṛhīta|dhauta|dhavala|valkalaś ca

saha|jyotsna iva saṃdhy"|ātapaḥ

kara|tala|nirdhūnana|viśada|jaṭaḥ

kamaṇḍalum āpūrya śucinā saro|vāriṇā

pratyagra|snān'|ārdra|jaṭena sakalena

tena muni|kumāraka|kadambaken' ânugamyamāno

māṃ gṛhītvā tapo|van'|âbhimukhaṃ śanair agacchat.

pick him up at once and take him down to the water.'
So saying he had me brought to the shore of the lake.
And going to the water,
putting his staff and pot to one side,
himself opening my mouth with his finger—
for any effort was beyond me—
he somehow got me to drink some drops of water.
And when I'd been sprinkled with water
and had come back to life,
he placed me in the shade of the leaf of a lotus plant
growing near the bank,
where the proximity of the water made it all the cooler,
and performed his customary ablutions.
And at the conclusion of his bath,
purified by many breath restraint exercises,
reciting quietly the sacred Vedic verses that remove sin,
standing, he lifted up his face to the divine sun,
and made an offering of freshly picked red lotuses
in a cup of *nálini* leaves.
And putting on a clean white bark garment,
becoming like evening twilight blended with moonlight,
he wrung out between his palms his glossy matted locks,
filled his pot with the pure lake water,
and all that crowd of young sages
wet-haired from their recent bathing
following behind him,
he picked me up and slowly went
in the direction of the penance grove.

an|atidūram iva gatvā

diśi diśi sadā|saṃnihita|kusuma|phalais

tāla|tilaka|tamāla|hintāla|bakula|bahulair

elā|lat"|ākulita|nālikerī|kalāpair

lola|lodhra|lavalī|lavaṅga|pallavair

ullasita|cūta|reṇu|paṭalair

ali|kula|jhaṃkāra|mukhara|sahakārair

unmada|kokila|kula|kalāpa|kolāhalibhir

utphulla|ketakī|rajaḥ|puñja|piñjaraiḥ

pūgī|latā|dol"|âdhirūḍha|vana|devatais

tārakā|varṣam iv' â|dharma|vināśa|piśunaṃ

kusuma|nikaram anila|calitam an|avaratam atidhavalam

utsṛjadbhiḥ,

saṃsakta|pādapaiḥ kānanair upagūḍham,

a|cakita|pracalita|kṛṣṇa|sāra|śata|śabalābhir,

utphulla|kamalinī|lohinībhir,

Mārīca|māyā|mṛg'|âvalūna|

rūḍha|vīrud|dalābhir,

Dāśarathi|cāpa|koṭi|kṣata|

kanda|garta|viṣamita|talābhir,

Daṇḍak'|âraṇya|sthalībhir

upaśobhita|prāntam

We hadn't gone very far before I saw
what was hugged by groves in every direction,
always with flowers and fruit in evidence
with lots of *tala*, *tílaka*, *hintála*, and *bákula* trees,
clumps of coconut trees covered in cardamom creeper,
waving leaves of *lodhra*, *lávali*, and *lavángas*,
rising clouds of mango pollen,
sahakára mango trees noisy
with the insistent hum of swarms of bees,
noisy with the commotion
of masses of flocks of impassioned *kókilas*,
tawny with heaps of pollen from blooming *kétakis*,
with woodland deities swinging on betel creepers,
incessantly shedding what seemed like
a shower of stars foreboding
Unrighteousness's destruction,
a mass of flowers, blown by the wind, really white—
such were the groves, their trees close packed together.
It was dappled
with hundreds of spotted antelopes roaming unafraid,
reddened with lotus plants in full bloom,
where the shrub leaves nibbled up by Marícha,
the illusory deer who lured Rama away from Sita,
had grown again,
where the surface of the ground was still pitted
with the holes from the root vegetables dug up
by the son of Dasha·ratha with the tip of his bow—
such were the grounds of the Dándaka forest
which adorned the further borders.

āgṛhīta|samit|kuśa|kusuma|mṛdbhir
adhyayana|mukhara|śiṣy'|ânugataiḥ
sarvataḥ praviśadbhir munibhir a|śūny'|ôpakaṇṭham,
utkaṇṭhita|śikhaṇḍi|maṇḍala|śrūyamāṇa|
jala|kalaśa|pūraṇa|dhvānam,
an|avarat'|ājy"|āhuti|prītaiś citra|bhānubhiḥ
sa|śarīram eva muni|janam amara|lokaṃ ninīṣubhir
uddhūyamāna|dhūma|lekhā|chalen'
ābadhyamāna|svarga|mārga|gamana|sopāna|setum iv'
ôpalakṣyamāṇam,
āsanna|vartinībhis
tapo|dhana|saṃparkād iv' âpagata|kāluṣyābhir
taraṃga|paraṃparā|saṃkrānta|ravi|bimba|paṅktibhis
tāpasa|darśan'|āgata|sapta|ṛṣi|mālā|vigāhyamānābhir iv'
âtivikaca|kumuda|vanam ṛṣi|janam upāsitum avatīrṇaṃ
graha|gaṇam iva niśās' ûdvahantībhir dīrghikābhiḥ
parivṛtam,
anil'|âvanamita|śikharābhiḥ praṇamyamānam iva
vana|latābhir,
an|avarata|mukta|kusumair abhyarcyamānam iva
pādapair,
ābaddha|pallav'|'âñjalibhir
upāsyamānam iva viṭapair,

Its precincts were by no means empty,
with sages coming in from all directions,
carrying firewood, *kusha* grass, flowers, and clay,
followed by their pupils
loudly reciting what they learned.
Circles of peacocks with their necks uplifted were
listening to the sound of the filling of water-pots there.
With the fires pleased with incessant offerings
of clarified butter, it looked as if a bridge
with steps leading all the way to heaven was being built
under the guise of the lines of smoke that rose up,
the fires wishing to transport the sages
bodily to the world of the gods.
Close at hand, free from any murkiness
as if because of the contact with the sages,
a row of round suns reflected in their rippling waves
as if the line of the Seven Sages
come to see the ascetics had plunged in;
at night bearing a grove of blooming *kúmuda* water-lilies
like the host of planets come down to worship the sages—
such were the pools surrounding it.
Forest creepers seemed to be bowing down to it
as the wind lowered their tops.
Trees seemed to be worshipping it,
incessantly dropping their flowers.
Shrubs seemed to be paying homage,
their foliage forming folded hands.

uṭaj'|âjira|prakīrṇa|śuṣyac|chyāmākam

upasaṃgṛhīt'|āmalaka|lavalī|karkandhū|kadalī|kuca|

panasa|cūta|tāla|phalam

adhyayan|mukhara|baṭu|janam,

an|avarata|śravaṇa|gṛhīta|vaṣaṭ|kāra|vācāla|śuka|kulam,

aneka|sārik'|ôdghuṣyamāṇa|Subrahmaṇyam,

araṇya|kukkuṭ'|ôpabhujyamāna|

Vaiśvadeva|bali|piṇḍam,

āsanna|vāpī|kalahaṃsa|pota|bhujyamāna|nīvāra|balim,

eṇī|jihvā|pallav'|ôpalihyamāna|muni|bālakam,

agni|kāry'|ârdha|dagdha|simi|simāyamāna|

samit|kuśa|kusumam,

upala|bhagna|nālikera|rasa|snigdha|śilā|talam,

acira|kṣuṇṇa|valkala|rasa|pāṭala|bhū|talaṃ,

rakta|candan'|ôpalipt'|āditya|maṇḍalaka|

nihita|karavīra|kusumam,

itas tato vikṣipta|bhasma|lekhā|kṛta|

muni|jana|bhojana|bhūmi|parihāraṃ,

paricita|śākhā|mṛga|kar'|ākṛṣṭi|niṣkāsyamāna|

praveśyamāna|jarad|andha|tāpasam,

ibha|kalabhak'|ârdh'|ôpabhukta|patitaiḥ

In the courtyards of the huts,
millet was spread out to dry.
Fruits had been harvested: *ámalaka*, *lávali*, *karkándhu*,
kádali, *kucha*, *pánasa*, mango, and coconuts.
Brahmin boys were noisily reciting their lessons.
Flocks of parrots were vociferously repeating
the *vashat* cry of the sacrificers they'd picked up
from incessantly hearing it. Lots of mynah birds
were singing out the 'Dear to brahmins'
sacrificial invocation, the Subrahmánya.
Wild cocks were enjoying
the rice balls offered to the All-gods.
Kala·hansa goslings from the nearby ponds
were eating the offerings of wild rice.
Does with their leaflike tongues
were licking the sages' children.
In the sacrificial fires the half burned firewood
with flowers and *kusha* grass on it hissed and spluttered.
The stone slabs were sticky with juice
from the coconuts smashed open on the breaking stones.
The ground was pink with the moisture
from freshly beaten bark. Sun disks
had been painted on the ground in red sandal-paste
and *karavíra* flowers laid on them.
Here and there the ground where the sages ate
was marked off and protected
by lines drawn with sacred ash.
Blind and doddering old sages
were being brought in and led away
by tame monkeys who pulled their hands.

Sarasvatī|bhuja|latā|vigalitaiḥ śaṅkha|valayair iva
mṛṇāla|śakalaiḥ kalmāṣitam,
ṛṣi|jan'|ârtham eṇakair viṣāṇa|śikhar'|ôtkhanyamāna|
vividha|kanda|mūlam ambu|pūrṇa|puṣkara|puṭair
vana|karibhir āpūryamāṇa|viṭap'|ālavālakam,
ṛṣi|kumārak'|ākṛṣyamāṇa|vana|varāha|daṃṣṭr"|ântarāla|
lagna|śālūkam,
upajāta|paricayaiḥ kalāpibhiḥ
P40 pakṣa|puṭa|pavana|saṃdhukṣyamāṇa|
muni|homa|hut'|āśanam,
ārabdh'|âmṛta|caru|cāru|gandham
ardha|pakva|puroḍāśa|puṇya|parimal'|āmoditam,
avicchinn'|ājya|dhār"|āhuti|huta|bhug|
jhaṃkāra|mukharitam,
upacaryamāṇ'|âtithi|vargaṃ, pūjyamāna|pitṛ|daivatam,
arcyamāna|Hari|Hara|Pitāmaham,
uddiśyamāna|śrāddha|kalpaṃ,
vyākhyāyamāna|yajña|vidyam,
ālocayamāna|dharma|śāstraṃ,
vācyamāna|vividha|pustakaṃ,
vicāryamāma|sakala|śāstr'|ârtham,
ārabhyamāṇa|parṇa|śālam,
upalipyamān'|ājiram,
upamṛjyamān'|ôṭaj'|âbhyantaram,

It was littered with bits of lotus fibers young elephants
had half eaten and then dropped,
like conch-shell bracelets slipped
from Sarásvati's creeper-like arms.
For the sages' benefit, deer were digging up
various root-vegetables with the points of their horns.
Wild elephants who'd charged their trunks with water
were filling the water basins round the trees.
The sages' little sons were pulling out lotus roots
stuck between the tusks of wild boar.
Peacocks who'd become really tame fanned
the sages' sacrificial fires with the wind from their wings. P40
There was the lovely smell coming from
the nectarous ghee and rice oblation being prepared.
The holy fragrance of half-cooked sacrificial cake
wafted about.
It was noisy with the crackling of fires receiving
oblations of clarified butter in unbroken streams.
Crowds of guests were being received with due honor.
The divine ancestors were being worshipped.
Vishnu, Shiva, and grandfather Brahma were worshipped.
The ritual of worship of the ancestors was being taught,
the science of sacrifice was being explained.
The *dharma·shastra* was being studied.
Various books were being read out.
The meaning of all the *shastras*
was being deliberated upon.
Leaf huts were being built,
courtyards were being covered with cow dung.
The huts were being swept out,

ābadhyamāna|dhyānaṃ,

sādhyamāna|mantram, abhyasyamāna|yogam,

upahriyamāṇa|vana|devatā|baliṃ,

nirvartyamāna|mauñja|mekhalaṃ,

kṣālyamāna|valkalam,

upasaṃgṛhyamāṇa|samidham,

upasaṃskriyamāṇa|kṛṣṇ'|âjinaṃ,

gṛhyamāṇa|vedhukaṃ,

śoṣyamāṇa|puṣkara|bījaṃ,

grathyamān'|âkṣa|mālaṃ,

nyasyamāna|vetra|daṇḍaṃ,

saṃskriyamāṇa|parivrājakam,

āpūryamāṇa|kamaṇḍalum,

a|dṛṣṭa|pūrvaṃ Kali|kālasy',

â|paricitam anṛtasy',

â|śruta|pūrvam Anaṅgasy',

Âbjayonim iva tribhuvana|vanditam,

Asurārim iva

prakaṭita/Varāha/Nara/siṃha/rūpaṃ,

Sāṅkhyam iva

Kapil'/âdhiṣṭhitaṃ,

Madhur"|ôpavanam iva

Bal'/âvalīḍha/darpita/Dhenukam,

meditation was being performed.
Mantras were proving efficacious, yoga was practiced.
Offerings were made to the forest deities.
Girdles of *munja* grass were being made up.
Bark garments were being washed.
Firewood was being collected.
Black antelope skins were being dressed.
Corn was being stored.
Lotus seeds were being dried.
Necklaces of holy *rudráksha* beads were being threaded.
Cane staffs were being bundled up.
Wandering ascetics were being consecrated.
Pots were being filled.
The Kali age had never seen it,
falsehood had never known it.
Bodiless Love had never heard of it.
Like lotus-born Brahma,
it was praised by the three worlds.
Just as Vishnu, the enemy of successive demons,
manifested his form as boar and then of the man-lion,
boars, men, and lions were visibly present there.
Just as the Sankhya philosophy
was founded by Kápila, the brown sage,
it *was inhabited by brown cows.*
Just as the groves around Máthura were *where*
Dhénuka in his pride was humbled by Bala·rama,
it *had cows who were proud of their calves*
and licked them zealously.[65]

Udayanam iv'

ānandita|Vatsa|kulaṃ,

kiṃpuruṣ'|âdhirājyam iva

muni|jana|gṛhīta|jala|kalaś'|

âbhiṣicyamāna|Drumaṃ,

nidāgha|samay'|âvasānam iva

pratyāsanna|jala|prapātaṃ,

jala|dhara|samayam iva

vana|gahana|madhya|sukha|supta|Hariṃ,

Hanumantam iva

śilā|śakala|prahāra|saṃcūrṇit'|

Âkṣ'|âsthi|saṃcayaṃ,

Khāṇḍava|vināś'|ôdyat'|Ârjunam iva

prārabdh'|âgni|kāryaṃ,

surabhi|vilepana|dharam api

satat'|āvirbhūta|havya|dhūma|gandhaṃ,

mātaṅga|kul'|âdhyāsitam api

pavitram,

ullasita|*dhūma|ketu|śatam* api praśānt'|ôpadravaṃ,

Just as Údayana *gave joy to the Vatsa lineage,*
it *gave joy to numerous calves.*
Like the kingdom of the nearly-men, the *kínnaras,*
where Druma was consecrated king
by ascetics holding pots of water,
it *had its trees sprinkled with water*
by the ascetics holding pots of water.
Just as the end of the hot season has *imminent rainfall,*
it had *waterfalls nearby.*
Just as the rainy season *has yellow Vishnu fast asleep*
in the middle of the deep waters of the oceans,
it has *lions fast asleep in the depths of its forest.*
Just as Hánuman smashed *all Aksha's bones*
by hurling rocks and boulders at him,
it *had heaps of rudráksha shells*
smashed *by rocks and boulders.*
Just as Árjuna prepared the destruction
of the Khándava forest by *starting fires,*
in it *fire sacrifices were being undertaken.*
The smell of the smoke from sacrificial offerings
was always apparent, though the place
had been smeared *with fragrant unguents*
—but, in reality, *with cow dung.*
It was pure, though it was inhabited
by families of matánga outcastes—
but, in reality, *by herds of elephants.*
Misfortune was allayed, though there blazed out
hundreds of comets—
but, in reality, *hundreds of fires.*

paripūrṇa|dvija|pati|maṇḍala|sanātham api

sadā|saṃnihita|taru|gahan'|ândhakāram,

atiramaṇīyam aparam iva

Brahma|lokam āśramam apaśyam.

yatra ca malinatā havir|dhūmeṣu na cariteṣu,

mukha|rāgaḥ śukeṣu na kopeṣu,

tīkṣṇatā kuś'|âgreṣu na sva|bhāveṣu,

cañcalatā kadalī|daleṣu na manaḥsu,

cakṣū|rāgaḥ kokileṣu

na para|kalatreṣu,

kaṇṭha|grahaḥ kamaṇḍaluṣu na surateṣu,

mekhalā|bandho vrateṣu

n' ērṣyā|kalaheṣu,

stana|sparśo homa|dhenuṣu

na kāminīṣu,

pakṣa|pātaḥ kṛka|vākuṣu

na vidyā|vivādeṣu,

bhrāntir anala|pradakṣiṇāsu

na śāstr'|ârtheṣu,

It was always dark
because of the thick groves of trees around it,
though it possessed *the disc of the full moon*—
but, in reality, *a large number of brahmins.*
Such was the hermitage upon which I gazed,
most delightful, like another Brahma's heaven.
And there dirtiness was in the smoke of oblations,
not in deeds.
Red faces were to be found on parrots, not angry people.
Sharpness was in the tips of *kusha* grass,
not in human nature.
Instability was in banana leaves, not in men's minds.
Parrots *had red eyes*, and *men did not direct*
impassioned glances at other men's wives.
Seizing by the neck took place in respect of pots,
not in love-making.
Putting on the girdle of munja grass took place
when men made the vow of asceticism, not women
binding their lovers with their girdles in jealous quarrels.
There was *touching of the teats* of the cows
who gave milk for the oblations,
but women's *breasts were not fondled.*
Crows *molted*, but there were no *closed minds*
in scientific and technical discussions.
There was *walking round*
in circumambulating the sacred fires, but there was
no *confusion* in interpretations of the *shastras*.

Vasu/saṃkīrtanaṃ divya|kathāsu
na tṛṣṇāsu,
gaṇanā rudr'|âkṣa|valayeṣu
na śarīreṣu,
muni/bāla/nāśaḥ kratu|dīkṣayā
na mṛtyunā,
Rām'/ânurāgo Rāmāyaṇena
na yauvanena,
mukha/bhaṅga|vikāro jarayā
na dhan'|âbhimānena.
yatra ca Mahābhārate
Śakuni/vadhaḥ,
purāṇe
Vāyu/pralapitaṃ,
vayaḥ|pariṇāme
dvija/patanam,
upavana|candaneṣu
jāḍyam,
agnīnāṃ *bhūtimattvam,*
eṇakānāṃ gīta|śravaṇa|vyasanaṃ,
śikhaṇḍināṃ *nṛtya/pakṣa/pāto,*
bhujaṃgānāṃ *bhogaḥ,*
kapīnāṃ *śrīphal'/âbhilāṣo,*
mūlānām *adho/gatiḥ.*

The praises of the Vasus
were sung in tales of the celestials,
while *wealth was not praised*
even in dreams of avarice.[66]
Counting was done using *rudráksha* necklaces,
but no *attention was paid* to the body.
The sages' hair was cut
during the initiatory part of sacrifices,
but *the sages' children were not lost through death.*
There was love for Rama *through the "Ramáyana,"*
not *resorting to beautiful women* through youth.
Old age *changed the face with wrinkles,*
not pride in wealth *with scowls.*
The only *killing of birds* in that place
was the *killing of Shákuni*
that occurs in the "Maha·bhárata."
Delirious ravings were only in the *purána*
where there is talk of Vayu, god of wind.
As people got older, *their teeth fell out,*
but there was *no lapse in behavior*
on the part of the twice-born.
The only *stupidity* was *the coolness* to be found
in the neighboring sandal groves.
The only *possession of wealth* was fires' *ashes.*
It was only deer
who were addicted to listening to singing.
It was only peacocks *who were addicted to dancing*
and *they dropped some feathers as they danced.*
The only *sensual enjoyment* was snakes' *coils.*
The only *longing for the fruits of wealth*

tasya c' âivaṃvidhasya madhya|bhāga|maṇḍalam
alaṃkurvāṇasy' ālaktakā|lohita|pallavasya
muni|jan'|ālambita|kṛṣṇ'|âjina|jala|karaka|sanātha|śākhasya
tāpasa|kumārikābhir mūla|bhāga|datta|pīta|piṣṭa|
pañc'|âṅgulasya,
hariṇa|śiśubhir āpīyamān'|ālavālaka|salilasya,
muni|kumārak'|ābaddha|kuśa|cīra|dāmno,
harita|go|may'|ôpalepana|vivikta|talasya,
tat|kṣaṇa|kṛta|kusum'|ôpahāra|ramaṇīyasya,
n' âtimahataḥ, parimaṇḍalatayā
vistīrṇ'|âvakāśasya, rakt'|âśoka|taror
adhaś|chāyāyām upaviṣṭam
atyugra|tapobhir bhuvanam iva sāgaraiḥ,
Kanakagirim iva kula|parvataiḥ,
kratum iva vaitāna|vahnibhiḥ,
kalp'|ânta|divasam iva ravibhiḥ,
kālam iva kalpaiḥ samantān,
maha|rṣibhiḥ parivṛtam.

was monkeys' *liking for bilva fruit.*
The only *degradation*
was the *downward movement* of roots.
And adorning the central area of the hermitage
which I have just described,
its leaves as scarlet as lac,
its branches hung with the black antelope skins
and water-pots the sages had put there,
on its roots the five-finger marks in yellow powder
the ascetics' daughters had applied,
young deer drinking the water in its irrigation basin,
garlanded by the sages' sons
with their garments of *kusha* grass,
the ground beneath it hallowed
with a smearing of green cow dung;
lovely with flower offerings that had just been made;
though not very high, covering a wide circle of ground—
such was the red *ashóka* tree beneath which,
in its shade, was seated a person,
like the earth surrounded by the oceans,
like the Golden Mountain
surrounded by subsidiary mountain chains,
like the sacrifice surrounded by the sacrificial fires,
like the day of universal destruction
at the end of the eon, encircled by multiple suns,
like time with the world-ages all around,
surrounded by great sages
who'd performed very severe asceticism.

ugra|śāpa|bhiy" êva
kampita/dehayā,
praṇayiny" êva
vihita/keśa/grahayā,
kruddhay" êva
kṛta/bhrū/bhaṅgayā,
mattay" êv' *ākulita/gamanayā,*
prasādhitay" êva *prakaṭita/tilakayā,*
jarayā gṛhīta|vratay" êva bhasma|dhavalayā
dhavalī|kṛta|vigraham,
āyāminībhiḥ palita|pāṇḍurābhis
tapasā vijitya muni|janam akhilaṃ,
dharma|patākābhir iv' ôcchritābhir,
amara|lokam āroḍhuṃ puṇya|rajjubhir iv'
ôpasaṃgṛhītābhir,
atidūra|pravṛddhasya puṇya|taroḥ
kusuma|mañjarībhir iv' ôdgatābhir
jaṭābhir upaśobhamānam,
uparacita|bhasma|tripuṇḍrakeṇa
tiryak|pravṛtta|Tripathagā|srotas|trayeṇ' êva
Himagiri|śilā|talena lalāṭa|phalaken' ôpetam,

Old age *was making his body tremble*
as if old age were a woman
trembling in fear of his fierce curse;
—had taken his hair
as if old age were a mistress who'd seized his hair;
—*wrinkled his brow*
as if old age were an angry woman *frowning*;
—*made his walk unsteady*
as if old age were a drunken woman *walking unsteadily*;
—*had given him moles all over*
as if old age were a woman all dolled up
with her *tílaka forehead mark displayed*;
—whitened his body
as if old age were an old woman who'd taken a vow
and whitened her body with ash.
Long, white with the grayness of old age,
like the flags of his righteousness raised
on conquering other sages in asceticism,
like ropes of merit strung together
to ascend to the world of the gods,
like rising clusters of blossom
on the tree of his merit which had grown very high—
with such matted hair he was resplendent.
Marked with three horizontal lines of ash,
like a stone slab of Himálaya
traversed by the triple stream
of the river Ganga
which passes through thc three worlds,
was the expanse of his forehead.

adho|mukha|candra|kal"|ākārābhyām
avalambita|vali|śithilābhyāṃ bhrū|latābhyām
avaṣṭabhyamāna|dṛṣṭim,
an|avarata|mantr'|âkṣar'|âbhyāsa|vivṛt'|âdhara|puṭatayā
nipatadbhir atiśucibhiḥ
satya|prarohair iva
svacch'|êndriya|vṛttibhir iva
karuṇā|rasa|pravāhair iva
daśana|mayūkhair dhavalita|puro|bhāgam,
udvamad|amala|Gaṅgā|pravāham iva Jahnum
a|virata|som'|ôdgāra|sugandhi|niśvās'|âvakṛṣṭair
mūrtimadbhir iva śāp'|âkṣaraiḥ
sadā mukha|bhāga|saṃnihitaiḥ
parisphuradbhir alibhir a|virahitam,
atikṛśatayā nimnatara|gaṇḍa|gartam,
unnatatara|hanu|ghoṇam, ōākarāla|tārakam,
avaśīryamāṇa|virala|nayana|pakṣma|mālam,
udgata|dīrgha|roma|ruddha|śravaṇa|vivaram,
ā|nābhi|lamba|kūrca|kalāpam
ānanam ādadhānam,
aticapalānām indriy'|âśvānām
antaḥ|saṃyamana|rajjubhir iv' ātatābhiḥ
kaṇṭha|nāḍībhir nirantara|saṃbaddha|kaṃdharaṃ,

Shaped like the downward pointing crescent of the moon,
flaccid with hanging folds of skin,
the creepers that were his brows obscured his eyes.
The aperture of his lips was open
in the constant repetition of the syllables of mantras,
and so spilling out, pure white,
like outgrowths of the tree of truth,
like the processes of his very pure senses,
like the streams of his compassion,
the rays of his teeth whitened the front of his body,
so that he looked like Jahnu
emitting Ganga's pure stream.
Attracted by his breath fragrant with his constant
exhalation of *soma*, like the syllables of his curses
taking on visible form, bees never left him,
flitting to and fro his mouth.
Such was his emaciation, the hollows of his cheeks
were deep indeed.
His jaw and nose were very prominent,
his eyeballs protruded,
his scanty eyelashes were dropping out,
his ear holes were blocked
by the long hairs growing from them,
his thick beard hung down to his navel.
That was the face he had.
Like reins for the inner restraint
of the all too skittish horses that are the senses,
the wide stretched veins on his throat
tightly bound his neck.

samunnata|viral'|âsthi|pañjaram
aṃs"|âvalambi|dhavala|yajñ'|ôpavītam
anila|vaśa|janita|tanu|taraṃga|bhaṅgam
utplavamāna|mṛṇālam iva Mandākinī|pravāham
a|kaluṣam aṅgam udvahantam,
amala|sphaṭika|śakala|ghaṭitam akṣa|valayam
ujjvala|sthūla|muktāphala|grathitaṃ Sarasvatī|hāram iva
calad|aṅguli|vivara|gatam āvartayantam
anavarata|bhramita|tārakā|cakram aparam iva Dhruvam,
unnamatā śirā|jālakena jarat|kalpa|tarum iva
pariṇata|latā|saṃcayena nirantara|nicitam,
amalena candr'|âṃśubhir iv',
âmṛta|phenair iva,
guṇa|saṃtāna|tantubhir iva nirmitena,
Mānasa|saro|jala|kṣālita|śucinā
dukūla|valkalena
dvitīyen' êva jarā|jālakena saṃchāditam,
āsanna|vartinā Mandākinī|salila|pūrṇena
tridaṇḍ'|ôpaviṣṭena
sphaṭika|kamaṇḍalunā vikaca|puṇḍarīka|rāśim iva
rāja|haṃsen' ôpaśobhamānaṃ,
sthairyeṇ' âcalānāṃ
gāmbhīryeṇa sāgarāṇāṃ
tejasā savituḥ
praśamena tuṣāra|raśmer
nirmalatay" âmbara|talasya
saṃvibhāgam iva kurvāṇaṃ,

His pale body, with each individual bone
in his rib cage prominent,
and the white sacred thread falling from his shoulder,
looked like the heavenly Ganga's stream
rippled by the wind, lotus fibers bobbing up and down.
Between his moving fingers revolving
a *rudráksha* necklace made of pieces of bright crystal
like Sarásvati's necklace strung with big shining pearls,
he was like another Dhruva, the Pole-star,
round which the circle of stars unceasingly revolve.
He was covered all over by a bulging network of veins,
like an aged *kalpa* tree by a maze of full-grown creepers.
Seemingly made of pure moonbeams,
froth of nectar,
threads of the cloth of his virtues;
pure from being washed in the waters of the Mánasa lake,
was the silky bark garment that clad him
like a second coating of old age.
He was resplendent with a crystal pot beside him
mounted on the tripod of his triple staff,[67]
full of water from the heavenly Ganga, as if he were
a cluster of blooming white *pundaríka* lotuses
with a royal goose beside it.
He seemed to share his stability with mountains,
his depth with the oceans,
his luster with the sun,
his mildness with the cold-rayed moon,
his freedom from stain with the sky's expanse.

Vainateyam iva sva|prabhāv'|ôpātta|
dvij'|âdhipatyaṃ,
Kamalāsanam iv'
āśrama/guruṃ,
jarac|candana|tarum iva
bhujaṃga/nirmoka/dhavala/jaṭ"/ākulaṃ,
praśasta|vāraṇam iva
pralamba/karṇa/vālaṃ,
Bṛhaspatim iv'
ājanma/saṃvardhita/Kacaṃ,
divasam iv'
ôdyad/arka/bimba/bhāsvara/mukhaṃ,
śarat|kālam iva
kṣīṇa/varṣaṃ,
Śaṃtanum iva *priya/Satyavratam,*
Ambikā|kara|talam iva
Rudr'/âkṣa/valaya/grahaṇa/nipuṇaṃ,
śiśira|samaya|sūryam iva
kṛt'/ôttar'/āsaṅgaṃ,
vaḍav'|ânalam iva
satata/payo/bhakṣaṃ,
śūnya|nagaram iva
dīn'/â/nātha/vipanna/śaraṇaṃ,
Paśupatir iva

Just as Gáruda, Vínata's son, by his might
gained lordship over *birds*, so too he over *brahmins.*
Just as lotus-seated Brahma is *the guru of life stages,*
he was *the guru of the hermitage.*
Just as an old sandal tree *may have tangled roots*
white with snake sloughs,
his *burden of matted locks was snake slough white.*
Just as a thoroughbred elephant *has long ears and tail,*
he *had long tufts of hair from his ears.*
Just like Brihas·pati, guru of the gods,
who cherished his son Kacha from birth,
his hair had been allowed to grow from birth.
Just like the day, *with the disk of the rising sun*
as its shining face,
his face shone like the disk of the rising sun.
Just as *the rains are over* by the fall,
his years were expended.
Just like King Shántanu *holding dear his son Bhishma*
who was true to his vow, he *held dear the vow of truth.*
Just like the hands of Ámbika, mother of the universe,
clever at covering fierce Shiva's eyes,
he *was skilled in counting his rudráksha* beads.
Just as the sun in the cold season, *moves to the north,*
he *had his upper body covered by a shawl.*
Just like the submarine fire *continuously consuming*
the waters, he *always drank milk.*
Just like a deserted city, *with its miserable dwellings*
uncared for, dilapidated, he *was a refuge*
for the poor, the helpless, and the afflicted.
Just like Shiva, lord of beasts, *his body white with ashes,*

bhasma|pāṇḍur'|Ôm"|āśliṣṭa|śarīraṃ
bhagavantaṃ Jābālim apaśyam.
avalokya c' âham acintayam.
‹aho prabhāvas tapasām! iyam asya śānt" âpi mūrtir
uttapta|kanak'|âvadātā parisphurantī
saudāmin" îva cakṣuṣaḥ pratihanti tejāṃsi.
satatam udāsīn" âpi mahā|prabhāvatayā
bhayam iv' ôpajanayati pratham'|ôpagatasya.
śuṣka|nala|kāśa|kusuma|nipatit'|ânala|caṭula|vṛtti
nityam asahiṣṇu tapasvināṃ tanu|tapasām api
tejaḥ prakṛtyā bhavati,
kim uta sakala|bhuvana|tala|vandita|caraṇānām
an|avarata|tapaḥ|kṣapita|malānāṃ
kara|tal'|āmalaka|phalavad akhilaṃ jagad ālokayatāṃ
divyena cakṣuṣā bhagavatām
evaṃ|vidhānām agha|kṣaya|kāriṇām.
puṇyāni hi nāma|grahaṇāny api mahā|munīnām.
kiṃ punar darśanāni.
dhanyam idam āśrama|padam ayam adhipatir yatra.
athavā bhuvana|talam eva dhanyam akhilam
anen' âdhiṣṭhitam avani|tala|Kamalayoninā.
puṇya|bhājaḥ khalv amī munayaḥ
yad ahar|niśam enam aparam iva Nalināsanam
apagat'|ânya|vyāpārā mukh'|âvalokana|niścala|dṛṣṭayaḥ
puṇyāḥ kathāḥ śṛṇvantaḥ samupāsate.

and embraced by his wife Uma,
his body was covered with ash-white hair.
Such was the blessed Jabáli as I beheld him.
And beholding him,
I reflected on the wonderful power of ascetics.
'Although his bodily form is peaceful,
white as molten gold,
it flickers and dazzles the eyes like lightning.
Although it's always indifferent, by its great might
it seems to terrify whoever sees it for the first time.
Its action as fast as fire on dried up reeds,
kusha grass and flowers,
ascetics' luster is in its very nature unstoppable,
even when they have done only minor austerities.
How much more so are ascetics such as this blessed man
and their feet are honored all over the world,
destroying sin with their unremitting austerities,
surveying the whole world with their divine eye,
as if it were an *ámalaka* fruit in the palm of their hand,
and bringing about the destruction of peoples' sins.
Even uttering the names of great sages is meritorious,
how much more actually seeing them.
Fortunate is this hermitage, where this one is in charge.
Or rather the whole world is fortunate
that he lives in the world,
a lotus-born Brahma on earth.
Assuredly these ascetics
are enjoying merits earned in previous lives
in that day and night they attend upon him
who is like a second Brahma sitting on his lotus seat,

Sarasvaty api dhanyā y" âsya tu satatam

atiprasanne karuṇā/jala/nisyandiny

a/gādha/gāmbhīrye

rucira/dvija/parivārā

mukha/kamala/saṃparkam anubhavantī

nivasati haṃs" îva *Mānase.*

catur|mukha|kamala|vāsibhiś catur|vedaiḥ

sucirād iva

dvitīyam idam aparam ucitam āsāditaṃ sthānam.

enam āsādya śarat|kālam iva

Kali|kāla|jalada|samaya|kaluṣitāḥ prasādam upagatāḥ

punar api jagati sarita iva sarva|vidyāḥ.

niyatam iha sarv'|ātmanā kṛt'|âvasthitinā

bhagavatā paribhūta|Kali|kāla|vilasitena Dharmeṇa

na smaryate Kṛta|yugasya.

dharaṇi|talam anen' âdhiṣṭhitam avalokya

na vahati nūnam idānīṃ sapta'|rṣa|maṇḍala|

nivās'|âbhimānam ambara|talam.

aho mahā|sattv" êyam jarā y" âsya

pralaya|ravi|raśmi|nikara|dur|nirīkṣye

rajani|kara|kiraṇa|pāṇḍura|śiro|ruhe jaṭā|bhāre

having no other duties than to look upon his face
with fixed gaze and listen to his holy discourses.
Sarásvati, too, is fortunate, for
like a goose *surrounded by equally lovely birds*
and enjoying touching lotuses with its beak
on Lake Mánasa which is always very clear,
compassionately overflowing with water,
unfathomable in its depth,
she, *enjoying the touch of his lotus-like mouth,*
amid his gleaming teeth, dwells in his mind
which is always very calm,
pouring forth the water of compassion,
unfathomable in its profundity.
The four Vedas who dwell in Brahma's four lotus faces
have at long last found this place
as a suitable second home.
Coming to him all the sciences in the world, muddied
as they are by the rainy season that is the Kali age,
become clear, just like rivers in the fall.
There can be no doubt
that living here and completely himself,
holy Dharma has defeated the wantonness of the Kali age
and has no call to remember the perfect Krita eon.
Looking down and seeing this man living on the earth,
assuredly the sky can now take no pride
in being the residence of the circle of the Seven Sages.
How great and good this old age must be that doesn't fear
to fall on his matted locks as difficult to look upon
as the mass of rays from the sun
at the dissolution of the universe,

phena|puñja|dhavalā Gaṅg" êva
Paśupateḥ kṣīr'|āhutir iva śikhā|kalāpe
vibhāvasor nipatantī na bhītā.
bahal'|ājya|dhūma|paṭala|malinī|kṛt'|āśramasya bhagavataḥ
prabhāvād bhītam iva ravi|kiraṇa|jālam api
dūrataḥ pariharati tapo|vanam.
ete ca pavana|lola|puñjī|kṛta|śikhā|kalāpā
racit'|âñjalaya iv' âtra mantra|pūtāni havīṃṣi
pratigṛhṇanty etat|prīty" āśuśukṣaṇayaḥ,
taralita|dukūla|valkalo 'yaṃ c'
āśrama|latā|kusuma|surabhi|parimalo manda|saṃcārī
sa|śaṅka iv' âsya samīpam upasarpati gandha|vāhaḥ.
prāyo mahā|bhūtānām api
durabhibhavāni bhavanti tejāṃsi.
sarva|tejasvinām ayaṃ c' âgraṇīḥ.
dvi|sūryam iv' ābhāti jagad
anen' âdhiṣṭhitaṃ mah"|ātmanā.
niṣkamp" êva kṣitir etad|avaṣṭhambhāt.
eṣa pravāhaḥ karuṇā|rasasya,
saṃtaraṇa|setuḥ saṃsāra|sindhor,
ādhāraḥ kṣam"|âmbhasāṃ,
paraśus tṛṣṇā|latā|gahanasya,
sāgaraḥ saṃtoṣ'|âmṛtasy',

hair white as moonbeams falling like Ganga,
white with masses of foam,
on to the matted locks of Shiva the lord of beasts,
falling like an oblation of milk
into the flames of the sacrificial fire.
This blessed one has darkened his hermitage
with clouds of smoke from lots of ghee
and as if fearful of his might
the sun's rays keep far from his penance grove.
And, their flames whipped up by the wind,
these sacrificial fires seem to fold their hands
and thank him, feeling affection for him
as they receive the oblations his mantras have consecrated.
And the wind,
scented with the fragrance of the hermitage's creepers,
rippling his silk-soft bark garment,
moves gently in his presence as if in fear of him.
Generally speaking even the five elements find it difficult
to overcome great men's personal radiance,
and this man is foremost of all illustrious ascetics.
Inhabited by this great soul,
the world seems to have two suns.
The earth is motionless, it seems,
because of this man's support.
This man is a river of compassion,
a causeway for crossing the ocean of repeated rebirth,
reservoir of the waters of forgiveness,
axe for cutting down the thicket
of the creepers of thirsty desires,
ocean of the nectar of contentment,

ôpadeṣṭā siddhi|mārgasy',
âsta|girir *a|sad|grahasya,*
mūlam upaśama|taror,
nābhiḥ prajñā|cakrasya,
sthiti|vaṃśo dharma|dhvajasya,
tīrthaṃ sarva|vidy"|âvatārāṇāṃ,
vaḍav'|ânalo lobh'|ârṇavasya,
nikaṣ'|ôpalaḥ śāstra|ratnānāṃ,
dāv'|ânalo rāga|pallavasya,
mahā|mantraḥ krodha|bhujaṃgasya,
divasa|karo moh'|ândhakārasy',
P45 ârgalā|bandho naraka|dvārāṇāṃ,
kula|bhavanam ācārāṇām,
āyatanaṃ maṅgalānām,
a|bhūmir mada|vikārāṇāṃ,
darśakaḥ sat|pathānām, utpattiḥ sādhutāyā,
nemir utsāha|cakrasy',
āśrayaḥ sattvasya, pratipakṣaḥ Kali|kālasya,
kośas tapasaḥ, sakhā satyasya,
kṣetram ārjavasya,
prabhavaḥ puṇya|saṃcayasy',
â|datt'|âvakāśo matsarasy', ârātir vipatter,
a|sthānaṃ paribhūter, an|anukūlo 'bhimānasy',
â|saṃmato dainyasy', ân|āyatto roṣasy',
â|vaśo viṣayāṇām,
an|abhimukhaḥ sukhānām.

teacher of the path of perfection,
sunset mountain *for the evil planet*
that is erroneous ideas,
root of the tree of forbearance,
hub of the wheel of wisdom,
flagstaff for Dharma's banner,
sacred site where all sciences
come down to earth,
submarine fire burning up the ocean of greed,
touchstone for the jewels that are the *shastra*s,
forest fire to passion's foliage,
sovereign mantra against the snake of anger,
light-bringing sun to the darkness of delusion,
crossbeam for closing up the doors of hell, P45
hereditary home of good conduct,
temple of auspicious things.
He gives no ground for passion's agitations.
He points out the paths the good should take.
He's the origin of goodness.
He's the rim of the wheel of energetic action.
He's the abode of greatness. He is the foe of the Kali age.
He is the treasury of religious austerity.
He's the friend of truth.
He's the home-ground of straightforwardness.
He's the source of all meritorious deeds.
He confiscates jealousy. He is bad luck's enemy.
He offers no scope for insult. He's inimical to pride.
He's not fond of meanness. He's oblivious to anger.
He's not in thrall to sense objects.
He pays no attention to pleasures.

asya bhagavataḥ prasādād ev'
ôpaśānta|vairam apagata|matsaraṃ tapo|vanam.
aho prabhāvo mah"|ātmanām.
atra hi śāśvatikam apahāya virodham upaśānt'|ātmānas
tiryañco' pi tapo|vana|vasati|sukham anubhavanti.
tathā hi:
eṣa vikaco'|ôtpala|vana|racan"|ânukāriṇam
utpatac|cāru|candraka|śataṃ
hariṇa|locana|dyuti|śabalam abhinava|śādvalam iva
viśati śikhinaḥ kalāpam ātap'|āhato niḥśaṅkam ahiḥ.
ayam utsṛjya mātaram a|jāta|kesaraiḥ kesari|śiśubhiḥ sah'
ôpajāta|paricayaḥ prakṣarat|kṣīra|dhāram
āpibati kuraṃga|śāvakaḥ siṃhī|stanam.
eṣa mṛṇāla|kalāp'|āśaṅkibhiḥ
śaśi|kara|dhavalaṃ saṭā|bhāram
āmīlita|locano bahu manyate
dvirada|kalabhair ākṛṣyamāṇaṃ mṛga|patiḥ.
idam iha kapi|kulam apagata|cāpalam
upanayati muni|kumārakebhyaḥ snātebhyaḥ phalāni.
ete ca na nivārayanti mad'|ândhā api
gaṇḍa|sthalī|bhāñji mada|jala|pāna|niścalāni
madhu|kara|kulāni jāta|dayāḥ karṇa|tālaiḥ kariṇaḥ.
kiṃ bahunā?
tāpas'|âgni|hotra|dhūma|lekhābhir utsarpantībhir
aniśam upapādita|kṛṣṇ'|âjin'|ôttar'|āsaṅga|śobhāḥ

It's by the grace of this holy man that the penance grove
allays animosity and dispels envy.
Wondrous is the power of great souls, for here
abandoning their age-old antipathies,
the very animals have become calm
and enjoy the happiness of living in the penance grove.
Instances of this abound:
Oppressed by the heat this snake enters a peacock's tail—
that resembles in its arrangement
a bed of blooming *útpala* water-lilies,
flickering with hundreds of beautiful iridescent circles,
dappled with the luster of a deer's eye—
enters it as if it were fresh grass.
This young antelope has parted from his mother
and fraternizing with lions cubs
whose manes haven't yet grown,
he drinks at the lioness's teat,
the stream of milk flowing for him.
Mistaking this lion's thick mane, moonbeam white,
for a pile of lotus fibers, young elephants are pulling at it,
and he closes his eyes and enjoys it.
Here this troop of monkeys has lost its natural fickleness
and is bringing fruits to the ascetics' young sons
who've been bathing.
And these elephants, though blind with rut,
feeling compassionate,
don't flap their ears to drive away the swarms of bees
clinging to their cheeks, comatose after drinking their rut.
What need to say more?
The lines of smoke

phala|mūla|bhṛto valkalino niścetanās taravo 'pi

sa|niyamā iva lakṣyante 'sya bhagavataḥ.

kiṃ punaḥ sa|cetanāḥ prāṇinaḥ.›

evaṃ cintayantam eva māṃ tasyām ev' âśoka|taror adhaś

chāyāyām eka|deśe sthāpayitvā

Hārītaḥ pādāv upagṛhya kṛt'|âbhivādanaḥ

pitur an|atisamīpa|vartini kuś'|āsane samupāviśat.

ālokya tu māṃ te sarva eva munayaḥ

‹kuto 'yam āsāditaḥ śuka|śiśur?› iti tam āsīnam apṛcchan.

asau tu tān abravīt:

‹ayaṃ mayā snātum ito gatena kamalinī|saras|tīra|

taru|nīḍa|patitaḥ śuka|śiśur ātapa|janita|klāntir

uttapta|pāṃsu|paṭala|madhya|gato

dūra|nipatana|vihvala|tanur alp'|âvaśeṣ'|āyur āsāditaḥ.

tapasvi|durārohatayā ca tasya vanaspater na śakyate

sva|nīḍam āropayitum iti jāta|dayen' ānītaḥ.

from the ascetics' sacrificial fires, rising up,
constantly give the trees
the look of wearing black antelope skins
as their upper garments.
And the trees, unconscious beings though they are,
source of fruits and roots,
like him, *subsisting on fruits and roots*, clad in bark,
seem to share the characteristics of this blessed man
and to observe religious vows.
How much more so conscious beings.
While I was thus reflecting,
Haríta put me down on the ground
in the shade of that *ashóka* tree,
and after touching his father's feet
and respectfully greeting him,
he sat down on a mat of *kusha* grass not too far away.
Seeing me, as soon as he'd sat down,
all the sages asked him where he'd got this young parrot.
He for his part replied to them,
'I found this young parrot when I'd gone off for my bath.
He'd fallen from his nest in the tree on the bank
of the lotus lake, and was worn out by the heat of the sun.
Lying amid a pile of burning hot dust,
his body exhausted after the long fall,
there was little life left in him.
Since no ascetic can climb that tree,
I couldn't put him back in his nest.
So I took pity on him and brought him back.

tad yāvad ayam a|prarūḍha|pakṣatir
a|kṣamo 'ntarīkṣam utpatituṃ
tāvad atr' âiva kasmiṃś cid āśrama|taru|koṭare
muni|kumārakair asmābhiś c' ôpanītena
nīvāra|kaṇa|nikareṇa phala|rasena ca saṃvardhyamāno
dhārayatu jīvitam.
a|nātha|paripālanaṃ hi dharmo 'smad|vidhānām.
udbhinna|pakṣatis tu gagana|tala|saṃcaraṇa|samartho
yāsyati yatr' âsmai rociṣyate.
ih' âiva v" ôpajāta|paricayaḥ sthāsyati.›
ity evam|ādikam asmat|saṃbaddham ālāpam ākarṇya
kiṃcid|upajāta|kutūhalo bhagavāñ Jābālir
īṣad|āvalita|kaṃdharaḥ puṇya|jalaiḥ prakṣālayann iva
mām atipraśāntayā dṛṣṭyā dṛṣṭvā suciram
upajāta|pratyabhijñāna iva punaḥ punar vilokya
‹svasy' âiv' â|vinayasya phalam anen' ânubhūyata,›
ity avocat.
sa hi bhagavān kāla|traya|darśī tapaḥ|prabhāvād
divyena cakṣuṣā sarvam eva kara|tala|gatam iva
jagad avalokayati.
vetti janm'|ântarāṇy atītāni,
kathayaty āgāminam apy artham,
īkṣaṇa|gocara|gatānāṃ ca
prāṇināṃ āyuṣaḥ pramāṇam āvedayati.
yataḥ sarv" âiva tāpasa|pariṣac chrutvā vidita|tat|prabhāvā
kīdṛśo 'nen' âvinayaḥ kṛtaḥ kim arthaṃ vā kṛtaḥ kva vā
kṛto janm'|ântare vā ko 'yam āsīd iti kautūhiny
abhavat. upanāthitavatī ca taṃ bhagavantam.
‹āvedaya prasīda, bhagavan,

While his wings haven't sprouted
and he can't fly up into the sky
let him stay here, in the hollow of some hermitage tree.
The ascetic boys and I will bring him handfuls
of wild rice and fruit juice, and get his strength back.
Protecting those who have no protector
is the duty of people like us.
And when his wings have grown and he can fly in the sky,
he can go where he pleases.
Or stay here, if he becomes attached to us.'
Hearing this conversation about me,
the divine Jabáli became a little curious, and
bending his neck a bit, as if washing me with holy water
he looked at me for a long while
with his exceedingly calm gaze.
He seemed to recognize me, looked harder, and said,
'He is receiving the fruit of his own misbehavior.'
For that blessed man by the power of his austerities
sees past, present and future, and with his divine eye
sees the whole world as if it were in the palm of his hand.
When living creatures are within range of his sight,
he knows all their former births,
he can foretell their future,
he can predict the length of their life.
The whole assembly of ascetics hearing this
and, well knowing his powers, were curious to know
what I'd done wrong, and why, and where,
and who I was in my previous birth.
And they entreated the blessed one,
'Tell us, please, O blessed one,

kīdṛśasy' â|vinayasya phalam
anen' ânubhūyate.
kaś c' âyam āsīj janm'|ântare?
vihaga|jātau katham asya saṃbhavaḥ?
kim abhidhāno v" âyam?
apanayatu naḥ kutūhalam.
āścaryāṇāṃ hi sarveṣāṃ bhagavān prabhavaḥ.›
ity evam upayācyamānas tu tapo|dhana|pariṣadā
sa mahā|muniḥ pratyavadat:
‹atimahad idam āścaryam ākhyātavyam.
alpa|śeṣam ahaḥ. pratyāsīdati ca naḥ snāna|samayaḥ.
bhavatām apy atikrāmati dev'|ârcana|vidhi|velā.
tad uttiṣhantu bhavantaḥ sarva eva
tāvad ācarantu yath"|ôcitaṃ divasa|vyāpāram.
apar'|âhṇa|samaye bhavatāṃ punaḥ kṛta|mūla|phal'|
âśanānāṃ viśrabdh'|ôpaviṣṭānām
āditaḥ prabhṛti sarvam āvedayiṣyāmi:
yo' yam, yac c' ânena kṛtam
aparasmiñ janmani, iha loke yath" âsya saṃbhūtiḥ.
ayaṃ ca tāvad apagata|klamaḥ kriyatām āhāreṇa.
niyatam ayam apy ātmano janm'|ântar'|ôdantaṃ
svapn'|ôpalabdham iva mayi kathayati
sarvam aśeṣataḥ smariṣyati.›
ity abhidadhad ev' ôtthāya saha munibhiḥ
snān'|ādikam ucitaṃ divasa|vyāpāram akarot.

what was the misbehavior
he's experiencing the fruit of?
And who was this parrot in his previous life?
How did he come to be born as a bird?
And what's his name?
You must satisfy our curiosity, for you are blessed
and capable of all miracles.'
Thus solicited by the assembly of ascetics,
the great sage replied,
'This is a very long story that I have to tell you.
Little of the day is left. The time for my bath is nigh,
and the time for your rites of divine worship is passing.
Therefore you should get up, everyone of you,
and first finish your daily routine, as is fitting.
In the evening, when you've eaten your roots and fruits
and are again sitting comfortably,
I will tell you everything from the beginning:
who he is, what he did in his former birth,
and how he came to be born in this world.
And in the meantime his fatigue
should be allayed by feeding him.
Assuredly, when I'm telling the story
of what happened in his previous life
he will remember everything completely,
as if he were living it in a dream.'
So pronouncing, he got up and with the other sages
performed his usual daily routine,
beginning with his bath.

anena ca samayena pariṇato divasaḥ.
snān'|ôtthitena muni|janen' ârgha|vidhim upapādayatā
yaḥ kṣiti|tale dattas tam ambara|tala|gataḥ
sākṣād iva rakta|candan'|âṅga|rāgaṃ ravir udavahat.
ūrdhva|mukhair arka|bimba|vinihita|dṛṣṭibhir
uṣmapais tapo|dhanair iva paripīyamāna|tejaḥ|prasaro
viral'|ātapo divasas tanimānam abhajat.
udyat|sapta|ṛṣi|sârtha|sparśa|parijihīrṣay" êva
saṃhṛta|*pādaḥ* pārāvata|caraṇa|pāṭala|rāgo
ravir ambara|talād alambata. ā|lohit'|āṃśu|jālaṃ
jala|śayana|gatasya Madhubhido vigalan|madhu|
dhāram iva nābhi|nalinaṃ pratimā|gatam apar'|ârṇave
sūrya|maṇḍalam alakṣyata. vihāya dharaṇi|talam
unmucya kamalinī|vanāni śakunaya iva divas'|âvasāne
tapo|vana|taru|śikhareṣu parvat'|âgreṣu ca
ravi|kiraṇāḥ sthitim akurvata. ālagna|rakt'|ātapa|cchedā
munibhir ālambit'|ālohita|valkalā iv' āśrama|taravaḥ
kṣaṇam aśobhanta.

astam upagate ca bhagavati
sahasra|dīdhitāv apar'|ârṇava|talād ullasantī
vidruma|lat" êva pāṭalā saṃdhyā samadṛśyata.

And by this time the day was drawing to a close.
Coming back from their baths, the sages performed
their usual rite of worship of the sun,
and the red sandal paste they put on the ground
the sun seemed actually to bear
on his own body in the sky.
While the ascetics lifted up their faces
and gazed at the disk of the sun,
as if they whose wealth was their ascetic heat,
were the Heat-drinking Ancestors
drinking up the diffusion of the day's radiance,
the day had little light left and shrank away.
As if wishing to avoid touching
the group of the Seven Sages who were rising up,
drawing in *its feet*, that is to say, *its rays,*
red as pigeon's feet, the sun fell from the sky.
Its network of rays reddened, the sun seemed to be
a reflection in the western ocean of Vishnu's navel lotus,
a reddish honey dripping from it,
as he, the slayer of Madhu, reclines on his watery couch.
Abandoning the ground, relinquishing the lotus groves,
at the end of the day, as birds do, the sun's rays
settled on the hermitage treetops and on the hilltops.
Patches of red sunshine clinging to the hermitage trees,
it seemed for a moment that the ascetics
had hung red bark garments on them.
And when the blessed thousand-rayed sun had set,
from the western ocean, gleaming like a creeper of coral,
pink twilight appeared.

yasyām ābadhyamāna|dhyānam eka|deśa|duhyamāna|
homa|dhenu|dugdha|dhārā|dhvanita|dhanyatar'|
âtimanoharam agni|hotra|vedī|vikīryamāṇa|harit|kuśam
ṛṣi|kumārikābhir itas tato vikṣipyamāṇa|
dig|devat"|āvali|siktham āśrama|padam abhavat.
kv' âpi vihṛtya divas'|âvasāne *lohita|tārakā*
tapo|vana|dhenur iva *kapilā* parivartamānā
saṃdhyā munibhir adṛśyata.
a|cira|proṣite savitari śoka|vidhurā kamala|mukula|
kamaṇḍalu|dhāriṇī haṃsa|sita|dukūla|paridhānā
mṛṇāpa|dhavala|yajñ'|ôpavītā
madhu|kara|maṇḍal'|âkṣa|valayam udvahantī
kamalinī dina|pati|samāgama|vratam iv' âcarat.
apara|sāgar'|âmbhasi patite dina|kare
patana|veg'|ôtthitam ambhaḥ|śīkara|nikaram iva
tārā|gaṇam ambaram adhārayat.
acirāc ca siddha|kanyakā|vikṣipta|saṃdhy"|ârcana|
kusuma|śabalam iva tārakitaṃ viyad arājata.
kṣaṇena c' ônmukhena muni|janen'

During the twilight, meditation was performed
in the hermitage which was delightful
with the very auspicious sound of streams of milk
from the oblation-cows being milked in one part of it,
and green *kusha* grass
was being scattered on the fire-offering altars,
and the ascetics' daughters were scattering
here and there boiled rice offerings
for the guardian deities of the directions.
Like a *tawny* hermitage cow *with red eyes*
coming back at the end of the day
after wandering off somewhere
was how the *tawny* twilight
that was reddening the stars looked to the sages.
The sun recently departed, the day-lotus bed,
overwhelmed with grief,
holding a pitcher in the form of a lotus bud,
wearing silk in the form of a white goose,
a white sacred thread of lotus fiber,
and a rosary of a ring of bees,
seemed to be carrying out a vow
to rejoin her husband the sun, lord of the day.
When the sun had fallen into the waters
of the western ocean the sky was filled
with the host of stars
as if with spray sent up by the velocity of its fall.
And it wasn't long before the heaven's expanse
was spangled with stars,
as if littered with the flowers of evening worship
strewn by the daughters of the siddhas.

ōrdhva|viprakīrṇaiḥ praṇām'|âñjali|salilaiḥ kṣālyamāna iv'

âgalad akhilaḥ saṃdhyā|rāgaḥ.

kṣayam upāgatāyāṃ saṃdhyāyāṃ tad|vināśa|duḥkhitā

kṛṣṇ'|âjinam iva vibhāvarī timir'|ôdgamam

abhinavam avahat.

apahāya muni|jana|hṛdayāni sarvam anyad

andhakāratāṃ timiram anayat.

krameṇa ca ‹ravir astam upāgata› ity

udantam upalabhya *jāta/vairāgyo*

dhauta/dukūla/valkala/dhaval'/âmbaraḥ

sa|tār'|ântaḥpuraḥ

paryanta|sthita|tanu|timira|tamāla|vana|lekhaṃ

Saptarṣi|maṇḍal'|âdhyuṣitam

Arundhatī/saṃcaraṇa/pavitram

upahit'/Āṣāḍham

ālakṣyamāṇa/Mūlam

ek'|ânta|sthita|*cāru/tāraka/Mṛgam*

amara|lok'|āśramam iva gagana|talam

amṛta|dīdhitir adhyatiṣṭhat.

And in a moment, the whole glow of twilight
flowed away, as if washed off by the water
from joined hands of obeisance
thrown high by the sages looking upwards.
When the twilight had disappeared, the night
underwent a new of augmentation of darkness,
as if, saddened by twilight's demise,
it had donned a black antelope skin.
Except for the sages' hearts,
the darkness made everything pitch black. And
in due course, receiving the news that the sun had set,
making the sky as white as birchbark or freshly washed silk,
in the midst of his harem, the stars,
the nectar-rayed moon occupied the sky
becoming pale : renouncing passion,
putting on a white garment of birchbark
which was like freshly washed silk,
as though occupying the hermitage of the celestials,
for the sky was bordered by a thin line of darkness
that might have been a line of *tamála* groves;
the circle of the Seven Sages, the Pleiades,
made it their home;
it was purified by the movements of the Arúndhati star,
seventh member of the Pleiades:
it was purified by the presence of Arúndhati;
it displayed the Ashádha constellation:
it was furnished with ascetics' staffs of palásha wood;
the Mula constellation was visible:
edible roots were to be seen;
and in one part of the sky

candr'/ābharaṇa/bhṛtas

tārakā|kapāla|śakal'|âlaṃkṛtād ambara|talāt

Tryambak'|ôttam'|âṅgād iva Gaṅgā sāgarān āpūrayantī

haṃsa|dhavalā dharaṇyām apataj jyotsnā.

hima|kara|sarasi vikaca|puṇḍarīka|site

candrikā|jala|pāna|lobhād avatīrṇo

niścala|mūrtir amṛta|paṅka|lagna iv' âdṛśyata hariṇaḥ.

timira|jala|dhara|samay'|âpagaman'|ânantaram

abhinava|sita|sinduvāra|kusuma|pāṇḍurair arṇav'|āgatair

agāhyanta haṃsair iva kumuda|sarāṃsi candra|pādaiḥ.

vigalita|sakal'|ôdaya|rāgaṃ rajani|kara|bimbam

ambar'|āpag"|âvagāha|dhauta|sindūram

Airāvata|kumbha|sthalam iva tat|kṣaṇam alakṣyata.

śanaiḥ śanaiś ca dūr'|ôdite bhagavati hima|tati|sruti,

sudhā|dhūli|paṭalen' êva dhavalī|kṛte candr'|ātapena jagaty,

avaśyāya|jala|bindu|patana|manda|gatiṣu

vighaṭamāna|kumuda|vana|kaṣāya|parimaleṣu

was the lovely Mriga constellation:
were lovely-eyed deer.
On to the earth, like Ganga falling
from Tryámbaka Shiva's head
that wears the moon as ornament, and filling the oceans,
the moonlight, white as a goose, fell
from the sky *that was ornamented with the moon,*
and was adorned with the stars
in place of the skulls that Shiva wears.
The moon's deer could be seen. Motionless,
it seemed to have come down into the lake
that was the cold-rayed moon,
white as blooming *pundaríka* water-lilies,
thirsting for the water of moonlight
and got stuck in the sludge of nectar.
Moonbeams, pale as fresh white *sinduvára* flowers,
alighted on the pools of white *kúmuda* lotuses,
like geese coming to the ocean,
once the rainy season that was the darkness had ended.
All the redness from its rising drained away,
the disc of the moon
looked for the moment like the forehead globe
of Indra's elephant, Airávata,
with its vermilion washed away
by plunging into the heavenly Ganga.
And when the one who sends out a stream of cold
was at long last far risen in the sky,
and the world was whitened by the moonlight
as if by a mass of plaster powder,
when the evening breezes were blowing,

samupoḍha|nidrā|bhar'|âlasa|tārakair
anyonya|grathita|pakṣma|puṭair
ārabdha|romantha|manthara|mukhaiḥ
sukh'|āsinair āśrama|mṛgair
abhinandit'|āgamaneṣu
pravahatsu niśā|mukha|samīreṣv
ardha|yāma|mātr'|âvakhaṇḍitāyāṃ vibhāvaryāṃ,
Hārītaḥ kṛt'|āhāraṃ mām ādāya
sarvais taiḥ saha munibhir upasṛtya
candr'|ātap'|ôdbhāsini tapo|van'|âika|deśe
vetr'|āsan'|ôpaviṣṭam anatidūra|vartinā
Jālapāda|nāmnā śiṣyeṇa
darbha|dhavitra|pāṇinā[68] mandam upavījyamānaṃ
pitaram avocat.
‹he tāta, sakale 'yam āścarya|śravaṇa|kutūhal'|ākalita|hṛdayā
samupasthitā tāpasa|pariṣad ābaddha|maṇḍalā pratīkṣate.
vyapanīta|śramaś ca kṛto 'yaṃ patatri|potaḥ.
tad āvedyatāṃ yad anena kṛtam aparasmiñ janmani.
ko 'yam abhūd bhaviṣyati ca?›
ity evam uktas tu sa mahā|munir
agrataḥ sthitaṃ mām avalokya tāṃś ca sarvān ek'|âgrāñ
chravaṇa|parān munīn buddhvā śanaiḥ śanair abravīt.
‹śrūyatāṃ yadi kutūhalam:

moving slowly because they were dropping dew,
fragrant with the scent
of the opening *kúmuda* water-lily groves,
their coming welcomed by the deer of the hermitage,
eyeballs lazy with the coming burden of sleep,
their eyelashes sticking together,
their mouths slowly ruminating, lying comfortably;
when the night had shortened
by a half watch of three hours,
and I'd finished my meal, Haríta took me and
in company with all those sages he approached his father.
His father was sitting in a cane chair
in a part of the hermitage illumined by moonlight,
slowly fanned by a pupil of his named Jala·pada
holding a fan made of *darbha* grass
in his hand, not very far from him.
Haríta said to his father,
'If you please, father, the assembly of ascetics
has gathered together in a circle,
their hearts filled with curiosity
to hear the wonderful tale; they are waiting.
And this young parrot's had his fatigue removed.
So, please inform us what he did in his former life.
Who was he, and who will he be?'
For his part that great sage, thus addressed,
looked at me standing in front of him
and knowing he had the undivided attention
of all those ascetics, spoke very slowly.
'If you are curious, then listen:

P50 asti sakala|tribhuvana|lalāma|bhūtā

prasava|bhūmir iva Kṛta|yugasy'

ātma|nivās'|ôcitā bhagavatā Mahākāl'|âbhidhānena

bhuvana|traya|sarga|sthiti|saṃhāra|kāriṇā

pramatha|nāthen' âpar" êva pṛthivī samutpāditā,

dvitīya|pṛthivī|śaṅkayā ca jala|nidhin" êva

rasā|tala|gambhīreṇa jala|parikhā|valayena parivṛtā,

Paśupati|nivāsa|prītyā

gagana|parisar'|ôllekhi|śikhara|mālena Kailāsa|giriṇ" êva

sudhā|sitena prākāra|maṇḍalena parigatā,

prakaṭa|śaṅkha|śukti|muktā|pravāla|marakata|maṇi|

rāśibhiś cāmī|kara|cūrṇa|vālukā|nikara|nicitair āyāmibhir

Agastya|paripīta|salilaiḥ sāgarair iva mahā|vipaṇi|pathair

upaśobhitā,

sur'|âsura|siddha|gandharva|vidyādhar'|ôrag'|âdhyāsitābhiś

citra|śālābhir a|virat'|ôtsava|pramad"|âvalokana|kutūhalād

ambara|tal'|âvatīrṇābhir divya|vimāna|paṅktibhir iv'

âlaṃkṛtā,

There is a city which is the ornament P50
of all the three worlds.
It's like the birthplace of the Krita·yuga, the perfect age.
It's like a second earth
produced as a suitable residence for himself
by the blessed one called Maha·kala, Shiva as time,
creator, preserver and destroyer of the three worlds,
lord of the *prámatha*s, the tormentors.
And it's surrounded by a moat
as deep as the subterranean world,
as if by the ocean mistaking it for a second earth.
It's encompassed by a circular rampart white with plaster
as if it were the Kailása mountain surrounding it
with its garlands of peaks
that scratch the surface of the sky out of affection for it
as a dwelling place of Shiva, the lord of beasts.
It's beautified with great long market streets
like the oceans when their water
had been drunk up by Agástya,
displaying piles of conches, mother-of-pearl,
pearls, coral, and emerald gems,
having mounds of gold in dust and in nuggets.
It's adorned with picture galleries
where the gods, demons, siddhas,
*gandhárva*s, *vidya·dhara*s, and snakes are present,
as if they'd descended from the sky
in lines of celestial chariots out of curiosity
to see the city's women in their unabating festival.

mathan'|ôddhata|dugdha|dhavalita|Mandara|dyutibhiḥ

kanaka|may'|âmala|kalaśa|śikharair

anila|dolāyita|sita|dhvajair

upari|patad|abhra|Gaṅgair iva Tuṣāragiri|śikharair

amara|mandirair virājita|śṛṅgāṭakā,

sudhā|vedik"|ôpaśobhit'|ôda|pānair

an|avarata|calita|jala|ghaṭī|yantra|

sicyamāna|harit'|ôpavan'|ândhakāraiḥ

ketakī|dhūli|dhūsarair upaśalyakair

upaśobhitā,

mada|mukhara|madhu|kara|paṭal'|ândhakārita|niṣkuṭā,

sphurad|upavana|latā|kusuma|parimala|surabhi|samīraṇā,

raṇita|saubhāgya|ghaṇṭair,

ālohit'|âṃśuka|patākair,

ābaddha|rakta|cāmarair,

vidruma|mayaiḥ,

pratibhavanam ucchritair makar'|âṅkair

madana|yaṣṭi|ketubhiḥ

prakāśita|Makaradhvaja|pūjā

Its crossroads are resplendent with temples
shining like the Mándara mountain whitened
with the milk tossed up during the churning of the ocean,
their spires topped with shining pots made of gold,
their white flags swinging in the wind,
resembling the peaks of the Himálaya mountain
upon which the celestial Ganga falls from above.
Their wells adorned with white plastered benches,
the darkness of their green groves
irrigated by constantly turning water wheels,
and gray with the pollen of *kétaki* flowers,
the surrounding areas of open ground
adorn it.
Its pleasure gardens are darkened
by swarms of bees noisy with intoxication.
It has breezes fragrant with the scent of the flowers
on the quivering creepers of its groves.
Auspicious bells tinkling on them,
with reddish silk banners,
red chowries tied to them,
studded with coral,
marked with the *mákara,*
raised high on every house
there flagstaff-signals
of thorn-apple wood
announce the worship
of *mákara*-bannered Love.

satata|pravṛtt'|âdhyayana|dhvani|dhauta|kalmaṣā,

stimita|muraja|rava|gambhīra|garjiteṣu

salila|śīkar'|āsāra|stabaka|racita|durdineṣu

paryasta|ravi|kiraṇa|racita|sura|cāpa|cāruṣu

dhārā|gṛheṣu matta|mayūrair

maṇḍalī|kṛta|śikhaṇḍais tāṇḍava|vyasanibhir

ābadhyamāna|kekā|kolāhalā,

vikaca/kuvalaya/kāntair

utphulla/kamala/dhaval'/ôdarair

a/nimiṣa/darśana/ramaṇīyair

Ākhaṇḍala|locanair iva sahasra|saṃkhyair

udbhāsitā sarobhir,

a|virala|kadalī|vana|kalitābhir

amṛta|phena|puñja|pāṇḍurābhir

diśi diśi danta|valabhikābhir dhavalī|kṛtā,

yauvana|mada|matta|Mālavī|kuca|kalaśa|lulita|salilayā

bhagavato Mahākālasya śirasi sura|saritam avalokya

samupajāt'|ērṣyay" êva

satata|samābaddha|taraṃga|bhru|kuṭi|lekhayā

kham iva kṣālayantyā Sipravā parikṣiptā,

In that city sins are washed away
by the sound of constant recitations of the Vedas.
In its rain houses, where the deep roaring of the water
silences the sound of drums,
where downpours are effected by clusters of spray jets,
which are beautiful when rainbows are formed
by the sun's rays passing through,
the intoxicated peacocks make a commotion
with their keka cries,
forming their tails into circles,
ardently engaged in dancing.
It shines with its thousands of ponds
lovely with their blooming kúvalaya water-lilies,
resembling Indra's thousand eyes
as lovely as blooming kúvalaya lotuses,
their interiors white with blooming kámala lotuses:
the whites of his eyes like blooming kámala lotuses,
delightful with fish visible in them:
delightful with their unblinking gaze.
In every direction it's whitened by its ivory terraces
as white as lumps of nectar foam,
and surrounded by dense groves of plantain trees.
Waters agitated by the pot-like breasts
of Malwa women drunk in the pride of their youth;
as if jealous at seeing Ganga, the river of the gods,
on the head of blessed Maha·kala,
constantly making the lines of frowns
that are its waves,
seeming to wash the sky,
the river Sipra encircles it.

sakala|bhuvana|khyāta|yaśasā,

Hara|jaṭā|candreṇ' êva

koṭi/sāreṇa,

Maināken' êv'

â/vidita/pakṣa/pātena.

Mandākinī|pravāheṇ' êva

prakaṭita/kanaka/padma/rāśinā,

smṛti|śāstreṇ' êva

sabh"|āvasatha|kūpa|prap"|ārāma|

sura|sadana|setu|yantra|*pravartakena,*

Mandareṇ' êv'

ôddhṛta/samasta/sāgara/ratna/sāreṇa,

saṃgṛhīta/gāruḍen' âpi

bhujaṃga/bhīruṇā,

khal'/ôpajīvin" âpi

praṇayi|jan'|ôpajīvyamāna|vibhavena,

vīreṇ' âpi vinayavatā,

priyaṃvaden' âpi satya|vādin",

The inhabitants of the city have their fame
celebrated through the whole world.
Like the moon in the matted locks of Shiva the destroyer,
which has prominently pointed ends,
they *were millionaires.*
Like the Maináka mountain,
who didn't have to experience
the cutting off of his wings, they *didn't know partiality.*
Like the stream of the heavenly Ganga,
which displays heaps of golden lotuses,
they *display heaps of gold and rubies.*
Like the law codes *which enjoin* the building
of assembly halls, stopping places for travelers,
wells, watering places for travelers,
parks, temples, bridges, and water wheels,
those constructions they *carry out.*
Like the Mándara mountain, *which brought out*
all the choice jewels in the ocean,
they *wear all the choice jewels from the ocean.*
Though they *have the antidote to poison,*
yet *they seem to be afraid of snakes,*
when in fact *they have emeralds* and *are afraid of rogues.*
Far from *employing scoundrels*, they *live on*
what they get from their threshing floor
and their wealth supports all who seek their help.
Though they're bold, they are well behaved.
Though they say what is pleasing,
they speak the truth.

âbhirūpeṇ' âpi sva|dāra|saṃtuṣṭen',

âtithi|jan'|âbhyāgam'|ârthin" âpi

para|prārthan'|ân|abhijñena,

kām'|ârtha|pareṇ' âpi

dharma|pradhānena,

mahā|sattven' âpi

para|loka|bhīruṇā,

sakala|vijñāna|viśeṣa|vidā,

vadānyena, dakṣeṇa, smita|pūrv'|âbhibhāṣiṇā,

parihāsa|peśalen', ôjjvala|veṣeṇa,

śikṣit'|âśeṣa|deśa|bhāṣeṇa, vakr'|ôkti|nipuṇen',

ākhyāyik"|ākhyāna|paricaya|catureṇa,

sarva|lipi|jñena,

Mahābhārata|purāṇa|Rāmāyaṇ'|ânurāgiṇā,

Bṛhatkathā|kuśalena,

dyūt'|ādi|kalā|kalāpa|pārageṇa,

śruta|rāgiṇā,[69]

subhāṣita|vyasaninā praśāntena,

surabhi|māsa|māruten'

êva *satata|dakṣiṇena,*

Though they're handsome
they are content with their own wives.
Though they ask people to visit them as their guests,
they're unacquainted with requests to others.
Though they're intent on love and wealth,
duty is the main thing.
Though they're very brave, they *fear other people,*
but actually *it's only the next world they fear.*
They have a detailed understanding
of all forms of knowledge.
They are generous, skilled in social intercourse,
smiling when they speak, knowing when to make a joke,
fashionably dressed,
and they've learned the languages of all countries.
Adept at witty repartee,
resourceful from their perusal of story literature,
knowing every alphabet,
passionate about the "Maha·bhárata,"
the *purána*s, and the "Ramáyana,"
knowing their way about the "Long Story;"
they've mastered gambling and other such arts,
they're passionate about revealed scripture,
they're addicted to elegant pithy verse.
They're self-controlled.
Like the wind of spring, the fragrant month
which *always blows from the south,*
they are *invariably courteous.*

Himagiri|kānanen' êv' *ântaḥ/saralena,*

Lakṣmaṇen' êva *Rām'/ārādhana/nipuṇena,*

Śatrughnen' êv' *āviṣkṛta/Bharata/paricayena,*

divasen' êva

mitr'/ânuvartinā,

Bauddhen' êva

sarv'/âsti/vāda/śūreṇa,

Sāṃkhy'|āgamen' êva

pradhāna/puruṣ'/ôpetena,

Jina|dharmeṇ' êva

jīv'|ânukampinā

vilāsi|janen' âdhiṣṭhitā;

sa|śail" êva prāsādaiḥ,

sa|śākhā|nagar" êva mahā|bhavanaiḥ,

sa|kalpa|vṛkṣ" êva sat|puruṣair,

darśita|viśva|rūp" êva citra|bhittibhiḥ,

Like the forest on the Himálaya, *full of pine trees,*
they're *honest-hearted.*
Just as Lákshmana was *adept in attending upon Rama,*
they're *adept at winning over ladies.*
Just as Shatrúghna *showed his affection*
for his brother Bhárata,
they *demonstrated their familiarity with dramaturgy.*
Just as the day *follows the sun, friend of all,*
they *follow their friends' advice.*
Like the Buddhist doctrine,
which boldly asserts everything exists,
they're *brave enough to say "Yes" to every supplicant.*
Like the Sankhya tradition,
which is provided with underlying mother nature
and the male consciousness,
they're amply provided with distinguished men.
Like the religion of the Jina, Jainism,
they have compassion for all living beings.
Such are the pleasure-loving people
who dwell in that city.
With its palaces it's like a mountain with its foothills.
With its grand houses, each a suburb in itself,
the city seems to be branching out.
With its good and generous men
it seems a city of wish-fulfilling *kalpa* trees.
With its wall paintings
it seems to be putting the universe on display.

saṃdhy" êva *padma/rāg'/ânurāgiṇy,*

Amarādhipa|mūrtir iva makha|śat'|ânala|dhūma|pūtā,

Paśupati|lāsya|krīḍ" êva *sudhā/dhaval'/âṭṭa/hāsā,*

vṛddh" êva

jāta/rūpa/kṣayā,

Garuḍa|mūrtir iv'

Âcyuta/sthiti/ramaṇīyā,

prabhāta|vel" êva

prabuddha/sarva/lokā,

śabara|vasatir iv'

âvalambita/cāmara/nāga/danta/dhavala/gṛhā,

Śeṣa|tanur iva

sad" āsanna/vasudhā/dharā

jaladhi|mathana|vel" êva

mahā|ghoṣa|pūrita|dig|antarā,

Like *ruby-colored* twilight,
it shines *with the color of its own rubies.*
Like the body of Indra, lord of the gods,
it's hallowed by the smoke
from the fires of a hundred sacrifices.
Like the gentle lascivious form
of the dance of Shiva, lord of beasts,
when he is playful, and *laughs loudly*
and flashes his teeth white as nectar,
the city *laughs a loud white laugh*
with its plastered buildings.
It might seem like an aging woman
whose beauty is withering away
but in reality *it's the abode of gold.*
We could say it's like Gáruda's body, *lovely*
because it's the seat of Vishnu the unfallen,
since *it's lovely on account of no lapses*
from good conduct on the part of its citizens.
Like the hour of sunrise *which awakens all the world,*
everybody in the city is enlightened.
Like a settlement of wild foresters,
where the dwellings are white
with elephants' tusks and yaks' tails hanging down,
the city's *houses are white with ivory*
and suspended chowries.
Like the body of the serpent Shesha
always close to the earth it supports,
it *is always excellently and freshly plastered.*
Like the time of churning the ocean to produce nectar,
the city fills the world to the horizon with its great din.

prastut'|âbhiṣeka|bhūmir iva

saṃnihita|kanaka|ghaṭa|sahasrā,

Gaur" îva

mahā/siṃh'/āsan'/ôcita/mūrtir,

Aditir iva

deva/kula/sahasra/sevyā,

mahā|varāha|līl" êva

darśita/Hiraṇyākṣa/pātā,

Kadrūr iv'

ānandita/bhujaṃga/lokā,

Harivaṃśa|kath" êv'

âneka/bāla/krīḍā/ramaṇīyā,

prakaṭ'/âṅgan'/ôpabhog"

âpy

a|khaṇḍita|caritrā,

Like the place where a royal consecration is prepared,
golden pots by the thousand are collected there.
Like Gauri, Shiva's wife who is also Durga
and *who is represented as riding on a great lion,*
its *form befits the great lion-throne*
of the monarch who rules there.
Like Áditi the boundless, mother of the gods, *whom*
the multitude of the gods in their thousands venerate,
the city *is worthy of visiting*
on account of its thousands of temples.
Like Vishnu's playful and gracious incarnation
as the great boar,
which enabled the world to see the downfall
of the demon Hiranyáksha, Golden-eyes,
the city *displays the throwing of golden dice.*
Like Kadru[70], the mother
in whom all snakes, her offspring, rejoice,
the city *delights the demimonde.*
Like the stories of *Hari·vansha,* "Vishnu's Lineage,"
continuation of the "Maha·bhárata,"
charming with the many playful deeds
of Krishna as a boy,
the city *is charming with the play*
of countless children.
Far from *women there being enjoyed in public,*
the public enjoys the courtyards
and their behavior is unblemished.

ratka/varṇ" âpi sudhā|dhaval",

âvalambita|muktā|kalāp" âpi

vi/hāra/bhūṣaṇā,

bahu/prakṛtir api

sthirā,

vijit'|âmara|loka|dyutir,

Avantīṣ' Ûjjayinī nāma nagarī.

yasyām

uttuṅga|saudh'|ôtsaṅga|saṃgīta|saṅginīnām aṅganānām

atimadhureṇa gīta|raveṇ'

ākṛṣyamāṇ'|âdho|mukha|turaṃgaḥ

puraḥ|paryasta|ratha|patākā|paṭaḥ

kṛta|Mahākāla|praṇāma iva pratidivasam

ālakṣyate gacchan bhagavān divasa|karaḥ.

yasyāṃ ca

saṃdhyā|rāg'|âruṇā iva sindūra|maṇi|kuṭṭimeṣu,

prārabdha|kamalinī|parimalanā iva marakata|vedikāsu,

gagana|tala|prasṛtā iva vaidūrya|maṇi|bhūmiṣu,

timira|paṭala|vighaṭan'|ôdyatā iva

kṛṣṇ'|âguru|dhūma|maṇḍaleṣv,

It may seem strange that the city is *red in color,*
when it's white with plaster,
but in reality it is that *all the different castes*
are contented.
It's festooned with pearls, and it might seem strange
that it's not adorned with necklaces,
but in fact *it's adorned with monasteries.*
Although it might seem *shifting in character,*
it *has a large population*, and is stable.
That city in the kingdom of Avánti
surpasses the splendor of heaven.
Újjayini is its name.
In that city the blessed sun, maker of the day,
as he traverses his course
can be seen each day
appearing to bow to Maha·kala,[71]
Shiva as the great God Time,
when his chariot pennon dips down ahead of him
since his horses lower their heads
being drawn by the excessively sweet sound
on the terraces of the lofty palaces
of women devoted to singing.
And there
as if red with the tint of evening,
they shine on the ruby floors;
as if they've pressed upon lotus ponds
and so got colored green,[72]
they shine on the emerald benches;
as if making their way across the heavens,
they shine on the lapis lazuli floors;

abhibhūta|tārakā|paṅktaya iva muktā|prālambeṣu,

vikaca|kamala|cumbina iva nitambinī|mukheṣu,

prabhāta|candrikā|madhya|patitā iva

sphaṭika|bhitti|prabhāsu,

gagana|sindhu|taraṃg'|ālambina iva sita|patāk"|âṃśukeṣu,

pallavitā iva sūrya|kānt'|ôpaleṣu,

Rāhu|mukha|kuhara|praviṣṭā iv'

êndra|nīla|vātāyana|vivareṣu,

virājante ravi|gabhastayaḥ.

yasyāṃ c' ân|upajāta|timiratvād

a|vighaṭita|cakra|vāka|mithunā

vyarthī|kṛta|surata|pradīpāḥ

saṃjāta|Madan'|ânala|dig|dāhā iva

kāminīnāṃ bhūṣaṇa|prabhābhir yānti

bāl'|ātapa|piñjarā iva rajanyaḥ.

yāṃ ca saṃnihita|Viṣamalocanām an|avaratam

atimadhuro Rati|pralāpa iva prasarpan

mukharī|karoti *Makaraketu/dāha/hetu/bhūto*

bhavana|kalahaṃsa|kula|kolāhalaḥ.

as if striving to break up the massed form of darkness,
they shine on circles of black *águru* smoke;
as if they were overcoming the serried stars,
they shine on festoons of pearls;
as if they were kissing lotuses in bloom,
they shine on the faces of wide-hipped women;
as if fallen amid bright moonlight,
they shine on the radiance of the crystals walls;
as if riding the waves of the celestial river,
they shine on the white cloth of the pennons;
as if sprouting, they shine on the sun-stones;
as if entering the cavern of Rahu's mouth,
the rays of the sun
shine in the gaps of the sapphire window grills.
And in that city,
because of the women's ornaments' bright luster
the nights seem yellow with the light of dawn,
as if the horizon's ablaze with Love's fire;
and lamps to illuminate love-making are unnecessary
and pairs of *chakra·vaka* ducks aren't separated at night
because darkness just doesn't happen.
And in that city where Three-eyed Shiva is present,
as if Rati's lament *at the burning up of her husband,*
mákara-bannered Love, was continuing,
the painfully sweet cries
of flocks of domestic *kala·hansa* geese
resound unendingly,
causing the burning fever of love.

yasyāṃ ca niśi niśi pavana|vilolair dukūla|pallavair ullasadbhir Mālavī|mukha|kamala|kānti|lajjitasy' êndoḥ kalaṅkam iv' âpanayanto dūra|prasārit'|ōrdhva|dhvaja|bhujāḥ prāsādā lakṣyante. yasyāṃ ca saudha|śikhara|śāyinīnāṃ paśyan mukhāni pura|sundarīṇāṃ madana|para|vaśā iva patitaḥ pratimā|chalena luṭhati bahala|candana|jala|seka|śiśireṣu maṇi|kuṭṭimeṣu mṛga|lāñchanaḥ. yasyāṃ ca niś"|âvasāna|prabuddhasya tārataram api paṭhataḥ pañjara|bhājaḥ śuka|sārikā|samūhasy' âbhibhūta|gṛha|sārasa|rutena vistāriṇā vilāsinī|bhūṣaṇa|raven' â|vibhāvyamānā vyarthī|bhavanti prabhāta|maṅgala|gītayaḥ. yasyāṃ c' *â/nivṛttir* maṇi|pradīpānām, *taralatā* hārāṇām, *a/sthitiḥ* saṃgīta|muraja|dhvanīnāṃ, dvandva|viyogaś cakra|nāmnāṃ, *varṇa/parīkṣā* kanakānām, *a/sthiratvaṃ* dhvajānāṃ, *mitra/dveṣaḥ* kumudānāṃ,

And in it every night the palaces
appear to be stretching out their arms—lofty banners—
as if to wipe away with the silken fringes
waving in the wind
the stain of the moon
which has been put to shame
by the beauty of the lotus-faces of Malwa women.
And seeing in it, as they recline
on the roofs of the palaces,
the faces of the women of the city,
the moon marked with the deer,
as if fallen down overwhelmed by love for them,
in the guise of his reflections
rolls about on the jeweled pavements
cool with abundant sprinklings of sandal water.
And in that city, waking at night's end,
the multitude of parrots and mynah birds
in their cages, though they call out very loudly,
have their auspicious dawn chorus
frustrated and distorted—
and the shrieking of the tame cranes is conquered—
by the widespread jingling of wanton ladies' ornaments.
And in that city the jewel-lamps *don't go out,*
and *there's no lack of quietude;*
pearl necklaces *have a central jewel,*
but *the citizens aren't fickle;*
there's *variation of beat* in the sounds of concert drums,
but *no instability anywhere else;*
the only couples to suffer separation
are *chakra·vaka* ducks;

kośa|guptir asīnām.

kiṃ bahunā?

yasyāṃ sur'|âsura|cūḍā|maṇi|marīci|cumbita|

caraṇa|nakha|mayūkho niśita|śūla|dārit'|Ândhaka|

mah''|âsuro Gaurī|nūpura|koṭi|ghṛṣṭa|śekhara|candra|

śakalas Tripura|bhasma|rajaḥ|kṛt'|âṅga|rāgo

Makaradhvaja|dhvaṃsa|vidhurayā Ratyā prasādayantyā

prasārita|kara|yugala|vigalita|valaya|nikar'|ârcita|caraṇaḥ

pralay'|ânala|śikhā|kalāpa|kapila|jaṭā|bhāra|bhrānta|

sura|sindhur Andhak'|ârātir bhagavān

utsṛṣṭa|Kailāsa|vāsa|prītir

Mahākāl'|âbhidhānaḥ svayaṃ nivasati.

the only *inquiry into caste membership*
is *inspecting the color of gold coins;*
the only *instability* is *the fluttering* of flags;
the only *hatred of a friend*
is the night-lotuses *shunning the sun;*
the only *guarding of treasures*
is that swords *remain sheathed.*
On this there's no need to say more.
There, the luster of his toe-nails kissed by the rays
from the crest-jewels of the gods and the demons,
he whose sharp trident destroyed
the great demon Ándhaka;
the crescent moon on his crest scraped
by the sharp points of Gauri's bracelets;
his body colored with dust from the ashes
from the demons' Triple City;
his feet receiving the offering of a heap of bangles
slipped from Rati's outstretched hands
as she tries to placate him,
made a helpless widow
by his destruction of her crocodile-bannered Love;
he who in whose burden of matted locks
red as the mass of flames of universal dissolution
roams Ganga, the river of the gods;
he, the foe of Ándhaka;
there he the blessed lord, who'd put aside
the pleasure of living on Kailása, dwells in person,
under the name of Maha·kala, Great Time.

tasyāṃ c' âivaṃ|vidhāyāṃ nagaryāṃ

Nala|Nahuṣa|Yayāti|Dhundhumāra|Bharata|Bhagīratha|

Daśaratha|pratimo bhuja|bal'|ôpārjita|bhū|maṇḍalaḥ

phalita|śakti|trayo

matimān utsāha|saṃpanno nīti|śāstr'|âkhinna|buddhir

adhīta|dharma|śāstras tṛtīya iva tejasā kāntyā ca

sūryā|candramasor aneka|sapta|tantu|pūta|mūrtir

upaśamita|sakala|jagad|upaplavo vihāya kamala|vanāny

a|vigaṇayya Nārāyaṇa|vakṣaḥ|sthala|vasati|sukham

utphull'|âravinda|hastayā śūra|samāgama|vyasaninyā

nirvyājam āliṅgito Lakṣmyā

mahā|muni|jana|saṃsevitasya Madhusūdana|caraṇa iva

sura|sarit|pravāhasya prabhavaḥ satyasya,

śiśirasy' âpi ripu|jana|saṃtāpa|kāriṇaḥ,

And in that city, just as I've described it,
there ruled a king,
the very image of Nala, Náhusha,
Yayáti, Dhundhu·mara,
Bhárata, Bhagi·ratha, and Dasha·ratha.[73]
The might of his arm had conquered the circle of the earth.
In him the three kinds of royal power bore fruit.
He was clever and vigorous. He had no trouble
in understanding the science of politics,
and he carefully studied the science of ethics.
In his radiance and his beauty
he came third to the sun and the moon.
His body was purified
by the many sacrifices he'd performed.
He'd alleviated all the world's calamities.
Leaving her lotus beds, scorning the pleasure of dwelling
on Naráyana Vishnu's chest,
Lakshmi, a blooming lotus in her hand,
openly embraced him,
addicted as she is to encounters with heroes.
He was the source of the truthfulness
that is practiced by all the great sages,
just as the foot of Vishnu, slayer of the demon Madhu,
was the cause of the descent to earth
of the river of the gods.
Just as the ocean was the nectar-producing moon's
place of origin, he was the place of origin of fame which
though cold burned his foes and their friends,

sthirasy' âpy an|avaratam̩ bhramato,

nirmalasy' âpi

malinī|kr̩t'|ârāti|vanitā|mukha|kamala|dyuter,

atidhavalasy' âpi *sarva|jana|rāga|kāriṇaḥ,*

sudhā|sūter iva jala|nidhir

udbhava yaśasaḥ,

pātālavad āśrito *nija|pakṣa|kṣati|bhītaiḥkṣiti|bhr̥t|kulaiḥ,*

graha|gaṇa iva *Budh'|ânugato,*

Makaradhvaja iv' *ôtsanna|vigraho,*

Daśaratha iva *Sumitr"|ôpetaḥ,*

Paśupatir iva *Mahāsen'|ânugato,*

bhujaga|rāja iva

kṣamā|bhara|gurur,

Narmadā|pravāha iva

mahā|vaṃśa|prabhavo,

'vatāra iva Dharmasya,

pratinidhir iva Puruṣottamasya,

parihr̥ta|prajā|pīḍo rājā Tārāpīḍo nām' âbhūt.

though constant, was ceaselessly roaming,
though stainless, sullied the luster of the day-lotuses
that were the faces of the women of the foes,
though very white, *colored all people,*
for *it made all his subjects love him.*
Like the nether regions
where the mountains sought refuge,
terrified at the prospect of their wings being cut off,
he was resorted to *by hosts of kings*
fearful of harm to their faction.
Like the group of the planets *followed by Mercury,*
he *was followed by wise men.*
Like *mákara*-bannered Love, *whose body was destroyed,*
he *had obliterated strife.*
Like Dasha·ratha *accompanied by his wife Sumítra,*[74]
he *had excellent friends.*
Like Shiva, lord of beasts, *followed by his son Karttikéya,*
the great general, he *led a great army.*
Like Shesha, king of snakes,
heavy with the burden of the earth,
his *extreme patience made him venerable.*
Like the course of the Nármada river,
which rises amid tall bamboos,
he *was the scion of a great lineage.*
He seemed the incarnation of the god of Righteousness.
He seemed the image of the supreme man, Vishnu.
He removed his subjects' woes,
and Tarapída, Star-crowned Moon, was his name.

yas *tamaḥ|prasara|malina|vapuṣā pāpa|bahulena*
Kali|kālena cālitam ā|mūlato dharmaṃ Daśānanen' êva
Kailāsaṃ Paśupatir iv' âvaṣṭabhya
punar api sthirī|cakāra.
yaṃ ca Rati|pralāpa|janita|day"|ārdra|hṛdaya|
Hara|nirmitam aparaṃ Makaraketum
amaṃsta lokaḥ.
yaṃ ca jala|nidhi|taraṃga|dhauta|mekhalāt,
pattr'|ântar|vicāri|tārā|gaṇa|dvi|guṇita|taṭa|taru|
kusuma|prakarād,
udyad|indu|bimba|vigalad|amṛta|bindu|
durdin'|ārdra|candanād,
a|śiśira|kara|ratha|turaga|khura|śikhar'|ôllekha|
khaṇḍit'|ôllasal|lavaṅga|pallavād,
Airāvata|kara|lūna|sallakī|kisalayād
ā śailād Udaya|nāmnaḥ,
kapi|bala|vilupta|virala|lavalī|latā|phalād,
udadhi|nirgata|jala|devatā|vandyamāna|Rāghava|pādād,
acala|pāta|dalita|śaṅkha|kula|śakala|tārakita|śilā|talān,
Nala|kara|tala|kalita|śaila|sahasra|saṃbhūtād
ā setu|bandhād,

The Kali age, *completely sullied*
by the spread of ignorance, abounding in sin,
had shaken righteousness to its very roots,
but he supported it and made it firm again,
just as Shiva, lord of beasts, did Kailása
when ten-headed Rávana,
his body as black as a mass of darkness,
full of sin,
tried to wrench it from its base.
People thought Rati's lament had softened Shiva's heart,
and that in his compassion
the Destroyer had created him for her
as another *mákara*-bannered Love.
From the mountain called Rising Mountain,
from which the sun rises, slopes washed by ocean waves;
where the mass of flowers on the trees on its flanks
are doubled by the throng of stars
moving between their leaves;
where sandal trees are moistened by showers of nectar
dripping from the disk of the rising moon;
where the shining leaves of the clove trees are broken
by the sharp-edged hooves of the horses
of the hot-rayed sun's chariot;
where Airávata plucks with his trunk the *sállaki* leaves;
from the causeway to Lanka
fashioned with thousands of mountains handled by Nala;[75]
where little fruit is left on the *lávali* creepers
the monkey forces plucked;
where the water deities rise from the ocean
to venerate the feet of Raghu's descendant, Rama;

accha|nirjhara|jala|dhauta|tārakā|sārthād,

amṛta|mathan'|ôdyata|Vaikuṇṭha|keyūra|pattra|makara|

koṭi|kaṣaṇa|masṛṇita|grāvṇaḥ,

sur'|âsura|helā|valayita|Vāsuki|samākarṣaṇ'|ārambha|

calita|caraṇa|bhara|dalita|nitambād,

P55 amṛta|śīkara|sikta|sānor Mandar'|âcalān;

Nara|Nārāyaṇa|caraṇa|mudr''|âṅkita|Badarik''|āśrama|

ramaṇīyāt Kubera|pura|sundarī|bhūṣaṇa|rava|

mukhara|śikharāt

sapta'|rṣi|saṃdhy''|ôpāsan'|āpūta|prasravaṇ'|âmbhaso

Vṛkodar'|ôddalita|saugandhika|khaṇḍa|sugandhi|maṇḍalād

ā Gandhamādanāt

sev''|âñjali|kamala|mukula|danturaiḥ śirobhiś

caraṇa|nakha|mayūkha|grathita|mukuṭa|

patra|latā|granthayo

bhaya|cakita|tarala|tāra|dṛśo bhuja|bala|vijitāḥ

praṇemur avanipāḥ.

where the surface of the rocks is spangled
with pieces of the masses of conch shells smashed
by the mountains as they fell into place;
from the Mándara mountain,
which washed the clusters of stars
with the clear waters of its streams,
its stones smoothed by the scraping of the sharp points
of the sea-monster leaf-work on Vishnu's arm-ornaments
when he was engaged in churning the nectar,
where the sides were broken by the friction
of Vásuki's underbody set in motion
once the gods and demons had without any problem
coiled him around it,
its peak sprinkled with drops of the nectar; P55
from the Gandha·mádana mountain,
lovely with the Bádarika hermitage marked
with the footprints of Nara and Naráyana,
its peaks resounding with the sound
of women's ornaments in Kubéra's city,[76]
the water of its streams purified
by the Seven Sages' twilight worship,
the whole region fragrant from the *saugándhika* blossoms
that wolf-bellied Bhima plucked for Dráupadi;[77]
—coming from these places, their heads half hidden
by the lotus buds of their hands folded in devotion,
the points on the ornamental leaf-work on their crowns
fastened to the rays from his toe-nails,
the darting pupils of their eyes trembling in fear,
already conquered by the might of his arms,
the kings bowed down before him.

yena

c' âneka|ratn'|âṃśu|pallavite

vyālambi|muktā|phala|jālake

dig|gajen' êva kalpa|tarāv ākrānte siṃh'|āsane

bhareṇa śilī|mukha|vyatikara|kampitā latā iva

nemur āyāminyaḥ sarva|diśaḥ.

yasmai ca manye sura|patir api spṛhayāṃ cakāra.

yasmāc ca dhavalī|kṛta|bhuvana|talaḥ

sakala|loka|hṛday'|ānanda|kārī Krauñcād iva

haṃsa|nivaho nirjagāma guṇa|gaṇaḥ.

yasya c' âmṛt'|āmoda|surabhi|parimalayā

Mandar'|ôddhata|bahula|dugdha|sindhu|phena|lekhay" êva

dhavalī|kṛta|sur'|âsura|lokayā daśasu dikṣu

mukharita|bhuvanam abhramyata kīrtyā.

yasya c' âtiduḥsaha|pratāpa|saṃtāpa|khidyamān" êva

kṣaṇam api na mumoc' ātapatra|cchāyāṃ rāja|lakṣmīḥ.

tathā ca yasya diṣṭi|vṛddhim iva śuśrāv'

ôpadeśam iva jagrāha

maṅgalam iva bahu mene

mantram iva jajāp'

āgama|vacanam iva

na visasmāra caritaṃ janaḥ.

And when he ascended the throne
which gave forth fronds of rays from many jewels
and had clusters of pearls hanging from it,
as when an elephant of the quarters attacks a wishing tree,
under his weight all the quarters,
far into the distance, shook,
like creepers shaken by contact with bees.
And I think even Indra, lord of the gods, envied him.
And from him, whitening the surface of the earth,
delighting the hearts of all the world,
like a flock of geese from the Krauncha mountain,[78]
a host of virtues came forth.
And, its perfume as fragrant as the scent of nectar,
like a line of thick foam Mándara had shot up
from the milk ocean, whitening
the world of the gods and the world of the demons,
his fame roamed in all the ten directions,
making the world resound.
As if she were suffering from the heat
of his altogether unbearable prowess,
royal glory didn't leave the shade of his parasol
even for a moment.
And so it was people listened to his deeds
as if they were words of congratulation to themselves.
They received them as if they were religious instruction.
They thought highly of them, as if they were auspicious.
They repeated them like a mantra.
As if they were the words of the Vedas,
they never forgot them.

yasmimś ca rājani

girīṇāṃ *vipakṣatā,*

pratyayānāṃ *paratvaṃ,*

darpaṇānām *abhimukh'|âvasthānaṃ,*

Śūlapāṇi|pratimānāṃ *durg'|āśleṣo,*

jala|dharāṇāṃ *cāpa|dhāraṇaṃ,*

dhvajānām *unnatir,*

dhanuṣām *avanatir,*

vaṃśānāṃ *śilīmukha|kṣatir,*

devatānāṃ *yātrā,*

kusumānāṃ bandhana|sthitir,

indriyāṇāṃ nigraho,

vana|kariṇāṃ *vāri|praveśas,*

taikṣṇyam asi|dhārāṇāṃ,

vratinām *agni|dhāraṇaṃ,*

grahāṇāṃ *tul"|ārohaṇam,*

Agasty'|ôdaye *viṣa|śuddhiḥ,*

keśa|nakhānām *āyati|bhaṅgo,*

And while he was king,
the only *enmity* was that mountains *had lost their wings;*
the only *feeling of alienation*
was *that parts of words came after prefixes;*
the only *facing a person down* that occurred
was *standing in front* of mirrors;
the only *besieging of fortresses* was
images of Shiva the trident-bearer *embracing Durga;*
the only *carrying of bows*
was clouds' *possession of the rainbow;*
the only *haughtiness* was *the hoisting up* of banners;
the only *humiliation* was *the bending* of bows;
the only *wounding by arrows*
was *insects boring* into bamboos;
the only *military expedition*
was *the procession of the gods* to and from temples;
the only tying up was of flowers;
the only restraint was of the senses;
the only *ordeal by immersion in water*
was *corralling* wild elephants;
the only *viciousness* was *the sharpness* of swords;
the only *ordeal by holding fire*
was ascetics' *maintenance of their sacrificial fires;*
the only *ordeal of mounting the balance beam*
was the planets *rising into Libra, the asterism of the scales;*
the only *proving purity by the ordeal of poison*
was *the purification of water*
at the rising of the star Agástya;[79]
the only *cutting short of men's futures*
was *cutting long* nails and hair;

jalada|divasānāṃ *malin'|âmbaratvaṃ,*

ratn'|ôpalānāṃ *bhedo,*

munīnāṃ *yoga|sādhanaṃ,*

Kumāra|stutiṣu *tārak'|ôddharaṇam,*

uṣṇa|raśmer *grahaṇa|śaṅkā*

śaśino *Jyeṣṭh'|âtikramo,*

Mahābhārate *duḥ|śāsan'|âparādh'|ākarṇanaṃ,*

vayaḥ|pariṇāme *daṇḍa|grahaṇam,*

asi|parivāreṣv *a|kuśala|yogo,*

vakratā kāminīnāṃ kuca|bhaṅgeṣu,

kariṇāṃ *dāna|vicchittir,*

akṣa|krīḍāsu *śūnya|gṛha*|darśanaṃ

pṛthivyām āsīt.

tasya ca rājño nikhila|śāstra|kal"|âvagāha|

gambhīra|buddhir, ā śaiśavād upārūḍha|nirbhara|

prema|raso, nīti|śāstra|prayoga|kuśalo,

bhuvana|rājya|bhāra|nau|karṇa|dhāro,

the only *dirty clothes* were rainy days' *dark skies;*
the only *dissension* was *drilling holes* in gems;
the only *use of magic tricks to gain one's end*
was sages' *practice of yoga*;
the only *plucking out of eyeballs*
was hymns of praise to Kumára
referring to his destruction of the demon Táraka;
the only *fear of imprisonment*
was the hot-rayed sun's *fear of eclipse;*
the only *ignoring the authority of the eldest brother*
was the moon *going beyond the Jyeshtha constellation*;
One only heard about incorrigible rogues
when one listened to Duhshásana's crimes
in the "Maha·bhárata";
the only *imposition of fines*
was *using a staff* when one got old;
the only *joining with evil*
was *sheathing dangerous swords* in scabbards;
the only *crookedness* was in the *convoluted* patterns
painted on women's breasts;
the only *cessation of generosity*
was when elephants *periodically ceased to rut*;
an empty house was only to be seen
as *an empty square on the board* in a game of dice.
So it was on earth while he was king.
And that king had a brahmin minister
who'd deeply studied all sciences and arts
and had a profound understanding of them;
from boyhood a feeling of strong affection
for the king had grown in him;

mahatsv api kārya|saṃkaṭeṣv a|viṣaṇṇa|dhīr,

dhāma dhairyasya,

sthānaṃ sthiteḥ,

setuḥ satyasya,

gurur guṇānām,

ācārya ācārāṇāṃ,

dhātā dharmasya,

Śeṣ'|âhir iva mahī|bhāra|dhāraṇa|kṣamaḥ,

salila|nidhir iva *mahā|sattvo,*

Jarāsandha iva *ghaṭita|saṃdhi|vigrahas,*

Tryambaka iva *prasādhita|Durgo,*

Yudhiṣṭhira iva *Dharma|prabhavaḥ,*

sakala|Veda|Vedāṅga|vid,

a|śeṣa|rājya|maṅgal'|âika|sāro,

Bṛhaspatir iva Sunāsīrasya,

Kavir iva Vṛṣaparvaṇo,

Vasiṣṭha iva Daśarathasya,

Viśvāmitra iva Rāmasya,

Dhaumya iv' Ajātaśatror,

skilled in the use of the science of politics,
helmsman of the whole world's ship of state,
his mind wasn't fazed even in grave and complex matters;
he was the home of courage,
constancy's dwelling place,
truth's causeway,
the teacher of good qualities,
instructor in good forms of behavior,
maintainer of dharma;
like the serpent Shesha he was capable
of supporting the burden of the earth;
like the ocean *which contains huge creatures within it,*
he *had great moral strength;*
like Jara·sandha, Jara's join, *the two halves of whose body*
were joined together by the demoness Jara,[80]
he'd *made declarations of war*
and arranged peace agreements;
just as three-eyed Shiva *placates Durga,*
he *subdued fortresses;*
just as Yudhi·shthira was *Dharma's son,*
he *was the source of dharma;*
he knew all the Vedas and the auxiliary texts;
he was the unique essence
of all the kingdom's auspicious things.
Like Brihas·pati for Indra,
like Kavi for the demon king Vrisha·parvan,
like Dasha·ratha's guru Vasíshtha,
like Vishva·mitra for Rama,
like Dhaumya for Yudhi·shthira,

Damanaka iva Bhīmasya,
Sumatir iva Nalasya,
sarva|kāryeṣv āhita|matir,
amātyo brāhmaṇaḥ
Śukanāso nām' āsīt.
yo Narak'|âsura|śastra|prahāra|bhīṣaṇe
bhraman|Mandara|nirdaya|niṣpeṣa|kaṭhin'|âṃsa|pīṭhe
Nārāyaṇa|vakṣaḥ|sthale 'pi sthitām
a|duṣkara|lābhām amanyata
prajñā|balena Lakṣmīm.
yaṃ ca samāsādya darśit'|âneka|rājya|phalā lat" êva
mahā|pādapam aneka|pratāna|gahanā
vistāram upayayau prajñā.
yasy' âneka|cāra|puruṣa|sahasra|saṃcāra|nicite
catur|udadhi|valaya|parikṣepa|pramāṇe dharaṇi|tale
bhavana iv' â|viditam ahar ahaḥ
samucchvasitam api rājñāṃ n' āsīt.
sa rājā bāla eva sura|kuñjara|kara|pīvareṇa
rāja|lakṣmī|līl'|ôpadhānena sakala|jagad|abhaya|pradāna|
yajña|dīkṣā|yūpena sphurad|asi|latā|marīci|jāla|jaṭilena
nikhil'|ārāti|kula|pralaya|dhūma|ketu|daṇḍena bāhunā

like Bhima's guru Dámanaka,
like Nala's guru Súmati,[81]
he bent his mind to all matters on the king's behalf.
Shuka·nasa, Parrot-nose, was his name.
Though she was on Naráyana Vishnu's chest frightful
from the scars of the demon Náraka's weapons,
and the god's shoulders were hardened by the pitiless
grinding against him of the Mándara mountain
as it revolved in the churning of the ocean,
he considered winning Lakshmi
by the power of his wisdom an easy thing.
Coming into contact with him, wisdom,
like a creeper growing round a great tree,
manifesting many fruits in the kingdom,
impenetrable with much branching out, spread widely.
The surface of the earth
whose extent is bounded by the four oceans
was covered by the movements
of his many thousand spies,
and on it, as if in his own palace, each and every day
not a sigh from its kings was not known to him.
That king while still a boy
with his arm as thick as the trunk
of the god Indra's elephant,
pillow graced by royal glory,
sacrificial post for the performance of the ritual
to give the whole world freedom from fear,
bristling with a web of rays
from his gleaming sword-blade,
the tail of a comet signifying destruction

vijitya sapta|dvīpa|valayāṃ vasuṃ|dharāṃ
tasmiñ Śukanāsa|nāmni mantriṇi suhṛd' îva
rājya|bhāram āropya susthitāḥ prajāḥ kṛtvā,
kartavya|śeṣam aparam a|paśyan
praśamit'|âśeṣa|vipakṣatayā vigat'|āśaṅkaḥ
śithilita|pṛthivī|vyāpāraḥ
prāyo yauvana|sukhāny anubabhūva.
tathā hi: kadā cid
ullasat|kaṭhora|kapola|pulaka|jarjarita|karṇa|pallavānāṃ
praṇayinīnāṃ candana|jala|cchaṭābhir iva
smita|sudhā|cchavibhir abhiṣicyamānaḥ,
karṇ'|ôtpalair iva locan'|âṃśubhis tāḍyamānaḥ,
kuṅkuma|dhūlibhir iv' ābharaṇa|prabhābhir
ākulī|kriyamāṇa|locano,
dhaval'|âṃśukair iva
kara|nakha|mayūkha|jālakair āhanyamānaś,
campaka|kusuma|dala|mālikābhir iva
bhuja|latābhir ābadhyamāno,

of the whole tribe of his foes,
conquered the earth with its seven continents,
and having made his subjects safe and content,
on that minister called Shuka·nasa,
as if indeed on a friend,
he placed the burden of state.
Not seeing anything else he had to do,
free from anxiety
since he had subdued all his enemies,
the need to concern himself
with the affairs of the world much reduced,
for the most part he enjoyed the pleasures of youth.
And it was like this. Sometimes,
to his loving ladies,
who—the blossoms on their ears falling apart
on their gleaming cheeks hardened by horripilation—
were consecrating him with the rays of light
from the nectar of their smiles
as if with quantities of sandal-water;
beating him with beams of light from their eyes,
as if with the lilies on their ears;
dazzling his eyes with the luster of their ornaments
as if with saffron pollen;
hitting him with masses of rays from their finger nails
as if with white silks;
entwining him with their arm-creepers
as with garlands of *chámpaka* blossom;

daṣṭ'|âdhar'|ādhūta|kara|tala|calan|maṇi|valaya|
kalakala|rava|ramaṇīyam atirabhasa|dalita|danta|pattra|
dala|danturita|śayanam
utkṣipta|caraṇa|galad|alaktaka|rakta|śekharaṃ
sarabhasa|kaca|graha|cūrṇita|maṇi|karṇa|pūram
ullasita|kuca|kṛṣṇ'|âguru|paṅka|pattra|lat"|âṅkita|
pracchada|paṭam accha|śrama|jala|kaṇik'|ālulita|
gorocanā|tilaka|pattra|bhaṅgam
Anaṅga|para|vaśaḥ suratam ātatāna.
kadā cin Makaraketu|kanaka|nārāca|paraṃparābhir iva
kāminī|kara|puṭa|vinirgatābhiḥ kuṅkuma|jala|dhārābhiḥ
piñjarī|kriyamāṇa|kāyo
lākṣā|jala|cchaṭā|prahāra|pāṭalī|kṛta|dukūlo
mṛga|mada|jala|bindu|śabala|candana|sthāsakaḥ
kanaka|śṛṅga|kośaiś ciraṃ cikrīḍa.
kadā cit kuca|candana|cūrṇa|dhavalit'|ōrmi|mālaṃ
caṭula|tulā|koṭi|vācāla|caraṇ'|ālaktaka|sikta|
haṃsa|mithunam alaka|nipatita|kusuma|śāraṃ
plavamāna|karṇa|pūra|kuvalaya|dalam
unnata|nitamba|kṣobha|jarjarita|taraṃgam
uddalita|nāla|paryasta|nalina|nipatita|dhūli|paṭalam
an|avarata|kar'|āsphālana|sphurat|phena|bindu|candrakitaṃ

he,
with the charming clinking of their jeweled bracelets
when he bit their lips and their hands trembled,
with ivory ear-ornaments violently smashed
and the bed studded with the bits,
with them kicking up their feet and
reddening the top of his head with the dripping lac,
with their jeweled ear-ornaments
pulverized by vicious hair pulling,
with gleaming breasts printing
black aloe leaf paintings on the bed sheets,
with leaf patterns and forehead marks
done in cow-yellow
smeared with drops of fresh sweat,
in thrall to Love, made love.
Sometimes, as if with flights of Love's golden arrows,
his body made yellow with showers of saffron water
issuing from his women's hands,
his silk clothes reddened by splashes of lac water,
his application of sandal-paste
blotched with drops of musk water,
he played for a long time with golden syringes.
Sometimes,
he garlanded the water with waves whitened
by sandal powder from women's breasts;
sprinkled pairs of geese with lac
from feet noisy with jingling anklets,
checkered the water with flowers fallen from their hair,
leaving lotus petals from ear-ornaments
to swim for themselves,

s'|âvarodha|jano jala|krīḍayā

gṛha|dīrghikāṇām ambhaś cakāra.

kadā cit

saṃketa|vañcitābhiḥ praṇayinībhir

ābaddha|bhaṅgura|bhrū|kuṭībhir

āraṇita|maṇi|pārihārya|mukhara|bhuja|latābhir

bakula|kusum'|āvalibhiḥ saṃyata|caraṇo

nakha|kiraṇa|vimiśraiḥ kusuma|dāmābhiḥ

kṛt'|âparādho divasam atāḍyata.

kadā cid bakula|tarur iva

kāminī|gaṇḍūṣa|sīdhu|dhār"|āsvāda|mudito

vikāsam abhajata.

kadā cid aśoka|pādapa iva yuvati|caraṇa|tala|prahāra|

saṃkrānt'|ālaktako *rāgam uvāha.*

kadā cin Musalāyudha iva *candana/dhavalaḥ*

kaṇṭh'|âvasakt'|ôllasal|lola|kusuma|mālaḥ

pānam asevata.

the force of broad hips breaking up the wave;
letting lots of pollen fall on the water from lotuses
they'd broken off their stalks and thrown about;
making it iridescent with gleaming drops of foam
from non-stop beating with their hands:
that is how, playing water games
with the women of his harem,
he treated the water of the palace pools.
Sometimes his loving ladies,
cheated of assignations with him,
curved brows frowning,
creeper-like arms noisy with jingling of ornaments,
fettered his feet with garlands of *bákula* flowers
and using flower garlands
mixed with the rays of their fingernails
beat the offender the whole day long.
Sometimes, like a *bákula* tree
he was pleasured with the taste of streams of wine
from his loving women's mouths
and he himself bloomed like a *bákula* tree.[82]
Sometimes, like an *ashóka* tree,
lac was transferred to him
by a kick from the sole of a woman's foot,
and like an *ashóka* tree made to *bear red blossom,*
he *became passionate.*
Sometimes,
like pestle-weaponed Bala·rama *white as sandal-paste*
he, *white with sandal-paste,*
a garland of bright flowers swinging from his neck,
drank heavily.

kadā cid gandha|gaja iva

mada/rakta|kapola/dolāyamāna/karṇa/pallavo

mada/kalaḥ kānanaṃ vikaca|vana|latā|kusuma|

surabhi|parimalaṃ jagāhe.

kadā cit *kvaṇita/maṇi/nūpura/ninād'/ānandita/Mānaso*

haṃsa iva kamala|vaneṣu reme.

kadā cin mṛga|patir iva *skandh'/âvalambi/kesara/mālaḥ*

krīḍā|parvateṣu vicacāra.

kadā cin madhu|kara iva vijṛmbhamāṇa|kusuma|

mukula|dantureṣu latā|gṛheṣu babhrāma.

kadā cin nīla|paṭa|viracit'|âvaguṇṭhano

bahula|niśā|pradoṣa|datta|saṃketāḥ

sundarīr abhisasāra.

kadā cic ca

vighaṭita|kanaka|kapāṭa|prakaṭa|vātāyaneṣv

an|avarata|dahyamāna|kṛṣṇ'|âguru|dhūma|raktair iva

pārāvatair adhyāsita|viṭaṅkeṣu

mahā|prāsāda|kukṣiṣu

katipay'|āpta|suhṛt|parivṛto

vīṇā|veṇu|muraja|manoharatamam

Sometimes, like a scent-elephant[83] in rut,
leaflike ears swinging
against cheeks red with rut, maddened,
he, *leaf-ornaments in his ears swinging against his cheeks*
reddened by intoxication, speech drunkenly slurred,
plunged into the forest fragrant with the scent
of the forest creepers' blooming flowers.
Sometimes, like a goose *whose cry*
like jeweled anklets jingling
rejoices the Mánasa lake, he, *heart rejoicing*
in the sound of jeweled anklets jingling,
took his pleasure amid the lotus beds.
Sometimes like a lion,
thick mane hanging over its shoulders,
he, *a bákula garland hanging from his shoulders,*
roamed his pleasure-hills.
Sometimes like a bee he went to and fro
in creeper-bowers bristling with buds beginning to unfurl.
Sometimes he made assignations with beautiful women
in the evening of the dark nights of the month,
disguised himself in dark clothes
and went out to meet them.
And sometimes
in the inner apartments of his great palace
with the golden shutters on the wide windows
thrown right open,
and the gray pigeons in the eaves
seeming colored by the smoke
from the black aloe incense constantly burning,
he, surrounded by a few select friends,

antaḥ|pura|saṃgītakaṃ dadarśa.
kiṃ ca bahunā? yad yad atiramaṇīyam abhimatam
a|viruddham āyatyāṃ tadātve ca
tat tad an|ākṣipta|cetāḥ
parisamāptatvād anyeṣāṃ pṛthivī|vyāpārāṇāṃ
siṣeve na tu vyasanitayā.
pramudita|prajasya hi parisamāpta|sakala|mahī|
prayojanasya nara|pater
viṣay'|ôpabhoga|līlā bhūṣaṇam
itarasya tu viḍambanā.
praj"|ânurāga|hetoś c' ântar" ântarā
darśanaṃ dadau
siṃh'|āsanaṃ ca nimitteṣv āruroha.
Śukanāso 'pi mahāntaṃ taṃ rājya|bhāram
an|āyāsen' âiva prajñā|balena babhāra.
yath" âiva rājā sarva|kāryāṇy akārṣīt
tadvad asāv api dviguṇī|kṛta|praj"|ânurāgaś cakre.
tam api calita|cūḍāmaṇi|marīci|mañjarī|jālibhir
maulibhir
āvarjita|kusuma|śekhara|cyuta|madhu|śīkara|
sikta|nṛpa|sabhaṃ
dūr'|âvanati|preṅkhita|maṇi|kuṇḍala|koṭi|
saṃghaṭṭit'|âṅgadaṃ
rājakam ānanāma.

attended a harem concert
most delightful with *vina*, flute, and drum.
What more need be said? Whatever was really pleasing,
just to his taste, and not counter
to his present and future interest,
with those things he occupied himself,
not that he became obsessed with them—
it was because he'd completed his other duties
in respect of the world, not through any addiction.
For a king who has made his subjects rejoice
and completed all his duties in respect of his kingdom,
the playful enjoyment of the objects of the senses
is an ornament,
though in the case of someone else
it would be somewhat disgraceful.
And out of love for his subjects
he from time to time gave audience,
and ascended the throne when occasion rose.
Shuka·nasa, for his part, by the force of his intellect
bore the great burden of state without strain.
Just as the king performed all his duties, so too did he,
doubling the people's affection for the king.
To him also, all the kings bowed down,
crowns streaming clusters of rays
from slipping crest jewels,
sprinkling the royal hall with drops of honey
falling from their chaplets of flowers,
bending so low
the swinging tips of their jeweled earrings
scraped against their armlets.

tasminn api calite

calita|caṭula|turaga|bala|mukhara|khura|rava|

badhirī|kṛta|bhuvan'|ântarālā,

bala|bhara|pracala|vasudhā|tala|dolāyamāna|girayo,

galan|mad'|ândha|gandha|gaja|

dāna|dhār"|ândhakārāḥ,

saṃsarpad|atibahala|dhūli|paṭala|

dhūsarita|sindhavaḥ,

pracala|padāti|bala|kalakala|rava|sphoṭita|śravaṇa|vivarāḥ,

sa|rabhas'|ôdghuṣyamāṇa|jaya|śabda|nirbharāḥ,

proddhūyamāna|dhavala|cāmara|sahasra|saṃchāditāḥ,

puñjita|nar'|êndra|vṛnda|kanaka|daṇḍ'|ātapatra|

saṃghaṭṭa|naṣṭa|divasā daśa diśo babhūvuḥ.

evaṃ tasya rājño mantri|

viniveśita|rājya|bhārasya

yauvana|sukham anubhavataḥ kālo jagāma.

bhūyasā ca kālen' ânyeṣām api

jīva|loka|sukhānāṃ

prāyaḥ sarveṣām antaṃ yayau.

ekaṃ tu suta|mukha|darśana|sukhaṃ na lebhe.

When he, for his part, set out,
all the ten directions felt the effect,
the world's arena deafened by the clattering hooves
of his cavalry's prancing horses on the move;
the mountains swinging to and fro
as the ground moved under the burden of his troops;
darkness brought on by the streams of rut
from his scent-elephants blind from flowing rut;
the rivers made gray
by the very thick clouds of dust spreading to them;
eardrums split
by the confused din of the foot-soldiers on the march;
overwhelmed by the vehement shouting of victory cries;
covered over with thousands of white chowries
shaken to and fro;
with the day disappearing
in the clashing
of the gold-handled parasols
of the kings crowded together.
So it was the king had placed the burden of state
on his minister
and spent his time experiencing the joys of youth.
And after a considerable time he had experienced
almost all the various pleasures
of this world of mortals.
But one happiness he didn't obtain—
looking at the face of a son.

tathā saṃbhujyamānam api
niṣphala|puṣpa|darśanaṃ
śara|vaṇam iv'
ântaḥ|puram abhūt.
yathā yathā ca yauvanam aticakrāma
tathā tathā viphala|manorathasy'
ân|apatyatā|janm"|âvardhat' âsya saṃtāpaḥ.
viṣay'|ôpabhoga|sukh'|êcchābhiś ca mano vijahe.
nara|pati|sahasra|parivṛtam apy
a|sahāyam iva
cakṣuṣmantam apy andham iva
bhuvan'|ālambanam api
nir|ālambanam iv' ātmānam amanyata.
atha tasya
candra|lekh" êva Hara|jaṭā|kalāpasya,
Kaustubha|prabh" êva Kaiṭabhārāti|vakṣaḥ|sthalasya,
vana|māl" êva Musalāyudhasya,
vel" êva sāgarasya,
mada|lekh" êva dig|gajasya,
lat" êva pādapasya,
kusum'|ôdgatir iva surabhi|māsasya,
candrik" êva candramasaḥ,
kamalin" îva sarasas,
tārakā|paṅktir iva nabhaso,
haṃsa|māl" êva Mānasasya,
candana|vana|rājir iva Malayasya,
phaṇā|maṇi|śikh" êva Śeṣasya

As has been described, he enjoyed his harem,
but his harem was like a cluster of *shara* reeds
displaying flowers but giving no fruit,
for the women menstruated
but their wombs were fruitless.
And as his youth passed away, his wish unfulfilled,
so the grief born of his lack of offspring increased.
And his mind lost the wish
for the pleasures of sensual enjoyments.
Though surrounded by thousands of kings,
he felt himself companionless,
though he had eyes he felt blind,
though he supported the world
he felt he had no support.
Now, just as the crescent of the moon is to
the piled up matted locks of Shiva the destroyer,
as the luster of the Káustubha gem is to
the chest of Vishnu, Káitabha's foe,
as the woodland garland to Bala·rama
whose weapon is the club,
as the shore to the ocean,
as its line of rut to an elephant of the quarters,
as a creeper to a tree,
as the appearance of flowers to the month of spring,
as moonlight to the moon,
as a bed of lotuses to a lake,
as the array of stars to the heavens,
as a flock of geese to the Mánasa lake,
as the line of sandal forests to the Málaya mountain,
as the flame of the jewels in his hoods to Shesha,

bhūṣaṇam abhūt tri|bhuvana|vismaya|
janani janan" îva vanitā|vibhramāṇāṃ
sakal'|ântaḥ|pura|pradhāna|bhūtā
mahiṣī Vilāsavatī nāma.
ekadā ca sa tad|āvāsa|gatas tāṃ
cintā|stimita|dṛṣṭinā śoka|mūkena parijanena parivṛtām,
P60 ārād avasthitaiś ca dhyān'|â|nimiṣa|locanaiḥ
kañcukibhir upāsyamānām,
an|atidūra|vartinībhiś c' ântaḥ|pura|vṛddhābhir
āśvāsyamānām,
a|viral'|âśru|bindu|pāt'|ārdrī|kṛta|dukūlām,
an|alaṃkṛtāṃ,
vāma|kara|tala|vinihita|mukha|kamalām,
a|saṃyat'|ākul'|âlakāṃ,
su|nibiḍa|paryaṅkik'|ôpaviṣṭāṃ,
rudatīṃ dadarśa.
kṛta|pratyutthānāṃ ca tāṃ tasyām eva paryaṅkikāyām
upaveśya svayaṃ c' ôpaviśy' â|vijñāta|bāṣpa|kāraṇo
bhīta|bhīta iva kara|talena vigata|bāṣp'|âmbhaḥ|kaṇau
kurvan kapolau bhū|pālas tām avādīt:
«devi, kim|artham antar|gata|guru|śoka|bhāra|mantharam
a|śabdaṃ rudyate?
grathnanti hi muktā|phala|jālakam iva
bāṣpa|bindu|nikaram etās tava pakṣma|paṅktayaḥ.

his queen, Vilásavati, was an ornament to him;
she who astonished the three worlds,
seeming the source of all womanly grace,
reigning peerlessly in the harem.
And one day when he went to her apartments
he beheld her surrounded by her attendants
staring at her anxiously in sad silence;
and close about her the chamberlains offered
their attentions, eyes unblinking in deep thought; P60
and hovering not far off the old women of the harem
were trying to console her.
Her silks were soaked
by the falling of her ceaseless teardrops.
She wore no ornaments.
The lotus of her face rested on the palm of her left hand,
her hair was untied and untidy,
she reclined on a hard bare couch, weeping—
that is how he saw her.
And as she made to rise he seated her back on the couch
and himself sat beside her,
not knowing the cause of her tears,
becoming more and more concerned about her,
the protector of the earth wiped the tears from her cheeks
with his hand and said to her,
"My queen, why are you weeping, without words,
slowly, burdened by a great grief you're concealing?
For your eye lashes are stringing together
a mass of tear drops like a network of pearls.

kim|artham ca, kṛś'|ôdari, n' âlaṃkṛt" âsi?
bāl'|ātapa iva rakt'|âravinda|kośayoḥ kim iti
na pātitaś caraṇayor alaktaka|rasaḥ?
Kusumaśara|saraḥ|kalahaṃsakau
kasmāt pāda|paṅkaja|sparśena
n' ânugṛhītau maṇi|nūpurau?
kiṃ|nimittam ayam apagata|mekhalā|kalāpa|mūko
madhya|bhāgaḥ?
kim iti ca hariṇa iva hariṇa|lāñchane na likhitaḥ
kṛṣṇ'|âguru|pattra|bhaṅgaḥ
payo|dhara|bhāre?
kena kāraṇena tanv" îyam
Hara|mukuṭa|candra|lekh" êva
Gaṅgā|srotasā na vibhūṣitā hāreṇa,
var'|ôru, śiro|dharā?
kiṃ vṛthā vahasi, vilāsini,
sravad|aśru|jala|lava|
dhauta|kuṅkuma|patra|lataṃ
kapola|yugam?
idaṃ ca komal'|âṅguli|dala|nikaraṃ
rakt'|ôtpalam iva
kara|talaṃ kim iti
karṇa|pūratām āropitam?
imāṃ ca kena hetunā, mānini, dhārayasy
an|uparacita|gorocanā|bindu|tilakām
a|saṃyamit'|âlakinīṃ lalāṭa|rekhām?

And why, my slender-bellied lady, are you not adorned?
Why hasn't liquid lac been put on your feet,
like morning sunlight on red lotus buds?
Why haven't your jeweled anklets,
that sound like two *kala·hansa* geese
on the lake of flower-arrowed Love,
been favored with the touch of your lotus feet?
What is the reason that this waist of your is dumb,
bereft of its elaborate girdle?
And again why are the black aloe leaf patterns
not drawn on your heavy breasts,
like the mark of the deer on the deer-marked moon?
O my lady with excellent thighs,
for what reason is this slender neck of yours
not adorned with a necklace,
just as the crescent moon
of Hara's crown is by Ganga's stream?
Why, my graceful playmate,
do you unbefittingly allow your cheeks
to have their leaf lines of saffron
washed off in streaks by flowing tears?
And this hand of yours with its groups of petals
that are your soft fingers,
why have you made it your ear ornament
as if it were a red lotus?
And what's the cause, my proud lady, you haven't placed
the round cow-yellow mark on your forehead,
and have left your locks unbound?

ayaṃ ca te bahula|pakṣa|pradoṣa iva
candra|lekhā|virahitaḥ
karoti me dṛṣṭi|khedam
atibahula|timira|paṭal'|ândhakāraḥ
kusuma|rahitaḥ keśa|pāśaḥ.
prasīda nivedaya, devi, duḥkha|nimittam.
ete hi pallavam iva *sa|rāgaṃ* mama hṛdayam
ākampayanti taralī|kṛta|stan'|âṃśukās
tav' āyatāḥ śvāsa|marutaḥ.
kva cin may" āparāddham anyena vā kena cid
asmad|upajīvinā parijanena?
atinipuṇam api cintayan na paśyāmi khalu
skhalitam alpam apy ātmanas tvad|viṣaye.
tvad|āyattaṃ hi me jīvitaṃ ca rājyaṃ ca.
kathyatāṃ, sundari, śucaḥ kāraṇam!»
ity evam abhidhīyamānā Vilāsavatī
yadā na kiṃ cit prativacaḥ pratipede
tadā vivṛddha|bāṣpa|hetum asyāḥ parijanam apṛcchat.
atha tasyās tāmbūla|karaṅka|vāhinī
satata|pratyāsannā
Makarikā nāma rājānam uvāca.
«deva, kuto devād alpam api pariskhalitam?
abhimukhe ca deve

And bereft of flowers your flowing locks,
like the early part of the night
in the dark half of the month
deprived of even the crescent of the moon,
dark as a mass of the thickest gloom,
pain my sight.
Please, my queen, let me know
the reason for your sorrow.
For these deep sighs of yours are winds
that flutter the silks on your breasts,
and reach as far as my *loving* heart
to shake it like a *red-tinged* blossom.
Can I have offended you,
or has any of the servants in our service?
Thinking it over most carefully,
I really can't see even a tiny fault
on my part in your respect.
For it's on you that both my life
and my kingdom depend.
Woman, you must tell me the cause of your sorrow."
When Vilásavati thus addressed
vouchsafed no answer at all,
then it was he asked her attendants
the cause of her excessive weeping.
Then her betel-box bearer, always at her side,
Mákarika by name, said to the king:
"Your Majesty, how could there be the slightest fault
on Your Majesty's part?
And Your Majesty being graciously disposed to her,
what power do her people

kā śaktiḥ parijanasy' ânyasya vā
kasya cid aparāddhum? kiṃ tu
‹mahā|graha|grast" êva
viphala|nar'|êndra|samāgam" âsm'› îty
ayam asyā devyāḥ saṃtāpaḥ.
su|mahāṃś ca kālaḥ saṃtapyamānāyāḥ.
prathamam api svāminī
dānava|śrīr iva
satata|nindita|suratā.
śayana|snāna|bhojana|bhūṣaṇa|parigrah'|ādiṣu
samuciteṣv api divasa|vyāpāreṣu
kathaṃ katham api parijana|prayatnāt
pravartyamānā sa|śok" êv' āsīt.
deva|hṛdaya|pīḍā|parijihīrṣyayā
na darśitavatī vikāram.
adya tu caturdaś" îti
bhagavantaṃ Mahākālam arcitum ito gatayā
tatra Mahābhārate vācyamāne śrutam
‹«a|putrāṇāṃ kila na santi lokāḥ śubhāḥ.
pun|nāmno
narakāt trāyata» iti puttra› iti.
etac chrutvā bhavanam āgatya parijanena
sa|śiraḥ|praṇāmam abhyarthyamān" âpi
n' āhāram abhinandati na bhūṣaṇa|parigraham ācarati

or anyone else have to harm her?
The fact of the matter is the queen feels
that her fruitless union with the king shows
she is under the influence of the great planet Saturn.
This is Her Majesty's anguish.
She has been in anguish for a very long time.
Right from the beginning of this our mistress,
like the demons' goddess of success
who always reviled the gods
has been constantly blaming her love making.
It's as if she were in mourning.
Only the efforts of her people
have kept her continuing
her daily task of sleeping, bathing,
eating, putting on ornaments and so on.
Anxious to prevent any pain to Your Majesty's heart,
she did not show how she has changed.
But she remembered that today is the 14th
and so went to worship
the blessed Shiva who is the great God Time.
There the "Maha·bhárata"
was being recited, and she heard,
'Truly the bright worlds
are not for those who have no sons.
The meaning of the word "son"
is "he who saves his parents from hell."'
When she heard that she came home
and despite her people bowing low in their entreaties
takes no interest in food, does not put on her jewels,
makes no response.

n' ôttaram pratipadyate.
kevalam a|virala|bāṣpa|bindu|durdin'|
ândhakārita|mukhī roditi.
etad ākarṇya devaḥ pramāṇam.»
ity abhidhāya virarāma.
virata|vacanāyāṃ tasyāṃ
bhūmi|pālas tūṣṇīṃ muhūrtam iva sthitvā
dīrgham uṣṇaṃ ca niśvasya nijagāda.
«devi, kim atra kriyatāṃ daiv'|āyatte vastuni?
atimātram alaṃ ruditena.
na vayam anugrāhyāḥ prāyo devatānām.
ātma|ja|pariṣvaṅg'|âmṛt'|āsvāda|sukhasya nūnam
a|bhājanam asmākaṃ hṛdayam.
anyasmiñ janmani na kṛtam avadātaṃ karma.
janm'|ântara|kṛtaṃ hi karma phalam
upanayati puruṣasy' êha janmani.
na hi śakyaṃ daivam anyathā kartum abhiyukten' âpi.
yāvan mānuṣyake śakyam upapādayituṃ
tāvat sarvam upapādyatām.
adhikāṃ kuru, devi, guruṣu bhaktim.
dvi|guṇām upapādaya devatāsu pūjām.
ṛṣi|jana|saparyāsu darśit'|ādarā bhava.
paraṃ hi daivatam ṛṣayaḥ.
yatnen' ārādhitā yathā|samīhita|phalānām
atidurlabhānām api varāṇāṃ dātāro bhavanti.

All she does is cry,
darkening her face in the ceaseless rain of her teardrops.
Your Majesty has heard, and must decide."
So saying, she fell silent.
When she'd stopped speaking
the king sat silent for a while.
Then giving vent to a long hot sigh he spoke.
"My queen, what can we do about it?
This matter is subject to fate.
You must not take weeping too far.
Probably the gods aren't going to favor us.
It seems to be the case
that our hearts won't partake of the happiness
of tasting the nectar of a son's embrace.
In another life we must have done no good deed,
for action done in another birth
bears fruit for a man in this life.
What is one's fate cannot be made otherwise,
however hard one tries.
Yet all that a human can do should be done.
My queen, give more devotion to elders,
redouble your worship of the gods.
Make sure you show your concern to pay homage
to the holy sages, for they are great divinities.
Propitiate them intently, and they will grant great boons
that yield the fruit we desire,
even though really hard to reach.

śrūyate hi purā Caṇḍakauśika|prabhāvān
Magadheṣu Bṛhadratho nāma rājā
Janārdanasya jetāram
a|tula|bhuja|balam a|pratiratham
Jarāsaṃdhaṃ nāma tanayaṃ lebhe.
Daśarathaś ca rājā pariṇata|vayā
Vibhāṇḍaka|mahā|muni|sutasya
Ṛṣyaśṛṅgasya prasādān
Nārāyaṇa|bhujān iv' â|pratihatān udadhīn iv'
â|kṣobhyān avāpa caturaḥ putrān.
anye ca rāja|rṣayas tapo|dhanān ārādhya
putra|darśan'|âmṛt'|āsvāda|
sukha|bhājo babhūvuḥ.
amogha|phalā hi mahā|muni|sevā bhavati.
aham api khalu, devi, kadā
samupārūḍha|garbha|bhar'|âlasām āpāṇḍu|mukhīm
āsanna|pūrṇa|candr'|ôdayām iva paurṇa|māsī|niśāṃ
devīṃ drakṣyāmi?
kadā me tanaya|janma|mah'|ôtsav'|ānanda|nirbharo
hariṣyati pūrṇa|pātraṃ parijanaḥ?
kadā hāridra|vasana|dhāriṇī
suta|sanāth'|ôtsaṅgā
dyaur iv' ôdita|ravi|maṇḍalā sabāl'|ātapā
mām ānandayiṣyati devī?

For we hear that in times past
through the power of the sage Chanda·káushika
in Mágadha a king named Brihad·ratha
obtained a son named Jara·sandha,
whose might in arms was unparalleled, a peerless warrior,
who defeated even Vishnu,[84] the agitator of men.
And Dasha·ratha was an aged king
when through the grace of Rishya·shringa,
son of the great sage Vibhándaka, he obtained four sons
like the four arms of Vishnu Naráyana,
invincible, and imperturbable like the four oceans.
And other royal sages,
when they'd conciliated ascetics
rich in ascetic power,
enjoyed the happiness of tasting
the nectar of the sight of a son.
For honor paid to great ascetics is unfailing in its fruits.
There's me too, my queen!
When shall I see Your Majesty
weary with the weight
of the child growing in your womb,
your face pale, like the night of the full moon
with the full moon about to rise?
When will your attendants, overwhelmed with joy
at the great festival of the birth of my son
carry off the full dish of auspicious gifts?
When will my queen clad in saffron robes,
her lap occupied by our son, make my heart rejoice
like the sky in early morning sunshine
when the disk of the sun has risen?

kadā sarv'|āuṣadhi|piñjara|jaṭila|keśo
nihita|rakṣā|ghṛta|binduni tāluni
vinyasta|gaura|sarṣap'|ônmiśra|bhūti|leśo
gorocanā|citra|kaṇṭha|sūtra|granthir
uttāna|śayo daśana|śūnya|smit'|ānanaḥ
putrako janasyiṣyati me hṛday'|āhlādam?
kadā gorocanā|kapila|dyutir
antaḥ|purikā|kara|tala|paramparā|
saṃcāryamāṇa|mūrtir
a|śeṣa|jana|vandito
maṅgala|pradīpa iva me śok'|ândhakāram
unmūlayiṣyati cakṣuṣoḥ?
kadā ca kṣiti|reṇu|dhūsaro maṇḍayiṣyati
mama hṛdayena dṛṣṭyā ca saha
paribhraman bhavan'|âṅgaṇam?
kadā kesari|kiśoraka iva
saṃjāta|jānu|caṅkramaṇ'|âvasthaḥ
saṃcariṣyat' îtas tataḥ
sphaṭika|maṇi|bhitty|antaritān
bhavana|mṛga|śāvakāñ jighṛkṣuḥ?
kad' ântaḥpura|nūpura|nināda|saṃgatān
gṛha|kalahaṃsakān anusaran
kakṣ"|ântara|pradhāvitaḥ
kanaka|mekhalā|ghaṇṭikā|rav'|ânusāriṇīm
āyāsayiṣyati dhātrīm?

When will a son generate joy in my heart
with his curly hair yellow with the all-herb mixture,
a lick of ash mixed with white mustard seed
placed on his fontanel
plus a drop of ghee to hold it in place;
a bright yellow string knotted round his neck,
lying on his back, smiling up without teeth in his mouth?
When will he, lustrous with cow-yellow,
like an auspicious lamp, his handsome body
passed round from hand to hand
by the women of the harem,
praised by everybody,
when will he uproot from my eyes
the darkness of sorrow?
And when, dirty with the dust of the earth,
will he adorn the courtyard of the palace,
as he crawls around,
taking with him my heart and my eyes?
When will his knees grow strong enough
for him to walk,
and roam here and there like a lion cub,
wanting to seize the tame young deer
separated from him by the crystal walls?
When will he run into the inner courtyard
after the tame *kala·hansa* geese who've followed
the jingling of the harem's anklets,
and wear out his nurse as she follows
the sound of the little golden bells on his girdle?

kadā kṛṣṇ'|âguru|paṅka|likhita|mada|lekh"|
âlaṃkṛta|gaṇḍa|sthalako,
mukha|ḍiṇḍima|dhvani|janita|prītir,
ūrdhva|*kara*|viprakīrṇa|candana|
cūrṇa|dhūli|dhūsaraḥ,
kuñcit'|âṅguli|śikhar'|âṅkuś'|ākarṣaṇa|
vidhūta|śirāḥ
kariṣyati matta|gaja|rāja|līlā|krīḍāḥ?
kadā mātuś caraṇa|yugala|rāg'|ôpayukta|śeṣeṇa
piṇḍ'|ālaktaka|rasena vṛddha|kañcukināṃ
viḍambayiṣyati mukhāni?
kadā kutūhala|cañcala|locano maṇi|kuṭṭimeṣv
adho|datta|dṛṣṭir anusariṣyati skhalad|gatir
ātmanaḥ pratibimbāni?
kadā nar'|êndra|sahasra|prasārita|bhuja|yugal'|
âbhinandyamān'|āgamano,
bhūṣaṇa|maṇi|mayūkha|lekh"|ākulī|kriyamāṇa|lola|dṛṣṭir
āsana|sthitasya me puraḥ paryaṭiṣyati sabh"|ântare?[85]
ity etāni ca manoratha|śatāni cintayato 'ntaḥ|
saṃtapyamānasya prayānti rajanyaḥ.
mām api dahaty ev' âyam ahar|niśam anala iv'
ân|apatyatā|samudbhavaḥ śokaḥ.

When will he—
his cheeks decorated
with lines of rut drawn
with black aloe paste,
taking pleasure in his nurse
making the sound
of a *díndima* drum with her mouth,
gray with the dust of powdered sandal
scattered over himself
by the upraised *elephant trunk* that is his *hand,*
shaking his head at his nurse drawing him to her
with the tip of the goad that is her curved finger—
play the game of pretending to be
a lead elephant in rut?
When will he streak the faces of the old chamberlains
with the remnant of the liquid from the balls of lac
after it has been used for coloring his mother's feet?
When, his eyes restless with curiosity, toddle about
looking down at the jeweled pavements
and following his own reflections?
When, his coming greeted by the outstretched arms
of thousands of kings, his restless eyes bewildered
by the rays from the jewels of the ornaments,
will he wander into the assembly hall
when I'm seated on the throne?
My nights are spent in anguish while I think
of hundreds of such wishes as these.
Me too day and night this sorrow of having no children
burns like a fire.
The world seems empty to me.

śūnyam iva me pratibhāti jagat.
a|phalam api paśyāmi rājyam.
a|pratividheye tu vidhātari kiṃ karomi?
tan mucyatām ayam, devi, śok'|ânubandhaḥ.
ādhīyatāṃ dhairye dharme ca dhīḥ.
dharma|parāyaṇānāṃ hi sadā samīpa|saṃcāriṇyaḥ
kalyāṇa|saṃpado bhavanti.»
ity evam abhidhāya salilam ādāya svayaṃ kara|talen'
âbhinava|pallaven' êva vikaca|kamal'|ôpamānam
ānanam asyāḥ s'|âśru|lekhaṃ mamārja.
punaḥ punaś ca priya|śata|madhurābhiḥ
śok'|âpanoda|nipuṇābhir dharm'|ôpadeśa|garbhābhir
vāgbhir āśvāsya suciraṃ sthitvā nar'|êndro nirjagāma.
nirgate ca tasmin mandī|bhūta|śokā Vilāsavatī
yathā|kriyamāṇ'|ābharaṇa|parigrah'|ādikam
ucitaṃ divasa|vyāpāram anvatiṣṭhat.
tataḥ prabhṛti sutarāṃ devat"|ārādhaneṣu
brāhmaṇa|pūjāsu guru|jana|saparyāsu c'
ādaravatī babhūva.
yad yac ca kiṃ cit kutaś cic chuśrāva
garbha|tṛṣṇayā tat tat sarvaṃ cakāra.
na mahāntam api kleśam ajīgaṇat.

I see the kingdom too as barren.
But since there is no appeal against the creator,
what can I do?
Therefore, my queen,
you must cease this persistent grieving.
Apply your mind to fortitude and duty.
For increase of blessings is always close at hand
to those intent on duty."
Having spoken thus, he took some water
and with a hand like a tender leaf he wiped
her tear-streaked face that resembled a lotus in bloom.
Again and again with words sweet
with a hundred endearments,
well chosen to dispel sorrow,
and full of instruction about duty,
he comforted her.
After spending a long time with her the king left.
And when he'd gone, her grief abated,
Vilásavati went back to her usual daily routine
such as putting on her jewelry.
But from that time she was unceasingly devoted
to propitiating the gods, honoring brahmins
and paying homage to holy people.
And in her thirst for a child
whatever she heard recommended,
from whatever source, she carried out completely.
She baulked at no difficulty, however great.

an|avarata|dahyamāna|
guggulu|bahula|dhūp'|ândha|kāriteṣu
Caṇḍikā|gṛheṣu dhaval'|âmbara|śuci|mūrtir upoṣitā
harita|kuś'|ôpacchadeṣu musala|śayaneṣu suṣvāpa.
puṇya|salila|pūrṇair
vividha|kusuma|phal'|ôpetaiḥ
kṣīra|taru|pallava|lāñchanaiḥ sarva|ratna|garbhaiḥ
śātakumbha|kumbhair go|kuleṣu
vṛddha|gopa|vanitā|kṛta|maṅgalānāṃ
lakṣaṇa|saṃpannānāṃ gavām adhaḥ sasnau.
pratidivisaṃ utthāy' ôtthāya
sarva|ratn'|ôpetāni haimāni
tila|pātrāṇi bhrāhmaṇebhyo dadau.
mahā|nar'|êndra|likhita|maṇḍala|madhya|vartinī
vividha|bali|dān'|ānandita|dig|devatāni
bahula|pakṣa|caturdaśī|niśāsu catuṣpathe
snapana|maṅgalāni bheje.
siddh'|āyatanāni
kṛta|vicitra|devat'|ôpayācitakāni siṣeve.
darśita|pratyayāni
saṃnidhāna|mātṛ|bhavanāni jagāma.
prasiddheṣu nāga|kula|hradeṣu mamajja.
aśvattha|prabhṛtīn upapādita|pūjān mahā|vanaspatīn
kṛta|pradakṣiṇā vavande.

In temples of Durga darkened with continuously burning
incense in which bdellium was prominent,
her pure body dressed in white clothes, fasting,
she slept on beds of spikes strewn with green *kusha* grass.
With golden pots full of holy water,
containing also various flowers and fruits,
decked with leaves of *kshira* trees,
with all sorts of jewels at the bottom,
in camps of cowherds she bathed
underneath cows endowed with lucky marks
and auspiciously decorated by the old cowherd wives.
Everyday, every time she got up,
she gave to the brahmins
golden pots of sesame seeds with all sorts of gems added.
On nights of the 14th of the dark fortnight
at a crossroads,[86]
standing in the center
of a circle drawn by a great magician,
she performed auspicious rites of bathing
that delighted the gods of the quarters
with various offerings.
She frequented the shrines
known to have fulfilled peoples' wishes,
and promised wonderful offerings to the deities.
She went to Mátrika shrines[87] in the region
which had demonstrated their efficacy.
She bathed in pools famous for their Naga families.
She honored great trees such as the *ashváttha*,
worshipping and circumambulating them.

dolāyamāna|maṇi|valayena
pāṇi|yugalena snātā svayam
a|khaṇḍa|siktha|saṃpāditaṃ rajata|pātre parigṛhītaṃ
vāyasebhyo dadhy|odana|balim adāt.
a|parimita|kusuma|dhūpa|vilep'|
âpūpa|palala|pāyasa|bali|lāja|kalitām
ahar ahar ambā|devī|saparyām ātatāna.
svayam upahṛta|piṇḍa|pātrān
bhakti|pravaṇena manasā
siddh'|ādeśān nagna|kṣapaṇakān papraccha.
vipraśnik"|ādeśa|vacanāni bahu mene.
nimitta|jñānān upacacāra.
śakuna|jñāna|vidām ādaram adarśayat.
aneka|vṛddha|paraṃpar"|āgam'|āgatāni
rahasyāny aṅgīcakāra.
darśan'|āgataṃ dvija|janam ātma|ja|darśan'|ôtsukā
veda|śrutīr akārayat.
an|avarata|vācyamānāḥ puṇya|kathāḥ śuśrāva.
gorocan"|ālikhita|bhūrja|pattra|garbhān
mantra|karaṇḍakān uvāha.
P65 rakṣā|pratisar'|ôpetāny oṣadhi|sūtrāṇi babandha.
parijano 'pi c' âsyāḥ satatam upaśrutyai
nirjagāma tan|nimittāni ca jagrāha.

With her own hands, jeweled bracelets swinging,
when she'd bathed she herself gave to the birds
an offering of curds and boiled rice
prepared from unbroken grains,
piled on a silver dish.
Every day in worship of the goddess Amba[88]
she made an offering comprising unlimited flowers,
incense, unguents, sweet cakes of barley flour,
sesame candy, and milk rice in sugar, as well as
the usual sacrificial offering of parched rice grains.
Herself filling their begging bowls,
with concentrated devotion
she questioned naked Jain monks
whose prophecies were known to come true.
She thought highly of the prophetic pronouncements
of female fortune tellers.
She waited upon experts in interpreting signs.
She showed her respect for those who were skilled
in the knowledge of interpreting the actions of birds.
She accepted the secret teachings handed down
in the scriptures of many ancient lineages of gurus.
When brahmins came to see her, she, eager to see a son,
made them recite the Veda to her.
She listened to the constant recital of holy tales.
She wore little mantra-caskets filled
with birchbark sheets written on with cow-yellow ink.
She tied on herself strings of medicinal herbs (p65)
joined with protective amulets.
Her attendants too went outside to listen
for significant sounds and interpreted them.

śivābhyo māṃsa|bali|piṇḍam
anudinaṃ niśi samutsasarja.
svapna|darśan'|āścaryāṇy ācāryāṇām ācacakṣe.
catvareṣu śiva|balim upajahāra.
evaṃ ca gacchati kāle kadā cid rājā
kṣīṇa|bhūyiṣṭhāyāṃ rajanyām
alpa|śeṣa|pāṇḍu|tārake
jarat|pārāvata|pakṣa|dhūmre nabhasi
svapne sita|prāsāda|śikhara|sthitāyā Vilāsavatyāḥ
kariṇyā iva bisa|valayam ānane
sakala|kalā|paripūrṇa|maṇḍalaṃ
śaśinaṃ praviśantam adrākṣīt.
prabuddhaś c' ôtthāya harṣa|vikāsa|sphītatareṇa cakṣuṣā
dhavalī|kṛta|vāsa|bhavanas tasminn eva kṣaṇe samāhūya
Śukanāsāya taṃ svapnam akathayat.
sa taṃ samupajāta|harṣaḥ pratyuvāca:
«deva, saṃpannāḥ su|cirād
asmākaṃ prajānāṃ ca manorathāḥ.
katipayair ev' âhobhir a|saṃdeham anubhavati svāmī
suta|mukha|kamal'|âvalokana|sukham.
adya khalu may" âpi niśi svapne dhauta|sakala|vāsasā
śānta|mūrtinā divy'|ākṛtinā dvijena vikacaṃ
candra|kal"|âvadāta|dala|śatam ālola|kesara|sahasra|jaṭālaṃ
makaranda|bindu|śīkara|varṣi puṇḍarīkam
utsaṅge devyā Manoramāyā nihitaṃ dṛṣṭam.

Every night she threw out an offering of meat
for female jackals.
She related the wonders seen in her dreams to gurus.
At crossroads she made auspicious offerings.
And time going by in this way, it chanced
when little of the night was left,
when the sky with a few pale stars
remaining was as gray as an old pigeon's wing,
the king saw in a dream Vilásavati
standing on the terrace of her white palace,
and like a ball of lotus fibers
going into the mouth of a cow elephant,
beheld the full circle of the moon
with all its digits going into her mouth.
On awakening he arose and made his bed-chamber
quite white with his wide open eyes beaming forth joy.
Straightaway calling Shuka·nasa, he told him the dream.
Shuka·nasa was filled with joy and replied,
"Your Majesty, at long last our wishes
and those of your subjects are fulfilled.
In just a few days, there can be no doubt,
my lord will experience the happiness
of beholding the lotus face of a son.
This very night I too saw in a dream a brahmin,
white robed, serene in appearance, of godly bearing,
place in the lap of my lady Mano·rama
a full-blown *pundaríka* lotus,
its hundred petals as white as the digits of the moon,
its thick cluster of a thousand filaments aquiver,
raining a shower of honey drops.

āvedayanti hi pratyāsannam ānanda|kāraṇam
agra|pātīni śubhāni nimittāni.
kiṃ c' ânyat priyataram adhik'|ānanda|kāraṇaṃ ato
bhaviṣyati? a|vitatha|phalāś ca prāyo
niś"|âvasāna|samaya|dṛṣṭā bhavanti svapnāḥ.
sarvathā na|cireṇa Māndhātāram iva dhaureyaṃ
sarva|rāja|rṣīṇāṃ bhuvan'|ānanda|hetum
ātma|jaṃ janayiṣyati devī.
śarat|kāla|kamalin" îv' âbhinava|kamal'|ôdgamena
gandha|gajam āhlādayiṣyati devam.
yen' êyaṃ dig|gaja|mada|lekh" êv'
âvicchinna|saṃtānā
kṣiti|bhāra|dhāraṇ'|ôcitā
bhaviṣyati kula|saṃtatiḥ svāminaḥ.»
ity evam abhidadhānam eva taṃ kareṇa gṛhītvā
nar'|êndraḥ praviśy' âbhyantaram
ubhābhyām api tābhyāṃ svapnābhyāṃ
Vilāsavatīm ānandayāṃ cakāra.
katipaya|divas'|âpagame ca
devatā|prasādāt
sarasīm iva pratimā|śaśī
viveśa garbho Vilāsavatīm.
yena Nandana|vana|rājir iva pārijātena
Madhusūdana|vakṣaḥ|sthal"
îva Kaustubha|maṇinā
sā sutarām arājata.

For auspicious omens befalling beforehand
inform us of the near approach of joy.
And what else can be dearer and a greater cause of joy?
And generally dreams seen at the close of night
don't fail to bear fruit.
It is exceedingly certain Her Majesty will soon give birth
to a son who will be like Mandhátri,[89]
foremost of all sage-like kings,
and a cause of joy to all the world.
Just as a pool of *kámala* lotuses in fall
delights a rutting elephant
with the springing up of fresh lotuses,
she will delight Your Majesty.
Through him the line of my lord's family,
fit to bear the weight of the world,
will be of unbroken succession
like the line of rut on an elephant of the quarters."
While he was continuing in this vein
the king took him by the hand,
entered the inner apartments
and delighted Vilásavati
with both the dreams.
And with the passing of some days
by the grace of the gods
a fetus entered Vilásavati,
as the reflection of the moon enters a lake.
With it, like the Nándana grove with the *parijáta* tree,
like Vishnu's chest with the Káustubha gem,
she shone most gloriously.

darpaṇa|śrīr iva garbha|cchalena saṃkrāntam
avani|pāla|pratibimbam uvāha.
śanaiḥ śanaiś ca pratidinam upacīyamāna|garbhā
nirbhara|paripīta|sāgara|salila|bhara|manthar" êva
megha|mālā mandaṃ mandaṃ saṃcacāra.
muhur muhur anubaddha|vijṛmbhikam ājihmita|locanā
s" âlasaṃ niśaśvāsa.
tath"|âvasthāṃ tām ahar ahaḥ svayam
aneka|rasa|vāñchita|pāna|bhojanāṃ prāvṛṣam iva
śyāmāyamāna/payodhara/mukhīṃ ketakīm iva
garbha/cchavi/pāṇḍurām
āloky' êṅgita|kuśalaḥ parijano vijñātavān.
atha tasyāḥ sarva|parijana|pradhāna|bhūtā
sadā rāja|kula|saṃvāsa|caturā
sadā ca rāja|saṃnikarṣa|pragalbhā
sarva|maṅgala|kuśalā
Kulavardhanā nāma mahattarikā
praśaste divase pradoṣa|velāyām
abhyantar'|āsthāna|maṇḍapa|gataṃ
gandha|tail'|âvaseka|jvalita|dīpikā|sahasra|parivāram
uḍu|nikara|madhya|vartinam iva paurṇa|māsī|śaśinam

Like a beautiful mirror, under the guise of the fetus
she carried the reflection of the king.
And each day as the fetus continued to grow,
little by little she moved about more and more slowly,
like a bank of clouds that is ponderous with the burden
of water it has thirstily drunk up from the ocean.
Again and again she gave a lazy sigh,
she yawned, her eyes unfocussed.
Her attendants, skilled in reading
every sign she gave,
took note of her condition day by day,
watching her eat and drink
the many different flavors she craved,
her nipples darkening like the rainy season
that begins with darkening clouds
while she *grew pale with the luster of pregnancy*
like the pale interior of a *kétaki* flower.
Then the chief of all the queen's servants,
having the skills
that come from constant residence in the court,
having the confidence
that comes from constant proximity to the king,
competent in every auspicious ceremony,
the senior handmaid named Kula·várdhana,
Family-increase,
on an auspicious day, at evening time,
approached the king who was in the harem hall,
surrounded by a thousand lamps
refreshed with fragrant oil,
like the full moon day's moon amid the myriad stars,

uraga|rāja|phaṇa|maṇi|sahasr'|ântarāla|sthitam iva
Nārāyaṇaṃ
mūrdh'|âvasiktaiḥ parimitaiḥ pradhāna|nar'|êndraiḥ
parivṛtam an|atidūr'|âvasthita|parijanam anantaram
uttuṅga|vetr'|āsan'|ôpaviṣṭena
dhauta|dhaval'|âmbara|paridhānen' ân|ulbaṇa|veṣeṇa
jala|nidhin" êv' â|gādha|gāmbhīryeṇa
samupārūḍha|viśrambha|nirbharās tās tāḥ kathāḥ
Śukanāsena saha kurvāṇaṃ bhūmi|pālam
upasṛtya rahaḥ karṇa|mūle viditaṃ
Vilāsavatī|garbha|vṛttāntam akārṣīt.
tena tu tasyā vacanen' â|śruta|pūrveṇ' â|saṃbhāvyen'
âmṛta|rasen' êva sikta|sarv'|âṅgasya,
sadyaḥ|prarūḍha|rom'|âṅkura|nikara|kaṇṭakita|tanor,
ānanda|rasena vihvalī|kriyamāṇasya,
smita|vikasita|kapola|sthalasya,
paripūrita|hṛday'|âtiriktaṃ harṣam iva
daśan'|âṃśu|vitāna|cchalena vikirato rājñaḥ
Śukanāsa|mukhe lola|tārakam
ānanda|jala|bindu|klinna|pakṣma|mālaṃ
tat|kṣaṇaṃ papāta cakṣuḥ.
an|ālokita|pūrvaṃ tu
harṣa|prakarṣam abhisamīkṣya bhū|pateḥ
Kulavardhanāṃ ca smita|vikasita|mukhīm
āgatāṃ dṛṣṭvā tasya c' ârthasya satataṃ
manasi viparivartamānatvād

like Naráyana Vishnu reclining under the thousand gems
on the hoods of Shesha, king of snakes.
A limited number of prominent crowned kings
surrounded him, his servants not very far away,
and Shuka·nasa was seated close beside him
on a high cane chair
dressed in clean white clothes, his get-up austere;
like the ocean, his depth unfathomable;
with whom he was conversing on topics
arising from their long intimacy—
and she whispered secretly in the king's ear
the news that Vilásavati was with child.
At her words, entirely new to his ears, hardly credible,
all his limbs felt bathed in nectar;
his body prickled as horripilation
immediately spread all over it;
he became befuddled with liquid bliss;
his cheeks blossomed into smiles;
in the guise of the spreading luster of his teeth
he seemed to disperse the overflow
from the joy filling his heart;
and his eyes, pupils quivering,
lashes awash with tears of joy,
at once fell upon the face of Shuka·nasa.
Shuka·nasa, for his part,
observing the king's excess of joy
such as he had not seen before,
and having seen Kula·várdhana
come in with a smiling face,
and because of the matter he constantly turned over

a|vidita|vṛttānto 'pi
tat|kāl'|ôcitam aparam atimahato harṣasya
kāraṇam a|paśyañ Śukanāsaḥ svayam utprekṣya
samutsarpit'|āsanaḥ samīpataram upasṛtya
n' âtiprakāśam ābabhāṣe:
«deva, kim asti kiṃ cit tasmin svapna|darśane satyam?
atyantam utphulla|locanā hi Kulavardhanā dṛśyate!
devasy' âp' îdaṃ priya|vacana|śravaṇa|kutūhalād iva
śravaṇa|mūlam upasarpad,
uparacayad iva nīla|kuvalaya|karṇa|pūra|śobhām
ānanda|jala|pariplutaṃ tarala|tārakaṃ vikasad
āvedayati mahat|praharṣa|kāraṇam
īkṣaṇa|yugalakam.
upārūḍha|mah"|ôtsava|śravaṇa|kutūhalam
utsuk'|ôtsukaṃ klāmyati me manaḥ.
tad āvedayatu devaḥ: kim idam?»
ity uktavati tasmin rājā vihasy' âbravīt.
«yadi satyam anayā yathā kathitaṃ
tathā sarvam a|vitathaṃ svapna|darśanam.
ahaṃ tu na śraddadhe!
kuto 'smākam iyatī bhāgya|saṃpat?
a|bhājanaṃ hi vayam īdṛśānāṃ priya|vacana|śravaṇānām.
a|vitatha|vādinīm apy ahaṃ Kulavardhanām
evaṃ|vidhānāṃ kalyāṇānām a|saṃbhāvitam ātmānaṃ
manyamāno viparītām iv' âdya paśyāmi.
tad uttiṣṭha svayam eva gatvā ‹kim atra satyam›
iti devīṃ pṛṣṭvā jñāsyāmi.»

in his mind, though he did not know what the news was,
not seeing any other cause for excessive joy
befitting that occasion, made his own surmise,
and pulling his chair closer,
moving right next to the king, spoke to him quietly:
"Your Majesty, is there some truth in that dream you had?
For one can see that Kula·várdhana's eyes are wide open!
And as for Your Majesty, your shining eyes,
reaching the lobes of your ears
as if in eagerness to hear the welcome news,
seeming to achieve the beauty
of blue *kúvalaya* water-lily ornaments for your ears,
swimming in tears of joy, pupils aquiver,
announce some cause of great joy.
Eagerness to hear that a great festival is nigh
exhausts my all too eager mind.
Therefore, may Your Majesty
let me know what this means?"
When he had said this the king smiled and said,
"If what she has told me is true,
then all the dream is not untrue.
But I cannot believe it!
How should such wonderful good luck befall us?
For we are not worthy of such good tidings.
Although Kula·várdhana doesn't say things
that aren't true,
I think myself unworthy of such auspicious things
and today I look on her as changed for the worse.
So, get up. I'll go myself, and ask the queen if it be true,
and then I'll know."

ity abhidhāya visarjya sakala|nar'|êndra|lokam

unmucya sv'|âṅgebhyo bhūṣaṇāni Kulavardhanāyai dattvā

tayā ca datta|prasād'|ânantaram

avani|tal'|āśliṣṭa|lalāṭa|lekhayā śiraḥ|praṇāmen' âbhyarcitaḥ,

saha|Śukanāsen' ôtthāya harṣa|viśeṣa|nirbhareṇa

tvaryamāṇo manasā pavana|calita|nīla|kuvalaya|dala|

līlā|viḍambakena dakṣiṇen' âkṣṇā parisphurat"

âbhinandyamānas,

tat|kāla|sevā|samucitena virala|viralena parijanen'

ânugamyamānaḥ,

puraḥ saṃsarpiṇīnām anila|lola|sthūla|śikhānāṃ

pradīpakānām ālokena

samutsāryamāṇa|kakṣ"|ântara|timira|saṃhatir

antaḥ|puram ayāsīt.

tatra ca sukṛta|rakṣā|saṃvidhāne

nava|sudh"|ânulepana|dhavalite

prajvalita|maṅgala|pradīpe

pūrṇa|kalaś'|âdhiṣṭhita|dvāra|pakṣake

pratyagra|likhita|maṅgaly'|ālekhy'|ôjjvalita|bhitti|bhāga|

manohāriṇy uparacita|sita|vitāne

vitāna|paryant'|âvabaddha|muktā|guṇe

maṇi|pradīpa|prahata|timire vāsa|bhavane

So saying, he dismissed all the kings,
and removing the ornaments from his limbs
gave them to Kula·várdhana.
And she on receiving his gracious gift paid homage
by bowing her head so low
her forehead touched the ground.
Rising with Shuka·nasa and hurried on
by his mind overcharged with special joy;
gladdened by his throbbing right eye resembling
the graceful beauty of a blue *kúvalaya* water-lily petal
stirred in the breeze;
followed by a very small number of attendants,
those who usually waited on him at that time of day;
the light of the lamps carried ahead of him,
their strong flames flickering in the wind,
driving back the darkness
in the rooms they passed through,
he proceeded to the harem.
And there in the bed chamber,
rituals of protection had been well performed,
whitened with a fresh layer of plaster,
auspicious lamps burning,
a pot full of water standing on either side of the door,
charming with its walls brightly decorated
with freshly painted auspicious pictures,
overhung with a white canopy,
with strings of pearls
hanging from the borders of the canopy,
jewel lamps driving back the darkness.

bhūti|likhita|pattra|latā|kṛta|rakṣā|parikṣepaṃ
śiro|bhāga|vinyasta|dhavala|nidrā|maṅgala|kalaśam
ābaddha|vividh'|āuṣadhi|mūla|yantra|pavitram
avasthāpita|rakṣā|śakti|valayam
itas tato viprakīrṇa|gaura|sarṣapam
avalambita|bāla|yoktra|grathita|lola|pippala|pattram
āsakta|harit'|âriṣṭa|pallavam
uttuṅga|pāda|pīṭha|pratiṣṭhitam
indu|dīdhiti|dhavala|pracchada|paṭam
acala|rāja|śilā|tala|viśālaṃ
garbh'|ôcitaṃ
śayana|talam adhiśayānāṃ,
kanaka|pātra|parigṛhītair
a|vicchinna|viral'|âvasthita|dadhi|lavair
jala|taraṃga|tarala|sita|śāli|siktha|nikarair
a|grathita|kusum'|âñjali|sanāthaiḥ
pūrṇa|bhājanair
a|khaṇḍit'|ānana[90]|matsya|paṭalaiś ca
pratyagra|piśita|piṇḍa|miśrair
a|vicchinna|salila|dhār"|
ânugamyamāna|mārgaiḥ
paṭalaka|prajvalitaiś ca śītala|pradīpair
gorocanā|miśra|gaura|sarṣapaiś ca
salil'|âñjalibhiś c'

The couch she was lying on had a protective circle
round it made of leaf and creeper patterns
drawn with holy ash.
At its head was placed an auspicious silver jar
to induce calm sleep.
It was hallowed with various herbs, roots,
and *yantra*s tied to it.
Rings with the power to protect were placed on it.
White mustard seed was scattered over it here and there.
From it swung *pippal* leaves
threaded on string made of human hair,
To it were fastened green *aríshta* leaves.
It stood on a base with high legs, and had a coverlet
as white as the rays of the moon.
It was as broad as a rock slab of the king of mountains.
It was fitting for a pregnant lady.
With lumps of curds in golden cups
placed at regular intervals,
with loaded dishes that had heaps of white boiled rice
undulating like waves of water,
and were topped with handfuls of loose flowers,
and heaps of fish with their heads not cut off
mixed with lumps of fresh meat
and the paths of these dishes could be followed
by the unbroken streams of water
poured on to the ground;
and with camphor lamps inside baskets,
and with white mustard seeds mixed with cow-yellow
and with handfuls of water,
the old women of the harem,

ācāra|kuśalen' ântaḥpura|jaratī|janena
kriyamāṇ'|âvataraṇaka|maṅgalām
dhaval'|âmbara|vivikta|veṣeṇa pramuditena
prastuta|maṅgalya|prāy'|ālāpena parijanen' ôpāsyamānām,
upārūḍha|garbhatay"
ântar|gata|kula|śailām iva kṣitim,
salila|nimagn'|Airāvatām iva Mandākinīm,
guhā|gata|siṃhām iva giri|rāja|mekhalām,
jala|dhara|paṭal'|ântarita|dina|karām iva divasa|śriyam
udaya|giri|tirohita|śaśi|maṇḍalām iva vibhāvarīm,
abhyarṇa|Brahma|kamala|vinirgamām iva
Nārāyaṇa|nābhim, āsann'|Âgasty'|ôdayām iva dakṣiṇ'|āśām,
phen'|āvṛt'|âmṛta|kalaśām iva kṣīr'|ôda|velām,
gorocanā|citrita|daśam an|upahatam atidhavalam
dukūla|yugalaṃ vasānāṃ Vilāsavatīṃ dadarśa.
sa|saṃbhrama|parijana|prasārita|kara|tal'|âvalamban'|
âvaṣṭambhena vāma|jānu|vinyasta|hasta|pallavāṃ
pracalita|bhūṣaṇa|maṇi|rava|mukharam
uttiṣṭhantīṃ Vilāsavatīm

proficient in customary rites were performing
the auspicious ritual of driving away bad spirits.
Her delighted servants were tending her.
They were wearing a distinctive dress of pure white cloth
and their talk was mainly about
the auspicious rituals that were being carried out.
Like the earth with the mountain chains
concealed within her,
like the heavenly Ganga with Indra's elephant Airávata
plunged beneath her waters,
like the curving sides of the king of mountains
with a lion lurking in the cave,
like the glory of the day
with the sun concealed within a bank of rain clouds,
like the night with the disc of the moon
concealed behind the rising mountain,
like Naráyana Vishnu's navel
with Brahma's lotus about to come forth,
like the southern quarter
when the star Agástya is about to rise,
like the shore of the milk ocean
with its pot of nectar covered over by foam,
wearing a new pair of very white silk garments,
painted on the hem with cow-yellow,
such was Vilásavati as he beheld her.
As Vilásavati was rising, leaning for support on the hand
a servant hurriedly stretched out,
placing her left hand on her knee,
clinking of her jeweled ornaments
as she set them in motion, the king said,

«alam alam atyādareṇa, devi, n' ôtthātavyam!»
ity abhidhāya saha tayā tasminn eva śayanīye
pārthivaḥ samupāviśat.
pramṛṣṭa|cāmīkara|cāru|pāde dhavalo'|ôpacchade c'
āsanne śayan'|ântare Śukanāso 'pi nyaṣīdat.
atha tām upārūḍha|garbhām ālokya
harṣa|bhara|manthareṇa manasā prastuta|parihāso rājā
«devi, Śukanāsaḥ pṛcchati yad āha Kulavardhanā
kim api tat kiṃ tath' âiva» ity uvāca.
ath' â|vyakta|smita|cchurita|kapol'|âdhara|locanā lajjayā
daśan'|âṃśu|jālaka|vyājen' âṃśuken' êva
mukham ācchādayantī Vilāsavatī tat|kṣaṇam
adhomukhī tasthau. punaḥ punaś c' ânubadhyamānā
«kiṃ mām atimātraṃ trapā|para|vaśāṃ karoṣi?
n' âhaṃ kiṃ cid api vedmi»
ity abhidadhānā tiryag|valita|tārakeṇa
cakṣuṣ" âvanata|mukhī
rājānaṃ s'|âbhyasūyam iv' âpaśyat.
a|parisphuṭa|hāsa|jyotsnā|viśadena mukha|śaśinā
bhū|bhujāṃ patir enāṃ bhūyo babhāṣe.
«sutanu, yadi madīyena vacasā tava trapā vitanyate
tad ayam ahaṃ sthito nibhṛtam.
asya tu kiṃ pratividhāsyasi
vighaṭamāna|dala|kośa|viśada|campaka|dyuteḥ

"No no, you pay me too much respect.
You mustn't get up;"
and sat down beside her on the bed.
Shuka·nasa for his part seated himself
on another couch nearby, with beautiful legs
of burnished gold, and a white coverlet.
Then seeing her swelling womb, his mind ponderous
with its burden of joy, adopting a humorous tone he said:
"My queen, Shuka·nasa is asking
whether something Kula·várdhana said is really true."
Then, an indistinct smile playing over cheek, lip and eye,
seeming to bashfully conceal her face with fine silk
in the guise of the net of rays from her teeth,
for the moment she remained looking down.
But when repeatedly pressed for a reply, she said,
"Why do you embarrass me so much?
I don't know anything."
And, her head still bowed, her eyes cast to the side,
she seemed to give the king a reproachful look.
With the moon of his face bright
with the moonlight of suppressed laughter,
the king of kings spoke to her again.
"My lady, your body is lovely!
If my words embarrass you,
I for my part will remain silent.
But how can you contradict
the paleness of the saffron coloring on your body—
a *chámpaka* flower's bright luster
as it opens its calyx of petals!

savarṇatayā parimal'|ânumīyamānasya
kuṅkum' âṅga|rāgasya
pāṇḍuratām āpadyamānasy',
ânayoś ca garbha|sambhav'|âmṛt'|âvaseka|nirvāpyamāna|
hṛdaya|śok'|ânala|prabhavaṃ dhūmam iva vamator
ānana|gṛhīta|nīl'|ôtpalayor iva cakravākayos
tamāla|pallava|lāñchita|mukhayor iva kanaka|kalaśayoḥ
sakṛd iv' ālikhita|kṛṣṇ'|âguru|paṅka|pattra|latayoḥ
śyāmāyamāna|cūcukayoḥ payo|dharayor,
asya ca pratidinam atigāḍhataratām āpadyamānena
kāñcī|kalāpena dūyamānasya naśyat|trivali|lekhā|valayasya
kraśimānam ujjhato madhya|bhāgasya?»
ity evaṃ bruvāṇam avani|pālam
antar|mukha|vinigūḍha|hāsaḥ Śukanāso
«deva, kim āyāsayasi devīm?
P70 iyam anayā kathay' âpi lajjate. tyaja
Kulavardhanā|kathita|vārtā|saṃbaddham ālāpam!»
ity abravīt.
evaṃ|vidhābhiś ca narma|prāyābhiḥ kathābhiḥ
suciraṃ sthitvā Śukanāsaḥ sva|bhavanam ayāsīt.
nar'|êndro 'pi tasminn eva vāsa|gṛhe
tayā saha tāṃ niśām atyavāhayat.

Now your body is the same color as saffron,
the saffron can only be inferred to be present
by its fragrance.
And, with their darkening nipples,
seeming to emit the smoke
from the fire of your heart's anguish
being extinguished as it is by the sprinkling of nectar
brought about by the fetus,
like two *chakra·vaka* ducks
each holding a blue lily in its beak,
like two gold pots with their openings
decked with a *tamála* leaf,
seemingly permanently painted
with leaf patterns in black *águru* paste,
how can you contradict those breasts of yours?
And your waist losing its thinness,
suffering as everyday the girdle becomes tighter,
the triple fold disappearing?"
To the king speaking in this fashion, Shuka·nasa,
hiding his laughter in his mouth, said:
"Your Majesty, why do you worry the queen?
She is embarrassed by this talk! Drop this chatter P70
about the news Kula·várdhana told you."
And after staying there a long time engaging in such talk,
joking for the most part,
Shuka·nasa went to his own home.
But the king spent the night with her
in that same bed-chamber.

tataḥ krameṇa yathā|samīhita|garbha|dohada|saṃpādana|
pramuditā pūrṇe prasava|samaye puṇye 'hany
an|avarata|galan|nāḍikā|kalita|kāla|kalair bahir
āgṛhīta|cchāyair gaṇakair gṛhīte lagne
praśastāyāṃ velāyām iraṃmadam iva
jala|dhara|mālā sakala|loka|hṛday'|ānanda|kāriṇaṃ
Vilāsavatī sutam asūta.

tasmiñ jāte
sarabhasam itas tataḥ pradhāvitasya parijanasya
caraṇa|śata|saṃkṣobha|calita|kṣiti|talo
bhū|pāl'|âbhimukha|prasṛta|skhalad|gati|
vikala|kañcuki|sahasro jana|saṃmarda|
niṣpiṣyamāṇa|patita|kubja|vāmana|kirāta|gaṇo
visphāryamāṇ'|ântaḥ|pura|jan'|ābharaṇa|
jhaṃkāra|manoharaḥ
pūrṇa|pātr'|āharaṇa|vilupyamāna|
vasana|bhūṣaṇaḥ saṃkṣobhita|nagaro
rāja|kule diṣṭi|vṛddhi|saṃbhramo 'timahān abhūt.
an|antaraṃ ca Mandara|mathyamāna|jaladhi|ghoṣa|
gambhīra|dundubhi|dhvāna|puraḥ|sareṇa
prahata|mṛdaṅga[91]|śaṅkha|kāhal'|ānaka|nivaha|

Then in due course, when she'd rejoiced
in the satisfaction of her pregnancy longings,
just as she wished,
when the period for gestation was complete,
on a holy day, at an auspicious hour,
with the exact moment noted by astrologers
using continuously flowing water clocks
measuring every forty-five minutes and sun dials,
just as a bank of rain clouds produces a lightning flash
Vilásavati gave birth to a son
who gave joy to the hearts of all the people.
When he was born—
the earth shaking under the impact of hundreds of feet
as the servants dashed here and there;
thousands of infirm chamberlains
starting to totter towards the king,
troops of hunchbacks, dwarfs and tribals
were knocked down and trampled on
in the crush of people;
with delightful jangling as the harem women's ornaments
were knocked about all over the place;
with clothes and jewels snatched
as the full plates of celebratory gifts were carried off;
shaking the city—
there was an almighty tumult of congratulations
in the royal household.
And thereupon, led by the beating
of the *dúndubhi* drums as deep as the roar
of the ocean being churned by Mount Mándara,
swollen by the strains of the numerous instruments

nināda|nirbhareṇa maṅgala|paṭaha|paṭu|rava|saṃvardhiten'
âneka|jana|sahasra|kalakala|bahulena
tribhuvanam āpūrayat" ôtsava|kolāhalena
sa|sāmantāḥ s'|ântaḥ|purāḥ
sa|prakṛtayaḥ sa|rāja|lokāḥ
sa|veśyā|yuvatayaḥ sa|bāla|vṛddhā
nanṛtur āgopālam
unmattā iva harṣa|nirbharāḥ prajāḥ.
pratidinam avardhata candr'|ôdayen' êva jaladhiḥ
kalakala|mukharo rāja|sūnor janma|mah"|ôtsavaḥ.
pārthivas tu
tanay'|ānana|darśan'|ôtsava|hṛta|hṛdayo 'pi
divasa|vaśena mauhūrtika|gaṇ'|ôpadiṣṭe praśaste muhūrte
nivārita|nikhila|parijanaḥ
Śukanāsa|dvitīyo
maṇi|maya|maṅgala|kalaśa|yugal'|â|śūnyen'
āsakta|bahu|putrik"|âlaṃkṛtena
vividha|nava|pallava|nivaha|nirantara|nicitena
saṃnihita|kanaka|maya|hala|musal'|ôkhalena[92]

being played: *mridánga* drums, conches,
káhala trumpets, *ánaka* drums, augmented
by the shrill beat of the auspicious *pátaha* drum,
added to by the hubbub of many thousand people—
such was the uproar of festival filling the universe,
to which the subjects danced as if frantic,
overwhelmed by joy,
including the feudatory kings,
including the women of the harem,
including the citizens,
including the royal servants,
including the courtesans,
including young and old, even the cowherds.
Day by day, the great festival of the birth of the king's son
increased, resounding with the roar natural to it,
like the ocean at the rise of the moon.
The king, for his part, though his heart was drawn
to the festival of seeing his son's face,
only on the day and specific auspicious moment
recommended by his troop of astrologers,
sending back all his attendants,
accompanied only by Shuka·nasa,
did he visit the birth-chamber.
Its doorway was resplendent, provided with
a pair of auspicious pots made of precious stones;
adorned with many little dolls attached to it; densely
hung with bundles of various kinds of fresh leaves;
with a plow, pestle and mortar,
all made of gold, placed there;

virala|grathita|sita|kusuma|miśra|dūrvā|pravāla|māl"|
âlaṃkṛten' âvalambit'|â|vikala|vyāghra|carmaṇā
vandana|māl"|ântarāla|ghaṭita|ghaṇṭā|gaṇena
dvāra|deśena virājamānam,
ubhayataś ca dvāra|pakṣakayor maryādā|nipuṇena,
gomaya|mayībhir uttāna|vinihita|varāṭaka|danturābhir
antar'|ântar'|ābaddha|vividha|varṇa|rāga|rucira|
kūrpāsa|kusuma|leśa|lāñchitābhiḥ
kusumbha|kesara|lav'|āśleṣa|lohitābhir lekhābhir
ālikhita|svastika|bhakti|jālam uparacayatā,
haridrā|drava|vicchuraṇa|paripiñjar'|âmbara|dhāriṇīṃ
bhagavatīṃ Ṣaṣṭhī|devīṃ kurvatā,
vikaca|pakṣa|puṭa|vikaṭa|śikhaṇḍi|pṛṣṭha|maṇḍal'|
âdhirūḍham ālola|lohita|paṭa|ghaṭita|patākam
ullasita|śakti|daṇḍa|pracaṇḍaṃ Kārtikeyaṃ saṃghaṭayatā,
vinyast'|ālaktaka|paṭala|pāṭala|madhya|bhāgau
sūryā|candramasāv ābadhnatā,
kuṅkuma|paṅka|piñjarī|kṛtām
ūrdhva|prota|kanaka|maya|yava|nikara|kaṇṭakitām
a|virala|lagna|gaura|siddh'|ârthaka|prakaratayā
kāñcana|rasa|khacitām iva
mṛn|maya|guṭikā|kadamba|mālāṃ vinyasyatā,

adorned with a loosely woven garland
of *durva* grass mixed with white flowers;
with a complete tiger-skin hanging down from it;
with a host of bells fixed at intervals
on its festoon of welcome.
And on either side of the panels of the door,
well versed in what custom demanded;
composing a network of swastika designs
drawn with lines of cow-dung studded
with cowrie shells, insides facing out,
and decked with pieces of cotton flowers
bright in varied colors fixed in at intervals,
red where they were embraced
by bits of *kusúmbha* filaments;
preparing an image of holy Shashthi,
goddess of the sixth day,
dressed in garments dyed yellow in liquid turmeric;
fashioning an image of Karttikéya mounted
on the back of his peacock which was formidable
with its two outspread wings,
his fluttering banner fashioned from a piece of red cloth,
fiercely brandishing his gleaming spear;
fashioning the sun and the moon, their middle portions
red with a mass of red lac poured into them;
laying out a garland of *kadámba* flowers
in the form of clay balls made tawny with saffron paste,
made spiky with a mass of golden barley grains
sticking up out of them,
and since they'd been rolled in thick yellow mustard seed
looking as if they were plated with liquid gold;

candana|jala|dhavaliteṣu bhitti|śikhara|bhāgeṣu
pañca|rāga|vicitra|cela|cīra|kalāpa|cihnām
āpīta|piṣṭa|paṅk'|âṅkitām vardhamāna|paramparām
anyāni ca prasava|gṛha|maṇḍana|maṅgalāni saṃpādayatā
puraṃdhri|vargeṇa samadhiṣṭhitam,
upadvāra|saṃyata|vividha|gandha|kusuma|māl"|
âlaṃkṛta|jarac|chāgam
akhila|vrīhi|madhy'|âvasthāpit'|ārya|vṛddh'|âdhyāsita|
śayana|śiro|bhāgam,
an|avarata|dahyamān'|ājya|miśra|
bhujaga|nirmoka|meṣa|viṣāṇa|kṣodam,
anala|pluṣyamāṇ'|âriṣṭa|taru|pallav'|ôllasita|
rakṣā|dhūma|gandham,
adhyayana|mukhara|dvija|gaṇa|viprakīryamāṇa|
śānty|udaka|lavam,
abhinava|likhita|Mātṛ|paṭa|pūjā|vyagra|dhātrī|janam,
aneka|vṛddh'|âṅgan"|ārabdha|sūtikā|maṅgala|
gītikā|manoharam upapādyamāna|svasty|ayanaṃ,
kriyamāṇa|śiśu|rakṣā|bali|vidhānam,
ābadhyamāna|dhavala|kusuma|dāma|śatam,
a|vicchinna|paṭhyamāna|Nārāyaṇa|nāma|sahasram,
amala|hāṭaka|yaṣṭi|pratiṣṭhāpitair
antaḥ śubha|śatān' îva niścala|śikhair

making on the upper parts of the walls
which they'd washed down with sandal water
a row of symbols of growth, formed out of
multiple strips of bright cloth of all five colors,
and dotted with yellow colored rice flour,
and other auspicious decorations
of a lying-in chamber—
a group of women doing all this occupied the room.
And tied up beside the door there was an old billy goat[93]
decorated with various fragrant flowers.
The space at the head of the bed
was occupied by a high-caste old lady
placed in the center of a circle of whole grains of rice.
Powder of snake sloughs and sheep horns
mixed with ghee was burned non-stop.
The fragrance of protective smoke was rising up
from leaves of neem trees burning in the fire.
Drops of holy water were sprinkled
by a number of brahmins loudly reciting the Vedas.
Nurses were busy worshipping a cloth
on which the Mothers[94] had been newly painted.
The chamber was charming with auspicious birth songs
which many old women had begun to sing,
with benedictions being offered, with offerings
for the protection of the infant being made, with
hundreds of garlands of white flowers being hung up.
The thousand names of Naráyana Vishnu
were being recited without interruption.
It was illuminated by auspicious lamps fastened to poles
of spotless gold, their flames motionless as if they were

dhyāyadbhir maṅgala|pradīpair
udbhāsitam,
utkhāt'|âsi|latā|sanātha|pāṇibhiḥ sarvato
rakṣā|puruṣaiḥ parivṛtaṃ
sūtikā|gṛham apaśyat.
ambhaḥ pāvakaṃ ca spṛṣṭvā viveśa.
praviśya ca prasava|parīkṣāma|pāṇḍu|mūrter
utsaṅga|gataṃ Vilāsavatyāḥ
sva|prabhā|samuday'|
ôpahata|garbha|gṛha|pradīpa|prabham,
a|parityakta|garbha|rāgatvād
udaya|paripāṭala|maṇḍalam iva savitāram,
apara|saṃdhyā|lohita|bimbam iva candramasam,
an|upajāta|kāṭhinyam iva kalpa|taru|pallavam,
utphullam iva rakt'|âravinda|rāśim,
avani|darśan'|âvatīrṇam iva lohit'|âṅgaṃ,
vidruma|kisalaya|dalair iva
bāl"|ātapa|cchedair iva
padma|rāga|raśmibhir iva racit'|âvayavam,
an|abhivyakta|mukha|pañcakam iva Mahāsenaṃ,
sura|vanitā|kara|paribhraṣṭam iv' âmara|pati|kumārakam,
uttapta|kalyāṇa|kārtasvara|bhāsvarayā sva|deha|prabhayā
pūrayantam iva vāsa|bhavanam,

meditating within themselves
on hundreds of blessings for the infant.
It was surrounded on all sides by guards
with unsheathed swords in their hands.
Such was the birth chamber he looked upon.
And after touching water and fire he entered.
And on entering, in Vilásavati's lap, her form emaciated
and pale after the delivery, he saw his son overpowering
the luster of the lamps in the lying-in chamber
with his own concentrated luster;
because he hadn't yet lost the redness of the womb
he was like the sun with its disc reddish in its rise,
like the moon with its disc ruddy in the western twilight,
like a leaf of the *kalpa* tree not yet toughened up,
like a heap of full blown red lotuses,
like the red-bodied planet Mars descended
to look at the earth;
his limbs seemed made out of pieces of coral twigs,
out of fragments of morning sunshine
or out of rays from rubies;
like the great general Karttikéya
with five of his faces hidden.
He seemed like Indra's son dropped
from the hands of a heavenly nymph;[95]
he seemed to be flooding the bedchamber
with the luster of his body
gleaming like refined gold being heated;

udbhāsamānaiḥ sahaja|bhūṣaṇair iva
mahā|puruṣa|lakṣaṇair upetam,
āgāmi|kāla|pālana|prahṛṣṭay' êva Śriyā samāliṅgitam,
āhlāda|hetum ātmajaṃ dadarśa.
vigata|nimeṣa|niścala|pakṣmaṇā muhur muhuḥ
pramṛṣṭa|saṃghaṭit'|ānanda|bāṣpa|paṭala|pluta|tārakeṇa
dūra|visphāritena snigdhena cakṣuṣā
pibann iv' ālapann iva spṛśann iva
manoratha|sahasra|prāpta|darśanaṃ
sa|spṛham īkṣamāṇas
tanay'|ānanaṃ mumude.
kṛta|kṛtyaṃ c' ātmānaṃ mene. samṛddha|manorathaḥ
Śukanāsas tu śanaiḥ śanair aṅga|pratyaṅgāny asya
nirūpayan prīti|vistārita|locano bhūmi|pālam avādīt:
«deva, paśya paśy' âsya kumārasya garbha|saṃpīḍana|vaśād
a|parisphuṭ'|âvayava|śobhasy' âpi māhātmyam
āvirbhāvayanti cakravarti|cihnāni.
tathā hi. asya saṃdhy"|âṃśu|rakta|
bāla|śaśi|kal"|ākāre lalāṭa|paṭṭe
nalina|nāla|bhaṅga|tantu|tanv"
îyam ūrṇā parisphurati.

he was endowed with the marks of a great man
shining like natural ornaments;
he was embraced by the goddess of beauty
who seemed thrilled by his future protection.
Such was his son, the cause of his rejoicing,
as he looked upon him.
With never a blink, lashes immobile,
eyeballs flooded with streams of tears of bliss
collecting as often as he wiped them away,
such were his eyes, widely dilated, affectionate;
with them he seemed to drink in his son's face,
with them he seemed to talk to it,
with them he seemed to touch it.
Longingly gazing on his son's face,
a sight obtained through a thousand wishes,
he rejoiced.
And he felt himself fulfilled. Shuka·nasa,
for his part, his wishes gloriously come to pass,
very slowly examined the infant's limbs and parts
before saying to the king, eyes wide with joy,
"Your Majesty, just look!
Although the beauty of this boy's limbs is not yet clear
because of the compression of the womb,
the marks of a sovereign emperor
bear witness to his greatness.
For instance, on his broad forehead,
which has the appearance of a young moon's crescent
reddened in the glow of twilight,
this circle of hair between the eyebrows[96] shimmers,
as thin as the fiber peeled from a broken lotus stalk.

etad vikaca|puṇḍarīka|dhavalaṃ karṇ'|ânt'|āyataṃ,
muhur muhur unmiṣitair
dhavalayat' îva vāsa|bhavanam
arāla|pakṣma locana|yugalam.
vijṛmbhamāṇa|kamala|kośa|parimala|manoharam iyam
asya sahajam ānan'|āmodam ājighrat' îva
dūrāyatā kanaka|lekh" êva nāsikā.
rakt'|ôtpala|kalik"|ākāram udvahat' îva c'
âsy' âdhara|rucakam.
rakt'|ôtpala|kalikā|lohita|talau bhagavato
viṣṭara|śravasa iva *śaṅkha|cakra|cihnau*
praśasta|lekhā|lāñchitau karau.
abhinava|kalpa|taru|pallava|komalaṃ
lekhāmayair dhvaja|ratha|turag'|ātapatra|kamalair
alaṃkṛtam aneka|nar'|êndra|sahasra|cūḍā|maṇi|cakra|
cumban'|ôcitaṃ caraṇa|yugalam.
eṣa ca dundubher iv' âtigambhīraḥ
svara|yogo 'sya rudataḥ śrūyate.»
ity evaṃ kathaty eva tasmin
sa|saṃbhram'|âpasṛtena rāja|lokena dvāri sthitena
datta|mārgas tvarita|gatir
āgatya praharṣ'|ôdgama|pulakita|tanuḥ
sphārī|bhavat|locano
Maṅgala|nāmā prahṛṣṭa|vadanaḥ puruṣaḥ
pādayoḥ praṇamya rājānaṃ vyajijñapat.
«deva, diṣṭyā vardhase! pratihatās te śatravaḥ,
ciraṃ jīva, jaya ca pṛthivīm!

Reaching as far as his ears, these eyes, white
as full-blown *pundaríka* lotuses, lashes curving,
all the time opening and shutting,
seem to whiten the bedchamber.
This nose of his like a streak of gold reaches down
as if smelling the natural fragrance of his mouth charming
as the scent of the opening calyx of a *kámala* lotus.
And his ornamental lower lip seems to bear
the likeness of a red *útpala* lotus bud.
His hands, palms as rosy as red lotus buds, marked
with auspicious lines, *have the signs of conch and wheel,*
like blessed far-famed Vishnu, *two of whose hands*
carry his insignia, the conch and the discus.
Soft as the fresh leaves of a *kalpa* tree, adorned
with lines forming a flag, a chariot, a horse, a parasol,
and a lotus, his feet are fit to be kissed by the circle
of innumerable crest-jewels of many thousand kings.
And here we hear, as he cries, his sonorous voice,
very deep like the sound of a *dúndubhi* drum."
Even as he was speaking thus,
the kings stationed at the door hastily drew aside
and made way as a man came dashing in,
his body thrilled with joy, his eyes wide-open.
Mángala was his name, his countenance was delighted.
The man bowed at the king's feet
and respectfully addressed him.
"Your Majesty, congratulations on your good fortune!
May your enemies be destroyed,
live long and conquer the world!

tvat|prasādād atra|bhavataḥ Śukanāsasy' âpi
jyeṣṭhāyāṃ brāhmaṇyāṃ Manoram'|âbhidhānāyāṃ
Rāma iva Reṇukāyāṃ tanayo jātaḥ.
śrutvā devaḥ pramāṇam» iti.
atha nṛpatir
amṛta|vṛṣṭi|pratimam ākarṇya tad|vacanaṃ
prīti|visphārit'|âkṣaḥ pratyavadat.
«aho kalyāṇa|paraṃparā! satyo 'yaṃ jana|pravādo
yad vipad vipadaṃ saṃpat saṃpadam anubadhnāt" îti.
sarvathā samāna|sukha|duḥkhatāṃ darśayatā vidhin" âpi
bhavat" êva vayam anuvartitāḥ.»
ity abhidhāya prīti|vikasita|mukhaḥ sarabhasam āliṅgya
vihasan svayam eva Śukanāsasy' ôttarīyaṃ
pūrṇa|pātraṃ jahāra.
tasmai ca prīta|manāḥ priya|vacana|śravaṇ'|ânurūpaṃ
puruṣāy' â|parimitaṃ pāritoṣikam ādideśa.
utthāya ca tath" âiva tena
caraṇa|vikuṭṭana|kvaṇita|nūpura|sahasra|
mukharita|dig|antareṇa,
sarabhas'|ôtkṣepa|calita|maṇi|valay'|āvalī|vācālita|
bhuja|laten' ōrdhvī|kṛtair uttāna|talaiḥ kara|puṭair
anila|lulitām ākāśa|kamalinīm iva
darśayatā paryasta|mṛdita|karṇa|pallavena,

By your grace, his excellency Shuka·nasa's eldest wife,
the brahmin lady named Mano·rama,
has given birth to a son,
like Rénuka[97] giving birth to Párashu·rama.
Having heard, Your Majesty must decide."
Then the king,
hearing these words from him like a shower of nectar,
responded,
"A succession of blessings! What people say is true:
Calamity follows calamity, success follows success.
Sharing the same happiness and woe,
fate has served us both
as you have served me, showing yourself the same
in happiness and in woe."
So saying, his face lighting up with joy,
he hugged Shuka·nasa
and snatched away Shuka·nasa's upper garment from him
as a congratulatory full-plate gift for himself.
And joyous-hearted on Shuka·nasa's account, he ordered
that the man should be given a reward beyond measure,
fit for the welcome news that had been heard.
And getting up just as he was,
followed by the harem maids
who made the heavens ring out as their thousand anklets
jangled with the pounding of their feet;
their creeper-like arms resounding
as they violently threw them about
and shook their rows of jeweled bracelets,
seeming to mime with their cupped hands lifted high,
palms up, a lotus pool in the sky, shaking in the wind;

paraspar'|âṅgada|koṭi|saṃghaṭṭa|daṣṭa|pāṭit'|
ôttarīy'|âṃśukena,
śrama|jala|dhaut'|âṅga|rāga|rañjita|navīna|vāsasā
kiṃ|cid|avaśiṣṭa|tamāla|pattreṇa,
vilasad|vāra|vilāsinī|hasitair unnidra|kairava|van'|
ânukāraṃ prathayatā sa|rabhasa|valgana|
skhalal|lola|hāra|latā|sphālita|kuca|sthalena,
sindūra|tilaka|lulit'|âlaka|lekhena,
viprakīrṇa|piṣṭātaka|pāṃśu|puñja|piñjarita|keśa|pāśena,
pranṛtta|kala|mūka|kubja|kirāta|vāmana|badhira|jaḍa|
jana|puraḥsareṇ',
ôttarīy'|âṃśuka|grīv'|ābaddh'|âvakṛṣṭa|
viḍambita|jarat|kañcuki|kadambakena,
vīṇā|veṇu|muraja|kāṃsya|tāla|lay'|ânugatena
kala|madhuram udgāyatā,
harṣa|nirbharatayā
matten' êv' ônmatten' êva
graha|gṛhīten' êva
vyapagata|vācy'|â|vācya|vivekena

throwing about and crushing
the leaves worn on their ears;
their silken upper garments pierced and ripped
as they were caught against the sharp points
of each other's armlets;
their new clothes colored red by the body paint
washed off by their perspiration, with only bits
of their *tamála* leaf forehead marks remaining;
with the gleaming white laughter
of the dancing girls spreading out the appearance
of a *káirava* lotus bed in full bloom,
their breasts struck by their long necklaces
swinging about and dropping off in their frantic jumping;
their rows of curls rubbing
against their vermilion forehead marks;
their long mass of hair turning yellow
from the heaps of *pishtátaka* powder scattered about;
preceded by people they'd set dancing, the deaf-mutes,
hunchbacks, *kiráta* tribals, dwarfs, the deaf, and the dim;
teasing the throng of old chamberlains
by tying their upper garments round their necks
and dragging them along;
singing sweetly
to the accompaniment of music of
vina, flute, drum and cymbal;
and who because of their joy's excess,
as if excessively drunk, delirious
and possessed by the planets
had given themselves up to dance and play,
and lost discrimination between what should be said

nṛtta|krīḍā|prasakten'
ântaḥpurikā|janena,
pracala|maṇi|kuṇḍal'|āhata|kapola|bhittinā ca
vighūrṇamāṇa|karṇ'|ôtpalen'
âdho|vigalita|vilola|śekhareṇa
dolāyamāna|vaikakṣaka|kusuma|mālena
nirdaya|prahata|bherī|mṛdaṅga|
mardala|paṭaha|ninād'|ânugata|kāhalā|śaṅkha|rava|
janita|rabhasena,
caraṇa|saṃnipātair dārayat" êva vasudhāṃ
rāja|parijanena,
pravṛtta|nṛttena ca cāraṇa|gaṇena
vividha|mukha|vādya|kṛta|kolāhalena
paṭhatā gāyatā c'
ânugamyamānaḥ
Śukanāsa|bhavanaṃ gatvā
dviguṇataram utsavam akārayat.
atikrānte ca ṣaṣṭhī|jāgare prāpte daśame 'hani
puṇye muhūrte gāḥ suvarṇaṃ ca koṭiśo
brāhmaṇasāt|kṛtvā
mātur asya mayā paripūrṇa|maṇḍalaś candraḥ svapne
mukha|kamalam āviśan dṛṣṭa iti svapn'|ânurūpam eva
rājā sva|sūnoś Candrāpīḍa iti nāma cakāra.

and what should not—
such were the women of the harem.
And the king's own servants followed him,
their cheeks struck by their swinging jeweled earrings,
their ear-lotuses rolling about,
their chaplets shaking and falling off,
the long garlands that hung from their shoulders
sliding to and fro,
excited by the sound of *káhala* drums and conches
accompanied by the beat of *bheri*, *mridánga*, *márdala*
and *pátaha* drums struck without pity;
seeming to shatter the earth
with the pounding of their feet;
and he was followed too by the host of bards
who'd begun to dance,
were making a great racket
with various sorts of trumpets,
as well as reciting and singing.
Followed by all these he went into Shuka·nasa's house
and ordered a festival to be held on twice the scale.
And the rite of keeping awake on the sixth day
from the birth performed,
on the tenth day, at an auspicious moment,
he bestowed cows and gold coins in vast numbers
on the brahmins;
and because he'd seen in his dream the full-orbed moon
entering the lotus-like mouth of his son's mother,
the king gave him a name in accord with his dream:
Chandrapída, Moon-crowned.

aparedyuḥ Śukanāso 'pi kṛtvā brāhmaṇ'|ôcitāḥ
sakalāḥ kriyā rāj'|ânumatam ātmajasya
vipra|jano'|ôcitaṃ Vaiśampāyana iti nāma cakre.
krameṇa kṛta|cūḍā|karaṇ'|ādi|bāla|kriyā|kalāpasya
śaiśavam aticakrāma Candrāpīḍasya.
Tārāpīḍaḥ krīḍā|vyāsaṅga|vighāt'|ârthaṃ bahir nagarād
anu|Sipram ardha|krośa|mātrāyām[98]
atimahatā tuhina|giri|śikhara|māl"|ânukāriṇā
sudhā/dhavalena prākāra|maṇḍalena parivṛtam,
anuprākāram āhitena mahatā parikhā|valayena
pariveṣṭitam,
P75 atidṛḍha|kapāṭa|saṃpuṭam
udghāṭit'|âika|dvāra|praveśam,
ekānt'|ôparacita|turaṃga|vāhy'|ālī|vibhāgam,
adhaḥ|kalpita|vyāyāma|śālam
amar'|āgār'|ākāraṃ vidyā|mandiram akārayat.
sarva|vidy"|ācāryāṇāṃ ca saṃgrahe
yatnam atimahāntam anvatiṣṭhat.
tatra|sthaṃ ca taṃ kesari|kiśorakam iva
pañjara|gataṃ kṛtvā pratiṣiddha|nirgamam
ācārya|kula|putra|prāya|parijana|parivāram
apanīt'|âśeṣa|śiśu|jana|krīḍā|vyāsaṅgam
an|anya|manasam akhila|vidy"|ôpādān'|ârtham
ācāryebhyaś Candrāpīḍaṃ śobhane divase
Vaiśampāyana|dvitīyam

The next day Shuka·nasa for his part
performed all the rituals befitting a brahmin,
and with the king's approval gave his son
a name suitable for a brahmin—Vaishampáyana.
In due course, Chandrapída's childhood went by,
with the whole set of childhood rituals,
tonsure and so on, performed for him.
Tarapída, in order to prevent over-indulgence in play,
outside the city on the bank of the Sipra river,
half a mile away, built a college, like a celestial mansion.
It was surrounded by a circular wall, *white with plaster,*
imitating the series of the snow mountain's peaks
white as nectar;
wrapped around by a great moat following the wall;
having a double door, with entrance provided P75
by one door left ajar;
one part of it sectioned off
for horses and rows of vehicles;
and underground
it had a specially designed gymnasium.
And he took great trouble to gather there
professors of every branch of learning.
And on an auspicious day
he entrusted Chandrapída,
with Vaishampáyana as his companion, to his teachers
in order for him to acquire knowledge
of all branches of learning,
putting him there like a lion cub
confined to a cage, forbidden to leave.
His entourage of servants were

arpayāṃ babhūva.

pratidinaṃ c' ôtthāy' ôtthāya saha Vilāsavatyā

virala|parijanas tatr' âiva gatv" âinam ālokayām āsa rājā.

Candrāpīḍo 'py an|anya|hṛdayatayā tathā niyantrito rājñ"

âcireṇ' âiva kālena yathā|svam ātma|kauśalaṃ

prakaṭayadbhiḥ pātra|vaśād upajāt'|ôtsāhair ācāryair

upadiśyamānāḥ sarvā vidyā jagrāha.

maṇi|darpaṇa iv' *âtinirmale* tasmin

saṃcakrāma sakalaḥ kalā|kalāpaḥ.

tathā hi pade vākye

pramāṇe dharma|śāstre rāja|nītiṣu

vyāyāma|vidyāsu cāpa|cakra|carma|kṛpāṇa|śakti|

tomara|paraśu|gadā|prabhṛtiṣu sarveṣv āyudha|viśeṣeṣu

ratha|caryāsu, gaja|pṛṣṭheṣu, turaṃgameṣu,

vīṇā|veṇu|muraja|kāṃsya|tāla|dardura|puṭa|prabhṛtiṣu

vādyeṣu, Bharat'|ādi|praṇīteṣu nṛtta|śāstreṣu,

Nāradīya|prabhṛtiṣu gāndharva|veda|viśeṣeṣu,

hasti|śikṣāyāṃ, turaga|vayo|jñāne, puruṣa|lakṣaṇeṣu,

citra|karmaṇi, pattra|cchedye,

mainly the sons of his teachers' families.
All possibilities for indulgence in children's play
were removed, so that he attended to nothing
but mastering all subjects.
And every day on rising he went
with Vilásavati and a small retinue
to see him there.
Chandrapída for his part, thus constrained by the king,
because his heart was set on nothing else grasped
all forms of knowledge in a short time,
taught by teachers who each displayed
their own expertise in their own department,
and who were enthused by such a worthy pupil.
The whole collection of the arts,
as into a *perfectly clear* jeweled mirror,
transferred itself to him who was *exceedingly bright.*
Thus it was, in grammar, in Mimánsa,
in logic, in law, in politics,
in the systems of gymnastics, in all types of weapons:
the bow, the discus, the shield, the sword, the javelin,
the spear, the axe, the club and so on,
in chariot driving, in riding on elephants, in horses,
in musical instruments: the *vina*, the flute, the drum,
the cymbals, the frog-pipe and so on,
in the works on dancing
written by Bhárata and others,
in the various treatises on music,
Nárada's and others,
in the training of elephants, in knowing how
to judge a horse's age, in the characteristic marks of men,

pusta|vyāpāre,[99] lekhya|karmaṇi,

sarvāsu dyūta|kalāsu, gandharva|śāstreṣu,

śakuni|ruta|jñāne, graha|gaṇite,

ratna|parīkṣāsu, dāru|karmaṇi,

danta|vyāpāre, vāstu|vidyāsv,

āyurvede, yantra|prayoge,

viṣ'|âpaharaṇe, suruṅg'|ôpabhede,

taraṇe, laṅghane, plutiṣv,

ārohaṇe, rati|tantreṣv, indra|jāle,

kathāsu, nāṭakeṣv, ākhyāyikāsu, kāvyeṣu,

Mahābhārata|purāṇ'|êtihāsa|

Rāmāyaṇeṣu, sarva|lipiṣu,

sarva|deśa|bhāṣāsu, sarva|saṃjñāsu,

sarva|śilpeṣu, chandaḥsv,

anyeṣv api kalā|viśeṣeṣu paraṃ kauśalam avāpa.

sahajā c' âsy' âjasram abhyasyato Vṛkodarasy' êva śaiśava ev'

āvirbabhūva sarva|loka|vismaya|jananī mahā|prāṇatā.

yad|ṛcchayā krīḍat" âpy anena

kara|tal'|âvalambita|karṇa|pallav'|âvanat'|âṅgāḥ

siṃha|kiśoraka|kram'|ākrāntā iva

gaja|kalabhāś calitum api na śekuḥ.

in painting, in making leaf patterns,
in plaster work, in engraving,
in all the forms of gambling,
in musicology, in interpreting bird calls,
in calculating the movements of the planets,
in examining precious stones, in carpentry,
in ivory carving, in the arts of building,
in the science of medicine, in mechanics,
in countering poisons, in the various forms of tunneling,
in swimming, in rowing, in jumping,
in climbing, in the erotic arts, in conjuring,
in stories, in dramas, in narratives, in poems,
in the "Maha·bhárata," the *purána*s, histories
and the "Ramáyana," in all forms of writing,
in in the languages of every country, in all sign languages,
in all crafts, in meter,
and in other cultural accomplishments
he attained the highest proficiency.
And, constantly exercising, he manifested
even in childhood, as did Wolf-belly Bhima,
great physical strength, innate to him,
arousing wonder in all people.
When, playing about, he pulled down
the bodies of young elephants
by tugging at their earflaps,
they could not budge, as if overpowered
by the spring of a lion cub.

ek'|âikena kṛpāṇa|prahāreṇa bāla eva tāla|tarūn

mṛṇāla|daṇḍān iva lulāva.

sakala|rājanya|*vaṃśa*|vana|dāv'|ânalasya

Paraśurāmasy' êv' âsya nārācāḥ

śikhari|*śilā*|*tala*|*bhido* babhūvuḥ.

daśa|puruṣa|saṃvāhana|yogyena c'

âyo|daṇḍena śramam akarot.

ṛte ca mahā|prāṇatāyāḥ sarvābhir anyābhiḥ kalābhir

anucakāra taṃ Vaiśampāyanaḥ.

Candrāpīḍasya tu sakala|kalā|kalāpa|

paricaya|bahu|mānena Śukanāsa|gauraveṇa

saha|pāṃśu|krīḍanatayā

saha|saṃvṛddhatayā ca

sarva|viśrambha|sthānaṃ

dvitīyam iva hṛdayaṃ

Vaiśampāyanaḥ paraṃ mitram āsīt.

nimeṣam api tena vinā sthātum ekākī na śaśāka.

Vaiśampāyano 'pi tam uṣṇa|karam iva vāsaro 'nugacchan

na kṣaṇam api virahayāṃ cakāra.

evaṃ tasya sarva|vidyā|paricayam ācarataś Candrāpīḍasya

tribhuvana|vilobhanīyo 'mṛta|rasa iva sāgarasya,

With a single blow of his sword, though just a boy,
he cut down palm trees as if they were lotus stalks.
Like the arrows of Párashu·rama—forest fire
to the *bamboos* that were every warrior *lineage*—
which split the rock of the Krauncha mountain,
his could split mountain boulders.
And he exercised with an iron rod
it took ten men to carry.
Apart from his great bodily strength,
in all other arts Vaishampáyana equaled him.
Vaishampáyana, because of Chandrapída's respect
for his acquaintance with the whole range of the arts,
because of his reverence for Shuka·nasa,
because they played in the dust together as children
and had grown up together, was Chandrapída's
best friend, repository of all his confidences,
like his second heart.
He could not remain alone without him
even for the blink of an eye,
while Vaishampáyana, following him
as day follows the sun,
did not leave him for a moment.
While Chandrapída was cultivating
all forms of knowledge,
as the nectar of immortality,
eagerly desired by the three worlds,
doubles the beauty of the ocean;

sakala|loka|hṛday'|ānanda|jananaś
candr'|ôdaya iva pradoṣasya,
bahu|vidha|rāga|vikāra|bhaṅguraḥ
sura|dhanu|kalāpa iva
jala|dhara|samayasya,
Makaradhvaj'|āyudha|bhūtaḥ
kusuma|prasava iva
kalpa|pādapasy',
âbhinav'|âbhivyajyamāna|rāga|ramaṇīyaḥ
sūry'|ôdaya iva
kamala|vanasya,
vividha|lāsya|vilāsa|yogyaḥ
kalāpa iva śikhaṇḍino,
yauvan'|ārambhaḥ prādur|bhavan
ramaṇīyasy' âpi
dviguṇāṃ ramaṇīyatāṃ puposa.
labdh'|âvasaro nava|sevaka iva
nikaṭī|babhūv' âsya Manmathaḥ.
lakṣmyā saha vitastāra vakṣaḥ|sthalam.
bandhu|jana|manorathaiḥ sah'
âpūryat' ōru|daṇḍa|dvayam.
ari|janena saha tanimānam abhajata madhya|bhāgaḥ.
tyāgena saha prathimānam ātatāna nitamba|bhāgaḥ.
pratāpena sah' āruroha roma|rājiḥ.
a|hita|kalatr'|âlaka|latābhiḥ saha
pralambatām upayayau bhuja|yugalam.

as the rise of the moon, causing joy to the hearts
of all the world, doubles the beauty of the evening;
as a series of rainbows, transient
in its transformation
of many different colors,
doubles the beauty of the season of rain-clouds;
as the appearance of its flowers,
which become the weapons
of *mákara*-bannered Love,
doubles the beauty of the *kalpa* tree;
as the rise of the sun,
lovely with its freshly manifesting glow,
doubles the beauty of a bed of *kámala* lotuses;
as its tail, apt for the graceful performance
of various dances,
doubles the beauty of a peacock;
the advent of adolescence doubled his beauty,
though he was handsome before.
Like a new servant finding employment
Love came to his side.
Along with his beauty, his chest expanded.
Along with the expectations of his family,
his thighs expanded.
Along with his foes, his waist became slim.
His buttocks developed along with his munificence.
Along with his prowess, the line of hair on his chest grew.
Along with the untied hair of his enemies wives,
his arms lengthened.

caritena saha dhavalatām abhajata locana|yugalam.
ājñayā saha gurur babhūva bhuja|śikhara|deśaḥ.
svareṇa saha gambhīratām ājagāma hṛdayam.
evaṃ ca krameṇa samārūḍha|yauvan'|ārambhaṃ
parisamāpta|sakala|kalā|vijñānam
adhīt'|âśeṣa|vidyaṃ c'
âvagamy' ânumoditam ācāryaiś
Candrāpīḍam ānetuṃ rājā
bal'|âdhikṛtaṃ Balāhaka|nāmānam āhūya
bahu|turaga|bala|padāti|parivṛtam
atipraśaste 'hani prāhiṇot.
sa gatvā vidyā|gṛhaṃ
dvāḥ|sthaiḥ samāveditaḥ praviśya
kṣiti|tal'|âvalambita|cūḍā|maṇinā śirasā praṇamya
sva|bhūmi|samucite rāja|samīpa iva sa|vinayam āsane
rāja|putr'|ânumato nyaṣīdat.
sthitvā ca muhūrta|mātraṃ Balāhakaś
Candrāpīḍam upasṛtya
darśita|vinayo vyajijñapat.
«kumāra, mahārājaḥ samājñāpayati:
‹pūrṇā no mano|rathāḥ.
adhītāni śāstrāṇi.
śikṣitāḥ sakalāḥ kalāḥ.
gato 'si sarvāsv āyudha|vidyāsu parāṃ pratiṣṭhām.
anumato 'si nirgamāya vidyā|gṛhāt sarv'|ācāryaiḥ.

Along with his conduct, his eyeballs became white.
Along with his command, his shoulders became great.
Along with his voice, his heart became deep.
And thus in due course realizing
that Chandrapída had reached adolescence,
had achieved knowledge of all the arts,
had studied all the sciences,
and won his teachers' applause,
the king summoned the commander of his army,
whose name was Baláhaka, and sent him
on a highly auspicious day with a large escort
of foot-soldiers and cavalry to bring back Chandrapída.
He went to the college,
was announced by the door-keepers,
and bowed so low his crest-jewel touched the ground.
With the prince's permission he sat on a seat
befitting his rank, and behaved as modestly
as if he were in the presence of the king.
After resting for a moment,
Baláhaka approached Chandrapída
and respectfully addressed him.
"Prince, His Majesty sends this message:
'Our wishes have been fulfilled.
You have studied the *shastra*s,
you have been instructed in all the arts.
You have become supremely skilled in all weapons.
All your teachers give you permission to leave the college.

upagṛhīta|śikṣaṃ
gandha|gaja|kumārakam iva
vāri|bandhād vinirgatam,
avagata|sakala|kalā|kalāpaṃ
paurṇa|māsī|śaśinam iva
nav'|ôdgataṃ paśyatu tvāṃ janaḥ.
vrajantu saphalatām
aticira|darśan'|ôtkaṇṭhitāni loka|locanāni.
darśanaṃ prati te samutsukāny atīva sarvāṇy antaḥ|purāṇi.
ayam atra|bhavato daśamo vatsaro vidyā|gṛham adhivasataḥ.
praviṣṭho 'si ṣaṣṭham anubhavan varṣam.
evaṃ sampiṇḍiten' âmunā ṣoḍaśena pravardhase.
tad adya|prabhṛti
nirgatya darśan'|ôtsukābhyo dattvā darśanam
akhilābhyo mātṛbhyo 'bhivādya ca gurūn
apagata|niyantraṇo yathā|sukham
anubhava rājya|sukhāni
nava|yauvana|lalitāni ca.
saṃmānaya rāja|lokam.
pūjaya dvi|jātīn.
paripālaya prajāḥ.
ānandaya bandhu|vargam.›
ayaṃ ca te tri|bhuvan'|âika|ratnam
anila|Garuḍa|sama|java
Indrāyudha|nāmā turaṃgamaḥ
preṣito mahārājena dvāri tiṣṭhati.
eṣa khalu devasya Pārasīk'|âdhipatinā
tri|bhuvan'|āścaryam iti kṛtvā jaladhi|jalād utthitam
a|yoni|jam idam aśva|ratnam āsāditaṃ mayā
mahā|rāj'|âdhirohaṇa|yogyam iti saṃdiśya prahitaḥ.

Let our subjects look upon you, fully trained
like a young scent-elephant released from the stockade,
having *mastered the whole range of the arts*
like the newly risen moon on the full-moon day,
possessed of all its digits.
Let the world's eyes, all too long longing to see you,
be fulfilled. All the women in the inner apartments
yearn for a sight of you.
This is the tenth year you've stayed in college.
You entered in your sixth year, and reckoning up,
you're in your sixteenth year of growth.
So, from today come out and show yourself
to all your mothers who are longing to see you;
and salute your elders.
Free from restraint, enjoy as it pleases you
the pleasures of the court
and the dalliances of adolescence.
Honor the tributary kings. Worship the brahmins.
Protect your subjects. Gladden your kinsfolk.'
And this horse, unique jewel of the three worlds,
as swift as the wind or Gáruda, Vishnu's eagle,
Indráyudha by name,
has been sent to you as a gift by His Majesty
and stands at the gate.
This horse, indeed, was considered
by the king of the Persians
to be the wonder of the three worlds,
and he sent him to His Majesty with the message
that he'd acquired this jewel of a horse,
risen up from the waters of the ocean,

dṛṣṭvā ca niveditaṃ lakṣaṇa|vidbhiḥ:
‹deva, yāny Uccaiḥśravasaḥ śrūyante lakṣaṇāni
tair ayam upeto n' âivaṃvidho bhūto bhāvī vā
turaṃgama› iti. tad ayam anugṛhyatām adhirohaṇena.
idaṃ ca mūrdh'|âbhiṣikta|pārthiva|kula|prasūtānāṃ
vinay'|ôpapannānāṃ śūrāṇām abhirūpāṇāṃ
kalāvatāṃ ca kula|kram'|āgatānāṃ rāja|putrāṇāṃ sahasraṃ
paricār'|ârtham anupreṣitaṃ turaṃgam'|âdhirūḍhaṃ
dvāri praṇāma|lālasaṃ pratipālayati.»
ity adhidhāya viracita|vacasi Balāhake
Candrāpīḍaḥ pitur ājñāṃ śirasi kṛtvā
nava|jala|dhara|dhvāna|gambhīrayā girā
«praveśyatām Indrāyudha» iti nirjigamiṣur ādideśa.
atha vacan'|ânantaram eva praveśitam,
ubhayataḥ khalīna|kanaka|kaṭak'|âvalagnābhyāṃ
pade pade kṛt'|ākuñcana|prayatnābhyāṃ puruṣābhyām
avakṛṣyamāṇam,
atipramāṇam ūrdhva|kara|puruṣa|prāpya|pṛṣṭha|bhāgam,
āpibantam iva saṃmukh'|āgatam akhilam ākāśam,

and not born from a womb,
and thought him worthy to be ridden by His Majesty.
And on seeing him, the experts in physiognomy
informed the king, 'Your Majesty,
this horse has exactly the characteristic possessed
by Ucchaih·shravas.
Such a horse there has not been before, nor will be again.'
Therefore honor this horse by mounting him.
And here waiting at the gate mounted on their horses,
are a thousand princes, scions of crowned kings,
well brought up, brave, handsome,
knowledgeable in the arts, hereditary in their service,
sent by the king to serve you,
and they're eager to bow down to you."
When Baláhaka had finished speaking
after delivering himself thus,
Chandrapída, acknowledging his father's command
with a bow of his head,
was eager to depart, and in a voice as deep
as the rumbling of a newly formed rain cloud
ordered Indráyudha to be brought in.
Then, brought in immediately on his command,
restrained by two men, one on each side,
holding on to the rings of his golden bridle bit,
straining to bend him back down at every step he made,
his size extraordinary—
only a man holding his hand high could reach his back—
trying to drink up all the space ahead of him,

atiniṣṭhureṇa muhur muhuḥ
prakampit'|ôdara|randhreṇa
heṣā|raveṇa pūrita|bhuvan'|ôdara|vivareṇa
nirbhartsayantam iv' âlīka|vega|durvidagdhaṃ
Garutmantam,
atidūram avanamatā pratikṣaṇam
atidūram unnamatā ca,
java|nirodha|sphīta|roṣa|ghuraghurāyamāṇa|
ghora|ghoṇena śiro|bhāgeṇa,
nija|java|darpa|vaśād ullaṅghan'|ârtham
ākalayantam iva tri|bhuvanam,
asita|pīta|harita|pāṭalābhir Ākhaṇḍala|cāp'|ânukāriṇībhir
lekhābhiḥ kalmāṣita|śarīram
āstīrṇa|vicitra|varṇa|kambalam iva kuñjara|kalabhaṃ,
Kailāsa|taṭ'|āghāta|dhātu|dhūli|pāṭalam iva
Hara|vṛṣabham,
asura|rudhira|paṅka|lekhā|lohita|
saṭam iva Pārvatī|siṃhaṃ,
raṃhaḥ|saṃghātam iva mūrtimantam,
an|avarata|parisphurat|protha|puṭ'|
ônmukta|sūt|kāreṇ'
âtijav'|āpītam anilam iva
nāsikā|vivareṇ' ôdvamantam,

with his really fierce repeated neighing
that shook the cavity of his belly,
that filled the empty hollows of the world,
seeming to mock Vishnu's eagle
as wrong-headed in his falsely claimed speed,
at every moment lowering his head right down
and raising it right up,
while his frightening nostrils were extended wide
and snorting in rage at the curtailment of his speed;
with his head generally he seemed to be measuring up
the triple world with the intention of jumping over it,
such was his pride in his own speed;
his body streaked with black, yellow, green and pink lines
like so many rainbows, bows of Indra the destroyer,
like a young elephant with a multicolored blanket
spread over his back;
like the bull of Shiva the destroyer,
ruddy with red lead dust
from butting the sides of Kailása;
like Párvati's lion with its mane reddened
with streaks of clotted blood from the buffalo demon;
seeming like the incarnation
of the concentrated essence of speed,
with the snorting sounds constantly released
from the folds of his quivering nostrils
he seemed to be expelling
through the openings of his nose
the wind he'd drunk in through his excessive speed;

antaḥ|skhalita|mukhara|khalīna|khara|śikhara|kṣobha|
janmano lālā|jala|bhuvaḥ phena|pallavān
udadhi|nivāsa|paripīt'|âmṛta|rasa|gaṇḍūṣān iv' ôdgirantam,
aty|āyatam ati|nirmāṃsatayā samutkīrṇam iva
vadanam udvahantam,
ānana|maṇḍala|nihit'|âruṇa|maṇi|samudgatair
aṃśu|kalāpair upeten' âvasakta|rakta|cāmareṇ' êva
niścala|śikhareṇa karṇa|yugalena virājamānam,
ujjvala|kanaka|śṛṅkhalā|racita|raśmi|kalāpa|kalitayā
lākṣā|lohita|lamba|lola|saṭā|saṃtānayā
jala|nidhi|saṃcaraṇa|lagna|vidruma|pallavay" êva
śiro|dharay" ôpaśobhitam,
atikuṭila|kanaka|pattra|latā|pratāna|bhaṅgureṇa
pade pade raṇita|ratna|mālena
sthūla|muktāphala|prāyeṇa
tārā|gaṇen' êva saṃdhyā|rāgam aruṇen'
âśv'|âlaṃkāreṇ' âlaṃkṛtam,
aśv'|âlaṃkāra|nihita|marakata|ratna|prabhā|
śyāmāyamāna|dehatayā gagana|tala|nipatita|
divasa|kara|ratha|turaṃgama|śaṅkām iv' ôpajanayantam,
atitejasvitayā java|nirodha|roṣa|vaśāt
pratiroma|kūpam udgatāni sāgara|paricayāl lagnāni
muktāphalān' îva sveda|lava|jālakāni varṣantam,

his saliva was turned into flakes of foam by the pounding
of the hard points of the bit that rattled
as he champed on it, and as he spat them forth
they seemed like mouthfuls of liquid nectar
he'd drunk in while living in the ocean;
his very long face was so devoid of flesh
it seemed like a work of sculpture,
splendid with his ears, tips motionless,
provided with a mass of rays
from the rubies encircling his head,
and seeming to have red chowries attached;
his neck was handsome,
overspread with a collection of rays
issuing from his bright golden chains,
and hanging on it the waving length of mane red as lac,
and seeming as a result to have shoots of coral clinging
after his gallops through the ocean.
Ornamented with a red horse ornament elegantly crisped
with extensive highly convoluted gold leaf work,
with strings of precious stones jingling at every step,
mainly consisting of large pearls,
he was like the red of evening with the host of stars.
As his body looked dark green from the luster
of the emeralds set in the horse ornament,
he gave the impression that he was one
of the sun's chariot steeds fallen from the sky.
So superabundant was his vitality,
in his anger at the restraint of his speed
he was showering sweat
in sheets of drops from every pore of his skin,

indra|nīla|maṇi|pāda|pīṭh'|ânukāribhir
añjana|śilā|ghaṭitair iv'
ânavarata|patan'|ôtpatana|janita|viṣama|khura|
mukha|ravaiḥ pṛthubhiḥ khura|puṭair
jarjarita|vasuṃ|dharair
muraja|vādyam iv' âbhyasyantam,
utkīrṇam iva jaṅghāsu,
vistāritam iv' ôrasi,
ślakṣṇī|kṛtam iva mukhe,
prasāritam iva kaṃdharāyām,
ullikhitam iva pārśvayor,
dviguṇī|kṛtam iva jaghana|bhāge,
java|pratipakṣam iva Garutmatas,
trailokya|saṃcaraṇa|sahāyam iva Mārutasy',
âṃś'|âvatāram iv' Ôccaiḥśravaso,
vega|sa|brahma|cāriṇam iva manasaḥ,
Hari|caraṇam iva
sakala|vasuṃdhar"|ôllaṅghana|kṣamaṃ,
Varuṇa|haṃsam iva *Mānasa|pracāraṃ,*
madhu|māsa|divasam iva *vikasit'|âśoka|pāṭalaṃ,*

as if he were showering pearls that had clung to him
from his residence in the sea.
With his huge hollow hooves,
resembling sapphire pedestals,
seemingly fashioned from rocks of antimony,
as they tried to shatter the earth to pieces,
continuously falling and rising back up
and generating irregular sounds with their front edges,
he seemed to be using them to practice
playing the *mridánga* drum.
Seeming sculptured in his shanks;
seeming broadened in his chest;
seeming polished on his face;
seeming stretched out in his neck;
seeming portrayed in a painting in his flanks;
seeming doubled in size in his haunches;
seeming to rival winged Gáruda in speed;
seeming like the wind's traveling companion
through the three worlds;
seeming like a partial incarnation
of Ucchaih·shravas, Indra's steed;
seeming the mind's fellow student in speed;
seeming like Vishnu's foot
able to bound over the whole earth;
just as Váruna's goose *swims in the Mánasa lake,*
moving with the speed of thought;
like a spring day
with ashóka and trumpet flower trees in bloom,
being pink as a blooming ashóka tree;

vratinam iva *bhasma|sita|puṇḍrak'|âṅkita|mukhaṃ,*

kamala|vanam iva *madhu|paṅka|piṅga|kesaraṃ,*

grīṣma|divasam iva mahā|yāmam ugra|tejasaṃ ca,

P80 bhujaṃgam iva sadā|gaty|abhimukham,

udadhi|pulinam iva śaṅkha|mālik"|ābharaṇaṃ,

bhītam iva *stabdha|karṇaṃ,*

vidyā|dhara|rājyam iva *cakra|varti|Naravāhan'|ôcitaṃ,*

sūry'|ôdayam iva *sakala|bhuvan'|ârgh'|ârham,*

aśv'|âtiśayam Indrāyudham adrākṣīt.

dṛṣṭvā ca tam a|dṛṣṭa|pūrvam

a|mānuṣa|lok'|ôcit'|ākāram

akhila|tri|bhuvana|rājy'|ôcitam

aśeṣa|lakṣaṇ'|ôpapannam

aśva|rūp|âtiśayam atidhīra|prakṛter api Candr'|āpīḍasya

pasparśa vismayo hṛdayam āsīc c' âsya manasi.

like a person observing a vow *who's marked his face*
with lines of white ash,
his *face marked with a blaze as white as ash*;
like a bed of *kámala* lotuses
with their filaments tawny with thick honey,
his mane as tawny as the lees of wine;
seeming like a summer's day,
being long and fiercely radiant;
seeming like a snake, being always ready to spring; P80
like the ocean beach, adorned with a string of conches;
like a terrified person *unable to take in what is said,*
his ears motionless;
like the kingdom of the *vidya·dharas*,
fit for its emperor Nara·váhana,[100]
being a mount worthy of an emperor;
just as the rise of the sun is *worthy of respectful reception*
on the part of the whole world,
being worth the price of the whole world—
such was the horse he beheld, Indráyudha,
more than a horse
And beholding that perfect horse,
such as had not been seen before,
in form fit for superhumans,
meet for the sovereignty of all the three worlds,
provided with all favorable physical marks,
though Chandrapída was very calm in character
wonder touched his heart and filled his mind.

«sa|rabhasa|vivartana|valita|Vāsuki|
bhramita|Mandareṇa
mathnatā jala|nidhi|jalam
idam aśva|ratnam an|abhyuddharatā
kiṃ nāma ratnam uddhṛtaṃ
sur'|âsura|lokena?
an|ārohatā ca Meru|śilā|tala|viśālam asya pṛṣṭham
Ākhaṇḍalena kim āsāditaṃ
trailokya|rājya|phalam?
Uccaiḥśravasā vismita|hṛdayo vañcitaḥ khalu
jala|nidhinā śata|makhaḥ.
manye ca bhagavato Nārāyaṇasya cakṣur|gocaram
iyatā kālena n' âyam upagataḥ,
yen' âdy' âpi tāṃ Garuḍ'|ārohaṇa|vyasanitāṃ
na parityajati.
aho khalv atiśayita|tridaśa|rāja|samṛddhir iyaṃ tātasya
rāja|lakṣmīḥ yad evaṃvidhāny api
sakala|tribhuvana|durlabhāni ratnāny
upakaraṇatām āgacchanti.
atitejasvitayā mahā|prāṇatayā ca
sa|daivat" êv' êyam asy' ākṛtiḥ.
yat satyam ārohaṇe śaṅkām iva me janayati.
na hi sāmānya|vājinām a|mānuṣa|lok'|ôcitāḥ
sakala|tribhuvana|vismaya|jananya
īdṛśyo bhavanty ākṛtayaḥ.

"When the gods and demons
wrapped Vásuki round Mándara
and violently pulling him to and fro
rotated the mountain and churned the ocean,
whatever jewel did they take out
that they did not take out this jewel of a horse?
And what fruit has Indra gained
from having the three worlds as his kingdom
when he has not mounted its back
as broad as a rock of Mount Meru?
Surely the god of a hundred sacrifices
was deceived by the ocean
when Ucchaih·shravas filled his heart with wonder.
And I think this one hasn't so far
come into blessed Naráyana's sight,
since even today he doesn't give up
his obsession for riding Gáruda.
Oh truly my father's royal glory surpasses the prosperity
of the king of the thirty gods, since such jewels,
hard to find in all the three worlds,
come into his service!
So superabundant is his radiant energy,
so great is his physical strength,
his shape seems to house a divinity
and to tell the truth seems to make me
afraid of mounting him.
For forms such as this that astonish all the three worlds
and befit superhumans
do not belong to ordinary horses.

daivatāny api hi muni|śāpa|vaśād
ujjhita|nija|śarīrakāṇi
śāpa|vacan'|ôpanītāni śarīr'|ântarāṇy adhyāsata eva.
śrūyate hi.
purā kila Sthūlaśirā nāma mahā|tapā munir
akhila|bhuvana|lalāma|bhūtām apsarasaṃ
Rambh"|âbhidhānāṃ śaśāpa.
sā sura|lokam apahāy' âśva|hṛdaye niveśy' ātmānam
Aśva|hṛday" êti vikhyātā vaḍavā Mṛttikāvatyāṃ
Śatadhanvānaṃ nāma rājānam upasevamānā
martya|loke mahāntaṃ kālam uvāsa.
anye ca mahātmāno
muni|jana|śāpa|paripīta|prabhāvā
nān"|ākārā bhūtvā babhramur imaṃ lokam.
a|saṃśayam anen' âpi mah"|ātmanā ken' âpi
śāpa|bhājā bhavitavyam.
āvedayat' îva mad|antaḥ|karaṇam asya divyatām.»
iti vicintayann ev' āruruksur āsanād udatiṣṭhat.
manasā ca taṃ turaṃgamam an|upasṛtya
«mah"|ātmann arvan, yo 'si so 'si namo 'stu te.
sarvathā marṣaṇīyo 'yam ārohaṇ'|âtikramo 'smākam.
a|parigatāni daivatāny apy
an|ucita|paribhava|bhāñji bhavant'» îty
āmantrayāṃ babhūva.

It happens that even divine beings through a sage's curses
give up their own bodies
and inhabit other bodies assigned to them by the curse.
The story goes that once upon a time
a sage of great ascetic power, Sthula·shiras,
Hard-head by name,
cursed an *ápsaras* called Rambha,
who was the ornament of the whole world.
She, leaving heaven and entering the heart of a horse,
as a mare became famous under the name of Horse-heart,
and served a king named Shata·dhanvan
in the city of Mrittikávati.[101]
She lived a very long time in the word of mortals.
And other great souls, their power sucked away
by the curses of sages
have taken on various forms
and wandered through this world.
There can be no doubt that this too
must be some great soul undergoing a curse.
My heart seems to tell me that his nature is divine."
Even as he thought these thoughts he rose from his seat
desiring to mount the horse.
And without going up to the horse
he mentally addressed him.
"O great-souled horse, whoever you may be, hail to you.
May our transgression in mounting you
be entirely forgiven!
Even deities when they are not recognized
undergo undeserved indignity."

vidit'|âbhiprāya iva sa tam Indrāyudhaś
caṭula|śiraḥ|kesara|saṭ"|āhaty|ākūṇit'|ākekara|tārakeṇa
tiryak|cakṣuṣā vilokya
muhur muhus tāḍayatā kṣiti|talam utkhāta|
dhūli|dhūsarita|kroḍa|roma|rājinā dakṣiṇa|khureṇ'
ārohaṇāy' āhvayann iva
sphurita|ghrāṇa|vivara|ghargharа|dhvani|miśraṃ
madhuram a|paruṣa|huṃkāra|paraṃpar"|ânubaddham
atimanoharaṃ heṣā|ravam akarot.
ath' ânena madhura|heṣitena
datt'|ārohaṇ'|âbhyanujña iv'
Êndrāyudham āruroha Candrāpīḍaḥ.
samāruhya taṃ prādeśa|mātram iva
trailokyam akhilaṃ manyamāno nirgatya
pralaya|jala|dhara|vimukt'|ôpal'|āsāra|paruṣeṇa
jarjarayat" êva rasā|talam,
atiniṣṭhureṇa khura|puṭānāṃ raveṇa
khura|rajo|niruddha|ghrāṇa|ghoṣeṇa ca heṣitena
badhirī|kṛta|sakala|bhuvana|vivaram,
a|śiśira|kiraṇa|dīdhiti|parāmarśa|sphurita|
vimala|phalaken' ōrdhvī|kṛtena kunta|latā|vanen'
ônnāla|nīl'|ôtpala|kalikā|vana|gahanaṃ sara iva
gagana|talam alaṃ|kurvāṇam,

Seeming to understand what he was thinking,
Indráyudha looked at him obliquely,
his eye slightly squinting,
partly closed by the lashing of his tossing mane,
again and again striking the ground with his right hoof,
making the line of hair on his chest
gray with the dust he dug up,
seeming to invite him to mount,
he gave a most charming neigh sweetly mingled
with a snorting sound from his quivering nostrils,
and followed by a mild series of grunts.
Then, as if by this sweet whinnying
he'd been given permission to mount,
Chandrapída mounted Indráyudha.
When he'd mounted him he felt
as if the three worlds of the universe
were just a span across, and rode out.
Like a harsh shower of hail stones
released from doomsday's rain clouds,
pulverizing the subterranean world,
the exceedingly harsh sound of hollow hooves
and the neighing distorted from noses blocked
by the dust from the hooves
deafened all the spaces in the world;
decorating the sky with a forest of creeper-like lances
held pointing upwards, their bright blades
flashing at the touch of the sun's rays,
like a lake half hidden by groves of blue water-lily buds
upraised on their stalks;

uddaṇḍa|māyūr'|ātapatra|sahasr'|ândhakārit'|
âṣṭa|diṅ|mukhatayā
sphurita|śata|manyu|cāpa|kalāpa|
kalmāṣam iva jala|dhara|vṛndam,
udvamat|phena|puñja|dhavalita|mukhatay"
ânavarata|valgana|caṭulatayā ca
pralaya|sāgara|jala|kallola|saṃghātam iva
samudgatam, a|dṛṣṭa|paryantam aśva|sainyam apaśyat.
tac ca sāgara|jalam iva candr'|ôdayena
Candrāpīḍa|nirgamena
sakalam eva saṃcacāl' âśvīyam.
aham|ahamikayā ca praṇāma|lālasāḥ
sarabhas'|âpanīt'|ātapatra|śūnya|śirasaḥ
paraspar'|ôtpīḍana|kupita|
turaṃgama|nivāraṇ'|āyastā
rāja|putrās taṃ paryavārayanta.
ek'|âikaśaś ca pratināma|grahaṇam
āvedyamānā Balāhakena
vipracalita|mukuṭa|padma|rāga|kiraṇ'|
ôdgama|cchalen' ânurāgam iv' ôdvamadbhiḥ
saṃghaṭita|sev"|âñjali|mukulatayā
yauva|rājy'|âbhiṣeka|kalaś'|
āvarjita|salila|lagna|kamalair iva
dūr'|âvanataiḥ śirobhiḥ praṇemuḥ.

because darkening the eight points of the directions
with thousands of parasols of peacock feathers
on poles held high
like a bank of clouds speckled
with masses of gleaming rainbows;
because its horses' mouths were white
with the mass of foam they were emitting,
and because of the restlessness of their ceaseless prancing
like the mass of waves of doomsday's ocean
risen up before him, no end to it in sight—
such was the cavalry force he beheld.
And like the water of the ocean at the rise of the moon,
when Chandrapída came out
the whole body of horse stirred.
Each saying "me first, me first,"
zealous to make their obeisances,
parasols violently discarded and their heads uncovered,
struggling to check their horses angered
by being pressed against each other,
the princes crowded round him.
And announced by name one at a time by Baláhaka,
they bowed to him with their heads bent very low,
as if they were pouring out their devotion to him
under the guise of the flashing forth of the red rays
from the rubies on their shaking crowns,
and since their hands folded in reverence formed buds,
their heads seemed to have lotuses clinging to them
from the water poured on to them
from the coronation pitchers
when they were crowned as heirs apparent.

Candrāpīḍas tu

tān sarvān mānayitvā yath"|ôcitam

anantaraṃ turaṃgam'|âdhirūḍhen' ânugamyamāno

Vaiśampāyanena,

rājya|lakṣmī|nivāsa|puṇḍarīk'|ākṛtinā

sakala|rājanya|kula|kumuda|khaṇḍa|

candra|maṇḍalen' êva

turaṃgama|senā|sravantī|pulināyamānena

kṣīr'|ôda|phena|dhavalita|

Vāsuki|phaṇā|maṇḍala|cchavinā

sthūla|muktā|kalāpa|jālak'|āvṛten' ôpari cihnī|kṛtaṃ

kesariṇam udvahat" âtimahatā kārtasvara|daṇḍena

dhriyamāṇen' ātapatreṇa nivārit'|ātapa,

ubhayataḥ samuddhūyamāna|cāmara|kalāpa|pavana|

nartita|karṇa|pallavaḥ,

puraḥ|pradhāvatā taruṇa|vīra|puruṣa|prāyeṇ'

âneka|sahasra|saṃkhyena padāti|parijanena

«jaya jīv'» êti ca madhura|vacasā

maṅgala|prāyam an|avaratam

uccaiḥ paṭhatā bandi|janena stūyamāno

nagar'|âbhimukhaḥ pratasthe.

Chandrapída, for his part—
when he had fittingly honored them all,
followed by Vaishampáyana
likewise mounted on a horse;
shielded from the heat of the sun by the parasol
which was held over him on a very long gold pole,
having the shape of the *pundaríka* lotus
where royal fortune dwells,
like the disc of the moon
to the beds of *kúmuda* night lotuses
that were the families of all those princes,
which was a sandbank amid the river of cavalry,
which had the hue of the circle of Vásuki's hoods
made all the whiter by the foam from the ocean of milk,
which had a lion painted on top of it,
and was fringed with festoons of fat pearls;
on either side of him bunches of chowries
being shaken, and the wind from them
shaking the sprouts that adorned his ears;
and being praised by the foot soldiers
who were his attendants for the moment,
for the most part virile young men,
many thousands of them, running ahead of him,
singing his praises along with the bards
who cried out in sweet tones without stopping
such auspicious things as "Victory to you,"
"Long life to you"
—set out in the direction of the capital.

kramena ca taṃ samāsādita|vigraham
Anaṅgam iv' âvatīrṇaṃ
nagara|mārgam anuprāptam
avalokya sarva eva parityakta|sakala|vyāpāro
rajani|kar'|ôdaya|paribudhyamāna|
kumuda|van'|ânukārī
janaḥ samajani.
«saty asmin saṃprati
mukha|kumuda|kadambaka|vikṛt'|ākṛtiḥ
Kārtikeyo viḍambayati kumāra|śabdam.»
«aho vayam atipuṇya|bhājaḥ.»
«yad imām a|mānuṣīm asy' ākṛtim
antaḥ|samārūḍha|prīti|rasa|nisyanda|vistāritena
kutūhal'|ôttānitena
locana|yugalen' â|nivāritāḥ paśyāmaḥ,
saphalā no 'dya jātā janmavattā.»
«sarvathā namo 'smai rūp'|ântara|dhāriṇe bhagavate
Candrāpīḍa|cchadmane Puṇḍarīkekṣaṇāya.»
iti vadann āracita|praṇām'|âñjalir nagara|lokaḥ praṇanāma.
sarvataś ca samupāvṛta|kapāṭa|puṭa|prakaṭa|
vātāyana|sahasratayā
Candrāpīḍa|darśana|kutūhalān nagaram api
samunmīlita|locana|nivaham iv' âbhavat.

And it came to pass, in due course, seeing him
arrived on the road to the city
like bodiless Love come down to earth
with his body restored,
they all abandoned everything they were doing
and became like a bed of *kúmuda*s, lilies of the night,
awaking at the rise of the moon, maker of the night.
"Now he is here, we can see that Karttikéya is deformed
by having a multiplicity of lotus-like faces
and that he makes the word *kumára*, 'prince,'
as applied to himself, ridiculous."
"Ah, we're enjoying the fruit
of very great merit in previous lives."
"Since we're getting an uninterrupted view
of his more than human form,
our eyes dilated with the flow of the emotion
of happiness that wells up within us,
and open wide with curiosity,
today our having been born has borne fruit."
"All hail, all hail to this divine being
who's assumed a new form,
to lotus-eyed Vishnu in the guise in Chandrapída."
Speaking thus, hands folded in reverence,
the citizens bowed before him.
And because thousands of windows were open
with their panels flung wide back
the city seemed to have opened innumerable eyes
in its curiosity to see Chandrapída.

anantaraṃ ca ‹samāpta|sakala|vidyo vidyā|gṛhān
nirgato 'yam āgacchati Candrāpīḍa›
iti samākarṇy' ālokana|kutūhalinyaḥ
sarvasminn eva nagare sa|saṃbhramam
utsṛṣṭ'|ârdha|parisamāpta|prasādhana|vyāpārāḥ,
kāś cid vāma|kara|tala|gata|darpaṇāḥ
sphurita|sakala|rajani|kara|maṇḍalā iva
paurṇa|māsī|rajanyaḥ,
kāś cid ārdr'|ālaktaka|rasa|
pāṭalita|caraṇa|puṭāḥ
kamala|paripīta|bāl'|ātapā iva
nalinyaḥ,
kāś cit sa|saṃbhrama|gati|vigalita|mekhalā|kalāp'|
ākulita|caraṇa|kisalayāḥ
śṛṅkhalā|saṃdāna|manda|manda|
saṃcāriṇya iva kariṇyaḥ,
kāś cij jala|dhara|samaya|divasa|śriya iv'
Êndr'|āyudha|rāga|rucir'|âmbara|dhāriṇyaḥ,
kāś cid ullasita|dhavala|nakha|mayūkha|pallavān
nūpura|rav'|ākṛṣṭa|
gṛha|kalahaṃsakān iva
caraṇa|puṭān udvahantyaḥ,
kāś cit kara|tala|sthita|sthūla|hāra|yaṣṭayo
Ratim iva Madana|vināśa|śoka|gṛhīta|
sphaṭik'|âkṣa|valayāṃ viḍambayantyaḥ,

And as soon as they heard
that Chandrapída had completed all his studies,
had left the college, and was coming by,
women throughout the whole city
were curious to see him
and in their hurry left their make-up half undone.
Some with their mirror in their left hand
seeming full-moon nights,
the disc of the moon gleaming with all its digits;
some, the soles of their feet
reddened with fresh lac liquid,
seeming like clusters of lotus plants who'd drunk up
the morning sunlight in their flowers;
some, their tender feet caught up
in the strands of their girdles
that had dropped down
in their hurried movements,
seeming like cow elephants moving very slowly
because fettered by their chains;
some, like the beauty of a day in the rainy season,
wearing garments brilliant with the colors of the rainbow;
some had feet, with the sprout-like rays
from their white toe-nails shining forth,
looking like tame *kala·hansa* geese
attracted by the sound of their anklets;
some carrying in their hands their strings of large pearls
and seeming to imitate Rati
when she was holding a crystal rosary
in her grief at the destruction of Love;

kāś cit payodhar'|ântarāla|galita|muktā|latās
tanu|vimala|sroto|jal'|ântarita|
cakravāka|mithunā iva
pradoṣa|śriyaḥ,
kāś cin nūpura|maṇi|samutthit'|
Êndr'|āyudhatayā
paricay'|ânugata|gṛha|mayūrikā iva virājantyaḥ,
kāś cid ardha|pīt'|ôjjhita|maṇi|caṣakāḥ sphurita|rāgair
madhu|rasam iv' âdhara|pallavaiḥ kṣarantyo,
harmya|talāni lalanāḥ samāruruhuḥ.
anyāś ca marakata|vātāyana|vivara|
vinirgata|mukha|maṇḍalā
vikaca|kamala|kośa|puṭām
ambara|tala|saṃcāriṇīṃ
kamalinīṃ iva darśayantyo dadṛśuḥ.
udapādi ca sahasā sa|rabhasa|saṃcalana|janmā,
madhura|sāraṇ"|āsphālita|vīṇā|rava|kolāhala|bahalo,
rasan"|ārav'|āhūta|gṛha|sārasa|rasita|saṃbhinnaḥ,
skhalita|caraṇa|tala|tāḍita|sopāna|jāta|gambhīra|dhvani|
prahṛṣṭānām avarodha|śikhaṇḍināṃ
kekā|ravair anugamyamāno,

some with their pearl necklaces
falling between their breasts seeming like
beautiful evenings when pairs of *chakra·vaka*s
are separated by a narrow stream of shining water;
some, because they had rainbows
rising from the jewels of their anklets,
looking as splendid as if they had tame peacocks
following them, liking to be with them;
some, who'd put down their jeweled goblets
when they'd only drunk half,
seeming to be spilling wine
from the blossom of their lips, shining red—
such were the elegant ladies
who climbed to the roofs of the palaces.
And other women, their round faces
protruding from the opening in emerald windows,
gazed at him, and seemed to present to the eyes
a *kámala* lotus bed with the petal cups
of its lotuses fully open, sailing through the sky.
And suddenly there arose,
born from their hasty movements,
augmented by the loud sound of *vina*s
struck sweetly on their chords,
blended with the cries of the house *sárasa* birds
the clinking of girdles had summoned,
followed by the cries of the harem peacocks
delighting in the deep reverberation
of the stairways beaten by stumbling feet,

nava|jala|dhara|rava|bhaya|cakita|
kalahaṃsa|kolāhala|komalo,
Makaradhvaja|vijaya|ghoṣaṇ'|ânukārī,
paraspara|vighaṭṭanā|raṇita|tāratara|hāra|maṇīnāṃ
ramaṇīnāṃ śrotra|hārī, harmya|kukṣiṣu
pratirava|nirhrādī bhūṣaṇa|ninādaḥ.
muhūrtād iva yuvati|jana|nirantaratayā
nārī|mayā iva prāsādāḥ,
s'|ālaktaka|pada|kamala|vinyāsaiḥ
pallava|mayam iva kṣiti|talam,
aṅganānām aṅga|prabhā|pravāheṇa
lāvaṇya|mayam iva nagaram,
ānana|maṇḍala|nivahena
candra|bimba|mayam iva gagana|talam,
ātapa|nivāraṇāy' ôttānita|kara|tala|jālakena
kamala|vana|mayam iva dik|cakravālam,
ābharaṇ'|âṃśu|kalāpen' Êndr'|āyudha|maya iv' ātapo,
locana|mayūkha|lekhā|saṃtānena
nīl'|ôtpala|dala|maya iva divaso babhūva.
kautuka|prasārita|niścala|locanānāṃ ca
paśyantīnāṃ tāsām ādarśa|mayān' îva
salila|mayān' îva

soft with the cries of the *kala·hansa* geese
agitated in their fear of what they thought
was the rumble of fresh rain clouds,
imitating the victory cry of *mákara*-bannered Love—
the ringing out of the women's ornaments
as the jewels of their necklaces
knocking against each other
jangled really loudly, charming to the ear,
its echoes resounding through the spaces of the palaces.
In a moment the palaces seemed walled with women,
so closely packed were the young women.
The earth seem made of blossom
on account of the red lac prints of their lotus feet.
The city seemed made of liquid beauty
through the flood of radiance from the women's bodies.
The sky seemed made of moon discs
thanks to the multitude of their round faces.
The circle of the quarters
seemed made of *kámala* lotus beds
through the networks of hands
spread out to ward off the sunlight.
The daylight seemed made of rainbows
by the massed rays of ornaments.
The day seemed made of blue lily petals
by the continuous succession
of lines of rays from their eyes.
And as the women looked at him,
their eyes wide open in curiosity and motionless,
the form of Chandrapída entered their hearts
as if they were made of mirrors

sphaṭika|mayān' îva
hṛdayāni viveśa Candrāpīḍ'|ākṛtiḥ.

āvirbhūta|madana|rasānāṃ c' ânyonyataḥ
sa|parihāsaḥ sa|viśrambhāḥ sa|saṃbhramāḥ
s'|ērṣyāḥ s'|ôtprāsāḥ s'|âbhyasūyāḥ sa|vilāsāḥ
sa|manmathāḥ sa|spṛhāś ca tat|kṣaṇaṃ ramaṇīyāḥ
prasasrur ālāpāḥ. tathā hi
«tvarita|gamane, mām api pratipālaya.»
«darśan'|ônmatte, gṛhāṇ' ôttarīyam.»
«ullāsay' âlaka|latām ānan'|âvalambinīṃ, mūḍhe.»
«candra|lekhām upāhar' ôpahāra|kusuma|
skhalita|caraṇā patasi, madan'|ândhe.»
«saṃyamaya, mada|niścetane, keśa|pāśam.»
«utkṣipa, Candrāpīḍa|darśana|vyasanini, kāñcī|dāmakam.»
«utsarpaya, pāpe, kapola|dolāyitaṃ karṇa|pallavam.»
«a|hṛdaye gṛhāṇa nipatitaṃ danta|pattram.»
«yauvan'|ônmatte vilokyase janena
sthagaya payodhara|bhāram.»
«apagata|lajje śithilībhūtam ākalaya dukūlam.»

as if they were made of water,
as if they were made of crystal.
And even as feelings of love manifested themselves
in the women, their charming conversation
between themselves straightway flowed forth,
joking, confidential, muddled,
jealous, ridiculing, envious, coquettish,
amorous, full of longing. Like this:
"You're going too fast, wait for me!"
"Have you gone crazy! Put on your upper garment
before you look at him."
"Your long hair's hanging down over your face.
Lift it up, you fool!"
"Put your moon-crescent ornament in the right place!
You're stumbling on the offering flowers!
You must be blind with love!"
"Passion's made you lose your head!
Tie up your long hair."
"You're getting dissolute
in your eagerness to see Chandrapída. Pull up your girdle."
"You wicked girl! Fasten up the spray on your ear—
it's swinging against my cheek."
"You've lost your heart! Pick up the ivory earring
you've dropped."
"Your youthfulness has made you lose your head!
People can see you—cover up your heavy breasts."
"Shameless wench! Your silken garment
has become loose—fasten it up."

«alīka|mugdhe drutataram āgamyatām.»

«kutūhalini dehi darśan'|ântaram.»

«a|saṃtuṣṭhe kiyad ālokayase.»

«tarala|hṛdaye parijanam apekṣasva.»

P85 «piśāci galit'|ôttarīyā hasyase janena.»

«rāg'|āvṛta|nayane, paśyasi na sakhī|janam.»

«aneka|bhaṅgi|vikāra|pūrṇe,

duḥkham a|kāraṇ'|āyāsita|hṛdayā jīvasi.»

«mithyā|vinīte, kiṃ vyapadeśa|vīkṣitair?

viśrabdham ālokaya.»

«yauvana|śālini, kiṃ pīḍayasi payodhara|bhāreṇa?»

«atikopane, purato bhava.»

«matsariṇi, kim ekākinī ruṇatsi vātāyanam?»

«Anaṅga|para|vaśe,

madīyam uttarīy'|âṃśukam uttarīyatāṃ nayasi.»

«rāg'|āsava|matte, nivāray' ātmānam.»

«ujjhita|dhairye, kiṃ dhāvasi guru|jana|samakṣam?»

«ullasat|svabhāve, kim evam ākulī|bhavasi?»

«mugdhe! nigūhasva madana|jvara|janita|pulaka|jālakam.»

«a|sādhv|ācaraṇe, kim evam uttāmyasi?»

"You're playing the fool! Hurry, come quick."
"You're too keen to see. Let me get a look at the prince."
"You're insatiable! How long
are you going to be looking?"
"Your heart's aflutter!
Remember the servants are watching you."
"You're behaving like a demoness! P85
Your upper garment has fallen off
and people are laughing at you."
"Passion fills your eyes! You can't see your friends."
"You're full of frowns and torments!
You're troubling your heart needlessly.
You're living in misery."
"Your modesty is false.
Why make pretexts to look at him?
Look at him freely."
"Young one, why are you hurting me
with your heavy breasts?"
"If you're so angry, go to the front."
"You greedy girl!
Why are you blocking up the window by yourself?"
"Slave of Love! It's my upper garment you're using."
"The wine of passion's made you drunk!
Control yourself."
"Impatient girl!
Why are you running in the presence of your elders?"
"You're a bright girl, why are you confused like this?"
"Silly girl! Hide the thrill love's fever's giving you."
"You're behaving badly! Why are you so tired!"
"You're very changeable! Wearing out your waist

«bahu|vikāre, vividh'|âṅga|bhaṅga|valan'|āyāsita|
madhya|bhāgā vṛthā khidyase.»
«śūnya|hṛdaye, sva|bhavanān nirgatam api
n' ātmānam avagacchasi.»
«kautuk'|āviṣṭe, vismṛt" âsi niśvasitum.»
«antaḥ|saṃkalpa|racita|rata|samāgama|sukha|rasa|
nimīlita|locane, samunmīlaya locana|yugalam
atikrāmaty ayam.»
«Anaṅga|śara|prahāra|mūrchite,
ravi|kiraṇa|nivāraṇāya
kuru śirasy uttarīy'|âṃśuka|pallavam.»
«ayi, satī|vrata|graha|gṛhīte,
draṣṭavyam a|paśyantī
vañcayasi locana|yugalam.»
«a|dhanye, hat" âsi para|puruṣa|darśana|parihāra|vratena.»
«prasīd' ôttiṣṭha, sakhi, paśya Rati|virahitaṃ sākṣād iva
bhagavantam a|gṛhīta|makara|dhvajaṃ Makaradhvajam.»
«ayam asya sit'|ātapatr'|ântareṇ'
âli|kula|nīle śirasi
timira|śaṅkā|nipatita iva śaśi|kara|kalāpo
mālatī|kusuma|śekharo 'bhilakyṣate.»
«etad asya karṇ'|ābharaṇa|marakata|
prabhā|śyāmāyitam
uparacita|vikaca|śirīṣa|kusuma|karṇa|pūram iva
kapola|talam bhāti.»

with this twisting and turning of your body,
you're uselessly troubling yourself."
"You're absent-minded, you don't realize
you've come outside your house."
"Full of curiosity! You've forgotten how to breathe."
"You've closed your eyes
to imagine the joy of sexual union with him!
Open your eyes, he's going past."
"You're fainting under the hits of Love's arrows!
To ward off the sun's rays, put the end
of your silken upper garment over your head."
"Ayi! You who're possessed by an evil planet
and've taken the vow to become a suttee,
you're cheating on your eyes
by not looking at what must be seen."
"Unlucky woman! You're accursed by your vow
to avoid looking at another man."
"Please get up, my friend, and see what seems to be
the blessed god of Love in person, separated from Rati,
and without his *mákara* banner."
"Here under his parasol,
on his head as black as a swarm of bees,
the chaplet of jasmine flowers
looks rather like a mass of moonbeams
mistaking his head for darkness."
"Made dark green
by the emerald luster of his ear ornament,
his cheek shines as if it has a blooming *shirísha* flower
as ear ornament hanging over it."

«ayam asya hār'|ântar|niviṣṭ'|āruṇa|maṇi|kiraṇa|kalāpa|
cchalena hṛdayaṃ vivikṣur
abhinava|yauvana|rāga iva bahiḥ parisphurati.»

«etad anena cāmara|kalāp'|ântarair ita eva vīkṣitam.»

«etat kim api Vaiśampāyanena saha samāmantrya
daśana|mayūkha|lekhā|
dhavalī|kṛta|dik|cakravālaṃ hasitam.»

«eṣo 'sya śuka|pakṣ'|âtiharita|rāgeṇ'
ôttarīy'|âṃśuka|prāntena
Balāhakas turaṃga|khura|calana|janmānam ālagnam
agra|keśeṣu reṇum apaharati.»

«ayam anena Lakṣmī|kara|kamala|komala|talaḥ
samutkṣipya tiryak|turaṃgama|skandhe
nikṣiptaś caraṇa|pallavaḥ.»

«sa|līlam ayam anena ca tāmbūla|yācan'|ârtham
uttānita|talo dīrgh'|âṅgulir
ātāmra|puṣkara|kośa|śobhī gajen' êva
śaivāla|kavala|grāsa|lālasaḥ prasāritaḥ karaḥ.»

«dhanyā sā yā Lakṣmīr iva
nirjita|kamalaṃ kara|talam
asya vasuṃ|dharā|sapatnī grahīṣyati.»

"Under the guise of the cluster of rays
from the rubies set in his necklace,
the passion of adolescence seems to hover around him,
wishing to enter his heart."
"In between the clusters of chowries
he's looking this way!"
"As he discusses something with Vaishampáyana,
his laugh whitens all directions
with the line of rays from his teeth."
"Here's Baláhaka with the hem
of his silken upper garment,
greener than a parrot's wing,
wiping from the tips of Chandrapída's hair
the clinging dust from the horses' trotting."
"Here he's lifting his shoot-like foot,
soft as the lotus in Lakshmi's hand,
and putting it sideways across his horse's back."
"How gracefully, signaling for betel, he stretches out
his long-fingered hand, palm upward,
as beautiful as the flower-cup of a pink púshkara lotus,
just as an elephant's trunk,
beautiful with the red cup of its tip,
reaches out for mouthfuls of *shaivála* grass.
"How fortunate will she be, who seeming like Lakshmi,
will hold in marriage his hand
that surpasses Lakshmi's lotus,
and be a co-wife to the earth."

«dhanyā ca devī Vilāsavatī

sakala/mahī/maṇḍala/bhāra/dhāraṇa/kṣamaḥ

kakubhā dig|gaja iva

garbheṇa yay" âyaṃ vyūḍhaḥ.»

ity evaṃ|vidhāni c' ânyāni ca vadantīnāṃ tāsām

āpīyamāna iva locana|puṭair,

āhūyamāna iva bhūṣaṇa|ravair,

anugamyamāna iva hṛdayair,

nibadhyamāna iv' ābharaṇa|ratna|raśmi|rajjubhir,

upahriyamāṇa iva nava|yauvana|balibhiḥ,

śithila|bhuja|latā|vigalita|

dhavala|valaya|nikaraiḥ

pade pade vivāh'|ânala iva kusuma|miśrair

lāj'|âñjalibhir avakīryamāṇaś,

Candrāpīḍo rāja|kula|samīpam āsasāda.

krameṇa ca yām'|âvasthitābhir

an|avarata|karaṭa|sthala|galita|mada|masī|paṅka|karībhir

añjana|giri|mālā|malinābhiḥ

kuñjara|ghaṭābhir

andhakārita|diṅ|mukhatayā jaladhara|divasāyamānam

"And how fortunate is queen Vilásavati
who carried in her *womb*
him who is able
to support the burden of the whole disk of the earth,
as each quarter of the sky carries *within itself*
its elephant *who supports the earth*"
While the women were saying such things,
and other things too,
seeming to be drunk in by the cups that were their eyes,
seeming to be summoned
by the jingling of their ornaments,
seeming to be followed by their hearts,
seeming to be tied up with the ropes that were
the rays from the jewels of their ornaments,
seeming to be worshipped
with their fresh youth as offering,
and at every step, bestrewn with masses of white bracelets
slipping off their slender arms
as if he were the fire at a wedding ceremony
bestrewn with cupped-handfuls
of parched rice mixed with flowers,
Chandrapída reached the vicinity of the palace.
And in due course reaching the king's door
which with its troops of elephants
on three-hour watches looked like a rainy day
because they so darkened the quarters,
making an inky mud from the rut oozing constantly
from their temples,
dirty as a row of black mountains of collyrium;

uddaṇḍa|dhaval'|ātapatra|sahasra|saṃkaṭam
aneka|dvīp'|ântar'|āgata|dūta|śata|samākulaṃ
rāja|dvāram āsādya turaṃgamād avatatāra.
avatīrya ca kara|talena kare Vaiśampāyanam avalambya
puraḥ sa|vinayaṃ prasthitena Balāhaken'
ôpadiśyamāna|mārgas
tri|bhuvanam iva puñjībhūtam,
āgṛhīta|kanaka|vetra|lataiḥ
sita|vārabāṇa|dhāribhiḥ
sit'|âṅga|rāgaiḥ
sita|kusuma|śekharaiḥ
sit'|ôṣṇīṣaiḥ sita|veṣa|parigrahatayā
Śvetadvīpa|saṃbhavair iva,
Kṛta|yuga|puruṣair iva mahā|pramāṇair,
divā|niśam ālikhitair iva
toraṇa|stambha|niṣaṇṇair
dvāra|pālair an|ujjhita|dvāra|deśam,
aneka|saṃjavana|candra|śālikā|viṭaṅka|vedikā|
saṃkaṭa|śikharair abhraṃkaṣair
apahasita|Kailāsa|śaila|śobhair amala|sudh"|âvadātaiḥ
sa|prāleya|śailam iva mahā|prāsādair
aneka|vātāyana|vivara|vinirgata|yuvati|bhūṣaṇa|kiraṇa|
sahasratayā kanaka|śṛṅkhalā|jālaken' êv'
ôpari vitatena virājamānam,

which was cluttered with thousands
of white parasols with the poles uppermost;
which was thronged with hundreds of messengers
come from many different continents,
he got down from his horse.
And when he'd dismounted
and was holding Vaishampáyana's hand in his,
Baláhaka respectfully preceded him and showed the way.
It was like the three worlds heaped up in one place.
The doorkeepers, holding golden canes,
wearing white armor, using white unguents,
wearing chaplets of white flowers, their turbans white,
because of the white dress they wore
looked like people from Shveta·dipa,
the White Continent.
Huge in size they looked like men
from the Krita·yuga, the Perfect Age.
Day and night never leaving the doorway,
as if painted in a picture,
they sat beside the pillars of its arch.
With its great roof terraces with numerous turrets,[102]
penthouses, pinnacles and balconies, putting to scorn
the beauty of the Kailása mountain,
so many peaks touching the sky,
white with shining plaster,
it seemed to possess snow mountains;
and with thousands of rays from its women's ornaments
coming out from the numerous window openings
so that there seemed to be spread above it
a network of golden chains as a canopy.

antar|gat'|āyudha|nivahābhir
āśī|viṣa|kula|saṃkulābhiḥ pātāla|guhābhir iv'
âtigambhīrābhir āyudha|śālābhir upetam,
abalā|caraṇ'|ālaktaka|rasa|rakta|
maṇi|śakalaiḥ
śikhara|nilīna|śikhi|kula|kṛta|
kekā|rava|kalakalaiḥ
krīḍā|parvatakair upaśobhitam,
ujjvala|varṇa|kambal'|âvaguṇṭhita|
kanaka|paryāṇābhiḥ
pralamba|cāmara|kalāpa|
cumbita|cala|karṇa|pallavābhiḥ
kula|yuvatibhir iv'
ôparūḍha|śikṣā|vinaya|nibhṛtābhir
yāma|kareṇukābhir a|śūnya|kakṣ"|ântaram,
ālāna|stambha|niṣaṇṇena nava|jala|dhara|ghoṣa|
gambhīram anugata|vīṇā|veṇu|rava|ramyam
āsphālita|ghargharikā|ghargharam
an|avarata|saṃgīta|mṛdaṅga|dhvanim
āmīlita|locana|tri|bhāgena
vāma|daśana|koṭi|niṣaṇṇa|hastena
niścala|karṇa|tālen' ākarṇayatā,
sa|līlam ubhayapārśv'|âvalambi|varṇa|kambalatayā,

It was resplendent.
It was provided with armories
with heaps of weapons in them,
very deep, like the caves of the subterranean world
crowded with families of serpents.
It was adorned with pleasure hills,
the inlaid slivers of precious stones there
reddened with the wet lac
from women's feet,
and resounding with the keka cry
made by flocks of peacocks
residing on their summits.
Its inner courtyards were never without
female elephants on guard duty,
their golden saddles given coverings
of brightly-colored carpets,
their moving leaf-like ears kissed
by numerous plumes hanging down over them,
standing still because of the training they had received,
just as young women of good family *are modestly behaved*
because of the training they have received.
Reclining against his tying post,
listening to the continual beat of the *mridánga* drum
as music was played,
deep as the rumbling of fresh rain clouds,
delightfully combined with the notes of *vina* and flute,
and the jingling of jingle bells,
the corners of his eyes partly closed,
trunk resting on the tip of his left tusk,
his ear flaps motionless;

Vindhya|giriṇ" êv' āviṣkṛta|dhātu|vicitrita|pakṣa|saṃpuṭen',

ādhoraṇa|gīt'|ānanda|kṛta|mandra|kaṇṭha|garjitena,

mada|jala|śabala|śaṅkha|śobhita|śravaṇa|puṭena,

rajani|kara|bimba|cumbi|saṃvartak'|âmbuda|vṛnda|

viḍambakena,

karṇ'|âvalambinā kāñcana|mayena

kṛta|karṇa|pūram iv' âṅkuśena mukham udvahatā,

mada|jala|malinena dvitīyen' êva karṇa|cāmareṇa

kapola|tala|dolāyamānena madhu|kara|kulen'

âlaṃkriyamāṇen',

âtyudagratayā pūrva|kāyasy' âtivāmanatayā ca

jaghana|bhāgasya Pātālād iva uttiṣṭhatā,

niśā|samayen' êva

parisphurat|s'|ârdha|candra|nakṣatra|mālena,

śarad|ārambheṇ' êva *prakaṭit'|âruṇa|cāru|puṣkareṇa,*

vāmana|rūpeṇ' êva *kṛta|tri|padavī|vilāsena,*

sphaṭika|giri|taṭen' êva *lagna|siṃha|mukha|pratimena,*

prasādhiten' êv' *ālola|karṇa|pallav'|āhata|mukhena,*

Gandhamādana|nāmnā gandha|hastinā

with his colored canopy
hanging down elegantly on either side
he looked like the Vindhya mountain
displaying the hollows of its flanks colored by red lead;
rumbling deep in his throat
in his delight at his driver's song,
the hollows of his ears decorated
with conch shells stained with rut
he resembled a bank of doomsday *samvártaka* clouds
kissing the disc of the moon,
his face seemed to have an ear-ornament fashioned for it
with the golden goad hanging down from his ear.
Like a second rut-stained ear plume
swinging over his cheek
he had a swarm of bees forming an ornament for him.
With his forepart very raised up
and his hindquarters very low,
he looked as if he was rising from the subterranean world,
seeming like night time
with the shining constellations of stars and the half moon,
with his gleaming constellation necklace
and a half-moon-plate decoration,
seeming like the advent of fall
displaying its beautiful púshkara lotuses which are so red,*
as he exhibited the beautiful tip of his trunk, delicately red.
Like Vishnu's dwarf form
performing the divine grace of making the three steps,
he *stood gracefully on three legs*
when he lifted up the fourth.
Like a crystal mountain *with lions' faces reflected on it,*

sanāthī|kṛt'|âika|deśam,

ujjvala|paṭṭa|kambala|paṭa|prāvārita|pṛṣṭhaiś ca

rasita|madhura|ghaṇṭikā|rava|mukhara|kaṇṭhair,

mañjiṣṭhā|lohita|skandha|kesara|vāla|pallavair

vana|gaja|rudhira|pāṭala|saṭair iva kesaribhiḥ,

puro|nihita|yavasa|rāśi|śikhar'|ôpaviṣṭa|mandurā|pālair,

āsanna|maṅgala|gīta|dhvani|datta|karṇair,

antaḥ|kapola|dhṛta|madhu|rasa|lava|lulita|lāja|kavalair,

bhū|pāla|vallabhair mandurā|gatais turaṃgamair

udbhāsitam,

adhikaraṇa|maṇḍapa|gataiś c' ārya|veṣair

atyucca|vetr'|āsan'|ôpaviṣṭair

dharma|mayair iva dharm'|âdhikāribhir

mahā|puruṣair adhiṣṭhitam,

adhigata|sakala|grāma|nagara|nāmabhir eka|bhavanam iva

jagad akhilam ālokayadbhir,

ālikhita|sakala|bhuvana|vyāpāratayā

dharma|rāja|nagara|vyatikaram iva darśayadbhir

he *had images of lions' faces on him.*
Like an ornamented person
with a trembling ear spray knocking against his cheek,
his flapping leaflike ears struck against his face.
Such was the scent-elephant named Gandha·mádana
who occupied one corner of the palace.
And,
their backs mantled in horse blankets of shining silk,
their necks vocal by sweetly jingling their little bells,
the spreading hairs of the mane on their shoulders
reddened by madder,
they were like lions with their manes
reddened by the blood of wild elephants;
the stable grooms were sitting on top
of the piles of fodder placed in front of them,
their ears pricked up at the sound
of the auspicious songs being sung not far away,
chomping between their cheeks
mouthfuls of fried grain mixed with drops of honey—
the palace was splendid with such horses,
very dear to the king, in its stables.
It had within it, in the hall of justice,
seated on very high cane chairs, great men,
in noble attire, administering justice
as if they themselves were made of justice.
Thousands of edicts were being written down
by the court clerks who knew the name of every village
and city, and who were as familiar with the whole world
as if it were a single dwelling;
in as much as they were writing down all the world's

adhikaraṇa|lekhakair ālikhyamāna|śāsana|sahasram,
abhyantar'|âvasthita|nara|pati|nirgama|pratīkṣaṇa|pareṇa ca
sthāna|sthāneṣu baddha|maṇḍalena
kanaka|may'|ârdha|candra|tārā|gaṇa|śata|śabalaiś
carma|phalakair niśā|samayam iva darśayatā
sphurit|niśita|karavāla|kara|praroha|karālit'|ātapen'
âika|śravaṇa|puṭa|ghaṭita|dhavala|danta|patreṇ'
ōrdhva|baddha|mauli|kalāpena
dhavala|candana|sthāsaka|khacita|bhuj'|ōru|daṇḍena
baddh'|âsi|dhenuken' Ândhra|Draviḍa|Siṃhala|prāyeṇa
sevaka|janen'
āsthāna|maṇḍapa|gatena ca yath"|ôcit'|āsan'|ôpaviṣṭena
prasārayatā durodara|krīḍām,
abhyasyat" âṣṭāpada|vyāpāram,
āsphālayatā parivādinīm,
ālikhatā citra|phalake bhūmi|pāla|pratibimbam,
ābadhnatā kāvya|goṣṭhīm,
ātanvatā parihāsa|kathāṃ,
vindatā bindumatīṃ,
cintayatā prahelikāṃ,

transactions, they seemed to be demonstrating
what goes on in the city of Death, the king of justice.
There too were servants whose chief concern was waiting
for their kings to come back from the inner chamber,
ranging themselves in various places,
with their leather shields checkered
with golden half-moons and hosts of stars
so that they seemed to be displaying night time,
who by the shooting rays
from their gleaming sharp swords
intensified the sunshine;
white ivory ornaments fastened to one ear lobe,
their hair tied high in an upright coil,
their muscular arms and thighs covered with a smearing
of white sandal-paste, wearing a dagger,
mostly men from Andhra, Drávida, and Sínhala.
Also to be found in the assembly hall,
seated according to their rank,
playing the game of throwing dice,
concentrating on chess matches,
strumming the *parivádini* lute,
sketching the portrait of the king
on their drawing boards,
forming a poetry group,
telling jokes,
finding hidden letters in verses,
pondering riddles,

bhāvayatā nara|pati|kṛta|kāvya|subhāṣitāni,

paṭhatā dvipadīm,

gṛhṇatā kavi|guṇān,

utkiratā patra|bhaṅgān,

ālapatā vāra|vilāsinī|janam,

ākarṇayatā vaitālika|gītam,

aneka|sahasra|saṃkhyena

dhaval'|ôṣṇīṣa|paṭ'|āśliṣṭa|vikaṭa|kirīṭa|saṃkaṭa|śirasā

sa|nirjhara|śikhar'|ālagna|bāl'|ātapa|maṇḍalen' êva

kula|parvat|cakravālena

mūrdh'|âbhiṣiktena sāmanta|loken' âdhiṣṭhitam,

āsthān'|ôtthita|bhūmi|pāla|saṃvartitānāṃ ca kuthānāṃ

ratn'|āsanānāṃ ca rāśibhir aneka|varṇair

Indr'|āyudha|puñjair iva virājita|sabhā|paryantam

amala|maṇi|bhūmi|saṃkrānta|

mukha|nivaha|pratibimbatayā

vikaca|kamala|puṣpa|prakaram iva saṃpādayatā

gati|vaśa|raṇita|nūpura|pārihārya|rasanā|svana|mukhareṇa

skandh'|âvasakta|kanaka|daṇḍa|cāmareṇa

nirgacchatā praviśatā c' ân|avaratam

vāra|vilāsinī|janen' ākulitam,

appreciating particularly fine observations on life
in poems written by the king,
reciting verses in *dvi·padi* meter,
appreciating the merits of poets,
making leaf decorations on their bodies,
chatting with dancing girls,
listening to the songs of the bards,
their heads wrapped round with white turbans
and sporting big crowns,
like the range of mountains that surrounds the world
with circles of morning sunlight playing on their peaks
from which streams descend—
such were the subordinate consecrated kings
to be found there,
several thousand of them in number.
And with the heaps of carpets that were rolled up
when the king rose from the assembly,
and piles of jeweled seats,
the sides of the hall shone brightly
as if with loads of multicolored rainbows.
Because of the images of their numerous faces
reflected in the bright jeweled pavement,
they seemed to be providing
an abundance of blooming *kámala* lotus flowers;
noisy with the sounds of their anklets, bracelets,
and girdles that rang out at their every movement,
the golden handles of their chowries
resting on their shoulders,
going out and coming back in all the time—
such were the dancing girls who thronged the palace.

eka|deśa|niṣaṇṇa|cāmī|kara|śṛṅkhalā|saṃyata|śva|gaṇam,

itas tataḥ pracalita|paricit'|â|mita|kastūrikā|kuraṅga|

parimala|vāsita|diṅ|mukham,

aneka|kubja|kirāta|varṣavara|badhira|

vāmanaka|mūka|saṃkulam,

upāhṛta|kiṃnara|mithunam,

ānīta|vana|mānuṣam,

ābaddha|meṣa|kukkuṭa|kurara|kapiñjala|lāvaka|

vartikā|yuddham utkūjita|cakora|kādamba|hārīta|kokilam,

ālapyamāna|śuka|sārikam,

ibha|pati|mada|parimal'|āmarṣa|jṛmbhitaiś ca niṣkūjadbhiḥ

śikhariṇāṃ jīvitair iva giri|guhā|nivāsibhir

gṛhītaiḥ pañjara|kesaribhir udbhāsyamānam,

uttrāsyamānaiḥ

kāñcana|bhavana|prabhā|janita|dāv'|ânala|śaṅkair

lola|tārakair bhramadbhir bhavana|hariṇa|kadambakair

locana|prabhayā śabalī|kṛta|dig|antaram,

uddāma|kekā|rav'|ânumīyamāna|

marakata|kuṭṭima|sthita|śikhaṇḍi|maṇḍalam,

atiśiśira|candana|viṭapi|cchāyā|niṣaṇṇa|

in one place lay a gaggle of dogs
restrained by golden chains;
everywhere was scented by the perfume
of the countless tame musk deer
wandering here and there;
it was crowded with many hunchbacks,
kiráta tribal people, eunuchs, deaf people,
dwarfs, and dumb people;
pairs of nearly-men had been brought there;
wild men had been led in;
fights was taking place between rams, between cocks,
between ospreys, between partridges, between quails,
between *vártika* sparrows;
chakóra partridges, *kádamba* geese, *haríta* pigeons,
and cuckoos were cooing;
parrots and mynah birds were conversing;
and it was resplendent with captured lions in cages,
growling, angrily aroused
by the smell of the bull elephants' rut,
living in mountain caves before they were captured
and looking like the very life force of mountains.
The golden luster of the palace
making them fear it was a forest fire,
with the luster of their eyes, black pupils darting about,
the wandering groups of palace deer, alarmed,
dappled it in every direction.
The presence of its groups of peacocks
standing on the emerald pavements
could only be inferred by their loud piercing cries.
There tame cranes sat asleep

nidrāyamāṇa|gṛha|sārasam
antaḥ|pureṇa ca bālikā|jana|prastuta|
kanduka|pañcālikā|krīḍen'
ân|avarata|saṃvāhyamāna|dolā|śikhara|kvaṇita|ghaṇṭā|
ṭaṃkāra|pūrit'|āśā|mukhena
bhujaga|nirmoka|śaṅkita|mayūra|hriyamāṇa|hāreṇa,
saudha|śikhar'|âvatīrṇa|pracalita|pārāvata|kulatayā
sthal'|ôtpalinī|vana|śobhiten' êv',
ântaḥ|purikā|jana|prastuta|nara|pati|carita|
viḍambana|krīḍen',
âśva|mandurā|paribhraṣṭ'|āgatair
avalupta|bhavana|dāḍimī|phalair
ākhaṇḍit'|âṅgaṇa|sahakāra|pallavair
abhibhūta|kubja|vāmana|kirāta|kara|talāc
chinnāni bhūṣaṇāni vikiradbhiḥ kapibhir ākulī|kṛtena
śuka|sārikā|prakāśita|surata|viśrambh'|ālāpa|
lajjit'|âvarodha|janena,
prāsāda|sopāna|samāroha|calitair a|balānāṃ
caraṇ'|âvasaktair maṇimayaiḥ pade pade raṇadbhis
tulā|koṭi|valayair dviguṇī|kṛta|kūjita|rutābhir
P90 bhavana|kalahaṃsa|mālābhir dhavalit'|âṅgaṇena,

in the very cool shade of the sandal trees.
And in the harem, little girls
were playing with balls and dolls.
Swings were being ridden non-stop and the bells ringing
on the top parts filled everywhere with their tinkling.
Peacocks were carrying off necklaces,
mistaking them for the sloughed skins of snakes.
Because flocks of pigeons
had come down from the roofs of the palace
and were walking about on the ground,
the harem seemed adorned
with clusters of land-growing lotuses.
Women in the harem had begun the game
of acting out the exploits of the king.
Monkeys had got in and were making a commotion.
They'd dropped down from the horses' stables,[103]
raided the palace pomegranate trees,
knocked down the mango blossom in the courtyard,
attacked the hunchbacks, dwarfs, and *kiráta* tribals,
and were throwing around the ornaments
they'd snatched from their hands.
Harem ladies were embarrassed
by their intimate talk during love-making
being broadcast by the parrots and mynah birds.
Lines of palace *kala·hansa* geese whitened the courtyards, P90
their honking cries reduplicated
by the jeweled 'beam-end' anklets
fastened to the women's feet,
swinging about as they ascended the stairs to the terraces,
jingling at every step.

dhṛta|dhauta|dhavala|dukūl'|ôttarīyaiḥ

kala|dhauta|daṇḍ'|âvalambibhiḥ

palita|pāṇḍura|maulibhir

ādhāra|mayair iva maryādā|mayair iva maṅgala|mayair iva

gambhīr'|ākṛtibhiḥ svabhāva|dhīrair

uṣṇīṣibhir vayaḥ|pariṇāme 'pi jarat|siṃhair iv'

â|parityakta|sattv'|âvaṣṭambhaiḥ

kañcukibhir adhiṣṭhitena samupet'|âbhyantaram,

jala|dhara|sanātham iva kṛṣṇ'|âguru|dhūma|paṭalaiḥ

sa|nīhāram iva yāma|kuñjara|ghaṭā|kara|śīkaraiḥ

sa|niśam iva tamāla|vīthik"|ândhakāraiḥ

sa|bāl'|ātapam iva rakt'|âśokaiḥ

sa|tārā|gaṇam iva muktā|kalāpaiḥ

sa|varṣā|samayam iva dhārā|gṛhaiḥ

sa|taḍil|latam iva hema|mayībhir mayūra|yaṣṭibhiḥ

sa|gṛha|daivatam iva śālabhañjikābhiḥ

Wearing freshly washed full-length garments of white silk,
leaning on their golden staffs,
heads white with gray hair,
like pure stability, pure propriety, pure auspiciousness,
profundity in person, innately wise,
wearing turbans, yet though advanced in years,
like aging lions *who haven't given up attacking beasts,*
they *hadn't given up maintaining their dignity.*
—Such were the chamberlains
who superintended the harem which was to be found
in the inner part of the palace.
With its billows of black *águru* incense,
the palace seemed to possess rain clouds.
With the spray from the trunks
of the numerous elephants on duty,
it seemed to have mists.
With its avenues of *tamála* trees so dark,
it seemed to have the night within it.
With its red *ashóka* trees,
it seemed to have the early morning sunshine.
With its festoons of pearls,
it seemed to have the hosts of stars.
With its shower houses,
it seemed to have the rainy season.
With its peacock perches made of gold,
it seemed to have flashes of lightning.
With its statues,
it seemed to have its household deities present.

Śiva|bhavanam iva

dvār'|âvasthita|daṇḍa|pāṇi|pratīhāra|gaṇam,

utkṛṣṭa|kavi|gadyam iva

vividha|varṇa|śreṇi|

pratipādyamān'|âbhinav'|ârtha|saṃcayam,

apsaro|gaṇam iva

prakaṭa|manoram'|ārambhaṃ,

divasa|kar'|ôdayam iv'

ôllasat|padm'|ākara|kamal'|āmodam,

uṣṇa|kiraṇam iva

nija|lakṣmī|kṛta|kamal'|ôpakāraṃ,

nāṭakam iva

prakaṭa|patāk"|âṅka|śobhitaṃ,

Śoṇitapuram iva

Bāṇa|yogya|vās'|ôpetaṃ,

With its numerous doorkeepers
at the door with staves in their hands,
it seemed like Shiva's home
where his ganas stand at the door,
staves in hand, as his doorkeepers.
Fresh loads of goods being brought in
by various castes and guilds,
it was like the prose poem of an excellent poet,
with a wealth of new meanings
achieved by various combinations of letters.
Charming undertakings so evident,
it seemed like a throng of heavenly nymphs
with Mano·rama and Rambha prominent among them.
Like the rising of the sun,
when the fragrance of the kámala lotus
spreads out from the lotus ponds,
there is delight in the lotus
in the hand of shining prosperity, the goddess Shri.
Like the hot-rayed sun *who through his own splendor*
benefits the kámala lotuses,
the palace *assisted the goddess of Fortune, lady of the lotus,*
with its own wealth.
Like a drama
which is splendid with clearly marked scenes and acts,
it was splendid with manifest devices on its banners.
Like the city of Shónita·pura
which had chambers fit for Bana,
its multi-armed ruler,
it *had chambers big enough for archery practice.*

purāṇam iva

yathā|vibhāg'|âvasthāpita|sakala|bhuvana|kośaṃ,

saṃpūrṇa|candr'|ôdayam iva

mṛdu|kara|sahasra|saṃvardhita|ratn'|ālayaṃ,

dig|gajam iv'

â|vicchinna|mahā|dāna|saṃtānaṃ,

Brahm'|âṇḍam iva

sakala|jīva|loka|vyavahāra|kāraṇ'|

ôtpanna|hiraṇya|garbham,

Īśāna|bāhu|vanam iva

mahā|bhogi|maṇḍala|sahasr'|âdhiṣṭhita|prakoṣṭhaṃ,

Mahābhāratam iv'

Ânanta|Gīt"|ākarṇan'|ānandita|Naraṃ,

Like a *purána which sets out*
the whole circle of worlds
according to their respective divisions,
it *had treasures from the whole world*
stored according to category.
Like the rise of the full moon
with its thousands of mild rays
making the ocean, repository of jewels, swell,
it *had its store of jewels*
augmented a thousandfold by light taxes.
Like an elephant of the quarters
whose flow of rut never ceases,
the continuity of its great gifts was unbroken.
Like Brahma's egg, the universe, *from which was born*
Brahma as the golden fetus,
cause of the proceedings of all living creatures in the world,
the palace *was full of gold produced*
by directing the legal processes of all the mortal world.
Like the forest of Shiva the lord's arms
when he is dancing,
with thousands of great snakes coiling round his forearms,
it *has thousands of groups of voluptuaries*
present in its courts.
Like the "Maha·bhárata" *wherein the man who is Árjuna*
delighted in hearing the "Bhágavad·gita,"
the song of Krishna who is endless Vishnu,
in it *men delighted to listen to songs unendingly.*

Yadu|vaṃśam iva

kula|kram'|āgata|

Śūra|Bhīma|Puruṣottama|Bala|paripālitaṃ,

vyākaraṇam iva

prathama|madhyam'|ôttama|puruṣa|

vibhakti|sthit'|ânek'|ādeśa|kārak'|

ākhyāta|saṃpradāna|kriy"|â|vyaya|prapañca|su|sthitam,

udadhim iva

bhay'|ântaḥ|praviṣṭa|

sa|pakṣa|bhūmi|bhṛt|sahasra|saṃkulam,

Uṣ"|Âniruddha|samāgamam iva

Citralekhā|darśita|vicitra|sakala|tri|bhuvan'|ākāram,

Bali|yajñam iva

Purāṇapuruṣa|Vāman'|âdhiṣṭhit'|âbhyantaraṃ,

Like the lineage of Yadu[104] *which was protected*
over successive generations by Shura, Bhima,
Krishna the supreme male, and Bala·rama,
it *was protected by a supreme force of formidable men,*
heroes whose service was hereditary.
Like the science of grammar
which is soundly based on the full range
of linguistic phenomena—first, second, and third persons,
substitutions occurring in the declensions,
the relations between nouns and verbs, verbs,
and indeclinables,
it was well founded on ample expenditure on gifts
recorded by the many officials stationed there and varying
as whether the recipient was low, middling, or excellent.
Like the ocean *when it was full of thousands of mountains*
which had plunged into it in fear of Indra
while they still had the wings that he was going to cut off,
it *was crowded with thousands of kings who were allies*
and had come in from fear of their foes.
Like the union of Usha and self-willed Anirúddha,[105]
which was brought about by Chitra·lekha showing Usha
all the diverse figures of men in the three worlds,
it *had displayed in paintings*
the multi-colored forms of all the three worlds.
Like Bali's sacrifice *into which came*
Vishnu, the primeval male, in his dwarf incarnation,
its interior was occupied by old men and dwarfs.

śukla|pakṣa|pradoṣam iva

vitata/śaśi/kiraṇa/kalāpa/dhaval'/âmbara/vitānaṃ,

Naravāhanadatta|caritam iv' *ântaḥ/saṃvardhita/*

priya/darśana/rāja/dārikā/Gandharvadatt"/ôtkaṇṭhaṃ,

mahā|tīrtham iva

sadyo 'neka/puruṣa/prāpt'/âbhiṣeka/phalaṃ,

prāg|vaṃśam iva

nān"/āsava/pātra/saṃkulaṃ,

niśā|samayam iv'

âneka/nakṣatra/māl"/âlaṃkṛtaṃ,

prabhāta|samayam iva

pūrva/dig/bhāga/rāg'/ânumeya/mitr'/ôdayaṃ,

gāndhika|bhavanaṃ

snāna|dhūpa|vilepana|varṇak'|ôjjvalaṃ,

tāṃbulika|bhavanam iva

kṛta|lavalī|lavaṅg'|âilā|kaṅkola|pattra|saṃcayaṃ,

prathama|veśyā|samāgamam iv'

Like a night of the waxing moon, *when the sky's expanse*
is white with the mass of spreading moonbeams,
it *has canopies of cloth*
as white as a mass of spreading moonbeams.
Like the story of the deeds of Nara·váhana·datta,
wherein he yearns in his heart
for the beautiful princess Gandhárva·datta,
it *makes even gandhárvas yearn*
for the beautiful princesses brought up within.
Like a great pilgrimage center *where many men*
obtain immediately the fruit of their bathing,
there *many people obtained immediately*
the fruit of the inauguration of the king.
Like an assembly pavilion at a fire sacrifice,
where various offering vessels are assembled,
it *was full of various kinds of wine cups.*
Like night time *which is adorned*
with many garlands of stars,
it *was adorned with many people wearing necklaces*
with constellations of precious stones.
Like the time of dawn *when the rise of our friend the sun*
can be inferred from the redness in the sky in the east,
there *the success of a friendship could be inferred*
from the affection shown in its beginning.
Like a perfumer's house it was splendid
with the bath incenses, unguents and cosmetics.
Like a betel-seller's house it stored
large quantities of *lávali* fruits, cloves,
cardamoms, and cubeb leaves.
Like the first union with a courtesan,

â|vidita|hṛday'|âbhiprāya|ceṣṭā|vikāraṃ,

kāmuka|janam iva

bahu|cāṭu|saṃlāpa|subhāṣita|ras'|āsvada|datta|tāla|śabdaṃ,

dhūrta|maṇḍalam iva

dīyamāna/maṇi/śata/sahasr'/âlaṃkaraṇa/kṛta/

lekhya/pattra/saṃcayaṃ,

dharm'|ārambham iv'

â|śeṣa|jana|manaḥ|prahlādanaṃ,

mahā|vanam iva

vividha/śvā/pada/dvij'/ôpaghuṣṭaṃ,

Rāmāyaṇam iva

kapi/kathā/samākulaṃ,

Mādrī|kulam iva

Nakul'/âlaṃkṛtaṃ,

saṃgīta|bhavanam iv'

âneka|sthān'|âvasthāpita|mṛdaṅgaṃ,

Raghu|kulam iva

Bharata/guṇ'/ānanditaṃ,

jyotiṣam iva

graha/mokṣa/kalā/bhāga/nipuṇaṃ,

there the difference between the heart's intention
and outer gestures was not understood.
As lovers do, the palace applauds
many words of praise in conversation, and
the tasting of poetic emotion in finely turned phrases.
Like a gambling den, *where detailed records are kept*
of the hundreds of thousands of jewels and ornaments
given as pledges,
it *had detailed records of the hundreds*
of thousands of jewels and ornaments that are given.
Like a religious undertaking
it gave great delight to all people.
Like a great forest
which resounds with various wild animals and birds,
it *resounded with various forms of humanity,*
from Shva·padas to brahmins.
Like the "Ramáyana"
which is filled with stories about monkeys,
it *was full of the chattering of monkeys.*
Like Madri's family *which was adorned by Nákula,*[106]
it *was adorned with mongooses.*
Like a concert hall
it had drums positioned in many places.
Like Raghu's family *which delighted in Bhárata's virtues,*
it *delighted in the merits of actors.*
Like the science of astronomy *which gives*
accurate information about the beginnings and ends
of eclipses and about the divisions of time,
its people *were skilled in the capture and release*
of prisoners and in the various kinds of arts.

Nāradīyam iv' āvarṇyamāna|rāja|dharmaṃ,

yantram iva vividha|śabda|rasa|labdh'|āsvadaṃ,

mṛdu|kāvyam iv'

ân|anya|cintita|svabhāv'|âbhiprāy'|āvedakaṃ,

mahā|nadī|pravāham iva

sarva/durit'/âpaharaṃ,

dhanam iva na kasya cin na kāṅkṣaṇīyaṃ,

saṃdhyā|samayam iva

dṛśyamāna/candr'/āpīḍ'/ôdayaṃ,

Nārāyaṇa|vakṣa|sthalam iva

Śrī/ratna/prabhā/bhāsita/dig/antaṃ,

Balabhadram iva

kādambarī/rasa/viśeṣa/varṇan'/ākula/mati,

brāhmaṇam iva

Padmāsan'/ôpadeśa/darśita/bhū/maṇḍalaṃ,

Skandam iva *śikhi/krīḍ"/ārambha/cañcalaṃ,*

Like Nárada's textbook,
the duties of kings were being expounded.
Like a musical instrument it allowed one to savor
the aesthetic emotions from varied sounds.
Like tender poetry it made known natures
and meanings not thought of by others.
Like the flow of a great river, *which removes all sins,*
it *did away with all discomfort.*
Like money, there was no one who doesn't desire it.
Like the time of twilight
when we behold the rise of its crest-jewel, the moon,
there *the appearance of Chandrapída could be seen.*
Like Naráyana's chest *which lights up the quarters*
with the luster of Lakshmi and the Káustubha gem,
it *lighted up the quarters*
with the luster of its beautiful gems.
Like auspicious Bala·rama, *its people gave much thought*
how best to describe
the particular qualities of the taste of wines,
as you the reader do to my Kadámbari.
Like a brahmin *who explains the world*
according to the teachings of lotus-seated Brahma,
there *particular places were pointed out*
as fitting for teaching the lotus-position.
Like Skanda *who sways when the peacock he rides on*
begins its amorous dance, there people *stirred*
when the peacocks began their amorous dances.

kul'|âṅganā|pracāram iva sarvad" ôpajāta|śaṅkaṃ,

veśyā|janam iv' ôpacāra|caturaṃ,

durjanam iv'

âpagata|para|loka|bhayam,

antyaja|janam iv'

â|gamya|viṣay'|âbhilāṣam,

a|gamya|viṣay'|āsaktam api

praśaṃsanīyam,

Antaka|bhaṭa|gaṇam iva

kṛt'|â|kṛta|sukṛta|vicāra|nipuṇaṃ,

sukṛtam iv' ādi|madhy'|âvasāna|kalyāṇa|karaṃ,

vāsar'|ārambham iva

parisphurat|padma|rāg'|âruṇī|kriyamāṇa|niś"|ântaṃ,

divya|muni|gaṇam iva

Kalāpi|sanātha|Śvetaketu|śobhitaṃ,

Bhārata|samaram iva

Kṛtavarma|śilīmukha|cakra|saṃbhāra|bhīṣaṇaṃ,

Like the behavior of a lady of good family,
people there were always reserved.
Like courtesans, people were skilled in obliging behavior.
As wicked people *have no fear of the next world,*
people there *had no fear of foes.*
Like people of the lowest caste
whose desires go in prohibited directions,
its *desire for conquest extends to inaccessible regions.*
Though seemingly *addicted to prohibited sexual practices,*
it was praiseworthy
for in fact its people
kept talking about inaccessible places now familiar.
Like the troop of Death's officials,
people there were skilled in discriminating
between what is done, not done, and well done.
Like a meritorious action it was productive of good
in the beginning, middle and end.
Like the beginning of the day *when the end of the night*
is reddened by the color of the opening kámala lotuses,
its *houses were reddened by gleaming rubies.*
Like the assemblage of the divine sages,
illustrious with Shveta·ketu along with Kalápin,[107]
it was *resplendent with white flags*
emblazoned with peacocks.
Like the Blárata war *which was frightening*
with Krita·varman[108] *and his large quantity of arrows,*
it *was fierce with its arsenals of armor, arrows,*
and discuses.

pātālam iva

mahā|kañcuki|sahasr'|âdhyāsitaṃ,

varṣa|parvata|samūham iv'

ântaḥ|sthit'|â|parimāṇa|Śṛṅgi|Hemakūṭaṃ,

mahā|dvāram api duṣ|praveśam,

Avanti|viṣaya|gatam api

Māgadha|jan'|âdhiṣṭhitaṃ,

sphītam api

bhraman|nagna|lokaṃ,

rāja|kulaṃ viveśa.

sa|saṃbhram'|ôpagataiś ca kṛta|praṇāmaiḥ

pratīhāra|maṇḍalair upadiśyamāna|mārgaḥ,

sarvataḥ pracalitena ca pūrva|kṛt'|âvasthānena

dūra|paryasta|mauli|śithilita|cūḍā|maṇi|marīci|cumbita|

vasudhā|talena rāja|lokena

pratyekaśaḥ pratīhāra|nivedyamānena

sādaraṃ praṇamyamānaḥ,

Like the subterranean world
which is inhabited by thousands of great snakes,
it *was administered by thousands*
of important chamberlains.
Like the group of continental mountain chains
that has within it the immeasurable mountains
Shringin and Hema·kuta,[109]
it *housed immeasurable gold in high heaps.*
Though it had a huge door, it was difficult to enter.
Though situated in the country of Avánti,
it might seem strange
it was inhabited by people from Mágadha,
but in fact *it was full of bards.*
Though it was prosperous,
naked people were wandering about there,
but in fact
wandering dig·ámbara Jain monks were there—
such was the royal palace that he entered.
And groups of doorkeepers rushed up to him,
bowing and showing him the way,
and the kings who'd been sitting down went up to him
from all sides, and respectfully saluted him,
kissing the surface of the earth with the rays
from their crest jewels that slipped
because they bent their heads so low,
and the doorkeepers announcing them
one by one to him,

pade pade c' âbhyantara|vinirgatābhir
ācāra|kuśalābhir antaḥ|pura|vṛddhābhiḥ
kriyamāṇ'|âvataraṇa|maṅgalo,
bhuvan'|ântarāṇ' îva
vividha|prāṇi|sahasra|saṃkulāni
sapta|kakṣ"|ântarāṇy atikramy'
âbhyantar'|âvasthitam,
an|avarata|śastra|grahaṇa|śyāmik"|ālīḍha|kara|talaiḥ
kara|caraṇa|locana|varjam asita|loha|jālak'|āvṛta|śarīrair
ālāna|stambhair iva gaja|mada|parimala|lobha|nirantara|
nilīna|madhu|kara|paṭala|jaṭilaiḥ,
kula|kram'|āgatair udātt'|ânvayair anuraktair
mahā|prāṇatay" âtikarkaśatayā ca dānavair iv'
āśay'|ākāra|saṃbhāvyamāna|parākramaiḥ
sarvataḥ śarīra|rakṣ"|âdhikāra|niyuktaiḥ puruṣaiḥ
parivṛtam,
ubhayato vāra|vilāsinībhiś c' ân|avaratam
uddhūyamāna|dhavala|cāmaram,
amala|pulina|tala|śobhini sura|kuñjaram iva
Mandākinī|vāriṇi
haṃsa|dhavala|śayana|tale
niṣaṇṇaṃ pitaram apaśyat.
«ālokay'» êti ca pratīhāra|vacan'|ânantaram
atidūr'|âvanatena calita|cūḍā|maṇinā śirasā kṛta|praṇāmam

and coming out of the inner apartments,
at every step the old women of the harem,
well versed in customary observances,
were performing the auspicious *ávatarana* ritual;
having passed through the seven interior courtyards,
like other worlds, full of thousands of varied creatures,
there was the king present inside.
Men whose hands were blackened
from constantly holding the sword,
their bodies, save only hands, feet and eyes,
covered in black chain-mail armor,
looking like elephants' tying posts bristling
with swarms of bees all over them
greedy for the scent of the elephants' rut;
hereditary retainers, of noble family, devoted to the king,
in their spiritedness and extreme toughness
they seemed like demons, their bearing and their bodies
making manifest their valor,
—such were the men appointed as the king's bodyguards,
surrounding him on all sides.
And on either side of him dancing girls
were constantly waving white chowries.
Like Airávata, the elephant of the god Indra,
resting in the water of the heavenly Ganga
shining with the white surfaces of its sandbanks,
he saw his father seated there on a goose-white couch.
And after the doorkeeper had said "Behold him!"
he made obeisance, bowing his head
so low his crest-jewel slipped.

«ehy eh'» îty abhidadhāno dūrād eva
prasārita|bhuja|yugalaḥ
śayana|talād īṣad|ucchvasita|mūrtir
ānanda|jal'|āpūryamāṇa|locanaḥ
samudgata|pulakatayā
sīvyann iv' âikī|kurvann iva pibann iva
taṃ pitā vinay'|âvanatam āliliṅga.
āliṅgit'|ônmuktaś ca pituś caraṇa|pīṭha|samīpe
piṇḍī|kṛtam uttarīyam ātma|tāmbūla|karaṅka|vāhinyā
sa|tvaram āsanī|kṛtam «apanay'» êti śanair vadann
agra|caraṇena samutsārya
Candrāpīḍaḥ kṣiti|tala eva niṣasāda.
anantara|nihite c' âsy' āsane rājñā suta|nirviśeṣam
upagūḍho Vaiśampāyano nyaṣīdat.
muhūrtam iva vismṛta|cāmar'|ôtkṣepa|niścalānāṃ
vāra|vilāsinīnāṃ s'|âbhilāṣair
anila|calita|kuvalaya|dala|dāma|dīrghair
ājihma|tarala|tāra|sārair avalupyamāna iva
dṛṣṭi|pātaiḥ sthitvā
«gaccha, vatsa, putra|vatsalāṃ mātaram abhivādya
darśana|lālasā yathā|kramaṃ sarvā jananīr
darśanen' ānanday'» êti
visarjitaḥ pitrā sa|vinayam utthāya

Saying, "Come to me, come to me,"
his father, even while he was at a distance
stretched out his arms to him, raising his body a little
from his couch, tears of joy welling in his eyes;
and as Chandrapída bent down in reverence
embraced him, his horripilation making it seem
he was stitching him tightly to himself,
becoming one with him, drinking him up.
And on release from his father's embrace,
Chandrapída pushed away with his toes
the upper garment his betel-box-girl
had quickly folded into a cushion for him,
softly telling her to remove it;
and sat down on the bare floor near his father's footstool.
On a seat placed next to him,
when the king had embraced him like his own son,
Vaishampáyana sat down too.
After he'd been there a while,
the dancing girls motionless,
forgetting to wave their chowries,
seeming to devour him with their impassioned glances,
long as strings of *kúvalaya* lily petals stirred in the wind,
flickering as their pupils darted sideways,
"Go, my dear, and greet your mother
who's aching for her son;
and gladden with your presence in due order
all your mothers who're longing to see you."

nivārita|parijano Vaiśampāyana|dvitīyo
'ntaḥpura|praveśa|yogyena
rāja|parijanen' ôpadiśyamāna|vartm"
ântaḥpuram āyayau.
tatra dhavala|kañcuk'|âvacchanna|śarīrair
aneka|śata|saṃkhyaiḥ Śriyam iva kṣīr'|ôda|kallolaiḥ
samantāt parivṛtāṃ śuddh'|ânt'|ântar|vaṃśikair,
atipraśānt'|ākārābhiś ca *kaṣāya/rakt'/âmbara/dhāriṇībhiḥ*
saṃdhyābhir iva sakala|loka|vandyābhiḥ
pralamba|śravaṇa|pāśābhir
vidit'|âneka|kathā|vṛttāntābhir
bhūta|pūrvāḥ puṇyāḥ kathāḥ kathayantībhir
itihāsān vācayantībhiḥ
pustakāni dadhatībhir
dharm'|ôpadeśān nivedayantībhir
jarat|pravrajitābhir vinodyamānām
uparacita|strī|veṣa|bhāṣeṇa gṛhīta|vikaṭa|prasādhanena
varṣa|dhara|janena saṃsevyamānām
an|avarata|vidhūyamāna|bāla|vyajana|kalāpām
aṅganā|janena ca vasan'|ābharaṇa|kusuma|paṭavāsa|
tāmbūla|tālavṛnt'|âṅga|rāga|bhṛṅgāra|dhāriṇā
maṇḍal'|ôpaviṣṭen' ôpāsyamānāṃ

With these words dismissed by his father,
he rose respectfully,
and bidding his suite not to follow him,
accompanied only by Vaishampáyana,
he entered the harem, the way being shown him
by the royal servants permitted to enter the harem.
There, their bodies clothed in white tunics,
many hundreds of them,
like waves surrounding the goddess Lakshmi,
the harem officials surrounded her on all sides.
And, exceedingly serene in appearance,
wearing red-dyed robes,
looking like so many dawns *reddening the sky,*
praised by all the world,
their long ear-lobes hanging down,
knowing many stories and narratives,
telling holy tales of times gone by,
reciting histories,
holding books,
expounding ethical teachings,
old female ascetics were entertaining her;
wearing women's clothes and talking like women,
holding big ornaments,
eunuchs were waiting upon her.
A mass of fans was being constantly waved around her;
and women carrying clothes, ornaments, flowers,
fragrant powders, betel rolls, palm-leaf fans, unguents,
and golden pitchers, encircled her, attending to her needs.

payodhar'|âvalambita|muktā|guṇām
acala|dvaya|madhya|pravṛtta|Gaṅgā|pravāhām iva medinīm
āsanna|darpaṇa|patita|mukha|pratibimbām
arka|bimba|praviṣṭa|śaśi|maṇḍalām iva divaṃ
samupasṛtya mātaraṃ nanāma.
sā tu taṃ sa|saṃbhramam utthāpya saty apy
ājñā|saṃpādana|dakṣe pārśva|parivartini parijane
svayam eva kṛt'|âvataraṇakā
prasruta|payodhara|kṣarat|payo|bindu|cchalena
dravī|bhūya sneh'|ākulena nirgacchat' êva
hṛdayen' ântaḥ śubha|śatāny abhidhyāyantī
mūrdhany upāghrāya
taṃ su|ciram āśiśleṣa.
an|antaraṃ ca tath" âiva kṛta|yath"|ôcita|samupacāram
āśliṣṭa|Vaiśampāyanā svayam upaviśya vinayād
avani|tale samupaviśantam ākṛṣya balād an|icchantam api
Candrāpīḍam utsaṅgam āropitavatī.
sa|saṃbhrama|parijan'|ôpanītāyām āsandyām
upaviṣṭe ca Vaiśampāyane
Candrāpīḍaṃ punaḥ punar āliṅgya
lalāṭa|deśe vakṣasi bhuja|śikharayoś ca
muhur muhuḥ kara|talena parāmṛśantī
Vilāsavatī tam avādīt:

She had a pearl necklace falling between her breasts,
as if she were the earth with Ganga's stream
passing between two mountains.
Her face was reflected in a nearby mirror,
so that she resembled the sky
when the circle of the moon
has entered into the disk of the sun.
He went up to his mother and bowed to her.
She for her part with some agitation raised him up
and though her attendants were beside her
and well able to carry out her commands
she herself performed the ceremony of welcoming a guest.
With her heart so overcome with love and melting
that it seemed to be coming out of her body
in the guise of drops of milk
trickling from her moist breasts,
and secretly wishing him hundreds of auspicious things,
she sniff-kissed him on the head and hugged him long.
And afterwards likewise with proper performance
of hospitality she embraced Vaishampáyana
and sitting down forcefully drew to herself Chandrapída
who was modestly about to sit on the ground,
and unwilling though he was placed him on her lap.
And when Vaishampáyana had sat on a cane chair
hurriedly brought in by the attendants,
embracing Chandrapída again and again,
and touching him again and again with her hands
on his forehead, on his chest, and on his shoulders,
Vilásavati said to him:

«vatsa, kaṭhina|hṛdayas te pitā yen' êyam ākṛtir īdṛśī tri|bhuvana|lālanīyā kleśam atimahāntam iyantaṃ kālaṃ lambhitā.
katham asi soḍhavān atidīrghām imāṃ guru|jana|yantraṇām? aho bālasy' âpi sataḥ kaṭhorasy' êva te mahad dhairyam!
aho vigalita|śiśu|jana|krīḍā|kautuka|lāghavam arbhake tvayi hṛdayam!
aho guru|janasy' ôpari bhaktir a|sādhāraṇā.
sarvathā yathā pituḥ prasādāt samastābhir upeto vidyābhir ālokito 'sy evam acireṇ' âiva kālen' ânurūpābhir vadhūbhir upetam ālokayiṣyāmi.»
ity evam abhidhāya lajjā|smita'|âvanatam ātma|mukha|pratibimba|garbhe vikaca|kamala|kṛta|karṇa|pallav'|âvataṃsa iva kapole paryacumbad enam.
evaṃ ca tatr' âpi n' âticiram eva sthitvā krameṇa sarv'|ântaḥpurāṇi darśanen' ānandayām āsa.
nirgatya ca rāja|kula|dvār'|âvasthitam Indrāyudham āruhya tath" âiva tena rāja|putra|loken' ânugamyamānaḥ Śukanāsaṃ draṣṭum āyāsīt.

"My dear boy, your father was hard-hearted
in making this body of yours,
which the three worlds should fondle,
undergo such great stress for so long.
How could you bear this restraint by teachers?
It was far too long. Ah, though but a boy,
you have the great firmness of a full grown man.
Ah, while you were still a little boy
your heart had lost its levity
and any zest for children's games.
Ah, you've an unparalleled devotion to your elders.
Exactly in the same way as through your father's grace
you've been seen to be provided
with all forms of knowledge,
so too in a short time I will see you
provided with suitable wives."
When she'd spoken thus to him,
his head bowed in a bashful smile,
she kissed him on the cheek, and her face reflected there
was like a blossom ornament for his ear
formed out of a blooming *kámala* lotus.
And without spending too long even there,
he gladdened all the women of the harem in due order
by showing himself to them.
And coming out and mounting Indráyudha
who was standing at the gate of the royal palace,
followed as before by that company of princes,
he went to see Shuka·nasa.

yām'|âvasthita|vividha|gaja|ghaṭā|saṃkaṭam
aneka|turaṃga|sahasra|saṃbādham,
a|parimita|jana|samūha|sahasra|saṃmarda|saṃkulam,
eka|deś'|ôpaviṣṭaiḥ sahasraśo nibaddha|cakra|vālair
aneka|kāry'|āgatair darśan'|ôtsukaiḥ
samantato vividha|śāstr'|âñjan'|ônmīlita|buddhi|locanaiś
cīvara|cchadmanā vinay'|ânurāgibhir
dharma|paṭair iv' âvaguṇṭhitaiḥ
P95 Śākyamuni|śāsana|patha|dhaureyai rakta|paṭaiḥ
Pāśupatair dvijaiś ca divā|niśam āsevyamānam,
abhyantara|praviṣṭānāṃ ca sāmantānāṃ jaghan'|ôpaviṣṭa|
puruṣ'|ôtsaṅga|sthita|dvi|guṇa|kuthābhir
aticir'|âvasthāna|nirveda|prasupt'|ādhoraṇābhiḥ
sa|paryaṇābhir niścal'|âvasthāna|pracālayitābhiḥ
śata|sahasraśaḥ kariṇībhir ākīrṇaṃ,
Śukanāsa|gṛha|dvāram āsādya
satvara|pradhāvitair dvāra|deś'|âvasthitaiḥ
pratīhāra|puruṣair a|nivāryamāṇo 'pi
rāja|kula iva rāja|putro bāhy'|âṅgaṇa eva
turaṃgād avatatāra.

It was packed with various groups of elephants
on guard duty; thronged with many thousand horses;
crammed with innumerable groups of people
in their thousands. And gathered together on one side,
formed into thousands of separate circles,
having arrived from all parts of the world
and eager to see Shuka·nasa on many matters,
their eyes of enlightenment opened by the salve of
many sciences, waiting there night and day,
were the chiefs of the followers
of the Buddha's preaching, wearing red robes, P956
showing their affection for discipline
under the guise of their ascetic garb,
seeming veiled in the cloths of their dharma;
and Páshupatas, and brahmins.
And it was crowded with cow elephants,
hundreds and thousands of them
belonging to the feudatory kings
who'd gone into the inner rooms,
the feudatories' men sitting on their hindquarters
with the elephants' covers folded in their laps,
the mahouts asleep, wearied by the long waiting,
the elephants themselves still wearing their harness,
swaying from side to side because kept stationary—
such was the door to Shuka·nasa's house.
On reaching it, though the doorkeepers stationed there
who quickly ran up did not prevent him riding in,
the prince, as he'd done at the royal palace
got down from his horse in the outer courtyard.

dvāra|deś'|âvasthāpita|turaṃgaś ca Vaiśampāyanam
avalambya pura|pradhāvitaiḥ samutsārita|parijanais
tath" âiva pratīhāra|maṇḍalair upadiśyamāna|mārgas,
tath" âiva calita|mukuṭa|koṭibhir nar'|êndra|vṛndaiḥ
sevā|samupasthitair utthāy' ôtthāya praṇamyamānas,
tath" âiva pracaṇḍa|pratīhāra|huṃkāra|
bhaya|mūkī|bhavat|parijanāni
pracalita|vetra|latā|cakita|sāmanta|cakra|
caraṇa|śata|calita|vasuṃdharāṇi kakṣ"|ântarāṇi
nirīkṣamāṇas,
tath" âiva nava|nava|sudh"|âvadāta|
prāsāda|sahasra|nirantaraṃ
dvitīyam iva rāja|kulaṃ
Śukanāsa|bhavanaṃ viveśa.
praviśya c' âneka|nar'|êndra|sahasra|madhy'|ôpaviṣṭam
aparam iva pitaram upadarśita|vinayo
dūr'|âvanatena maulinā Śukanāsaṃ vavande.
Śukanāsas taṃ sa|saṃbhramam utthāy' ânupūrvyeṇ'
ôtthita|rāja|lokaḥ s'|ādaram
abhimukha|datt'|âvirala|padaḥ
praharṣa|visphārita|locan'|āgat'|ānanda|jala|kaṇaḥ
saha Vaiśampāyanena premṇā gāḍham ālilinga.

Leaving his horse at the threshold,
and leaning on Vaishampáyana,
his path was cleared by groups of doorkeepers
running ahead of him
and driving away the other servants,
just as had happened in his father's palace.
Just as before, their crested crowns slipping,
the hosts of kings assembled to pay homage to Shuka·nasa
jumped up and bowed to Chandrapída.
Just as before, he got a look at the inner apartments
where the servants fell silent in fear
at the doorkeepers' fierce hisses,
where the earth shook
under the feet of the numerous feudatories
startled by the brandished long staffs.
Just as before, everywhere the thousands of walls
were white with very fresh plaster.
The palace of Shuka·nasa that Chandrapída entered
was like a second royal palace.
And on entering he showed his respect
as if to another father to Shuka·nasa
who was seated amid many thousand kings,
saluting him with his head bent very low.
Shuka·nasa hurriedly rose,
followed by the kings around him,
and respectfully advanced more than a few steps
towards him; his eyes wide open in delight
and welling with tears of joy,
he affectionately embraced him
as well as Vaishampáyana.

âliṅgit'|ônmuktaś ca s'|ādar'|ôpanītam apahāya
ratn'|āsanam avanāv eva rāja|putraḥ samupāviśat
tad anu ca Vaiśampāyanaḥ.
samupaviṣṭe ca rāja|putre
Śukanāsa|varjam anyad akhilam
avani|pāla|cakram ujjhita|nij'|āsanam
avani|talam abhajata.
sthitvā ca tūṣṇīṃ kṣaṇam iva Śukanāsaḥ
samudgata|prīti|pulakair aṅgair
āvedyamāna|hṛdaya|harṣa|prakarṣas tam abravīt.
«tāta Candrāpīḍ', âdya khalu devasya Tārāpīḍasya
samāpta|vidyam upārūḍha|yauvanam ālokya bhavantaṃ
sucirād bhuvana|rājya|phala|prāptir upajātā.
adya samṛddhāḥ sarvā guru|jan'|āśiṣaḥ.
adya phalitam
aneka|janm'|ântar'|ôpāttam avadātaṃ karma.
adya prasannāḥ kula|devatāḥ.
na hy a|puṇya|bhājāṃ bhavādṛśās tri|bhuvana|
vismaya|hetavaḥ putratāṃ pratipadyante.
kv' êdaṃ vayaḥ? kv' êyam amānuṣī śaktiḥ?
kva c' êdam a|śeṣa|vidyā|grahaṇa|sāmarthyam?
aho dhanyāḥ prajā yāsāṃ
Bharata|Bhagīratha|pratimo

The king's son, embraced and released,
avoided the jeweled seat
that was respectfully brought for him,
and sat down on the ground; and following him,
Vaishampáyana did so too.
And when the king's son had sat down,
the whole circle of kings, everybody else,
except Shuka·nasa,
left their own seats and sat down on the ground.
And standing silent for a moment, Shuka·nasa,
the excess of joy in his heart
revealed by his horripilating limbs,
said to him,
"Chandrapída, my dear boy, surely it is only today
that His Majesty Tarapída, seeing you
complete your education and reach maturity,
has at long last obtained the fruit
of his sovereignty of the world.
Today all the hopes of your elders have been fulfilled.
Today has born fruit the pure action
accomplished in many previous births.
Today the household deities have shown their favor.
For such as you,
causing astonishment to the three worlds,
do not become the sons of those who are without merit.
What a great difference there is between this age of yours
and your more than human strength.
And this ability of yours to master all the sciences.
Oh, blessed are the subjects
whose protector you were born to be,

bhavān utpannaḥ pālayitā!

kiṃ khalu kṛtam avadātaṃ karma

vasuṃdharayā yay" âsi bhartā samāsāditaḥ?

Hari|vakṣaḥ|sthala|nivās'|â|sad|graha|vyasaninī hatā khalu

Lakṣmīr yā vigrahavatī bhavantaṃ n'ôpasarpati.

sarvathā kalpa|koṭīr Mahāvarāha iva

daṃṣṭrā|valayena

vaha bāhunā vasuṃdharā|bhāraṃ saha pitrā.»

ity abhidhāya ca svayam ābharaṇa|vasana|kusum'|

âṅga|rāg'|ādibhir abhyarcya visarjayāṃ cakāra.

visarjitaś c' ôtthāy' ântaḥ|puraṃ praviśya dṛṣṭvā

Vaiśampāyana|mātaraṃ Manoram'|âbhidhānāṃ

nirgatya samāruhy' Êndrāyudhaṃ

pitrā pūrva|kalpitaṃ

praticchandakam iva rāja|kulasya

dvār'|âvasthita|sita|pūrṇa|kalaśam

ābaddha|harita|vandana|mālam

ullasita|sita|patākā|sahasram

abhyāhata|maṅgala|tūrya|rava|paripūrita|dig|antaram

you who are the image of Bhárata and Bhagi·ratha.
What excellent deed did the earth do,
that you have now become her lord?
Surely Lakshmi is accursed,
addicted as she is to her unfortunate whim
of residing on Hari's chest,
rather than taking corporal form and approaching you!
Carry, with your father,
the burden of the earth in its entirety
on your arm for ten million eons,
as Vishnu the great boar did on his curved tusk."
And when he'd said this,
Shuka·nasa himself honored Chandrapída
with ornaments, clothes, flowers, unguents,
and other such things, and gave him leave to depart.
And given leave to depart
he got up and entered the harem,
and visited Vaishampáyana's mother,
whose name was Mano·rama.
Coming out, the prince mounted Indráyudha
and went to the palace his father had earlier
had built for him, like a replica of the royal palace.
Silver pots of water stood at the door.
Green garlands of welcome were strung up.
Thousands of white flags were fluttering over it.
The sound of the playing of auspicious
musical instruments filled every part of it.

uparacita|vikaca|kamala|kusuma|prakaram
acira|kṛt'|âgni|kāryam ujjvala|vivikta|parijanam
upapādit'|â|śeṣa|gṛha|praveśa|maṅgalaṃ
kumāro bhavanaṃ jagāma.

gatvā ca śrī|maṇḍap'|âvasthite śayane
muhūrtam upaviśya saha tena rāja|putra|loken'
âbhiṣek'|ādikam aśan'|âvasānam
akarod divasa|vidhim.
abhyantare ca sva|śayanīya|gṛha ev' Êndrāyudhasy'
âvasthānam akalpayat.
evaṃ|prāyeṇa c' âsy' ôdantena
tad ahaḥ pariṇatim upayayau.

gagana|talād avatarantyā divasa|śriyaḥ
padma|rāga|nūpuram iva
sva|prabhā|pihita|randhraṃ
ravi|maṇḍalam *unmukta/pādaṃ* papāta.
salila|pravāha iva ratha|cakra|mārg'|ânusāreṇa
divasa|karasya vāsar'|ālokaḥ pratīcīṃ kakubham agāt.
abhinava|pallava|lohita|talena kareṇ' êv'
âdho|mukha|prasṛtena divasa|kara|bimbena
vāsaraḥ kamala|rāgam aśeṣaṃ mamārja.

Flower offerings of blooming *kámala* lotuses
were being made.
Fire sacrifices had just been performed.
The servants were bright and clean.
All the auspicious rites required
for entering a newly built house for the first time
had been performed.
And going in, when he'd sat for a while on a couch
in the beautiful reception pavilion with his royal retinue,
in the company of the other princes
he completed his daily duties,
beginning with the bath and ending with dinner.
And he arranged for Indráyudha to be stabled
inside the house, indeed in his own sleeping quarters.
And with suchlike doings on his part
that day came to its end.
As if it were a ruby anklet
slipping from the foot of the glorious beauty of the day
as she came down from the sky,
with its hollow center masked by its own radiance,
the disc of the sun fell down *shorn of its rays.*
As if it were a stream of water
following the path of the sun's chariot,
the light of the day went to the west.
As if with a hand, palm as red as new blossom,
stretched down, the day wiped away
all the red color of the *kámala* lotuses
with the sun as it sank down.

kamalinī|parimala|paricay'|
āgat'|âli|māl"|ākulita|kaṇṭhaṃ
kāla|pāśair iva cakra|vāka|mithunam
ākṛṣyamāṇaṃ vijaghaṭe.
kara|puṭair ā|divas'|ântam
ā|pītam aravinda|madhu|rasam iva
rakt'|ātapa|cchalena gagana|gamana|khedād iva
divasa|kara|bimbaṃ vavāma.
krameṇa ca pratīcī|karṇa|pūra|rakt'|ôtpale lok'|ântaram
upagate bhagavati gabhasti|mālini, samullasitāyām
ambara|taṭāka|vikaca|kamalinyāṃ saṃdhyāyāṃ,
kṛṣṇ'|âguru|paṅka|pattra|latāsv iva timira|lekhāsu
sphurantīṣu diśāṃ mukheṣv,
ali/kula/malinena kuvalay|vanen' êva rakta|kamal'|ākare
timira|nikareṇ' *ôtsāryamāṇe* saṃdhyā|rāge,
kamalinī|nipītam ātapam unmūlayitum
andhakāra|pallaveṣv iva
viśatsu rakta|kamal'|ôdarāṇi
madhu|kara|kuleṣu,

Their necks encumbered by garlands of bees
come because of their fondness
for the fragrance of the lotus beds,
the pairs of *chakra·vaka* ducks as they separated
seemed dragged apart
by the nooses of the god of death.
The sun's disc, under the guise of its reddened sunshine,
seemed to vomit forth, from fatigue,
the lotus honey it had as it were been drinking up
right until the end of day
with the cupped *hands* that were its *rays.*
And in due course, when the blessed ray-wreathed sun,
red lotus ear ornament for the west,
had gone to the other world;
when the twilight was shining forth,
a blooming *kámala* lotus bed in the lake of the sky;
when streaks of darkness
like leaf and creeper decorations in black aloe paste
were appearing on the faces of the quarters;
when twilight's red *was being driven away*
by dense darkness, *black as a swarm of bees,*
just as a bed of closing red *kámala* lotuses
belonging to the day,
is *surpassed* by a grove of blue *kúvalaya* lilies
when they open in the night
and are *dark with swarms of bees*;
when swarms of bees are entering
the insides of red *kámala* lotuses
as if they were strips of cloth used by darkness
to pull out the sunshine drunk in by the lotus plants;

śanaiḥ śanaiś ca niśā|vilāsinī|mukh'|âvataṃsa|pallave

galite saṃdhyā|rāge,

dikṣu dikṣu vikṣipteṣu

saṃdhyā|devat"|ârcana|bali|piṇḍeṣu,

śikhara|deśa|lagna|timirāsv an|ārūḍha|mayūrāsv api

mayūr'|âdhiṣṭhitāsv iva mayūra|yaṣṭiṣu,

gavākṣa|vivara|nilīneṣu

prāsāda|lakṣmī|karṇ'|ôtpaleṣu pārāvateṣu,

vigata|vilāsinī|saṃvāhana|niścala|kāñcana|pīṭhāsu

mūkī|bhūta|ghaṇṭā|svarāsv antaḥ|pura|dolāsu,

bhavana|sahakāra|śākh'|âvalambita|pañjareṣu

vigat'|ālāpeṣu śuka|sārikā|nivaheṣu,

saṃgīta|virāma|viśrānta|ravās' ûtsāryamāṇāsu vīṇāsu,

yuvati|nūpura|śabd'|ôpaśama|nibhṛteṣu

bhavana|kalahaṃseṣv,

apanīyamāna|karṇa|śaṅkha|cāmara|nakṣatra|mālā|

maṇḍaneṣu madhu|kara|kula|śūnya|kapola|bhittiṣu

matta|vāraṇeṣu,

and when twilight's red glow, blossom ornament
for the face of lovely lady night,
had very slowly flowed away;
when rice ball offerings
for the worship of the deity of twilight
had been scattered in all directions;
when the peacocks' perches,
though no peacocks were mounted on them,
darkness clinging to their tops,
seemed to have peacocks sitting there;
when the pigeons, blue *útpala* lilies
for the glorious beauty of the palaces,
had reposed themselves in the gaps of the lattice windows;
when, their burden of ladies departed,
the harem swings had their golden seats
motionless and the tinkling of their bells silenced;
when the multitudes of parrots and mynahs in their cages
hanging from the branches of the palace mango trees
had stopped their conversations;
when, their sounds silenced at the end of the concert,
the *vinas* were being put aside;
when the palace *kala·hansa* geese were silent
on the cessation of the sound of the women's anklets;
when the rut elephants
were having their ornaments taken off—
their ear conch shells, chowries,
and constellation necklaces—
and their broad cheeks were devoid of the swarms of bees;

pradīpyamānṣu rāja|vallabha|turaṃgama|
mandurā|pradīpeṣu,
praviśantīṣu prathama|yāma|kuñjara|ghaṭāsu,
kṛta|rāja|svasty|ayaneṣu niṣkrāmatsu purohiteṣu,
visarjita|rāja|loka|virala|parijaneṣu vistāriteṣv iva
rāja|kula|kakṣ"|ântareṣu,
prajvalita|dīpikā|sahasra|pratibimba|cumbiteṣu
kṛta|vikaca|campaka|dal'|ôpahāreṣv iva
maṇi|bhūmi|kuṭṭimeṣu,
nipatita|dīp'|ālokāsu ravi|virah'|ārta|nalinī|vinodan'|āgata|
bāl'|ātapāsv iva bhavana|dīrghikāsu,
nidr"|âlaseṣu pañjara|kesariṣu,
samāropita|kārmuke gṛhīta|sāyake yāmika iv'
ântaḥpura|praviṣṭe Makaraketāv,
avataṃsa|pallaveṣv iva *sa|rāgeṣu* karṇe
kriyamāṇeṣu surata|dūtī|vacaneṣu,
sūrya|kānta|maṇibhya iva
saṃkrānt'|ânaleṣu jvalatsu
māninīnāṃ śoka|vidhureṣu hṛdayeṣu,

when lamps were being lit
in the stables of the king's favorite horses;
when the troops of elephants
for the first watch of the night were coming in;
when the priests who'd performed
the *svasty·áyana* rites for the king were filing out;
the interior rooms of the royal palace
seeming to have expanded, only a few servants
remaining after the kings had been dismissed;
when the jeweled floor pavements,
kissed by the reflections of the thousands
of glowing lamps, seemed to have on them
offerings of full blown *chámpaka* petals;
with the light of the lamps fallen into them as reflections,
the palace pools seeming visited
by the early morning sunshine
come to distract the lotus-plants
distressed by separation from the sun;
the lions in their cages lazily asleep;
when, stringing his bow and taking up his arrows,
like a night-watchman, *mákara*-bannered Love
entered the harem;
when *impassioned* messages relating to love making
were being delivered by go-between girls to the ear,
as if they were ornaments of *red* blossoms for it;
when haughty ladies' hearts, overcome with grief
at the absence of their lovers, were burning,
as if the fire from the sun stone jewels
had been transferred to them;

pravṛtte pradoṣa|samaye Candrāpīḍaḥ
prajvalita|dīpikā|cakravāla|parivāraś
caraṇābhyām eva rāja|kulaṃ gatvā
pituḥ samīpe muhūrtaṃ sthitvā dṛṣṭvā ca Vilāsavatīm
āgatya sva|bhavanam aneka|ratna|prabhā|śabalam
uraga|rāja|phaṇā|maṇḍalam iva Hṛṣīkeśaḥ
śayana|talam adhiśiśye.
prabhātāyāṃ ca niśīthinyāṃ samutthāya
samabhyanujñātaḥ pitr",
âbhinava|mṛgayā|kautuk'|âvakṛṣyamāṇa|hṛdayo
bhagavaty anudita eva sahasra|raśmāv
āruhy' Êndrāyudham
agrato bāleya|pramāṇān ākarṣadbhiś
cāmī|kara|śṛṅkhalābhiḥ kauleyakāñ,
jarad|vyāghra|carma|śabala|
vasana|kañcuka|dhāribhir,
aneka|varṇa|paṭṭa|cīrik"|
ôdbaddha|maulibhir,
upacita|śmaśru|gahana|mukhair,
eka|karṇ'|âvasakta|hema|tālī|puṭair,
ābaddha|nibiḍa|kakṣair,
an|avarata|śram'|ôpacit'|ōru|piṇḍikaiḥ,
kodaṇḍa|pāṇibhiḥ,
śva|poṣakair an|avarata|kṛta|kolāhalaiḥ pradhāvadbhir
dviguṇī|kriyamāṇa|gaman'|ôtsāho

when night had thus manifested itself,
his entourage holding a circle of lighted torches,
Chandrapída went on foot to the king's palace.
He stayed in his father's presence for a while,
visited Vilásavati, and returned to his own palace
where he slept on a bed checkered with the radiance
of many jewels, like Vishnu, lord of the senses,
on the circle of the snake king's hoods.
And when the night had begun to lighten he got up,
his heart drawn by eagerness for hunting
which he hadn't done before
and, his father having given him permission,
even though the blessed thousand-rayed sun hadn't risen,
he mounted Indráyudha,
and with the huntsmen ahead of him—
holding back on golden chains
hounds the size of donkeys,
themselves clad in tunics and cloths
discolored like old tiger-skins,
their heads wrapped round
with strips of cloth of various colors,
their faces covered in heavy beards,
each with a gold *tali·puta* ornament in one ear,
their thighs and calves developed by constant exercise,
their loins tightly girded,
bows in their hands,
running about and raising a continuous din,
such were the huntsmen, and they redoubled
his enthusiasm for going—

bahu|gaja|turaga|padāti|parivṛto vanaṃ yayau.

tatra ca karṇ'|ânt'|âvakṛṣṭa|muktair

vikaca|kuvalaya|palāśa|kāntibhir bhallair

mada|kala|kalabha|kumbha|bhitti|bhiduraiś ca

nārācaiś cāpa|ṭaṃkāra|rava|bhaya|

cakita|vana|devat''|ârdh'|âkṣa|vīkṣito

vana|varāhān kesariṇaḥ śarabhāṃś

camarān|aneka|kuraṅgakāṃś ca sahasraśo jaghāna.

anyāṃś ca jīvata eva

mahā|prāṇatayā sphurato jagrāha.

samārūḍhe ca madhyam ahnaḥ savitari

vanāt snān'|ôtthiten' êva

śrama|salila|bindu|varṣam an|avaratam ujjhatā

muhur muhur daśana|vighaṭṭanaiḥ

khaṇakhaṇāyita|khara|khalīnena

śrama|śithila|mukha|galita|phenila|rudhira|lavena

paryāṇa|paṭṭak'|ânusār'|ôtthita|phena|rājinā,

karṇ'|âvataṃsī|kṛtam

utphulla|kusuma|śabalam

ali|paṭala|jhaṃkāra|rava|mukharaṃ

vana|gamana|cihnaṃ pallava|stabakam udvahat''

he went to the forest surrounded by many elephants,
horses, and foot soldiers.
And there, with *bhalla* arrows shining
like blooming *kúvalaya* lily petals, drawn back
as far as his ear and then released, and *narácha* arrows
that could pierce a young rut elephant's temple,
while forest divinities trembling in fear
at the twanging of his bow
looked on with half-closed eyes.
He killed by the thousand wild boar, lions,
*shárabha*s, yak, and many kinds of deer.
And other animals, such was his great physical strength,
he captured, alive and trembling.
And when the sun had risen to mid-day,
being carried from the wood by Indráyudha—
who as if he'd just emerged from a bath
was continuously shedding a shower of sweat drops,
again and again making his hard bridle clank
with the gnashing of his teeth,
his mouth hanging open loose from fatigue
drops of blood mixed with foam falling from it,
raising a line of lather along the edge of his saddle cloth;
wearing a cluster of sprouts,
souvenir of the visit to the forest,
which formed an ornament for his ears
spotted with blooming flowers
and noisy with the humming of a swarm of bees—

Êndrāyudhen' ôhyamānaḥ
samudgata|svedatay" ântar'|ārdrī|kṛta|maṇḍalena
mṛga|rudhira|lava|śata|śabalena vāravāṇena
dvi|guṇataram upajanita|kāntir,
aneka|rūp'|ânusaraṇa|saṃbhrama|paribhraṣṭa|
cchattra|dhāratayā chattrī|kṛtena nava|pallavena
nivāryamā'|ātapo,
vividha|vana|latā|kusuma|reṇu|dhūsaro
vasanta iva vigrahavān,
aśva|khura|rajo|malina|lalāṭ'|âbhivyakt'|
âvadāta|sveda|lekho,
dūra|vicchinnena padāti|parijanena
śūnyī|kṛta|purobhāgaḥ,
prajavi|turaṃgam'|âdhirūḍhair alp'|âvaśiṣṭaiḥ
saha rāja|putrair
«evaṃ mṛga|patir, evaṃ varāha,
evaṃ vana|mahiṣa, evaṃ śarabha,
evaṃ hariṇa»
iti tam eva mṛgayā|vṛttāntam uccārayan
sva|bhavanam ājagāma.
avatīrya ca turaṃgamāt sa|saṃbhrama|pradhāvita|
parijan'|ôpanīte samupaviśy' āsane vāravāṇam avatāry'
âpanīya c' âśeṣaṃ turaṃgam'|âdhirohaṇ'|ôcitaṃ
veṣa|parigraham itas tataḥ pracalita|tālavṛnta|pavan'|

from his armor Chandrapída was enjoying
a double liquid embellishment:
its curved interior was wet with collected sweat,
and it was spotted on the outside
with hundreds of drops of the blood of wild animals.
Since his parasol bearer was lost in the confusion
of chasing numerous wild beasts,
he kept the sun off himself by using
a fresh sprig of foliage as a parasol.
Dusty with pollen
from the flowers of various wild creepers
he was like spring in human form.
White lines of sweat were clearly visible on his forehead
which was dirty with the dust raised by horses' hooves.
Ahead of him was empty ground,
for his servants who went on foot
now cut off from him were far in the rear.
With the few princes who remained with him
being mounted on fast horses,
he discussed the events of the hunt—
"That was how the lion was killed,
how the boar was killed,
how the wild buffalo, the *sharabha,*
the deer, and so on"—
as he made his way to his own abode.
And getting down from his horse, his servants
hurriedly running up and bringing a seat,
he sat down on it and got out of his armor,
and removed the rest of his riding gear.
While his fatigue was removed by fans waved to and fro

âpanīyamāna|śramo muhūrtaṃ viśaśrāma.
viśramya ca maṇi|rajata|kanaka|kalaśa|śata|sanāthām
antar|vinyasta|kāñcana|pīṭhāṃ snāna|bhūmim agāt.
nirvartit'|âbhiṣeka|vyāpārasya ca vivikta|vasana|
parimṛṣṭa|vapuṣaḥ svaccha|dukūla|pallav'|ākalita|mauler
gṛhīta|vāsasaḥ kṛta|dev'|ârcanasy'
âṅga|rāga|bhūmau samupaviṣṭasya
rājñā visarjitā mahā|pratīhār'|âdhiṣṭhitā
rāja|kula|paricārikāḥ Kulavardhanā|sanāthāś ca
Vilāsavatī|dāsyaḥ sarv'|ântaḥpura|preṣitāś c'
ântaḥpura|paricārikāḥ
paṭalaka|vinihitāni vividhāny ābharaṇāni mālyāny
aṅga|rāgān vāsāṃsi c' ādāya
P100 puratas tasy' ôpatasthur upaninyuś ca.
yathā|kramam ādāya ca tābhyaḥ prathamaṃ svayam
upalipya Vaiśampāyanam uparacit'|âṅg|rāgo dattvā ca
samīpa|vartibhyo yath"|ârham
ābharaṇa|vasan'|âṅga|rāga|kusumāni
vividha|maṇi|bhājana|sahasra|sāraṃ śāradam
ambara|talam iva sphurita|tārā|gaṇam
āhāra|maṇḍapam agacchat.

he rested for a while.
And when he'd rested he went to the bathing room
provided with hundreds of pitchers, jeweled, silver,
and golden, and furnished with a seat of gold.
When he'd finished bathing and had had his body
rubbed dry with clean towels and had his head
wrapped round with a turban cloth of shining silk,
he put on his clothes and worshipped the gods,
and seated himself in the unguent room.
There came to him servants from the royal palace
sent by the king under the supervision
of the chief doorkeeper, and Vilásavati's maids
with Kula·várdhana at their head,
and the harem servants sent
by all the women of the harem.
Bringing baskets packed with all sorts of ornaments,
garlands, unguents and clothes,
they came before him and presented them to him. P100
He accepted the gifts in due order,
and when he'd himself
first anointed Vaishampáyana,
finished his own anointing.
And giving to the people around him,
each as he deserved,
ornaments, clothes, unguents and flowers,
he went to the dining pavilion which was equipped
with thousands of different kinds of jeweled vessels,
like the fall sky with its hosts of glittering stars.

tatra ca dviguṇī|kṛta|kuth"|āsan'|ôpaviṣṭaḥ
samīp'|ôpaviṣṭena tad|guṇa'|ôpavarṇana|pareṇa
Vaiśampāyanena
yath"|ârha|bhūmi|bhāg'|ôpaveśitena rāja|putra|loken'
«êdam asmai dīyatām, idam asmai dīyatām»
iti prasāda|viśeṣa|darśana|saṃvardhita|sevā|rasen'
āhāra|vidhim akarot.
upaspṛśya ca gṛhīta|tāmbūlas tasmin muhūrtam iva sthitv"
Êndrāyudha|samīpam agamat.
tatra c' ânupaviṣṭa eva tad|guṇ'|ôpavarṇana|prāy'|ālāpāḥ
kathāḥ kṛtvā saty apy ājñā|pratīkṣaṇ'|ônmukhe
pārśva|parivartini parijane tad|guṇa|hṛta|hṛdayaḥ
svayam ev' Êndrāyudhasya puro yavasam ākīrya
nirgatya rāja|kulam ayāsīt.
ten' âiva krameṇ' âvalokya rājānam
āgatya niśām anaiṣīt.
aparedyuś ca prabhāta|samaya eva
sarv'|ântaḥpur'|âdhikṛtam avani|pateḥ
parama|saṃmatam anumārg'|āgatayā,
prathame vayasi vartamānayā,
rāja|kula|saṃvāsa|pragalbhay" âpy anujjhita|vinayayā,
kiṃ|cid|upārūḍha|yauvanayā,
śakra|gopak'|ālohita|rāgeṇ' âṃśukena racit'|âvaguṇṭhanayā,
sa|bāl'|ātapay" êva pūrvayā kakubhā,

And there he sat down on a seat of folded carpets,
and took his meal with Vaishampáyana
who was seated close to him and
intent on describing Chandrapída's merits,
and the princes seated in such places as each deserved,
their delight in serving Chandrapída increased
by him showing them special favors:
"Serve this to him, serve that to him."
And when he'd rinsed his mouth, taken a betel roll,
and stayed a while in the dining pavilion,
he went to Indráyudha.
And there, without sitting down, he talked for a while,
mainly extolling Indráyudha's merits,
and though there were servants at his side eagerly
awaiting his command, he himself, his heart captivated
by Indráyudha's merits, spread fodder before him.
After he left him he went to the royal palace.
In due order, having seen the king, he came home
and spent the night there.
And the next day, right at dawn, he saw approaching
the person in charge of the whole harem,
in high favor with the king,
followed by a very young woman.
Though self-assured through residence in the royal palace
she had not lost her modesty.
She'd just reached maturity.
Clad in a silken robe reddened with cochineal dye,
she looked like the east in the early morning sunshine.

pratyagra|dalita|manaḥ|śilā|cūrṇa|varṇen'
âṅga|lāvaṇya|prabhā|pravāheṇ'
âmṛta|rasa|nadī|pūreṇ' êva bhavanam āpūrayantyā,
jyotsnay" êva Rāhu|graha|grāsa|bhayād
apahāya rajani|kara|maṇḍalaṃ gām avatīrṇayā,
rāja|kula|devatay" êva mūrtimatyā,
kvaṇita|maṇi|nūpur'|ākulita|caraṇa|yugalayā
kūjat|kalahaṃs'|ākulita|kamalay" êva kamalinyā
mah"|ārha|hema|mekhalā|kalāpa|kalita|jaghana|sthalayā,
n' âtinirbhar'|ôdbhinna|payodharayā,
mandaṃ mandaṃ bhuja|latā|vikṣepa|preṅkhita|
nakha|mayūkha|cchalena dhārābhir iva
lāvaṇya|rasam an|avarataṃ kṣarantyā,
diṅ|mukha|visarpiṇi hāra|latānāṃ
raśmi|jāle nimagna|śarīratayā
kṣīra|sāgar'|ônmagna|vadanay" êva Lakṣmyā,
bahula|tāmbūla|kṛṣṇik"|
ândhakārit'|âdhara|lekhayā,
sama|suvṛtta|tuṅga|nāsikayā,
vikasita|puṇḍarīka|dhavala|locanayā.

With the flowing luster of the beauty of her body,
the color of freshly powdered red lead,
she seemed to be filling the palace
with the flooding waters of a river of liquid nectar.
She was like moonlight who'd abandoned
the disc of the moon
in fear of being swallowed up by the planet Rahu,
and come down to earth.
She was like the guardian deity of the royal palace
in human form.
Her feet burdened with ringing jeweled anklets,
she was like a *kámala* lotus pool with its lotuses
burdened with cackling *raja·hansa* geese.
Tied on her buttocks
was a costly multi-stringed girdle of gold.
Her breasts had appeared but weren't very prominent.
In the guise of the rays of light from her fingernails
swinging about as she very slowly moved her arms
she seemed incessantly pouring out in streams
the liquid of her beauty.
As her body was submerged in the mass of rays
from her pearl necklaces which spread to the quarters
she looked like Lakshmi when her face
was rising up out of the ocean of milk.
The line of her lower lip was darkened
with the black stain of many betel-rolls.
Her nose was even, well-rounded and high.
Her eyes were white like a *pundaríka* lotus in bloom.

maṇi|kuṇḍala|makara|patra|bhaṅga|koṭi|kiraṇ'|
ātap'|āhata|kapolatayā sa|karṇa|pallavam iva
mukham udvahantyā,
paryuṣita|dhūsara|candana|rasa|tilak'|âlaṃkṛta|
lalāṭa|paṭṭayā, muktā|phala|prāy'|âlaṃkārayā,
Rādheya|rājya|lakṣmy" êv' *ôpapādit'|Âṅga|rāgayā,*
nava|vana|lekhay" êva *komala|tanu|latayā,*
trayy" êva *su|pratiṣṭhita|caraṇayā,*
makha|śālay" êva *vedi|madhyayā,*
Meru|vana|latay" êva kanaka|patr'|âlaṃkṛtayā,
mah"|ânubhāv'|ākāray"
ânugamyamānaṃ kanyakayā
Kailāsa|nāmānaṃ kañcukinam āyāntam apaśyat.
sa kṛta|praṇāmaḥ samupasṛtya
kṣiti|tala|nihita|dakṣiṇa|karo vijñāpayām āsa.
«kumāra, mahā|devī Vilāsavatī samājñāpayati:
‹iyaṃ khalu kanyakā mahārājena pūrvaṃ
Kulūta|rāja|dhānīm avajitya Kulūt'|ēśvara|duhitā
Patralekh"|âbhidhānā bālikā
satī bandī|janena sah' ānīy'
ântaḥ|pura|paricārikā|madhyam upanītā.

Since her cheeks were struck by the sunshine of the rays
from the points of the ornamental leaf-work *mákaras*
on her jeweled earrings,
her face seemed to have leaf sprays for the ears.
Her broad forehead was adorned with a *tílaka* mark
in sandal paste put on the night before and now gray.
Her ornaments were mostly pearls.
She was like Karna's regal glory
beloved by the people of Anga,[110]
in that *she had used unguents.*
Like a line of young woodland *with soft slim creepers,*
her *slim body was soft.*
Like the three Vedas *with their well established schools,*
she *put her feet down elegantly.*
Like a sacrifice hall *with the altar in the middle of it,*
her *waist was shaped like an altar.*
Like a creeper in the forest on Mount Meru
she was adorned with golden leaves.
Her bearing was very noble.
Such was the girl
following the chamberlain named Kailása.
The chamberlain bowed, approached, and kneeling down
with his right hand placed on the ground said,
"Your Highness, the great queen Vilásavati commands:
'This maiden is the daughter
of the ruler of the Kulútas.[111]
Her name is Patra·lekha. When our great king
earlier conquered the royal capital of the Kulútas
she was brought here as a little girl
with the other captives, and was placed

sā mayā vigata|nāthā rāja|duhit" êti samupajāta|snehayā
duhitṛ|nirviśeṣam iyantaṃ kālam upalālitā saṃvardhitā ca.
«tad iyam idānīm ucitā bhavatas tāmbūla|karaṅka|vāhin"»
îti kṛtvā mayā preṣitā.
na c' âsyām āyuṣmatā parijana|sāmānya|dṛṣṭinā
bhavitavyam. bāl" êva lālanīyā.
sva|citta|vṛttir iva cāpalebhyo nivāraṇīyā.
śiṣy" êva draṣṭavyā. suhṛd iva
sarva|viśrambheṣv abhyantarī|karaṇīyā.
dīrgha|kāla|saṃvardhita|snehatayā sva|sutāyām iva
hṛdayam asyām asti me.
balavān asyāṃ pakṣa|pātaḥ.
mah"|âbhijana|rāja|vaṃśa|prasūtā c' ârhat' îyam
evaṃ|vidhāni karmāṇi.
niyataṃ svayam ev' êyam
ativinītatayā katipayair eva divasaiḥ kumāram ārādhayiṣyati.
kevalam aticira|kāl'|ôpacitā
balavatī me prema|pravṛttir asyām
avidita|śīlaś c' âsyāḥ kumāra iti saṃdiśyate.
sarvathā tathā kalyāṇinā prayatitavyaṃ
yath" êyam aticiram ucitā paricārikā te bhavati.› »

among the female attendants in the harem.
Seeing her, a king's daughter without a protector,
she won my affection and I cherished her
and brought her up as if she were my own daughter
for all this time.
Now thinking that she is fit to be your betel-box bearer,
I send her to you.
And you, long-lived may you be, should not look on her
as an ordinary servant.
She is to be cherished like a child.
Like your own mind,
she should be restrained from rash acts.
She should be looked upon as a pupil. Like a friend
she should be brought into all your confidential matters.
Because my affection has grown over a long time,
my heart is attached to her
as if she were my own daughter.
My partiality for her is strong.
She is daughter of a great and noble line of kings
and she deserves appropriate behavior on your part.
Assuredly she is so very well-behaved
she will herself please the prince in just a few days.
Only because my affectionate feelings for her
have developed over a very long time and are very strong,
and as her character is unknown to the prince
do I send this message.
Prince, may you be prosperous! you should strive
in every way for her to be an appropriate attendant
for you for a very long time.'"

ity abhidhāya virata|vacasi Kailāse
kṛt'|âbhijāta|praṇāmāṃ Patralekhām a|nimiṣa|locanaṃ
suciram ālokya Candrāpīḍo «yath" ājñāpayaty amb"»
êty evam uktvā kañcukinaṃ preṣayām āsa.
Patralekhā tu tataḥ|prabhṛti darśanen' âiva
samupajāta|sevā|rasā na divā na rātrau
na suptasya n' āsīnasya n' ôtthitasya
na bhramato na rāja|kula|gatasya
cchāy" êva rāja|sūnoḥ pārśvaṃ mumoca.
Candrāpīḍasy' âpi tasyāṃ darśanād ārabhya pratikṣaṇam
upacīyamānā mahatī prītir āsīt.
abhyadhikaṃ ca pratidivasam asyāḥ prasādam akarot.
ātma|hṛdayād a|vyatiriktām iva c' âināṃ
sarva|viśrambheṣv amanyata.
evaṃ samatikrāmatsu keṣu cid divaseṣu,
rājā Candrāpīḍasya yauva|rājy'|âbhiṣekaṃ cikīrṣuḥ
pratīhārān upakaraṇa|saṃbhāra|saṃgrah'|ârtham ādideśa.
samupasthita|yauva|rājy'|âbhiṣekaṃ ca taṃ
kadā cid darśan'|ârtham āgatam
ārūḍha|vinayam api
vinītataram icchañ Śukanāsaḥ sa|vistaram uvāca.

When Kailása had thus spoken and was silent,
Chandrapída looked long and steadily at Patra·lekha
who had made a dignified bow, and with the words,
"It shall be as my mother commands,"
he dismissed the chamberlain.
Patra·lekha for her part from then on,
filled with devotion at first sight,
neither by day nor by night, not when he was asleep,
not when he was sitting, not when he was standing,
not when he was walking about,
not when he was in the king's palace,
as if she were his shadow,
did she quit the side of the prince.
Chandrapída for his part from the time he first saw her
felt for a great affection for her,
growing at every moment.
And every day he showed her greater favor.
And in all confidential matters he considered her
no different from his own heart.
When some days had gone by in this way,
desiring to crown Chandrapída heir apparent,
the king directed his doorkeepers
to collect the requisite materials.
And, his coronation as heir apparent nigh,
Chandrapída came one day to see Shuka·nasa.
Although Chandrapída was already well trained,
Shuka·nasa wanted him yet better trained,
and spoke to him at length.

«tāta Candrāpīḍa, vidita|veditavyasy'
âdhīta|sarva|śāstrasya
te n' âlpam apy upadeṣṭavyam asti.
kevalaṃ ca nisargata ev' a|bhānu|bhedyam
a|ratn'|ālok'|ôcchedyam
a|pradīpa|prabh"|âpaneyam
atigahanaṃ tamo yauvana|prabhavam.
apariṇām'|ôpaśamo dāruṇo lakṣmī|madaḥ.
kaṣṭam an|añjana|varti|sādhyam
aparam aiśvarya|timir'|ândhatvam.
a|śiśir'|ôpacāra|hāryo
'tyanta|tīvro darpa|dāha|jvar'|ôṣmā.
satatam a|mūla|mantra|gamyo
viṣamo viṣaya|viṣ'|āsvāda|mohaḥ.
nityam a|snāna|śauca|vadhyo
balavān rāga|mal'|âvalepaḥ.
ajasram a|kṣap"|âvasāna|prabodhā ghorā ca
rājya|sukha|saṃnipāta|nidrā bhavati.
ity ato vistareṇ' âbhidhīyase.
garbh'|ēśvaratvam abhinava|yauvanatvam
a|pratima|rūpatvam a|mānuṣa|śaktitvaṃ c' êti
mahat" îyaṃ khalv an|artha|paraṃparā.
sarv'|â|vinayānām ekaikam apy eṣām āyatanam.
kim uta samavāyaḥ.

"Chandrapída, my dear boy, there is nothing remaining
for you to be taught, even fine points,
for you have learned all there is to be learned,
and you have studied all the *shastras*.
Yet it's only natural, the sun can't pierce through it,
the radiance of jewels can't break through it,
the light of lamps can't dispel it
—very deep is the darkness arising from youth.
The intoxication of wealth Lakshmi brings
is terrible and doesn't get better
as one gets older.
Then again there's the grievous blindness
from the cataract-darkness of lordship,
not to be removed by any collyrium pencil.
Not to be removed by cooling remedies
is the all too fierce heat of pride's burning fever.
Forever beyond primary mantras is the vexatious stupor
from tasting the poison of sense objects.
Never removed by bathing or purification
is the strong coating of passion's stain.
The multitude of pleasures a kingdom brings
is a perpetual nightmare, a sleep
from which there's no waking when night ends.
So I must tell you about it at some length.
To be rich from birth, to be very young,
to have matchless beauty and more than human might—
this is indeed a series of disasters.
Any one of these is the home of all bad behavior.
How much more their conjunction!

yauvan'|ārambhe ca prāyaḥ
śāstra|jala|prakṣālana|nirmal" âpi
kāluṣyam upayāti buddhiḥ.
an|ujjhita|dhavalat" âpi
sa|rāg" âiva bhavati yūnāṃ dṛṣṭiḥ.
apaharati ca vāty" êva śuṣka|patraṃ
samudbhūta|rajo|bhrāntir
atidūram ātm'|êcchayā
yauvana|samaye puruṣaṃ prakṛtiḥ.
indriya|hariṇa|hāriṇī ca
satatam ati|dur|ant" êyam
upabhoga|mṛga|tṛṣṇikā.
nava|yauvana|kaṣāyit'|ātmanaś ca salilān' îva
tāny eva viṣaya|sva|rūpāṇy āsvādyamānāni
madhuratarāṇy āpatanti manasaḥ.
nāśayati ca diṅ|moha iv'
ônmārga|pravartakaḥ
puruṣam atyāsaṅgo viṣayeṣu.
bhavādṛśā eva bhavanti bhājanāny upadeśānām.
apagata|male hi manasi
sphaṭika|maṇāv iva rajani|kara|gabhastayo
viśanti sukham upadeśa|guṇāḥ.
guru|vacanam amalam api salilam iva mahad upajanayati
śravaṇa|sthitaṃ śūlam a|bhavyasya.

And in early adolescence, as a rule, even if purified
by being washed in the waters of the *shastra*s,
the intellect is muddied.
Though they don't lose their whiteness, young men's eyes
are in fact *reddened*, that is to say *impassioned.*
And just as the wind *whirls up a column of dust*
and blows far away a dried up leaf,
in the time of youth a man's nature
is *confused by passion,*
and at its own whim carries him far away.
And luring away the deer that is his senses,
this mirage of sensual pleasure always ends really badly.
And for one who is sullied and poisoned by fresh youth,
these very forms of sense objects
are the sweeter to his mind
the more he tastes them, like water.
And like disorientation *sending one on the wrong road,*
excessive attachment to sense objects
destroys a man,
sending him morally astray.
It is indeed persons such as yourself
who are fit to receive advice.
For into a mind freed from impurities
the merits of advice penetrate easily,
like moonbeams into a crystal.
For a person who isn't fit for it, an elder's discourse
though pure causes pain when heard,
like water in the ear.

itarasya tu kariṇa iva śaṅkh'|ābharaṇam
ānana|śobhā|samudayam adhikataram upajanayati.
harati ca sakalam atimalinam apy andhakāram iva
doṣa|jātaṃ pradoṣa|samaya|niśākara iva
gur'|ûpadeśaḥ.
praśama|hetur vayaḥ|pariṇāma iva
palita|rūpeṇa śirasija|jālam
amalī|kurvan guṇa|rūpeṇa
tad eva pariṇamati.
ayam eva c' ân|āsvādita|viṣaya|rasasya
te kāla upadeśasya,
Kusumaśara|śara|prahāra|jarjarite hi hṛdaye
jalam iva galaty upadiṣṭam.
a|kāraṇaṃ ca bhavati duṣ|prakṛter
anvayaḥ śrutaṃ vā vinayasya.
candana|prabhavo na dahati kim analaḥ?
kiṃ vā praśama|hetun" âpi
na pracaṇḍatarī|bhavati vaḍav'|ânalo vāriṇā?
gur'|ûpadeśaś ca nāma puruṣāṇām
akhila|mala|prakṣālana|kṣamam a|jalaṃ snānam
an|upajāta|palit'|ādi|vairūpyam
a|jaraṃ vṛddhatvam
an|āropita|medo|doṣaṃ gurū|karaṇam
a|suvarṇa|viracanam a|grāmyaṃ karṇ'|ābharaṇam
atīta|jyotir āloko
n' ôdvega|karaḥ prajāgaraḥ.

But for another it makes his face the more beautiful,
as a conch-shell ornament does an elephant.
An elder's advice takes away the whole range of faults,
even the most reprehensible,
just as the moon when night begins
dispels even the blackest darkness.
Like old age it makes one calm,
and just as old age cleans all one's hair
by making it white,
it purifies those faults
by transforming them into virtues.
You haven't yet tasted the pleasures of the senses,
and this is just the time to advise you,
for when the heart is damaged by the impact
of the arrows of flower-arrowed Love
what one has been taught flows away like water.
In the case of a man of evil disposition,
neither birth nor education
is the cause of good behavior.
Does not fire from sandalwood burn one?
Does not water, though it puts out fire,
make the submarine fire yet fiercer?
And verily an elder's instruction is for men
a bath that can wash away all blemish without water.
It's old age without getting old, without
the occurrence of deformities such as gray hair.
It gives gravitas without the ills of obesity.
It's an elegant ornament for the ear not made
out of gold, a light that goes beyond flame,
a waking up that doesn't produce anxiety.

viśeṣeṇa tu rājñām, viralā hi teṣām upadeṣṭāraḥ.

pratiśabdaka iva rāja|vacanam anugacchati jano bhayāt.

uddāma|darpa|śvayathu|sthagita|śravaṇa|vivarāś c'

ôpadiśyamānam api te na śṛṇvanti.

śṛṇvanto 'pi ca gaja|nimīliten' âvadhīrayantaḥ

khedayanti hit'|ôpadeśa|dāyino gurūn.

ahaṃkāra|dāha|jvara|mūrcch"|ândhakāritā

vihvalā hi rāja|prakṛtiḥ.

alīk'|âbhimān'|ônmāda|kāriṇi dhanāni.

rājya|viṣa|vikāra|tandrā|pradā rāja|lakṣmīḥ.

ālokayatu tāvat kalyāṇ'|âbhiniveśī

Lakṣmīm eva prathamam,

iyaṃ hi subhaṭa|khaḍga|maṇḍal'|ôtpala|vana|

vibhrama|bhramarī[112] Lakṣmīḥ.

kṣīra|sāgarāt pārijāta|pallavebhyo *rāgam*

indu|śakalād *ekānta/vakratām*

Uccaiḥśravasaś *cañcalatāṃ*

Especially in the case of kings,
for very few are those who admonish kings.
People follow what kings say like echoes, out of fear.
Those who are ears are blocked
by the tumor of unbridled arrogance
do not hear the advice they're given.
And when they do listen to elders
who are giving them good advice,
they cause them distress by closing their eyes
in the way an elephant does.
For it's the nature of kings to be paranoid,
losing consciousness
and being blinded in egoism's burning fever.
Riches generate the delirium of false pride.
Regal glory leads to the lassitude
that is the ill-effect of royal power's poison.
One disposed to what is right and proper should first
take a careful look at Lakshmi, the goddess of fortune,
for this Lakshmi moves like a bee
restlessly around the lotus beds
that are the circle of brave warriors' swords.
It was from the ocean of milk that she arose.
From the leaves of the *parijáta* tree,
the redness that is her *passion*;
from the crescent of the moon, *the special curvature*
that is *her extreme crookedness*;
from the horse Ucchaih·shravas,
the readiness of movement that is *her unsteadiness*;

kāla|kūṭān *mohana/śaktiṃ*
madirāyā madaṃ
Kaustubha|maṇer *atinaiṣṭhuryam*
ity etāni saha|vāsa|paricaya|vaśād
viraha|vinoda|cihnāni gṛhītv" âiv' ôdgatā.
na hy evaṃ|vidham aparam a|paricitam iha jagati
kiṃ cid asti yath" êyam an|āryā.
labdh" âpi khalu duḥkhena paripālyate.
dṛḍha|guṇa|pāśa|saṃdāna|nispandī|kṛt" âpi naśyati.
uddāma|darpa|bhaṭa|sahasr'|ôllāsit'|âsi|latā|
pañjara|vidhṛt" âpy apakrāmati.
mada|jala|durdin'|ândhakāra|gaja|ghaṭita|
ghana|ghaṭā|paripālit" âpi prapalāyate.
na paricayaṃ rakṣati.
n' âbhijanam īkṣate.
na rūpam ālokayate.
na kula|kramam anuvartate.
na śīlaṃ paśyati.
na vaidagdhyaṃ gaṇayati.
na śrutam ākarṇayati.
na dharmam anurudhyate.
na tyāgam ādriyate.

from hashish, the black lump poison,
the altered state of consciousness that is her *infatuation*;
from wine, her intoxication;
from the Káustubha gem, *the extreme hardness*
that is *her extreme cruelty*—
these are the mementoes she brought with her,
to ease the pain of separation from the milk ocean,
because they'd become familiar to her as neighbors.
But there is nothing else in this world
so inscrutable as this wicked woman.
When won, it's difficult to protect her.
Though bound so tight with the ropes
that are one's merits that she can't move, she vanishes.
Though secured in the cage of creepers
that are the swords brandished
by thousands of warriors unbridled in their pride,
she escapes.
Though guarded by close ranked elephants
dark with their showers of liquid rut,
she slips away.
She doesn't preserve intimacy.
She has no regard for noble birth.
She pays no attention to beauty.
She doesn't follow family tradition.
She doesn't look at character.
Cleverness doesn't count with her.
She has no ear for learning.
Righteousness doesn't please her.
She has no respect for liberality.

na viśeṣa|jñatām vicārayati.

n' ācāraṃ pālayati.

na satyam anubudhyate.

na lakṣaṇaṃ pramāṇī|karoti.

gandharva|nagara|lekh" êva paśyata eva naśyati.

ady' âpy ārūḍha|Mandara|parivart'|āvarta|bhrānti|

janita|saṃskār" êva paribhramati.

kamalinī|saṃcaraṇa|vyatikara|lagna|nalina|nāla|kaṇṭak" êva

na kva cin nirbharam ābadhnāti padam.

atiprayatna|vidhṛt" âpi param'|ēśvara|gṛheṣu

vividha|gandha|gaja|gaṇḍa|madhu|pāna|matt" êva

pariskhalati.

P105 *pāruṣyam* iv' ôpaśikṣitum asi|dhārāsu nivasati.

viśva|rūpatvam iva grahītum āśritā Nārāyaṇa|mūrtim.

a|pratyaya|bahulā ca divas'|ânta|kamalam iva

samupacita|mūla|daṇḍa|kośa|maṇḍalam api

muñcati bhū|bhujam.

She has no time for discrimination.
She doesn't protect tradition.
She takes no account of truth.
Auspicious marks carry no weight with her.
Like the skyline of the *gandhárvas'* city,
she disappears even as one looks at her.
The whirlpool created by the churning
of Mount Mándara made her giddy
and even today she wanders about
as if still suffering the after effects.
Nowhere does she put her foot down firmly,
as if she had a thorn from the stalk of a *nálina* lotus
sticking in her
from her walking around on lotus beds.
Though she's kept under tremendous restraint
in the palaces of supreme monarchs,
she staggers away, as if drunk from drinking the wine
from the cheeks of various rut elephants.
She dwells on sword blades as if to learn from them P105
the sharpness that is *cruelty.*
She resorts to Naráyana's body,
which has the power to manifest itself
as the whole universe,
as if to get from him *the power to take on any form.*
Never having much confidence in any one,
she abandons a king
though he has enlarged his inherited territory, his army,
his treasury and the number of kings subordinate to him,
just as she does at the end of the day a lotus
though it has a well developed root, stalk, circular pericarp.

lat" êva *viṭapakān* adhyārohati.

Gaṅg" êva *Vasu|janany api taraṃga|budbuda|cañcalā.*

divasa|kara|gatir iva

prakaṭita|vividha|saṃkrāntiḥ.

pātāla|guh" êva tamo|bahulā.

Hiḍimb" êva *Bhīma|sāhas'|âika|hārya|hṛdayā.*

prāvṛḍ iv' *âcira|dyuti|kāriṇī.*

duṣṭa|piśāc" îva

darśit'|âneka|puruṣ'|ôcchrāyā

svalpa|sattvam unmattī|karoti.

Sarasvatī|parigṛhītam īrṣyay" êva

n' āliṅgati janam.

guṇavantam a|pavitram iva na spṛśati.

udāra|sattvam a|maṅgalam iva na bahu manyate.

As a creeper *climbs up trees,*
she dwells *with the patrons of parasites.*
Like Ganga *who, though the mother of the eight Vasus,*[113]
is in constant movement with her waves and foam,
she, *though she generates wealth*
is as evanescent as foam on a wave.
Like the motion of the sun,
with its traversing the various sectors
of the zodiac plain to see, she *flaunts her various flittings.*
Like a cave in the subterranean world,
she's full of darkness.
Like the demoness Hidímba[114] *whose heart was*
entirely won by Bhima's daring deeds,
her *heart is won only by savage recklessness.*
Like the rainy season *producing lightning flashes,*
her *illumination is transitory.*
Like a depraved flesh-eating demoness *who shows herself*
as several times the height of a man
and *drives the timid into a frenzy of fear,*
she *shows many men the way to prosper* and *gives*
miserable specimens of mankind delusions of grandeur.
As if it's because of jealousy, she doesn't embrace
a man favored by Sarásvati, goddess of learning.
As if he were unclean, she doesn't touch
the man of merit.
She doesn't think much of the man of noble character,
treating him as inauspicious.

su|janam a|nimittam iva na paśyati.

abhijātam ahim iva laṅghayati.

śūraṃ kaṇṭakam iva pariharati.

dātāraṃ duḥ|svapnam iva na smarati.

vinītaṃ pātakinam iva n' ôpasarpati.

manasvinam unmattam iv' ôpahasati.

paraspara|viruddhaṃ c' êndra|jālam iva darśayantī

prakaṭayati jagati nijaṃ caritam.

tathā hi: satatam *uṣmāṇam āropayanty* api

jāḍyam upajanayati.

unnatim ādadhān" âpi nīca|svabhāvatām āviṣ|karoti.

toya|rāśi|saṃbhav" âpi tṛṣṇāṃ saṃvardhayat'.

Īśvaratāṃ dadhān" âpy

a/Śiva/prakṛtitvam ātanoti.

bal'|ôpacayam āharanty api laghimānam āpādayati.

amṛta|sah'|ôdar" âpi *kaṭuka/vipākā.*

As if he were a bad omen, she doesn't look
at the good man.
The well-born man she skips over as if he were a snake.
The brave man she avoids as if he were a thorn.
She forgets the generous man as if he were a bad dream.
She doesn't go near the well-behaved man
as if he were a criminal.
She mocks at the intelligent man as if he were mad.
She exhibits her deeds in this world
as if she were performing conjuring tricks
which cancel each other out, one after the other.
For example: though she's forever *producing heat*
she *generates cold*, which is to say
while making a man full of ardor
she *makes him morally and intellectually torpid.*
Though raising up high
she reveals a person's low character.
Though she was born from the ocean
she increases one's thirst.
Though making one the lord Shiva,
she *reveals one's nature to be other than Shiva.*
That is to say, *though she makes a man a millionaire,*
she *shows his character to be grudging.*
Though bringing an increase of strength
she makes one trivial.
Though nectar's sister, having the same source,
she *has a bitter taste*, and *her consequences are disastrous.*

vigrahavaty apy

a|pratyakṣa|darśanā.

puruṣ'|ôttama|rat" âpi

khala|jana|priyā.

reṇu|may" îva svaccham api kaluṣī|karoti.

yathā yathā c' êyaṃ capalā dīpyate

tathā tathā dīpa|śikh" êva *kajjala|malinam* eva

karma kevalam udvamati.

tathā h' îyaṃ saṃvardhana|vāri|dhārā

tṛṣṇā|viṣa|vallīnāṃ,

vyādha|gītir indriya|mṛgāṇāṃ,

parāmarṣa|dhūma|lekhā sac|carita|citrāṇāṃ,

vibhrama|śayyā moha|dīrgha|nidrāṇāṃ,

nivāsa|jīrṇa|valabhī dhana|mada|piśācikānāṃ,

timir'|ôdgatiḥ śāstra|dṛṣṭīnāṃ,

puraḥ|patākā sarv'|âvinayānām,

utpatti|nimnagā krodh'|āvega|grāhāṇām,

āpāna|bhūmir viṣaya|madhūnāṃ,

saṃgīta|śālā bhrū|vikāra|nāṭyānām,

āvāsa|darī doṣ'|āśī|viṣāṇām,

utsāraṇa|vetra|latā sat|puruṣa|vyāhārāṇām,

Though she *has a bodily form* she *cannot be seen clearly,*
that is to say, she *fosters strife* and *makes one want to see*
a state of affairs that isn't feasible.
Though *taking pleasure in the best men,* she *loves rogues,*
that is to say, *she's attached to Vishnu, the supreme male,*
and *she's dear to the wicked.*
As if made of dust, she soils even the pure.
And the more this fickle lady shines,
the more she vomits forth action *as dirty as lamp black,*
just as the more a lamp flickers *the more soot it sheds.*
Furthermore,
this lady is the stream of water that nourishes
the poison creepers of thirsty desire,
the hunter's luring song to the deer of the senses,
an obscuring column of smoke
to the paintings of good deeds,
the soft bed of pleasure to the long sleep of infatuation,
an old turret that provides living quarters
for the flesh-eating demonesses of pride in wealth,
the cataract to the eyes of the *shastra*s,
the banner carried ahead of acts of insolence,
the river that is the breeding place
for the crocodiles of paroxysms of wrath,
the drinking hall for the wines of sense objects,
the concert hall for the dance of frowns,
the cave that is home to the pythons of faults,
the cane stick for driving away
good men's words of advice,

a|kāla|prāvṛḍ guṇa|kalahaṃsakānāṃ,
visarpaṇa|bhūmir lok'|âpavāda|visphoṭakānāṃ,
prastāvanā kapaṭa|nāṭakasya,
kadalikā kāma|kariṇo,
vadhya|śālā sādhu|bhāvasya,
Rāhu|jihvā dharm'|êndu|maṇḍalasya.
na hi taṃ paśyāmi
yo hy a|paricitay" ânayā
na nirbharam upagūḍho
yo vā na vipralabdhaḥ.
niyatam iyam ālekha|gat" âpi calati,
pusta|mayy[115] ap' îndra|jālam ācaraty
utkīrṇ" âpi vipralabhate,
śrut" âpy abhisaṃdhatte,
cintit" âpi vañcayati.
evaṃ|vidhay" âpi c' ânayā dur|ācārayā katham api
daiva|vaśena parigṛhītā viklavā bhavanti rājānaḥ.
sarv'|â|vinay'|âdhiṣṭhānatāṃ ca gacchanti.
tathā hi:
abhiṣeka|samaya ev' âiṣāṃ
maṅgala|kalaśa|jalair iva
prakṣālyate dākṣiṇyam.

unseasonal rain for the *kala·hansa* geese of good qualities,
the hotbed for the boils of public scandal,
the prologue to the drama of deceit,
the pennant on love's elephant,
the slaughterhouse of good intentions,
the tongue of Rahu the eclipse
to the moon disc of righteousness.
I don't see, indeed I don't, anyone
who's been passionately embraced by her—
and she does this
without knowing the person beforehand—
who's not been deceived by her.
It's all too true she'll go away,
even when painted in a picture.
Even when made of clay, she performs her magic.
Even when carved as a stature she deceives.
Even when just listened to she cheats.
Even when just thought about she deceives.
And even though this is how she is,
somehow by the will of fate
kings are controlled by this wicked woman,
and become helpless
and become the home of all wickedness.
For it is thus:
At the very time of their coronation shower,
as if by the waters from the auspicious jars,
their courtesy is washed away.

agni|kārya|dhūmen' êva malinī|bhavati hṛdayam.

purohita|kuś'|âgra|saṃmārjanībhir iv' âpanīyate kṣāntiḥ.

uṣṇīṣa|paṭṭa|bandhen' êv' ācchādyate

jarā|gamana|smaraṇam.

ātapatra|maṇḍalen' êv' âpavāryate para|loka|darśanam.

cāmara|pavanair iv' âpahriyate satya|vāditā.

vetra|daṇḍair iv' ôtsāryante guṇāḥ.

jaya|śabda|kalakalair iva tiraskriyante sādhu|vādāḥ.

dhvaja|paṭa|pallavair iva parāmṛṣyate yaśaḥ.

tathā hi:

ke cic chrama|vaśa|śithila|śakuni|gala|puṭa|

capalābhiḥ khadyot'|ônmeṣa|muhūrta|manoharābhir

manasvi|jana|garhitābhiḥ saṃpadbhiḥ pralobhyamānā,

dhana|lava|lābh'|âvalepa|vismṛta|janmāno,

'neka|doṣ'|ôpacitena duṣṭ'|âsṛj" êva

rāg'|āveśena bādhyamānā,

As if by the smoke from the fire ritual
their heart is darkened.
As if the tips of the *kusha* grass had become brooms,
their patience is swept away.
As if by the winding on of their turbans,
acknowledgment of the approach of old age
is blotted out.
As if by the disc of the royal parasol,
sight of the next world is hidden from them.
As if by the breezes from their chowries,
speaking the truth is blown away.
As if by the cane staffs,
merits are driven away.
As if by the din of shouts of victory,
words of good advice are drowned.
As if by the streaming pennants of their banners,
their fame is wiped away.
This is how it is:
Riches, which are as unsteady as a bird's neck
hanging slackly from exhaustion,
delightful only for a moment, like a firefly's flash,
reprobated by the high-minded,
tempt some, who forget the status they were born to
in the arrogance caused by the acquisition
of a scrap of wealth,
who are handicapped by being possessed by passion,
as if by the tainted blood
from multiple physiological imbalances.

vividha|viṣaya|grāsa|lālasaiḥ pañcabhir apy
aneka|sahasra|saṃkhyair iv' êndriyair āyāsyamānāḥ,
prakṛti|cañcalatayā labdha|prasareṇ' âiken' âpi
śata|sahasratām iv' ôpagatena manas" ākulī|kriyamāṇā
vihvalatām upayānti. grahair gṛhyante.
bhūtair iv' âbhibhūyante.
mantrair iv' āveśyante.
sattvair iv' âvaṣṭabhyante.
vāyun" êva viḍambyante.
piśācair iva grasyante.
Madana|śarair marm'|âbhihatā iva
mukha|bhaṅga|sahasrāṇi kurvate.
dhan'|ôṣmaṇā pacyamānā iva viceṣṭante.
gāḍha|prahār'|āhatā iv' âṅgāni na dhārayanti.
kulīrā iva tiryak paribhramanti.
a|dharma|bhagna|gatayaḥ paṅgava iva
pareṇa saṃcāryante.
mṛṣā|vāda|vipāka|saṃjāta|mukha|rogā iv'
âtikṛcchreṇa jalpanti.
sapta|cchada|tarava iva kusuma|rajo|vikārair
āsanna|vartināṃ śiraḥ|śūlam utpādayanti.
āsanna|mṛtyava iva bandhu|janam api n' âbhijānanti.
utkupita|locanā iva tejasvino n' êkṣante.

Though it is the five senses that harry them,
each of the five being eager to taste multiple sense objects,
there seem to be many thousands of them.
Given free reign, the mind allows them no rest—
though one, owing to its natural fickleness
it becomes a hundred thousand.
They become miserable. Evil planets take them over.
They seem overpowered by ghosts.
They seem possessed by spells.
They seem taken over by spirits.
They seem mocked by delirium.
They seem swallowed up by flesh-eating demons.
As if wounded in their vital parts by Love's arrows,
they contort their faces in a thousand ways.
As if boiled by the warmth of their wealth, they twitch.
As if belabored with hard blows,
they cannot lift their limbs.
Like crabs they crawl sideways.
Their progress impeded by their lack of righteousness,
like the lame they have to be supported by someone else.
As though they have mouth ulcers caused
by the infection of their lying speech,
they speak with very great difficulty.
As if they were *sapta·cchada* trees,
with the harmful effect of the pollen of their flowers
they give a headache to those who are near them.
As if near death, they don't recognize even their relatives.
As if they had sore eyes,
they cannot look upon illustrious men.

kāla|daṣṭā iva mahā|mantrair api na pratibudhyante.

jātuṣ"|ābharaṇān' îva *s'|ôṣmāṇam* na sahante.

duṣṭa|vāraṇā iva

mahā|māna|stambha|niścalī|kṛtā

na gṛhṇanty upadeśam.

tṛṣṇā|viṣa|mūrcchitāḥ

kanaka|mayam iva sarvaṃ paśyanti.

iṣava iva

pāna|vardhita|taikṣṇyāḥ para|preritā

vināśayanti.

dūra|sthitāny api

phalān' îva *daṇḍa|vikṣepair* mahā|kulāni śātayanti.

a|kāla|kusuma|prasavā iva manohar'|ākṛtayo 'pi

loka|vināśa|hetavaḥ.

śmaśān'|âgnaya iv' *âtiraudra|bhūtayaḥ.*

taimirikā iv' â|dūra|darśinaḥ.

upasṛṣṭā iva *kṣudr'|âdhiṣṭhita|bhavanāḥ.*

As if bitten by a black snake, they cannot be
restored to consciousness, even by powerful mantras.
As if they were ornaments made of lac,
they cannot bear *the heat that is a man of ardor.*
Like rogue elephants *tied fast to posts of huge size,*
they do not take instruction,
deprived of movement by the post of their great pride.
Like people delirious from *the poison that produces thirst*
who see everything as *golden in color,*
they, delirious from *the poison of greed,*
see everything *in terms of gold.*
Like arrows *sharpened on a whetstone, shot at the foe,*
they, *their cruelty increased by drinking,*
urged on by others, destroy.
Sending off their armies they destroy great families
though they're remote, as if they were knocking down fruit
out of their reach by throwing sticks.
Like the growth of flowers out of season,
even though charming in appearance,
they are the cause of people's destruction.
Like the fires in burning grounds,
the ashes very much Shiva's,
their prosperity is extremely frightful.
Like people with cataracts on their eyes,
they cannot look far ahead.
Like people possessed by evil spirits
whose houses are invaded by bees,[116]
their palaces are occupied by mean-spirited people.

śrūyamāṇā api preta|paṭahā iv' ôdvejayanti.

cintyamānā api mahā|pātak'|âdhyavasāyā iv'

ôpadravam upajanayanti.

anudivasam āpūryamāṇāḥ pāpen' êv'

ādhmāta|mūrtayo bhavanti.

tad|avasthāś ca vyasana|śata|śaravyatām upagatā

valmīka|tṛṇ'|âgr'|âvasthitā jala|bindava iva

patitam apy ātmānaṃ n' âvagacchanti.

apare tu sv'|ârtha|niṣpādana|parair

dhana|piśita|grāsa|gṛdhrair āsthāna|nalinī|bakair

dyūtaṃ vinoda iti,

para|dār'|âbhigamanaṃ vaidagdhyam iti,

mṛgayā śrama iti,

pānaṃ vilāsa iti,

pramattatā śauryam iti,

sva|dāra|parityāgam a|vyasanit" êti,

guru|vacan'|âvadhīraṇam a|para|praṇeyatvam iti,

a|jita|bhṛtyatā sukh'|ôpasevyatvam iti,

nṛtya|gīta|vādya|veśy"|âbhisaktī rasikat" êti,

Even the sound of them, like the drums
of a funeral procession, causes revulsion.
Even the thought of them, like resolving
to commit a heinous sin, brings disaster.
Sated every day, as if inflated with sin
their bodies become bloated.
And such being their condition,
the targets of hundreds of vices,
they do not realize they have fallen,
like drops of water standing on the tips of blades of grass
on an anthill, about to be absorbed in it.
Others, for their part, are told by people
intent on gaining their own ends,
vultures devouring the flesh of their wealth,
cranes in the lotus pool of the assembly hall,
that gambling is a pastime,
that seducing other men's wives is cleverness,
that hunting is exercise,
that drinking is elegant sport,
that carelessness is bravery,
that neglect of one's wife is rejection of sexual addiction,
that disregarding elders' advice
is refusal to be led by others,
that not chastising bad servants
is being a pleasure to serve,
that addiction to dancing, vocal and instrumental music,
and the company of harlots is being a connoisseur,

mah"|âparādh'|âvakarṇanaṃ mah"|ânubhāvat" êti,

paribhava|sahatvaṃ kṣam" êti,

svacchandatā prabhutvam iti,

dev'|âvamānanaṃ mahā|sattvat" êti,

bandi|jana|khyātir yaśa iti,

taralat" ôtsāha ity a|viśeṣa|jñatā pakṣa|pātitvam iti,

doṣān api guṇa|pakṣam adhyāropayadbhir antaḥ

svayam api vihasadbhiḥ pratāraṇa|kuśalair dhūrtair

a|mānuṣ'|ôcitābhiḥ stutibhiḥ pratāryamāṇā

vitta|mada|matta|cittā

niścetanatayā tath" âiv' êty

ātmany āropit'|âlīk'|âbhimānā

martya|dharmāṇo 'pi

divy'|âṃś'|âvatīrṇam iva

sa|daivatam iv' âtimānuṣam

ātmānam utprekṣamāṇāḥ

prārabdha|divy'|ôcita|ceṣṭ"|ânubhāvāḥ

sarva|janasy' ôpahāsyatām upayānti.

âtma|viḍambanāṃ c' ânujīvinā janena kriyamāṇām

abhinandanti.

manasā devat"|âdhyāropaṇa|pratāraṇād

a|sad|bhūta|saṃbhāvan'|ôpahatāś c'

that being unmoved when hearing of atrocious crime
is showing great dignity,
that putting up with insults is patience,
that willfulness is assertion of authority,
that despising the gods shows great strength of character,
that bards' applause is fame,
that rashness is being energetic,
that inability to discriminate is impartiality,
So they are told by rogues superimposing
the label of merit upon faults
while themselves laughing inwardly,
expert as they are in deception.
Misled by praises befitting immortals,
minds intoxicated by their pride in their wealth,
their lack of understanding leads them to assent
when false measures are applied to themselves;
when, mortal creatures though they are,
they fancy themselves to be more than men,
as if incarnations of a portion of divinity,
as if possessing divinity,
they assume the dignity
due to the performance of divine actions.
Everybody finds them ridiculous.
When their servants imitate them in their actions
they welcome it.
And through the deception of deification
seduced into believing what isn't true,

ântaḥ|praviṣṭ'|âpara|bhuja|dvayam iv'

ātma|bāhu|yugalaṃ saṃbhāvayanti.

tvag|antarita|tṛtīya|locanaṃ

sva|lalāṭam āśaṅkante.

darśana|pradānam apy anugrahaṃ gaṇayanti.

dṛṣṭi|pātam apy upakāra|pakṣe sthāpayanti.

saṃbhāṣaṇam api

saṃvibhāga|madhye kurvanti.

ājñām api vara|pradānaṃ manyante.

sparśam api pāvanam ākalayati.

mithyā|māhātmya|garva|nirbharāś

ca na praṇamanti devatābhyaḥ.

na pūjayanti dvijātīn. na mānayanti mānyān.

n' ârcayanty arcanīyān.

n' âbhivādayanty abhivādan'|ârhān.

n' âbhyuttiṣṭhanti gurūn.

an|arthak'|āyās'|ântarita|viṣay'|ôpabhoga|sukham

ity upahasanti vidvaj|janam.

jarā|vaiklavya|pralapitam iti paśyanti vṛddha|jan'|ôpadeśam.

ātma|prajñā|paribhava ity asūyanti saciv'|ôpadeśāya.

they become convinced that their two arms
conceal a second pair.
They imagine their forehead
has a third eye hidden under the skin.
They consider allowing themselves to be seen
to be an act of grace.
Letting their eye fall on someone,
they count as conferring a benefit.
Even conversing with someone
they classify as giving a bonus.
Even a command they count as conferring a boon.
Even their touch they put down as purification.
And puffed up by pride
by false hymns to their own glory,
they don't bow to the gods.
They don't worship the brahmins.
They don't honor the honorable.
They don't worship those
who ought to be worshipped.
They don't salute those who ought to be saluted.
They don't get up to receive their elders.
They laugh at learned men for shielding themselves
from the joy of sensual pleasures
through their profitless exertion.
They see the advice of old people as what they call
'the prattle of senility.'
They take ill the advice of ministers,
thinking it an insult to their intelligence.

kupyanti hita|vādine.
sarvathā tam abhinandanti,
tam ālapanti, taṃ pārśve kurvanti,
taṃ saṃvardhayanti,
tena saha sukham avatiṣṭhante, tasmai dadati,
taṃ mitratām upanayanti,
tasya vadanaṃ śṛṇvanti, tatra varṣanti,
taṃ bahu manyante, tam āptatām āpādayanti,
yo 'har|niśam an|avaratam
uparacit'|âñjalir
adhidaivatam iva
vigat'|ânya|kartavyaḥ stauti
yo vā māhātmyam udbhāvayati.
kiṃ vā teṣāṃ a|sāṃpratam[117] yeṣām
atinṛśaṃsa|prāy'|ôpadeśa|nirghṛṇaṃ
Kauṭilya|śāstraṃ pramāṇam,
abhicāra|kriyā|krūr'|âika|prakṛtayaḥ
purodhaso guravaḥ,
par'|âbhisaṃdhāna|parā mantriṇa
upadeṣṭāro,
nara|pati|sahasra|bhukt'|ôjjhitāyāṃ
Lakṣmyām āsaktir,
māraṇ'|ātmikeṣu śāstreṣv abhiyogaḥ,
sahaja|prem'|ārdra|hṛday'|ânuraktā
bhrātara ucchedyāḥ?
tad evaṃ|prāye 'tikuṭila|kaṣṭa|ceṣṭā|sahasra|
dāruṇe rājya|tantre 'smin
mahā|moha|kāriṇi ca yauvane, kumāra,

They get angry with someone
offering them friendly counsel.
In every way they welcome, him they talk to,
him they put at their side, him they advance,
with him they stay with pleasure, to him they give,
him they make their friend, his words they heed,
on him they shower down,
him they honor,
him they make their trusted confidant,
who day and night, without interruption,
folding his hands in the gesture of worship
as if they were gods,
putting aside all other business, praises them;
or who makes up hymns of praise to their glory.
What won't they do, those kings whose authority
is Kautílya's science of pitiless politics,
its advice almost entirely cruel;
whose spiritual guides are priests entirely ruthless
in character from their practice of malevolent magic;
whose teachers are ministers intent on deceiving others;
who are devoted to Lakshmi who's been enjoyed
and then abandoned by thousands of kings;
who apply themselves to the text-books
devoted to murder;
whose brothers, attached to them with their hearts
full of natural affection, are to be cut down?
Therefore, my prince,
in the administration of the kingdom,
which is for the most part as I have just described,
dreadful with thousands of crooked

tathā prayatethā
yathā n' ôpahasyase janair,
na nindyase sādhubhir,
na dhik|kriyase gurubhir,
n' ôpālabhyase suhṛdbhir,
na śocyase vidvadbhiḥ.
yathā ca na prahasyase viṭair
na pratāryase kuśalair
n' āsvādyase bhujaṃgair
n' âvalupyase sevaka|vṛkair
na vañcyase dhūrtair, na pralobhyase vanitābhir,
na viḍambyase Lakṣmyā,
na nartyase madena,
n' ônmattī|kriyase Madanena
n' ākṣipyase viṣayair,
na vikṛṣyase rāgeṇa, n' âpahriyase sukhena.
kāmaṃ bhavān prakṛty" âiva dhīraḥ.
pitrā ca mahatā prayatnena
samāropita|saṃskāraḥ.
tarala|hṛdayam a|pratibuddhaṃ ca
madayanti dhanāni.
tath" âpi bhavad|guṇa|saṃtoṣo
mām evaṃ mukharī|kṛtavān.
idam eva ca punaḥ punar abhidhīyate.

and reprehensible actions,
and in this youthfulness of yours,
which can lead to great infatuation,
you should strive to so conduct yourself
that you are not laughed at by people,
nor censured by the good,
not reprobated by your elders,
nor reproached by your friends,
nor grieved for by the wise.
And that you may not be mocked by sycophants;
nor taken in by clever swindlers;
nor preyed upon by the dissolute;
nor torn to pieces by the wolves who are servants;
nor deceived by rogues; nor enticed by women;
nor made ridiculous by Lakshmi;
nor set dancing by arrogance;
nor driven mad by the god of Love;
nor overthrown by sense objects;
nor drawn away by passion; nor entirely lost to luxury.
I willingly admit that you are steadfast in nature,
and your father has paid great attention
to giving you a sound education.
It is the fickle-hearted and the unenlightened
whom riches infatuate.
All the same, it was my satisfaction at your virtues
which has made me so garrulous.
But this much should be said again and again.

vidvāṃsam api, sa|cetanam api,

mahā|sattvam apy,

abhijātam api, dhīram api, prayatnavantam api,

puruṣam iyaṃ dur|vinītā

khalī|karoti Lakṣmīr iti.

sarvathā kalyāṇaiḥ pitrā kriyamāṇam

anubhavatu bhavān yauva|rājy'|âbhiṣeka|maṅgalam.

kula|kram'|āgatām udvaha

pūrva|puruṣair ūḍhām dhuram.

avanamaya dviṣatāṃ śirāṃsi.

unnamaya bandhu|vargam.

abhiṣek'|ânantaraṃ ca prārabdha|dig|vijayaḥ

paribhraman vijitam api tava pitrā

sapta|dvīpa|bhūṣaṇāṃ punar vijayasva vasuṃdharām.

P110 ayaṃ ca te kālaḥ pratāpam āropayitum.

ārūḍha|pratāpo hi rājā trailokya|darś" îva

siddh'|ādeśo bhavat'»

îty etāvad abhidhāy' ôpaśaśāma.

upaśānta|vacasi Śukanāse Candrāpīḍas

Though a man be learned, though he be wary,
though he be of high character,
though he be of noble birth,
though he be industrious,
this ill-educated woman Lakshmi
can turn him into a rogue.
May you enjoy the auspicious ceremony
of your installation as heir apparent
that your father's performing with every refinement.
Bear the yoke that was borne by your ancestors,
and has come to you through hereditary succession.
Bend down the heads of your foes.
Raise the host of your relatives.
And after your coronation
begin the conquest of the quarters.
And in the course of your marches,
though it has been conquered by your father,
conquer again
the earth ornamented with its seven continents.
And this is the time for you to establish your prowess. P110
For a king whose prowess is established is like a sage
who sees all the three worlds at once:
what he describes is proven to be true;
and what the king orders is carried out."
Having said this much, he ceased.
When Shuka·nasa's speech had drawn to a close,
Chandrapída,

tābhir amalābhir upadeśa|vāgbhiḥ prakṣālita iv'
ônmīlita iva svacchī|kṛta iva
nirmṛṣṭa iv' âbhiṣikta iv'
âbhilipta iv' âlaṃkṛta iva
pavitrī|kṛta iv' ôdbhāsita iva
prīta|hṛdayo muhūrtaṃ sthitvā
sva|bhavanam ājagāma.

as if those words of advice had washed him,
had opened his eyes, had made him clean,
had polished him, had bathed him,
had anointed him, had adorned him,
had purified him, had made him sparkle,
his heart delighted, staying for a short while,
went to his own palace.

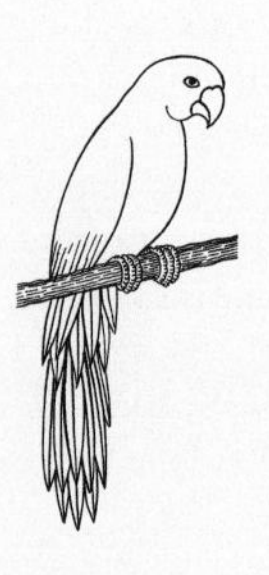

NOTES

Bold *references are to the English text;* ***bold italic*** *references are to the Sanskrit text.*

1 Bana died before completing "Princess Kadámbari," so it is not certain that he wrote these verses. PETERSON thinks that his son wrote them. However, they resemble those that preface the "Deeds of Harsha," and to my mind differ in style and manner from those that preface the son's concluding part of the *kathā*. Presumably Bana felt some kinship with the demon who was his namesake. They were both devotees of Shiva. He refers to Bana the demon also at 1.19 and 1.384; and to the demon's daughter Usha on 1.387. Bana is eldest son of the much more famous demon Bali, whom Vishnu in his dwarf incarnation pushed down into the subterranean world. Shiva granted him the boon of having a thousand hands, but Krishna sliced them off with his discus. Worshipping Shiva's feet, one is freed from rebirth.

2 ***sāmanta***: vassal kings; in the descriptions of courts that follow, *sāmanta*s are heirs of vassal kings, held as hostages. Cf P82.5.

3 **Bharvu**: Is this Bana's guru? He makes no mention of him in the "Deeds of Harsha." PETERSON suggested taking *Bharvoḥ* as the genitive dual of *Bharu*, meaning Hari·hara, the joint form of Vishnu and Shiva. In "The Deeds of Harsha" Harsha's father marries his daughter into the Máukhari dynasty, saying, "Now at the head of all royal houses stand the Múkharas, worshipped, like Shiva's foot-print, by all the world" (trans. p. 122).

4 **Rahu**: "Seizer." Rahu was a demon who at the churning of the ocean joined with the gods in drinking the nectar that had been produced, but the sun and the moon recognized him and informed the gods. Vishnu immediately struck off his head, but since he had tasted nectar he became immortal. As this bodiless head Rahu continues to attempt to swallow the sun and moon, attempts visible to us as eclipses.

5 **Káustubha** was one of the 14 jewels churned from the ocean. Vishnu placed it on his chest.

6 *śayyā*, "bed" is also a technical term in Sanskrit poetics, signifying the unity of word and meaning, "the expression of just the right idea in just the right way" (Gerow 1971). Bana uses the same pun in an introductory verse to "The Deeds of Harsha."

7 The **Guptas** ruled over almost the whole of Northern India in the 4th and 5th centuries. By Bana's day they had been superseded by the Máukhari dynasty, and then by Harsha. Cf. the homage received by Bharvu.

8 *jagur*: lit. "they sang," applies to the "Sama Veda," but not to the "Yajur."

9 **Checked on every word**: or perhaps, "when in doubt they were kept right" by the birds.

10 **All forms of literature**: the principal form of speech is the Veda.

11 **Anxious boys**: the final position of *śaṅkitāḥ* stresses the boys' anxiety. The reference to the linguistic capabilities of these birds foreshadows the fact that a parrot is going to be a principal narrator in this *kathā*.

12 High praise indeed for Bana's ancestor. In "The Deeds of Harsha," Bana is less effusive: "there was in due time born … a certain twice-born man, Kuvéra by name, devoted as the son of Vínata to his guru. He begat four sons…." (trans. p. 31). Note that the comparison with the son of Vínata, that is, Gáruda, is again made here, but in respect of Kubéra's grandson, Artha·pati, not Kubéra.

13 **From him**: i.e. from Kubéra. But according to "The Deeds of Harsha," Kubéra is the grandfather, whose son Pashu·pati, unmentioned here, is the father of Artha·pati. Probably, as Kane suggests, a verse is missing from "Princess Kadámbari."

14 The Pravárgya sacrifice is centered on a non-iconic earthen pot, the *mahā/vīra* vessel, which glowing in the sacrificial fire is the "all encompassing hero," Maha·vira, the Sun.

15 Or should *śruti/śāstra* be science of music?

16 ***sphaṭik'/ôpal'/âmalaṃ***: the reading of some manuscripts and the Calcutta editions, in place of PETERSON and NSP ed.'s *sphaṭik'/ ôpal'/ôpamam*. *Śleṣa* in the verse is less likely with the latter reading.

17 **His other noble and most excellent sons**: in "The Deeds of Harsha," Bana tells us that Chitra·bhanu had ten brothers.

18 **The seven worlds**: there are seven upper worlds (*bhūḥ*, *bhuvaḥ*, *svaḥ*, *mahaḥ*, *janaḥ*, *tapaḥ*, *satyam*), and seven lower worlds.

19 **That has no parallel** (*atidvayī*) can be either the best or the worst. KANE suggests it might refer to "surpassing the two preceding *kathās*," namely Gunádhya's "Long Story" (*Bṛhatkathā*) and Subándhu's *Vāsavadattā*, both of which Bana praises in the introduction to "The Deeds of Harsha." H. TIEKEN (forthcoming: 6) suggests that the alternative meaning is rather that both parts of "Princess Kadámbari" are by Bana himself: "the author could be saying that he has produced in the *Kādambarī* a work which goes against the rule of the genre by being divided into two."

20 The sage **Bhagi·ratha** performed great deeds of asceticism in order to bring Ganga down from the heavens. He then led the holy river to the sea, she following behind his chariot.

21 **Wet with the gifts** (*ārdrīkṛta*): water was given at the same time as a gift.

22 Note the priority given to literary tastes. He was the best of archers, but archery was of little importance in his scheme of things.

23 **Prithu** was the virtuous son of the wicked king Vena. A divine bow fell from heaven for him at his birth. He leveled the earth and made husbandry possible.

24 **Súdraka**: a legendary person, quaintly named for a king, supposedly author of the play "The Little Clay Cart" (*Mṛcchakaṭika*), translated for the Clay Sanskrit Library by DIWAKAR ACHARYA, 2009.

25 ***viśvarūpākṛti***: a reference to chapter 11 of the "Bhagavad Gīta" where Krishna showed his universal form to Árjuna and identified himself with all the gods and various objects.

26 This list of twelve expands the list given in the "Laws of Manu" 7.4 where a king was in the beginning created from particles of Indra and the seven other great *devas* who are guardians of the world, *lokapālas*.

27 **Vídisa**: an ancient city, capital of Eastern Malwa, situated on the confluence of the rivers Bes and Betwa.

28 **His jeweled bracelets swinging**: the *mridánga* drum has two heads, and is held horizontally. It might be assumed that the king had bracelets on both hands. However KANE remarks, "Even now rich men wear golden and jeweled bracelets on their left forearms." In "The Deeds of Harsha" we read of foot soldiers "with sparkling golden bracelets on their left forearms." But soldiers would need to keep their right hands unencumbered.

29 **The puránas**: the one *purāṇa* that Bana mentions by name in both "Princess Kadámbari" and "The Deeds of Harsha" is the *Vāyu*.

30 **Sages who had come to see him**: note that the visits of holy men are sandwiched between painting, music, and literary and puzzles. The implication is that holy men are not of great moment for the king.

31 **Finding the missing syllable** (*akṣara/cyutaka*): KANE gives the example of a verse (*Vāgbhaṭālaṃkāra* 4.13) ostensibly about dust (*reṇu*), but which makes even better sense when *ka* added and the verse is seen to be about an elephant (*kareṇu*).

32 **Finding the missing character** (*mātrā*): *mātrā* here is not "meter," as LAYNE takes it, but rather a stroke of writing. In both the examples KANE cites from commentaries the point is to replace an *a*, the default vowel after a consonant which does not require to be written, with an *i*. This can have far-reaching effects, as KANE's example from Rúdrata's *Kāvyālaṅkāra* 5.28 shows, where the change from *kala* to *kila*, made by adding *i* to blank space,

changes a sentence from referring to a coward being unable to face battle to a woman of good family restricted to the women's apartments being unable to see the archway of the gateway to her palace.

33 **Supplying missing consonants**: literally, [filling in the missing] "dots" (*bindu*), consonants being represented by dots, and the vowels correctly written in.

34 **Uncovering the last quarter of a verse**: some of the letters in the first three quarters will, when rearranged, provide the fourth quarter.

35 **Kings' heads**: Bana frequently refers to the tributary kings resident in the court as simply "kings," using exactly same word, *rāja*, as he does for the ruling king, whether Shúdraka or Tarapída.

36 **Párashu·rama** killed the brahmin Kartavírya for stealing the cow of his father Jamad·agni. The sons of Kartavírya in revenge killed Jamad·agni in the absence of Párashu·rama, who then vowed to extirpate the kshatriyas, and did so with his axe no less than 21 times. Is there an animus against the warrior caste here? Harsha was not kshatriya but vaishya by caste.

37 **Tri·shanku** was a king who wished to go to heaven with his mortal body. His guru Vasíshtha told him this was impossible. He then went to another guru, Vishva·mitra, who raised him to heaven, but when he got there Indra told him to fall headfirst back to earth. It is appropriate that the *chandála* maiden is compared to the royal glory of Tri·shanku since Tri·shanku had been made a *chandála* by a curse, and we discover later that she herself was a *chandála* or *matánga* only as the result of a curse. See also *Uttarabhāga*, ed. PETERSON, p. 337.

38 Mountains used to have wings, until Indra cut them off with his thunderbolt.

39 **Madhu and Káitabha** were two demons born from Vishnu's earwax when he was absorbed in yogic sleep at the end of the eon. They were about to devour Brahma who sat in the lotus growing

from Vishnu's navel. The latter woke up Vishnu, who crushed them on his thigh. Solid ground was formed from their bodies.

40 **Cow-yellow** (*go/rocanā*): bright yellow pigment prepared from cows' urine.

41 In his "Birth of Kumára," Kali·dasa describes Shiva's destruction of Kama with fire from his third eye when Kama is about to shoot his flower arrow at Shiva. Bana frequently refers to Kama's destruction. Later on in "Princess Kadámbari" King Tarapída and his son Chandrapída are both compared to Kama in handsomeness.

42 **At the sound of a falling coconut**: the Sanskrit is simply *tāla/śabdena*. PETERSON suggests, "May not the meaning be 'the sound of the clapping of the ears' (of a rogue elephant or the leader of another herd)?" He also notes that in Kali·dasa's *Raghuvaṃśa* 9.71 the clapping of elephants' ears (*karṇa/tāla*) is compared to sharp drum beats.

43 Elephants' tongues cannot be protruded outwards. When the gods sought Agni to send him against the demon Táraka, he hid. An elephant told the gods where he was, and he cursed elephants to have reversed tongues. Then a parrot told the gods where Agni was hiding next, and he cursed parrots to lose their power of perfect speech.

44 **The half hour** (*nāḍikā/ccheda*): literally, "the twenty-four minutes," a *nāḍikā* being half a *muhūrta* of forty-eight minutes, and thirty *muhūrtas* making a day in the standard time measurement of ancient India.

45 ***pratīhāryā ... kara/talaṃ kareṇa***: I emend here to the text of PETERSON's C (one of two Deccan College MSS used by him) and India Office Sanskrit 3300 (IOSan3300).

46 **Cigar** (*dhūma/varti*): made of aromatic ingredients (*dhūpa*) such as cardamom, sandalwood, and aloe wood, plus resin and thin tree bark. Tobacco was introduced into India by the Portuguese in the seventeenth century.

47 **Aloe paste** is black in color. The other references to it in "Princess Kadámbari" refer to it as *kṛṣṇ'|âguru*, black aloe paste.

48 **Hundreds of officials holding cane staffs**: the Sanskrit says simply "hundreds of cane staffs" (*vetra|latā|śata*).

49 **The demon Vatápi**: Vatápi and his brother Ílvala were demons who had a routine for killing brahmins whereby Ílvala became a brahmin and Vatápi a goat. Ílvala would kill the goat and feed brahmins with the flesh. Then he would call out to Vatápi who would come tearing out of the stomach of the brahmin who had eaten him. Agástya put a stop to this by digesting Vatápi.

50 **Náhusha** was a human king who replaced Indra and became lord of the gods. To thwart his attentions, Indra's wife persuaded him to come to her in a palanquin carried by sages. Finding the sages too slow, the king kicked Agástya, the shortest, and said, "Hurry up" (*sarpa sarpa*). Whereupon Agástya cursed him to become a serpent (*sarpa*). Bana's version differs from Náhusha's own account in the "Maha·bhárata," where he says that when he was in Indra's position in heaven, and Agástya was carrying his palanquin, he kicked Agástya. "An unseen being then called out angrily, 'Perish, you Snake!'" ("Maha·bhárata" 3.178.37, translated by J.A.B. van Buitenen (1981: 367). For what happened later, see note 52 below.

51 **Agástya, the pot-born**: at the sight of the nymph Úrvashi the seed of the god Mitra fell into a pot. Agástya was born from the pot.

52 **Náhusha's boa constrictor body**: as described above in note 50, Náhusha, risen to Indra's role in heaven, insulted Agástya, and came to earth as a snake. Agástya foretold that Yudhi·shthira would free him from his curse. In the "Maha·bhárata" 3.178, Yudhi·shthira answers correctly the questions that the boa constrictor, wrapped tightly around Bhima, poses, about Brahman and brahminhood. Thereupon Náhusha releases Bhima, assumes a celestial form and goes up to heaven.

53 **The place on the circle of the earth**: the indentation in the surface of the earth made by the Boar's snout as he lifted up the earth from the ocean.

54 ***madhyacāriṇāṃ***: the reading of IOSan3300, rather than *madhyacāriṇā* of printed ed.

55 **Rama's curse**: lamenting his loss of Sita, Rama is supposed to have cursed happy pairs of *chakra·vaka* birds for not sharing his grief. Subándhu's *Vāsavadattā* (ed. Hall, 1859: 185) seems to be the earliest statement that Rama made such a curse.

56 **Árjuna the son of Krita·virya** was granted by his guru Datta·treya the boon of having a thousand arms. Sporting with his wives one day in the river Nármada, he raised the water level by damming the river with his arms. This submerged Rávana who was worshipping Shiva on a sandbank of the river.

57 In the "Ramáyana," Rama asks Agástya why the Dándaka forest is bereft of animals and birds. Agástya tells him Ikshváku gave this region to his badly behaved son Danda. Danda there raped Ara, the daughter of the sage Úshanas, and her father called down the wrath of Indra. Seven days were allowed the inhabitants to leave, then the king and all his kingdom were reduced to ashes. "Ramáyana" 7.78–81.

58 **Khara**, "Donkey,:" chief of the *rákshasas* sent by Rávana to occupy Jana·sthana, the land of ascetics, at the time when Rama is exiled to the neighboring Dándaka forest. Rama kills him in a duel after having massacred the 14,000 *rákshasas* that Khara sent against him (3.30). He is a brother of Rávana, without doubt a cousin by one of his maternal great-uncles. The name Khara makes him a parody of the sacrificial horse. See Biardeau & Porcher (1999: 1,521).

59 **Dúshana**: general in charge of the expedition prepared by Khara to attack Rama in Jana·sthana. He is killed by Rama in the attack of the 14,000 *rákshasas*.

60 In the "Maha·bhárata" **Eka·lavya**, "Single-aim," is a prince of a wild Nisháda tribe, who is rejected as an archery student by

Drona. Worshipping a clay image of Drona, he teaches himself. His exceptional prowess is revealed when he seals a barking dog's mouth with arrows, and the Pándavas see the dog. Árjuna, the great bowman, fears his supremacy is compromised. Drona is angry that Eka·lavya ignored his rejection and took him for his teacher anyway; and demands as payment Eka·lavya's right thumb, which Eka·lavya at once cuts off and gives to Drona.

61 **Mánasa·vega**: the chief villain of the "Long Story," who carries off Nara·váhana's favorite wife.

62 **Sanat·kumára, the shining youth**: the best-known of Brahma's four mind-born sons, who are eternal, independent, unattached to worldly life, and have knowledge of the future.

63 **Ashva·tthaman, followed by the warrior Kripa**: these two, along with Krita·varman, were the three surviving Káurava warriors after the last great battle of the "Maha·bhárata," and carried out an attack on the Pándava camp at night. Kripa was Ashva·tthaman's maternal uncle and the teacher of the Káuravas and Pándavas before Drona took on that role.

64 **Náraka** was the son of the earth and king of Pragjyótisha, Assam. He took Váruna's umbrella, and Áditi's earrings. At Indra's request Vishnu killed him. Bana describes Náraka as follows in "The Deeds of Harsha:" "In former times, ... the holy earth, having through union with the boar [incarnation of Vishnu] become pregnant, gave birth in hell to a son called Náraka. Before this hero's feet, while he was still in his boyhood, the crest-jewels of the lords of nations were apt to bow. Without the command of this stout-armed ruler of the world the sun himself, though scanned with angrily bent side-glances by the female *chakra·vaka*s of the domestic lotus tanks, went not to his setting, and Áruna reversed his chariot wheels in fear. It was he who won this umbrella, this external heart of Váruna." It is a descendant of Náraka who sends the wonderful umbrella, his family heirloom, to Harsha. COWELL AND THOMAS (1897: 216f.).

65 **Proud of their calves and licked them zealously** (*bal'/âvalīḍha/darpita/Dhenukam*): possibly simply "strong and proud cows"

but this ignores the resonance of *līḍha*, "licked," in connection with milch cow. LAYNE translates here "proud cows who forcefully licked." I take the compound as "where there were cows [who had calves whom] they licked hard [and of whom] they were proud," the calves being understood.

66 **In dreams of avarice**: the Sanskrit is simply *tṛṣṇāsu*, "in greed," "in cases of greed," but *tṛṣṇā*, in itself and even more so in the plural, reads oddly here.

67 The **triple staff** (*tri/daṇḍa*) of an ascetic is bound together near the top, and can be opened out to form a tripod.

68 ***darbha/dhavitra/pāṇinā***: PETERSON and other editions have *darbha/pavitra/dhavitra/pāṇinā*. I suspect scribal repetition. Either we should read *darbha/pavitra/pāṇinā*, "holding a strainer made of *darbha* grass [as a fan]," or *darbha/dhavitra/pāṇinā*, "holding a fan made not of leather but of *darbha* grass." *dhavitra* is rare in *kāvya* texts. Kṛṣṇamohana notes that *dhavitra* does not occur in some MSS of "Princess Kadámbari."

69 ***śruta/rāgiṇā***: a strange expression. Unlikely the Vedas are referred to here, unless sarcastically. Passionate about gossip? About music (*śruta* for *śruti*)?

70 **Kadru**, wife of the sage Káshyapa, gave birth to a thousand snakes who were the ancestors of all snakes.

71 **Maha·kala**: this famous Shiva temple is often referred to in literature from Kali·dasa's "Cloud Messenger" onwards. It was destroyed in the thirteenth century.

72 **And so got colored green**: this is implicit in the Sanskrit, *prārabdha/kamalinī/parimalanā*, "they've pressed upon lotus ponds," and is needed to make sense of the sentence. For this usage of *parimalana*, cf. *Kādambarī*, *Uttarabhāga*, ed. PETERSON, 271.15–17: *vinidra/kumudinī/parimalana/lagna/parimale .... mātariśvani*.

73 **Nala ... Dasha·ratha**: these are all notable kings. The story of **Nala**, king of Níshadha, and his adventures due to the ill-will of

Kali, personification of the Kali yuga, are well-known, not least from being the first reading of most western students of Sanskrit. He and his future wife Damayánti fell in love before they met, because of what they had heard about each other. For **Náhusha** see note 52 above. **Yayáti** was the second son of Náhusha. For long an extreme sensualist, he was through his sons Yadu and Puru the founder of the two great lineages that took their names from those sons, the Yádavas (Krishna the most famous descendant) and the Páuravas (the Káuravas; and the Pándavas, most notably Yudhi·shthira and Árjuna). **Dhundhu·mara** was, as his name says, the slayer of the demon Dhundhu. **Bhárata**, "He who supports his subjects," the son of Dushyánta and Shakúntala, whose origin is described in Kali·dasa's play *Śakuntalā*, was the supreme ruler from whom India takes its name, Bharat. **Bhagi·ratha** was a warrior king who practiced asceticism for a thousand years in order to bring the celestial Ganga down to earth so that he could perform funeral rites for his 60,000 ancestors who had been destroyed by the sage Kápila.

74 **Sumítra** was Dasha·ratha's second wife, mother of the twins Lákshmana and Shatrúghna. Lákshmana was especially devoted to Rama, and accompanied him in his exile.

75 **Nala**: the monkey son of the divine architect Vishva·karman, from whom he inherited his construction skills.

76 **Kubéra** is the god of wealth; Álaka is his city.

77 **Bhima**, one of the five Pándava brothers, heroes of the "Maha·bhárata," was such a hearty eater he was given the name Wolf-belly. **Gandha·mádana** is a mountain to the east of Meru famous for its fragrant forests. Once **Dráupadi** found a fragrant lotus carried by the wind and asked Bhima to bring her more. Bhima went to Saugándhika·vana, fought with the guardians there and brought back the flowers.

78 Párashu·rama or Skanda shot an arrow through the **Krauncha mountain** and made a passage through which it was believed that geese passed from the plains to the Mánasa lake and back.

79 **The star Agástya**: Canopus, the second brightest star in the night sky.

80 **Jara·sandha**, "Put-together-by-Jara" was a son of Brihad·ratha, the king of Mágadha. Brihad·ratha's two wives, long barren, given two halves of a mango by the sage Chanda·káushika, gave birth to two halves of a boy. These two abortions were thrown away. Jara, a cannibal demoness, picked up the pieces, put the boy together, and kindly gave him back to his parents.

81 **Like Brihas·pati for Indra ... Nala's guru Súmati**: the famous gurus of famous kings: Indra's Brihas·pati, Vrisha·parvan's Kavi, Dasha·ratha's Vasíshtha, Rama's Vishva·mitra, Yudhi·shthira's Dhaumya, Bhima's Dámanaka, Nala's Súmati.

82 **Bloomed like a bákula tree**: it was a poetic convention that *bakula* trees put forth buds when sprinkled with wine from lovely women's mouths.

83 **Scent elephant**, *gandha/gaja*: a technical term for a bull elephant whose scent inspires fear in other elephants.

84 **Jara·sandha ... who defeated even Vishnu**: For details of Jara·sandha's birth, see note 80 above. Jara·sandha besieged Krishna in Máthura eighteen times. It was Bhima who killed Jara·sandha.

85 ***āsana/sthitasya***: my conjectural emendation for *āsthāna/sthitasya*, the reading everywhere. ***sabh"/ântare***: the reading of PETERSON's MS B, instead of the reading *sabh"/ântareṣu* found in all editions. Elsewhere in "Princess Kadámbari" Bana invariably speaks of the *āsthāna* as *āsthāna/maṇḍapa* (eleven times) or *-bhavana* (once), except that he also refers to carpets being rolled up when the king "rose from the assembly" (*āsthān'/ôtthita/bhūmi/pāla*, p. 404.) *sabhā* and *āsthāna* are equivalent terms, though the passage just cited goes on to speak of the "sides of the hall" (*sabhā/paryantam*) shining, thus suggesting a connection between *āsthāna* and being seated, since the king rises from the *āsthāna*. The unemended text would be translated, "When I'm in the assembly hall" (*āsatha/sthitasya*) ... "on the occasions of meetings" (*sabh"/ântareṣu*).

86 SHARAD PATIL (1974: 39), refers to Vilásavati's bathing at a crossroads, and remarks, "Though dying out, the custom still persists in Indian countryside. In order that the fertilizing waters should touch every part of the body, childless women strip themselves completely naked." And with regard to "pools famous for their Naga families," PATIL says that she "knows of such a pond near Sakri in Dhulia district, Maharashtra, and it is known as Nāga-āī or Cobramother." (p.52).

87 **Mátrika shrines**: shrines to the seven or eight mother goddesses who form a powerful group. See note 94 below.

88 Immediately following mention of Jain monks, **Amba** must be Ámbika, the Jain version of Durga.

89 **Mandhátri**: a royal sage (*rāja'|ṛṣi*), who ruled wisely and well. Bana refers to him six times in "The Deeds of Harsha." Harsha's horoscope is said to resemble that of Mandhátri, COWELL AND THOMAS (1897: 110).

90 PETERSON *akhaṇḍit'|ānana*. IOSan3300 reads *akhaṇḍit'|āma*, fish that are "whole, raw."

91 I have emended *prahata|mṛdu|mṛdaṅga* to ***prahata|mṛdaṅga***, on the grounds that *mṛdu* is scribal repetition. I cannot find *mṛdu* used in respect of drumming anywhere; and it makes no sense in this context.

92 All editions have *musala|yugena*. PETERSON's MS A reads *musala|yugalena*. I here conjecturally emend to ***musal'|ôkhalena***. Plow, pestle, and mortar commonly symbolize fruitful human life. The mortar is essential here.

93 The **goat** is to be sacrificed, after the birth of a son.

94 **Mothers** (*mātṛkās*): a group of seven or eight goddesses, female versions (*śaktis*) of particular male gods, who are powerful and sometimes dangerous. The earliest account of them is in the *Devīmāhātmya*.

95 **Indra's son dropped from the hands of a heavenly nymph**: this seems to be a hypothetical occurrence, rather than an actual

event. Indra had several sons, including Árjuna. A legendary king of Újjayini, Gandhárva·sena, was a son of Indra, but he was a young man, and his father sent him to earth in the form of an ass for laughing at an *apsaras*.

96 The **circle of hair** (*ūrṇā*) is a curved thin line of hair resembling wool between the eyebrows, regarded as indicative of a future world-ruler.

97 **Rénuka**: wife of Jamad·agni and mother of Párashu·rama, an avatar of Vishnu, perfect example of the warrior brahmin. Párashu·rama decapitates his mother at the order of his father, then asks as recompense her resurrection. Is Bana smiling to himself here? This son Vaishampáyana in the event is not very warlike. Or is does this relate to an anti-kshatriya feeling on those around Harsha, the vaishya emperor?

98 Reading ***ardha/krośa/mātrāyām*** with IOSan3300 in place of PETERSON's *ardha/krośa/mātr'/āyāmam*. It is not credible that this building was half a *krośa* in length.

99 ***pusta/vyāpāre***: the reading of IOSan3300, rather than *pustaka/ vyāpāre*, the reading of all editions; supported by *pusta/maya* PETERSON 276.21, and *pusta/kṛt* in Bombay edition of *Harṣacarita*, 47.11, and *pusta/karman* ibid. 86.10. *pustaka/mayy* on p. 490 is likewise to be emended to *pusta/mayy*.

100 **Nara·váhana**: hero of the "Long Story."

101 **Mrittikávati**: the country of the Bhojas, beside the Banas river in Malwa. This story seems lost, apart from a brief account given by Bhanu·chandra, the sixteenth century commentator on "Princess Kadámbari," wherein the sage curses the *ápsaras* because she delays her marriage to him.

102 **Turrets**: *saṃjavana*, usually taken to mean "quadrangle," but that does not fit here—nor, for that matter, does it in the "Ramáyana," where at 5.3.10 Lanka is described as having doors which, provided with beautiful *saṃjavanas*, seemed to soar into the sky.

103 **Monkeys ... from the horses' stables**: a monkey was kept in stables to ward off the evil eye. Cf. the Persian proverb "The misfortune of the stable be on the monkey's head."

104 **The lineage of Yadu**: Krishna and his elder brother Bala·rama are the two most famous descendants of Yadu, the founder of the Yádavas. Shura is the grandfather of Krishna. It is not known who the Bhima referred to here is.

105 **Like the union of Usha and Anirúddha**: Usha was the daughter of Banásura. In a dream she saw a prince and fell in love with him. In order to find out who the prince of the dream was, Chitra·lekha, the friend of Usha, drew the pictures of all the princes of the world. Usha recognized Anirúddha, son of Pradyúmna and grandson of Krishna, to be her lover. By her yogic powers Chitra·lekha brought Anirúddha to Usha's bedroom. Banásura imprisoned Anirúddha, but Krishna rescued him.

106 **Madri's family**: Madri was the sister of the king of the Madras, and second wife of Pandu to whom she bore the twins Nákula and Saha·deva.

107 **Shveta·ketu along with Kalápin**: Kalápin is a sage who founded a Vedic school (*caraṇa*), chosen here simply because of the pun his name suggests. Shveta·ketu, on the other hand, figures later in the "Princess Kadámbari" in person. He is, indirectly, the father of Pundaríka, one of the principal characters of "Princess Kadámbari." He said to be extremely handsome. See vol. 3 of this translation and edition. He is best known as the young sage to whom in the "Chandogya Upanishad" his father explains the true meaning of the words *tat tvam asi*. In the "Maha·bhárata" Shveta·ketu prescribes monogamy for both men and women. In the "Kama Sutra," Shveta·ketu is said to have written a earlier version of the science of love.

108 **Krita·varman**: a great archer who fought on the side of the Káuravas and accompanied Ashva·tthaman in the night attack on the Pándavas' camp.

109 **Shringin and Hema·kuta**: two of the mountains that divided one continent from another. Hema·kuta is near the eastern ocean, and

not far from Mount Kailása. Chandrapída visits Hema·kuta in vol. 2 and meets Kadámbari there.

110 **Karna**, son of the sun, half-brother of the Pándavas, was the king of Anga. Anga is the region around Bhogalpur in Bihar. It is said in the "Ramáyana" that Shiva burned up Kama at this place.

111 **Kulúta**: Kulu, to the northeast of Kangra, in the Punjab. Its capital was Sushárma·pura. It is a sacred site where one of Sati's breasts is said to have fallen to earth. The country is north of Kalínda·desha where the Yámuna has its source.

112 ***vibhrama | bhramarī***: PETERSON, KANE and the NSP edition print *viśrama|bhramarī*, the other editions and IOSan3300 have *vibhrama|bhramarī*.

113 **Ganga, mother of the eight Vasus**: the Vasus are a group of eight deities, originally personifications of natural phenomena, who attend on Indra. Once they tried to steal Vasíshtha's cow Kama·dhenu and were condemned by the sage to be born as men. The Vasus then asked Ganga to be their mother. Ganga, in the form of the wife of king Shántanu, threw each Vasu as she gave birth to him, into the river Ganga, until the last, whom she gave to her husband. He afterwards became known as Bhishma.

114 **Hidímba**: a demoness in the "Maha·bhárata," sent by her brother to lure the Pándavas to him but she fell in love with Bhima. She offered to carry him away to safety on her back, but Bhima refused and killed her brother. By his mother's desire Bhima married her, and by her had a son named Ghatótkacha.

115 ***pusta|mayy***: the reading of IOSan3300, in place of *pustaka|mayy*. See note 99 above.

116 **Houses are invaded by bees**: KANE notes that "Beehives attaching to private dwellings are even now looked upon as inauspicious."

117 ***a|sāṃpratam***: a variant reading given in the NSP edition. PETERSON has *sāṃpratam*.

THE CLAY SANSKRIT LIBRARY

For further details please consult the CSL website.

1. The Emperor of the Sorcerers (*Bṛhatkathāślokasaṃgraha*) (vol. 1 of 2) by *Budhasvāmin*. SIR JAMES MALLINSON
2. Heavenly Exploits (*Divyāvadāna*). JOEL TATELMAN
3. Maha·bhárata III: The Forest (*Vanaparvan*) (vol. 4 of 4) WILLIAM J. JOHNSON
4. Much Ado about Religion (*Āgamaḍambara*) by *Bhaṭṭa Jayanta*. CSABA DEZSŐ
5. The Birth of Kumára (*Kumārasaṃbhava*) by *Kālidāsa*. DAVID SMITH
6. Ramáyana I: Boyhood (*Bālakāṇḍa*) by *Vālmīki*. ROBERT P. GOLDMAN
7. The Epitome of Queen Lilávati (*Līlāvatīsāra*) (vol. 1 of 2) by *Jinaratna*. R.C.C. FYNES
8. Ramáyana II: Ayódhya (*Ayodhyākāṇḍa*) by *Vālmīki*. SHELDON I. POLLOCK
9. Love Lyrics (*Amaruśataka, Śatakatraya & Caurapañcāśikā*) by *Amaru, Bhartṛhari & Bilhaṇa*. GREG BAILEY & RICHARD GOMBRICH
10. What Ten Young Men Did (*Daśakumāracarita*) by *Daṇḍin*. ISABELLE ONIANS
11. Three Satires (*Kaliviḍambana, Kalāvilāsa & Bhallaṭaśataka*) by *Nīlakaṇṭha, Kṣemendra & Bhallaṭa*. SOMADEVA VASUDEVA
12. Ramáyana IV: Kishkíndha (*Kiṣkindhākāṇḍa*) by *Vālmīki*. ROSALIND LEFEBER
13. The Emperor of the Sorcerers (*Bṛhatkathāślokasaṃgraha*) (vol. 2 of 2) by *Budhasvāmin*. SIR JAMES MALLINSON
14. Maha·bhárata IX: Shalya (*Śalyaparvan*) (vol. 1 of 2) JUSTIN MEILAND
15. Rákshasa's Ring (*Mudrārākṣasa*) by *Viśākhadatta*. MICHAEL COULSON

16. Messenger Poems (*Meghadūta, Pavanadūta & Haṃsadūta*)
by *Kālidāsa, Dhoyī & Rūpa Gosvāmin.* SIR JAMES MALLINSON
17. Ramáyana III: The Forest (*Araṇyakāṇḍa*)
by *Vālmīki.* SHELDON I. POLLOCK
18. The Epitome of Queen Lilávati (*Līlāvatīsāra*) (vol. 2 of 2)
by *Jinaratna.* R.C.C. FYNES
19. Five Discourses on Worldly Wisdom (*Pañcatantra*)
by *Viṣṇuśarman.* PATRICK OLIVELLE
20. Ramáyana V: Súndara (*Sundarakāṇḍa*) by *Vālmīki.*
ROBERT P. GOLDMAN & SALLY J. SUTHERLAND GOLDMAN
21. Maha·bhárata II: The Great Hall (*Sabhāparvan*)
PAUL WILMOT
22. The Recognition of Shakúntala (*Abhijñānaśākuntala*) (Kashmir Recension) by *Kālidāsa.* SOMADEVA VASUDEVA
23. Maha·bhárata VII: Drona (*Droṇaparvan*) (vol. 1 of 4)
VAUGHAN PILIKIAN
24. Rama Beyond Price (*Anargharāghava*)
by *Murāri.* JUDIT TÖRZSÖK
25. Maha·bhárata IV: Viráta (*Virāṭaparvan*)
KATHLEEN GARBUTT
26. Maha·bhárata VIII: Karna (*Karṇaparvan*) (vol. 1 of 2)
ADAM BOWLES
27. "The Lady of the Jewel Necklace" & "The Lady who Shows her Love" (*Ratnāvalī & Priyadarśikā*) by *Harṣa.*
WENDY DONIGER
28. The Ocean of the Rivers of Story (*Kathāsaritsāgara*) (vol. 1 of 7)
by *Somadeva.* SIR JAMES MALLINSON
29. Handsome Nanda (*Saundarananda*)
by *Aśvaghoṣa.* LINDA COVILL
30. Maha·bhárata IX: Shalya (*Śalyaparvan*) (vol. 2 of 2)
JUSTIN MEILAND
31. Rama's Last Act (*Uttararāmacarita*) by *Bhavabhūti.*
SHELDON POLLOCK. Foreword by GIRISH KARNAD

32. "Friendly Advice" (*Hitopadeśa*) by *Nārāyaṇa* &
 "King Víkrama's Adventures" (*Vikramacarita*). Judit Törzsök
33. Life of the Buddha (*Buddhacarita*)
 by *Aśvaghoṣa*. Patrick Olivelle
34. Maha·bhárata V: Preparations for War (*Udyogaparvan*) (vol. 1 of 2)
 Kathleen Garbutt. Foreword by Gurcharan Das
35. Maha·bhárata VIII: Karna (*Karṇaparvan*) (vol. 2 of 2)
 Adam Bowles
36. Maha·bhárata V: Preparations for War (*Udyogaparvan*) (vol. 2 of 2)
 Kathleen Garbutt
37. Maha·bhárata VI: Bhishma (*Bhīṣmaparvan*) (vol. 1 of 2)
 Including the "Bhagavad Gita" in Context
 Alex Cherniak. Foreword by Ranajit Guha
38. The Ocean of the Rivers of Story (*Kathāsaritsāgara*) (vol. 2 of 7)
 by *Somadeva*. Sir James Mallinson
39. "How the Nagas were Pleased" (*Nāgānanda*) by *Harṣa* &
 "The Shattered Thighs" (*Ūrubhaṅga*) by *Bhāsa*.
 Andrew Skilton
40. Gita·govínda: Love Songs of Radha and Krishna (*Gītagovinda*)
 by *Jayadeva*. Lee Siegel. Foreword by Sudipta Kaviraj
41. "Bouquet of Rasa" & "River of Rasa" (*Rasamañjarī & Rasataraṅ-giṇī*) by *Bhānudatta*. Sheldon Pollock
42. Garland of the Buddha's Past Lives (*Jātakamālā*) (vol. 1 of 2)
 by *Āryaśūra*. Justin Meiland
43. Maha·bhárata XII: Peace (*Śāntiparvan*) (vol. 3 of 5)
 "The Book of Liberation" (*Mokṣadharma*). Alexander Wynne
44. Little Clay Cart (*Mṛcchakaṭikā*) by *Śūdraka*.
 Diwakar Acharya. Foreword by Partha Chatterjee
45. Bhatti's Poem: The Death of Rávana (*Bhaṭṭikāvya*)
 by *Bhaṭṭi*. Oliver Fallon
46. "Self-Surrender," "Peace," "Compassion," and "The Mission of the Goose": Poems and Prayers from South India (*Ātmārpaṇastuti, Śāntivilāsa, Dayāśataka & Haṃsasaṃdeśa*) by *Appayya Dīkṣita, Nīlakaṇṭha Dīkṣita & Vedānta Deśika*.

Yigal Bronner & David Shulman
Foreword by Gieve Patel

47. Maha·bhárata VI: Bhishma (*Bhīṣmaparvan*) (vol. 2 of 2)
Alex Cherniak

48. How Úrvashi Was Won (*Vikramorvaśīya*) by *Kālidāsa*
Velcheru Narayana Rao & David Shulman

49. The Quartet of Causeries (*Caturbhāṇī*)
by *Śūdraka, Śyāmilaka, Vararuci & Īśvaradatta.*
Csaba Dezső & Somadeva Vasudeva

50. Garland of the Buddha's Past Lives (*Jātakamālā*) (vol. 2 of 2)
by *Āryaśūra*. Justin Meiland

51. Princess Kadámbari (*Kādambarī*) (vol. 1 of 3)
by *Bāṇa*. David Smith

52. The Rise of Wisdom Moon (*Prabodhacandrodaya*)
by *Kṛṣṇamiśra*. Matthew T. Kapstein
Foreword by J.N. Mohanty

53. Maha·bhárata VII: Drona (*Droṇaparvan*) (vol. 2 of 4)
Vaughan Pilikian

54. Maha·bhárata X & XI: Dead of Night & The Women
(*Sauptikaparvan & Strīparvan*). Kate Crosby

55. Seven Hundred Elegant Verses (*Āryāsaptaśatī*)
by *Govardhana*. Friedhelm Hardy

56. Málavika and Agni·mitra (*Mālavikāgnimitram*) by *Kālidāsa.*
Dániel Balogh & Eszter Somogyi